SUGAR MOMMY ON TOP

JUDE E. MCNAMARA

COPYRIGHT

Twitter: @judeemcnamara

Instagram: iamtwojudes

Two Judes Publishing (A division of Two Judes Media)

668 Stony Hill Road Suite 339

Yardley, Pennsylvania, 19067

ISBN: 978-0-9972863-7-3

ACKNOWLEDGMENTS

I am beyond grateful to everyone who was part of the process of creating *Sugar Mommy on Top*. Thank you to:

My loyal and diligent beta readers: Nicole Arnold, Jeanine Hillesland, Donna Harden Nelson, Erica McCarty; all of who read multiple versions of the story, providing me helpful feedback until I felt it was right.

My editor: Michelle Phinney-Smith for all her work, without which there would be rambling and other grammatical offenses. My proofreader Keyanna Butler for the second set of eyes every author needs.

Donna Sebastian: the inspiration for the name Two Judes Publishing.

Britter, whose "bright green smiley-faced" note that's been on my door four years now and reads "Keep Writing," reminds me not to quit and to keep doing what I'm doing.

Candy Cane for helping me sort through tons of imagery for all things graphic. Your talents are never lost on me. I see you.

Tymoney, Diva. and Tootsie Pop: You're the best fan club ever.

A special thanks to Lani Diane Rich and Alastair Stephens. You guys are my first and my last word on all things story.

To my readers: To all those who purchased my novel and those who have shared my stories on your book blogs and with your book clubs, thank you for your unfailing love and support. You rock, and I am eternally grateful.

And last, but not least: To my mother for your undying love, motivation, and support throughout my entire writing life. To my father who is with me always in spirit.

DEDICATION

To Mico . . .you will forever remain a matter of the heart.

Will the man who spends his days and nights bringing new life into the world be able to heal himself while mending her broken heart, igniting an unexpected flame of love between them?

Julianna Becker

Thirty-one-year-old Julianna Becker's world is suddenly shattered when her long-standing relationship with the man she thought she would marry comes to a staggering halt. Reeling from the loss and betrayal, everything changes when Julianna breaks past the family's golden cage, landing herself in an unexpected encounter with the handsome, engaged, renowned New York Obstetrician, Dr. Elliot Fischer.

Dr. Elliot Fischer

Vanity Fair's most eligible bachelor, Dr. Elliot Fischer, knows he's headed down the road to disaster with his engagement to the former Ms. New York. Elliot struggles to convince himself that a marital future with a gold digging trophy wife-to-be is everything he wants and needs. His nuptial path derails quickly when he finds himself on a collision course with the very wealthy, petite stick of dynamite, Julianna Becker.

ulianna

"**A**re you sitting down?"

I sensed in my gut that those words meant nothing good would follow.

"I wanted to let you know I got married.'

And there it was. Three God-awful words: "I got married." Was he kidding me? Okay, so it was Halloween, and this felt like he was playing a bad trick; but it wasn't even time to hand out treats, and this was worse than any trick I'd ever gotten.

My heart sank in disbelief. I swear that I felt a physical blow to my gut; it was as if a giant invisible fist had been launched directly at my navel. Could I even breathe anymore? Had all the air suddenly been sucked out of the room? Why had everything become a blur? And why was everything happening so quickly? I needed to get off the fucking phone. I couldn't hear any more from him.

"I want to remain friends."

Had he lost his mind? Had I lost my mind? Why was I even still listening?

It was bad enough that I'd invested three years into loving him, hanging on his every word. I listened to him all the time sounding like a scratched record on repeat. He was sure that there was nowhere for our relationship to go but marriage. Of course, he didn't ever want to marry, or so he'd always said.

When I finally got the courage to end it, he decided it was best to keep his toe in the pond, staying near the front and center of my world, stoking the embers of love in my heart, never letting the fire go out completely. He would never fully release me. And now this? Surely I had *fool* written across my forehead. Pretend you love me. Play with me. Screw me. Never marry me. The prick.

"Congratulations, I wish you all the best."

How I managed to belt those words out as strong as I did, I'll never know. I was already hurting, but he hadn't hurt me enough. No, he had to turn the knife, had to twist it in my back some more. He wanted to kill what little life was left in me completely. He insisted on sharing the details about her, about the two of them.

"I want you and me to stay friends. I'll call you in a couple of weeks," he said, ending the call.

Seriously? Mr. Heartcracker, who is currently extracting every bit of life from me, thinks we're going to "remain friends?" Oh hell no. My head was dizzy. The walls of my bedroom were starting to close in on me, getting closer and closer, as each paralyzing second ticked by.

I needed to get out of here. I was struggling to breathe, and I couldn't stand being in my own skin, let alone being home alone. It was time for me to use my lifeline, my *phone a friend*. I needed my girlfriends now more than ever. My promise of tomorrow, my man-future, my everything had just come crashing down all around me, shattering me into a thousand little pieces. I burst into tears, sobbing aloud.

It was time for me to call my roadies. Time for us to find the nearest hot spot so I could drown in an endless row of tequila shots, where I could silence those ugly words. Until then, "I got married" would be on constant replay in my ears.

I grabbed my black leather messenger bag, twisting it over my shoulder against my favorite navy blue, leather-trimmed, quilted Burberry jacket. I stuffed some extra tissues in my dark five-pocket denim jeans to wipe my runny nose. I slid on my black suede Louboutin shoe boots with the four-inch heels. I pulled my red cashmere scarf off the bed, wrapped it around my neck, and stuffed the matching red boy cap into the side of my bag.

Maya and Logan would surely remind me that the best revenge was looking good. If I was going to die of a broken heart, I needed to at least look like every penny's worth of the million dollar princess he'd let slip right through his fingers.

I keyed the alarm codes into my security system in order to leave, which would put my brother's bodyguard goons on high alert. I slammed the heavy oak double doors behind me and stepped into the hallway, then headed for the gold-framed private elevator, pulling out my key card. I pushed the *down* button repeatedly, mentally willing the elevator to rise as quickly as possible to the seventy-fifth floor of Becker Towers. But even a private, express, non-stop elevator to my door wasn't quick enough for moments like these.

I cursed my father under my breath for demanding that I move into this building after I'd returned to the States. Our family owned tons of real estate all over Manhattan; I could have lived anywhere else. But no, he wanted me here with the family where one of my brothers could act as a watchdog.

Becker Towers was an ultra-luxurious condominium property overlooking Central Park. My father's intentions for putting me here were clear; my older brother and his family lived eleven floors up in the Presidential Penthouse Suite. This was yet another one of my father's overprotective methods of keeping tabs on me. The one saving grace was that the building was well known for its panoramic view of Central Park and the glittering New York skyline. I loved the view, especially at night.

I tapped my foot nervously, hoping that my brother's security team wasn't looking at close-ups on the security monitors, getting peeks at my bewildered, tear-stained face. I resisted looking directly into the monitors or giving them a wave.

The elevator doors opened. I jumped in, placing my key card into the mouth of the scanner, sliding it in and out of the slot, and pushing the express button to the ground floor. As the doors opened at my destination, I pulled my huge, Jackie O sunglasses down off my auburn tresses to cover my tear-soaked eyes. I blew past the concierge's desk with quickness, knowing that if I looked anything but normal my brother would get a report back immediately, at which point the family bodyguards would be all over me, on my trail like bloodhounds on the hunt.

I gave a quick wave to the doorman, Rick. I intentionally bit my lip to hold back the flood of tears that was still welling up inside me. My heart felt like it was beating so loud it might jump out of my chest.

"Good afternoon, Ms. Becker. Shall I have Silas come around?" he said genially, tipping his hat.

"No thanks, Rick. I'm going to walk today."

"It's no problem for me to call Silas, Ms. Jules."

Silas was my brother's limousine driver. My brother didn't approve of my taking public transportation. Everyone that worked in the building knew my brother's rules, and an important one was *no public transportation for Julianna.*

I rushed off as fast as I could, before Rick got a chance to ask me anything else.

I scurried outside, the brisk chill of the fall's windy air slamming against my tear-soaked face, the first signs of winter just starting to show themselves. I pulled the collar of my jacket up around my neck, trying to hold back the muffled sounds of anguish that were building in my throat, dying to let out the painful wail that was bubbling up in my soul.

The glow of the October sun wasn't bright enough to warm the dark and wounded places of my heart. By now, you might have thought I could deal with man-pain better, surrounded as I was by an overprotective father and two workaholic brothers. This was what mothers were for, and I didn't have one of those.

Sadly, this wasn't my first trip to this heartbreak rodeo. Still, things seemed different; things seemed worse than they had in the past because I had really, truly cared for him. Just this once, love had snuck in, had snuck past the closed gates of my heart with silent treachery. Love had melted the ice-filled places, overpowered all my rules and standards, had parked itself in the center of my heart, and now it refused to leave. Worse, I'd encouraged love to stay there, failing to call in the heart police to save the day, to drag his never-gonna-get-married ass away. I needed another term at the school of men. In particular, I needed to repeat all the lessons about putting men on proverbial pedestals; it seemed I must have slept through class the first time.

*A*s the wind whistled around my ears, I attempted to three-way call my best friends Maya and Logan to suggest an early-evening bar crawl before heading to our pre-planned Halloween party at Luigi's later.

I don't know if it was the fact that my fingers were trembling too hard to dial, or that the non-stop ringing in my head coupled with the tears streaming down my face were blurring my vision, but I never made the call. I raced the ten feet to the curb, and jumped into the nearest taxi without looking, the first step of a desperate plan for a certified hangover.

"You're going to have to open your legs wider, honey. It's going to hurt a bit, but you have to trust me. I'm not going to let anything bad happen to you. You can do this," the man said, then turned to yell at the cabbie to hurry up.

His piercing gray eyes honed in on me like laser beams; I felt his gaze with momentary surprise, but had already climbed into the back-seat, slamming the door shut behind me.

"Grab her hands. Prop her shoulders up against your chest," Gray Eyes barked at me.

I was sure that I'd stopped breathing again; my brain struggled to process what was going on around me.

"Now I need you to push, Dana," he said to the young woman in my lap whose face portrayed excruciating pain, her panting on the brink of hyperventilating, her hands gripping the upholstery.

"Oh hell no! Let me out of this cab right now!" I screamed loudly, banging like a wild woman on the Plexiglas partition that separated us from the cab driver.

"Keep driving," he ordered the cabbie. "And you . . . you need to shut the fuck up," Gray Eyes admonished me, his voice deep and stern. "Reach in my jacket pocket there, and hold the phone up to my ear."

Gray Eyes punched in a few numbers. The young woman let out an earth-shattering scream.

"This is Dr. Elliot Fischer. I'm five minutes out from the hospital in a cab with a nineteen year old patient, Dana Kilpatrick. Her contractions are one minute apart and she's almost fully dilated. I'll need obstetric and pediatric teams on standby upon arrival."

The cabbie was weaving in and out of the afternoon rush-hour traffic like a madman, forcing me to grab hold of one of the dangling loops above my head to keep from falling onto her. The cab took another sharp turn. She slid hard against me, causing both of us a fair deal of pain.

Did somebody say doctor? Yes, that's it. *I* damn sure needed a doctor. I began banging on the Plexiglas window again, alternating hysterically with groping for the door handle. My head was spinning in widening circles. This couldn't be happening to me. Was I really trapped in a cab in the middle of Manhattan's high-noon rush hour with a woman in labor and a crazy gray-eyed arrogant commando barking orders at me? I banged harder and harder on the partition.

"Lady, you've got to stop banging your fist on the glass," the cab driver said. "I'm trying to get us there as fast as I can."

"I can't breathe. I'm going to have a heart attack. I need a doctor!" I screamed through the clear screen, now in a state of absolute panic.

"No, I'm the one who can't breathe!" the young woman shouted at me through her apparent pain.

"Don't worry, Dana," Gray Eyes said in a soothing voice. "I need you to make one big push now, honey. The baby's head is crowning," he said, rubbing the top of her belly in small circles.

"Wipe her brow and pull her hair back," Gray Eyes snapped at me.

"I'm going to die, I tell you!" I shrieked.

"You're not going to die or have a heart attack. A panic attack, yes, a heart attack, no. Take deep breaths so you can slow your heart rate down. Now do as I say," he commanded.

I started taking long deep breaths, which seemed absurd when juxtaposed to the short, rapid breaths the young woman was taking. My head was spinning like that of a woman possessed. I was getting confused. But still, I pulled the young woman's sweaty hair back, wishing I had someone to pull my own sweaty hair back as well.

And who was ever gonna pull my sweaty hair back? My sweaty-hair-puller-backer got fucking married for Christ's sake. Who was gonna be there for me? Don't they know that I sweat too?

The young woman groaned loudly, this time arching her back into my chest, forcing me to push my backside up against the door. I held her hands tightly so that neither of us would fall onto the other, certain the driver was turning the corner on two wheels. Sweat was dripping down the side of my face. As I slid my tongue across my lips, I could taste the saltiness of my own dried tears, contrasting with my throat, now dry as a desert.

Gray Eyes unzipped his pewter-colored fleece hoodie, kicking it to the floor out of his way, his eyes never losing focus.

"This is the big one now, Dana. Push hard this time," Gray Eyes spoke softly to the young woman.

"I can't do this," I yelped.

Squeezing my hands tightly, the young woman let out another earth-shattering scream. I let out my own ear-piercing wail, just as a gush of fluid poured out of her and the sound of a fresh, sharp cry filled the air.

Gray Eyes caught the tiny brown baby in his big open palms. He

7

unbuttoned his blue Oxford shirt, pulled his arms out of the sleeves one at a time, and swaddled the brown baby in a bundle.

"You have a daughter, Dana," he said, smiling a megawatt grin. He placed the baby on the new mom's belly, easing her a bit upright, instructing her to elevate her heart.

"I told you things would work out just fine," he said, a look of relief washing over him. "Dana, I'm gonna cut the cord next and help you pass the afterbirth, sweetie."

*T*he cab driver turned on what felt like two wheels again, coming to a screeching halt in front of the emergency doors of New York Presbyterian Hospital.

"Good timing," Gray Eyes muttered to himself as a sea of folks dressed in blue scrubs and wheeling a gurney rushed to open the cab doors.

New life had come into the world just as my own life was crumbling into tattered pieces around me. I was done for at thirty-one. Oh, how I wished I could close my eyes and stop existing. My hopes and dreams had abandoned me, marrying someone else.

Gray Eyes took the baby girl from the young mother's arms, handing her over to one of the nurses, backing his body out of the crouched position and onto the pavement. He moved aside while the miniature army of women and men dressed in blue placed the young woman on the gurney.

One of the men in blue grinned at Gray Eyes and chuckled. "I see it didn't take you long to start rolling this morning, E. Thought this was your day off?"

"No rest for the weary," Gray Eyes growled back. "Take care of her and that baby. She's family."

"And what about that one?" the man in blue quizzed, with raised eyebrows, tilting his head towards me.

Gray Eyes rolled his eyes up to the heavens and shook his head.

"I'll leave that one to you. No baby there. My job is done."

"I don't know, E—a cutie like that ought to be somebody's baby, if you know what I mean," the man in blue joked, elbowing him in the ribs. The man bent down, sticking his head into the cab, taking a good, long, hard look at me.

"Done with this," Gray Eyes barked again.

Done? Did he say he's done? No, I'm the one who's done! Done with Mr. Heartcracker. Done with Commander Gray Eyes. Done with life. I was done with everything, all of me shattered to slivers. So I closed my eyes; I willed myself out of existence. But then it occurred to me that I'd best keep one eye open. And it's a good thing I did— otherwise I would have missed what was coming next.

Gray Eyes made a slow, confident power stretch, forcing his strikingly tall and muscular frame upright, then letting out a deep sigh. He appeared to be a couple of inches over six feet, which made me think of some professional basketball players. Maybe he was a professional basketball player. Maybe that was why he was so good at catching little brown balls that were thrown his way.

Gray Eyes raised his arms over his head, rolled his neck from side to side, his bare, caramel-colored, sun-kissed chest on full display, his pants drenched in fluids. My eyes immediately locked in on the well-toned chest—not an ounce of fat on it. I had a full frontal peek at his beautiful, super-tight six-pack, with a magnificent V of muscle hugging his pelvis, a glimpse of which took my breath away.

By now, the sea of blue people had fully surrounded the cab. I was suspended in my tracks like a slow fish in a deep freeze. Gray Eyes put a firm grip on my hand and yanked me hard towards him, jerking me out of the cab. I shrank in his arms. His unbridled testosterone overcame me as he paused to stare down into my eyes. I knew that he was judging me. I hoped he was.

My legs felt like the blood had run out of them, and I wasn't sure my feet could move. Gray Eyes put his hand around my back for support, fixing me in his arms.

"Who the hell are you, exactly? And where did you come from?" he growled, his jaw tensing between syllables.

I winced at the sight of those gorgeous gray eyes, the color of a blooming storm at dawn. I opened my mouth to protest, but nothing came out. I was falling, but I was also rising up; this is what the arms of angels must feel like, as they bear us through the pearly gates.

And then everything began to fade to black. The last thing I saw was his large, well-manicured hands and strong muscular arms stretching to catch my body as it crashed down to the ground.

ulianna

"*J*told you I can walk," I pleaded with the stocky nurse who was rolling me in a wheelchair towards the hospital's exit doors.

"Sorry honey, hospital rules require me to wheel you out like this. It isn't every day that a woman faints in the arms of Dr. EZ," the middle-aged, stocky African American nurse said with a wicked grin.

"Dr. EZ?"

"Yeah, Doctor *Easy On The Eyes* Elliot Fischer," she chuckled heartily. Most of the young gals around here would have traded their left arm to find themselves in your position."

"Dr. Elliot Fischer? You mean the man in the cab isn't a basketball player? He's really a doctor?"

"Yes ma'am, he's a doctor all right. But he's not just any ole doctor. He's one of Vanity Fair's twenty-five most eligible African American Bachelors. That is, up until last year, before that former Ms. New

Yorker crazy woman got a hold of him. He's head of our hospital's new obstetrics wing. The Becker Wing."

"The Becker Obstetrical Wing?"

"Yup, that's the one."

I couldn't believe what I was hearing.

"Some fat cat money bagger donated several million dollars six years ago to build it as a result of his wife giving birth to twins," she said. "Fat Cat's wife was having a complicated delivery. Dr. EZ performed the delivery. Story goes Fat Cat was beyond grateful because his own mother had died in childbirth."

"The Becker Wing," I murmured softly, still in a state of disbelief at the coincidence. And I barely believed in coincidences. I believed everything happened for a reason.

"So the hospital got a new wing from all that gratitude," the nurse continued. "Now that handsome specimen of a man, Dr. EZ, Mr. Very Easy On The Eyes, heads the hospital's new multi-million dollar obstetrical wing. Word is, Dr. EZ is now good friends with the Fat Cat's wife."

"Oh my," I gulped loudly.

What the nurse didn't know was that Fat Cat's mother was *my* mother too. My mother, Julianna Giraurd Becker, had died during childbirth getting *me* here. When my brother Nicholas's wife Harper went into labor in the middle of a crisis, Nicholas went berserk like a crazy man threatening anyone and everyone to get his babies here safely. He had no intention of losing his wife Harper in the process. Mountains got moved that day at this hospital.

I glanced down at myself, relieved to be out of that horrid gray hospital gown that flashed my butt cheeks when I stood. It felt good to be back in my own clothes. I fingered the hospital wrist tag still on me, looking around for a way to get the wretched thing off.

"The nurses on Dr. EZ's wing have a pool going as to whether or not his engagement will last. A lot of us doubt that marriage will ever happen."

"What marriage?" I said, having lost my focus on the thread of this conversation that was going down gossip row. I didn't want to hear any more about marriage today.

"Why, Dr. EZ and the former Ms. New York."

"Oh yeah, that," I said, still stuck on the news that Gray Eyes was Chief of Obstetrics.

"Rumor is, his fiancée is slow rolling the wedding plans. He's looking none too happy these days."

The nurse continued with the hospital gossip as she rolled me down the long hall ever so slowly. She made a tsk tsk sound with her tongue emphasizing the words, "none too happy."

"None too happy" might explain all that barking he was doing at me, refusing to let me out of that cab, I thought.

"I want out of here as soon as possible. This day's been over for me since it began," I whined. "It was more than I could bear being stuck in a cab with Mister . . . Doctor . . . " I paused, conflicted. "Never mind," I said, shaking my head. I wasn't sure what the hell I thought of him. Maybe "Beautiful Asshole" were the words that I was missing.

"Well, don't worry sweetie. We're officially cutting you loose." She patted the top of my shoulder with her hand so as to reassure me, rolling me towards the lobby area doors.

"Your friends are waiting in the lobby to pick you up. Seems you've managed to create a bit of a stir yourself."

"How so?" I chirped with a bit of sarcasm in my voice, totally not surprised by anything at this point.

"One of the emergency room doctors, Doctor DeLuca, wanted to keep you around until tomorrow for observation. Seems your girl-friends raised a pretty big ruckus with the folks in the ivory tower. Phones starting ringing. The hospital big wigs in administration got all up in arms. Everybody started running around like this place was on fire."

"So let me just walk on out of here then. Why must I stay in this wheelchair like an invalid? I'm perfectly capable of walking out of here on my own steam."

I was getting impatient. I started to pout. I never was good at having my freedom restrained, being confined to small spaces—antiseptic hospital rooms especially—and most of all stuck in a cab in the middle of the day coaxing seven pound bundles of joy to make their appearance. This whole scene felt like a horror movie—and I hated horror movies.

I needed my freedom back, so I could finish getting myself out of Mr. Heartcracker's orbit, complete my crash into the wall, and permanently turn off my heart lights. I was tired of getting hurt. Tired of loving. Tired of losing. Tired of letting yet another man get into my soul, then abandoning me for someone else.

"I've got orders to treat you, Ms. Thang, with special care. You know, the kid glove treatment, baby. You're pretty special 'round these parts for some reason."

"That's because my name is Julianna Becker. My friends call me Jules."

The nurse stopped the wheelchair so abruptly, my entire torso jerked forward, then back again, making me grab the arms of the chair tightly so as not to be flung onto the floor.

"Becker? As in the Becker of the "Becker Obstetrical Wing" Becker?" she asked, eyes big, eyebrows raised, mouth opened wide.

"Yes *that* Becker. As in my brother Nicholas Becker who dropped ten million dollars in that wing that Mister Crazy Commando Doctor EZ whatever, who trapped me in his cab, apparently now runs."

"Well shut yo mouth," the nurse said. "Who'da thunk it." She laughed uncontrollably.

The nurse's demeanor lifted as she continued wheeling me toward the doors. She suddenly had a new pep in her step. I figured I had given her *the* prize piece of gossip that was going to land the title of Crown Jewel Gossiper, the keeper of the best information around here. My stock magically went up five hundred points with her, and somehow that pleased us both.

*S*he rolled me through the double doors that automatically opened with the press of a huge button located on the left wall. I sensed my girlfriends Maya and Logan had to be close by, once I laid eyes on my brother Nicky's driver, Silas. I could see Silas through the glass windows, standing outside near the long black stretch limousine wearing his uniformed black hat, black suit, and black gloves, looking sharp as a tack.

I heard Maya's stilettos clacking down the hospital lobby's linoleum-tiled floors first, with Logan right behind.

Maya Matthews and Logan Kennedy were my best friends. The three of us were thick as thieves since meeting at London's Winchester Boarding School in England. After boarding school, we stayed in England, each continuing on with our studies at Oxford University. We were born into some of New York's oldest money families, making us New York's next generation of trust fund babies.

We thought of ourselves at the "artsy gals." After graduation we stayed in England to pursue our "artsy professions." I landed at Le Cordon Bleu, trained in the Culinary Arts profession, morphing myself into the properly trained pastry chef. Maya studied Art History, Graphic Design, and Photography. Logan was a gifted classically trained pianist, now recognized in both New York and London.

My father, Blake Ross Becker II, aka "Big Daddy" to the family, was king of America's largest chicken processing dynasty. Maya's parents owned the largest African American law firm in the country, and Logan's people were world renowned shipping tycoons. Logan's father's shipping conglomeration was considered to be one of the finest in the world.

"Nothing but the best for the best," my brother Nicky would say. The acquisition of my brother's magnanimous yacht, *"The Julianna,"* was managed by Logan's father personally. Hence the three of us were tied at the hip on a lot of other levels beyond being old school chums. Family business interests connected us as well.

It didn't take much for Maya, Logan, and myself to bond and forge what has turned out to be a lifelong friendship.

"Jules!" both Maya and Logan screamed in unison. "Are you okay?"

They each took turns saying "Omigod," in a flurry of excited chatter.

I'd phoned Logan a few hours earlier, sobbing about my phone call with the Heartcracker Oliver Banks, letting her know I was here, all while begging her to get me out of this place.

"What happened to you? They wanted to keep you overnight but we were having none of it," Logan said looking at the nurse as if anyone with a brain could logically conclude that she, Logan, was the real one in authority. "This place is absolutely antiseptic."

"We had to call Nicholas," Maya spoke apologetically. "He insisted upon talking to the doctors himself, but at the end of the day we managed to get you sprung," she said, practically jumping up and down in excitement.

"God Maya, you called Nicky? Seriously?"

"Well what else would you have me do? He was the only surefire way to get you out of here," she said, shrugging her shoulders. "Whaaaat? You wanted us to leave you here?"

"Telling Nicky means I have to listen to him bitch about my taking public transportation. You know how he hates it when I do that. He might sic his guard dogs back on me again," I groaned.

"We had to choose, Jules," Maya huffed, crossing her arms in front of her and shifting her weight to one foot. "Freedom from these blue-deviled-dressed muckity-mucks, or Nicky. We picked the lesser of the two evils."

I rolled that idea around in my head for a minute, not convinced that was true. Nicky was going to turn up the heat with my security after this.

"Nicky's like a God. He can do anything. You're free. Get over it babe, it's done now," Logan said, looking around, giving the hospital the once over. "I hate hospitals."

She stepped behind the wheelchair, nudging the nurse out of the way so that she could push the wheelchair.

"No, *I* hate hospitals, which is why I need to get out of here."

"Me too," Maya said. "A gal could get sick up in here. Too many germs and all."

"Omigod, we heard you delivered a baby," Logan cackled. "How could you even manage such a huge feat after that devastating phone call from that good-for-nothing Oliver Banks?"

"Now's not the time Logan," Maya scolded. "We need some liquid courage first before we can do *that* conversation justice; just in case we need to go spray paint Oliver's new Corvette with obscenities tonight."

Logan snapped her hand and pointed her index finger at Maya. Then she and Maya slapped each other a sideways high five, palm first, backhand second.

"Please don't bring his name up to me anymore," I winced, feeling tears forming in the back of my eyes.

"You're done with him now Jules? Right? You're really done with him this time," Maya said, repeating herself in a fairly insistent tone.

"Yeah, color me done," I said, mustering up as much conviction that I could ring out of my body from what was left of today's stormy rollercoaster.

Stocky Nurse was fiddling nearby with a clipboard, but part of me was convinced she was taking in our every word.

"You're a hero Jules, delivering a baby and all," Logan said, flinging her long blonde curls over her shoulder, forcing a change in the subject. She reached down to my level in the wheelchair and planted a soft kiss on top of my forehead. I was certain she knew that I was fighting back tears.

Logan was real good at getting our little clan off anger-fueled topics and sore subjects when the three of us got together. I could always count on her to properly move the ball at the most opportune moments. She really needed to go into politics. She was very skilled at reading the temperature in a room. Not many wars would ever break out on Logan's watch.

"I really didn't do anything," I said, feeling terribly conflicted. Maya and Logan hadn't seen me lose my mind in that cab.

"Let's blow this joint," Maya said.

"Just a second ladies, your girlfriend has to sign these release papers first or she's going nowhere tonight," the nurse said, putting a halt to my rolling wheelchair.

She pushed a clipboard under my nose with her hands on her hips, giving Maya and Logan the evil stare.

"It's okay," I said to the girls, who were both silently throwing their own eye darts back at the nurse. "It's hospital procedure," I said, hoping to put an end to the stink eye stare-down by both sides.

"Yes, hospital procedure," the nurse repeated.

I signed my name quickly, beyond ready to get this show on the road.

"Thank you very much . . . ah . . . " I said, looking for the nurse's name tag.

"Barbara, but my friends call me Babs," she said, using her index finger to point out her name. "You can call me Babs too," she smiled.

I nodded, giving her a big smile back. "Thank you Babs."

Babs bent down close to my ear and whispered, "The best way to get over a man is to get under a new one."

Then she patted me lovingly on the shoulder again.

I smiled, figuring if I had a mother, that might be something she would say. I made a mental note to record that in my diary just in case I ever had to say that to my own daughter one day.

"*Now*, you're free to go," she said with full authority.

I stood up, just as Silas entered the lobby and took my hand to escort me out.

"Come now Ms. Julianna," Silas said. "Your brother is on pins and needles, waiting to hear from you. He would have come himself, but Superman and Wonder Woman had him wrapped up in "Doc McStuffin."

Silas was referring to my brother Nicholas's six-year-old twins, Miles and Milania's Halloween costumes. I totally forgot this was Halloween night.

"Yeah, yeah yeah," I said, waving my hand dismissively, noticing I still had the hospital tag on my wrist. "So much for Halloween," I lamented.

Silas opened the limousine doors and I slid into the back seat first. The temperature outside was much colder from earlier this afternoon, so I was pleased the limousine was warm and comfortable.

Silas coughed out loud to get Maya and Logan's attention, interrupting their conversation.

"Ahem. Ladies," Silas nodded to Maya and Logan. They both jumped inside behind me, each taking a seat on either side of me.

"*J*ules, don't even think about bailing out on Halloween because the universe dealt you a dirty blow today," Logan said. "We're still going to the Halloween party tonight at Luigi's. Everybody that's anybody knows Luigi's has the best Halloween Party in all of Manhattan. It'll help take your mind off things."

"Yeah Jules. One monkey does not stop a show," Maya insisted.

"Yeah, even a married monkey," Logan said.

Maya and I looked at each other, not sure we thought Logan was making any sense. Logan often said things from time to time that scrambled our brains.

"We brought the costumes. We're going to put them on, we're going to go out, get wasted, have fun, and then tomorrow you're going to finally put that heartbreaking loser to rest," Maya demanded.

"And what costumes are we all going to be wearing tonight Maya?" I ask, pursing my lips, scared to know the answer to the question.

"Well, I'm going to be . . . "

"No, let me tell it Maya. You're going to scare Jules out of going, and we can't have that," Logan said, her own level of excitement barely contained.

"Damn bitch, a woman can't ever be first whenever you're around." Maya sulked, throwing shade, popping her fingers in the air with her signature top to bottom snapping motion.

"Oh the hell with it, you tell it then Maya. Don't take all day," Logan surrendered, waving her hand in dismissal at Maya.

"*Somebody* tell it please," I demanded.

"Nah, let Logan tell it. She'll die ten deaths if she doesn't tell her cockamamie ideas first."

My confidence in the outcome of this story was eroding fast.

"Okay then Maya."

Logan straightened her back and cleared her throat as if she were getting ready to make a speech in front of Toastmasters. I briefly closed my eyes, not sure I wanted to hear what was coming out of it next.

"Maya's going to be a sexy Laker Girl. I'm going to be a hottie Swat Team gal, and . . . you're . . . you're . . . "

"And I'm going to be what?" I said, looking for some tequila in the limousine wet bar. I had a feeling I was going to need it. Surely my brother stocked tequila in here. Yes, he did. Found it. Gonna drink it now.

"You're going to be Tinkerbell," Logan said, looking so proud you would have thought she was getting ready to accept her Oscar at the Academy Awards.

Oh hell to the no.

"Tinker-fucking-bell?" I said. "You've got to be kidding. You guys get to be hot sexy sirens and I get to be freakin' Tinkerbell?!?"

"Yes Jules. You know how Tinkerbell watched over Peter Pan," Logan said.

"And that means *what* in this instance?"

"In means somebody has to keep the bad girls out of trouble, right?" she said, turning both hands over with the palms up, a quizzical look on her face that screamed 'Why don't you get it?'

There was a pregnant pause in the air as they both waited for me to respond.

"Do I get some fairy dust?" I grinned.

"Pink edible glitter-like candy dust," Maya said casually, while opening the tequila bottle, turning it up to her lips.

Logan clapped her hands together in satisfaction.

"Logan's stupid idea. Next year *I* get to pick the costumes," Maya grunted.

"I love it, Maya being a cheerleader and all," I laughed. "It's poetic justice."

"Why the hell can't I be Catwoman or something? I hate pom poms," Maya mumbled.

"We all need a cheerleader in life, Maya," Logan said, passing around three shot glasses between us. She slapped Maya's hand for not accepting the shot glass readily. "And God knows Jules could use some cheering up right now."

"I need more than a cheerleader and some fairy dust, that's for sure. I need a new life."

"Now, we're going to turn the page tomorrow Jules," Maya said in her best motherly voice. "Tonight is about fun, remember. Besides, you might get lucky and meet a hot guy tonight. Everybody that's anybody will be at Luigi's."

Maya poured each of us a shot of tequila.

"Who's going to know who's who," I said. "Folks will be running around in costume. With my luck I'll pick up Peter-Fucking-Pan. A man that never wants to fucking grow up," I laughed wryly, taking a swig of my shot.

We all starting laughing out loud. Logan laughed so hard she spit her tequila out all over herself, coughing and spurting liquor everywhere.

It was nice to be able to laugh at them and myself. That's what good friends were for, despite the fact I couldn't guarantee I might not start crying all over again any minute now. But for the time being, I'd take what I could get. One hour at a time.

---

*T*he limousine phone rang and a hush fell over the car. We knew who was calling. I could see my brother Nicky's name come up on the screen. I put my index finger to my lips, motioning for Maya and Logan to be quiet. That was too much to ask. They both starting giggling like idiots.

"Hey Nicky," I said, trying to sound serious, the tequila giving me a bit of false confidence.

"Julianna, sweetheart, how are you feeling?"

"Well it's been a rough day, but I'm better now, Nicky. I'm glad I was able to get out of that hospital. Thanks for pulling strings today."

My brother Nicholas was the master puppeteer. He could talk the white off rice. He had the gift of gab that made him the successful man that he was, and it didn't hurt that he was *very* successful. His net worth was close to a half a billion dollars now, due to the rise of his angel investment company, Milk Money.

Maya and Logan started giggling loudly, again pouring each of us more shots. I signaled for them to be quiet with my hand, but they snickered even more.

"I hear your girlfriends in the background. I'm glad you're not alone. Frankly, I would have preferred that you stayed put at the hospital overnight, just to be sure you're okay, but your posse was all over me."

"You know how I feel about hospitals Nicky. Really I'm fine. Honestly. I was overwhelmed over Oliver's news. And then the cab ride, the baby being born, it was all too . . . "

"Julianna, how many times do I have to tell you that you need to make use of the family's transportation fleet? I don't like the idea of your using public transportation. I can't keep you safe. Too many of my enemies have unsavory interests in my family's whereabouts. Your taking public transportation will be viewed by them as one of my vulnerabilities."

"I need to be as normal as I can Nicky."

"That's not your life, sweetheart. I need to feel like I can protect you. And after what happened to Harper, it's even more important that you try to play by the rules. If Big Daddy knew I agreed to let you use public transportation, he'd string both our asses up permanently. Try to help me out here Julianna."

Harper Montgomery Becker was my brother's wife. They had six-year-old twins. He loved his wife more than life. She was the very oxygen he breathed. I wanted that for myself, but my picker was off. I had wasted time loving men that didn't love me the same way I loved them, and I was clueless as to what mistakes I was making. I didn't know what was keeping me from getting the outcome that I wanted, but Nicky had somehow figured it out. I didn't know how to get what he had. His wife Harper thought the sun rose and shined in his every move.

"I'm sorry. I was just so upset over the news from Oliver that's all," I said, dropping my voice level several octaves lower.

"Yes, your girls read me in. I'm sorry you had to go through that loss Julianna. It's just as well. He wasn't good enough for you. The man didn't deserve you."

"I know," I murmured.

"He had an oversized ego. He played games with your heart for way too long. Never committing, but never wanting to let you go either. He wouldn't know a good woman if she came up and slapped him across the face. It's all for the best Julianna. In time, you'll see that."

That was the one thing that I loved about my brother Nicholas. He always had my back, even when I was a kid growing up. I was my mom's mid-life baby. Even though there was a ten-year difference in age between us, I always felt close to Nicky. He understood me. He got me. My other brother Blake was two years older than Nicholas, and closest to my father, which kept him largely preoccupied with all things "Big Daddy," but Nicholas was the one who was there for me. He was more than a brother. He was my protector. My friend.

"Are you on your way to the Towers?"

"Yes, we're almost there. We plan to change into our costumes and head straight over to Luigi's."

"Thank God. Blake and Big Daddy won't be around tonight. Lucky for us, they hate Halloween. Hell, I'm not sure why I indulge in the madness myself. I do it for Harper. She drags me into this nonsense every year," he grumbled.

My brother Blake Ross Becker III, aka "Three," was the family lawyer for the chicken processing empire. Nicholas had done his own thing, building a multi-million-dollar empire as an Angel Investor.

Nicky led everyone he interacted with to believe that he was a "God," making miracles happen and helping people to fulfill their lifelong dreams. But Nicholas was serious as a heart attack. He did exactly that every day. He led his life in such a way that he contributed to a better world by helping humanity with his wealth. He paid it forward. But his family came first, and he would climb Mount Everest for his family.

Me, I was still scratching around life's highways trying to figure out who I was, what I needed. Right now, all of my life's most important fronts were in a shambles. Besides my relationship crumbling, my professional life wasn't too much better right now. I had failed at making a couple of business enterprises work over in England, despite the fact I was certain my next venture would be a hit.

I was going to build a pastry empire. I had even worked out the branding. People were gonna love *Sugar Mommy's*. I knew that in my heart and soul, because whenever I baked cookies or cakes, I couldn't get rid of Maya and Logan. They begged me for everything sweet whenever I made pastry samples, in anticipation of what I'd plan to put on the menu. I wanted to talk to Nicky about my thoughts about building my pastry business, but this wasn't the time.

My love life was a zero. Oliver had left me, marrying someone else. I was internally fighting feelings of inadequacies and basically feeling not good enough. I was working hard to put on a good face, but deep in my heart I was crushed to the core. I needed to talk to Nicky about business when I was stronger internally. Nicky didn't accommodate character weakness nor whiney boo-boos when it came to business, life, and love. I needed to first get over this blow Oliver dealt me.

"We're at the Towers, Nicky. I need to go."

"I'll meet you at Luigi's, Julianna. Harper's preparing the twins for bed. Their nannies just brought them in to my study for their good-night kiss."

"Who should I look for?"

I could hear my brother hugging and kissing his kids, both giggling in the background.

"Tinkerbell, Hot Swat Momma, and a Lakers Cheerleader."

"And you are . . . "

"Tinkerbell, who else?"

Nicky laughed heartily.

"I'll look for you Julianna."

"And, who am I looking for this year? God and the Mother Mary?"

Nicholas laughed at my sarcasm.

"Bond. James Bond," he said in his deepest, sexiest voice. "And I'll have a very gorgeous Bond Girl attached to my hip with my vodka shaken, not stirred."

"You are so my brother," I giggled.

"Love you Julianna."

"Love you Nicky."

We hung up. I smiled. My heart was warmed after a very ugly day.

"Shall I wait here Ms. Julianna?" Silas asked as he eased the limousine curbside in front of Becker Towers.

"Yes please, Silas. The next time you see us, we'll look different. Will you recognize us?"

"I'll know you, Ms. Julianna. A beautiful woman like you is hard to miss."

Silas was good for my ego. He was so comforting. No wonder Nicky felt comfortable letting Silas drive me.

"Thank you Silas," I said as Maya, Logan, and I headed into Becker Towers to change and re-make ourselves.

Too bad the other men in my life that mattered didn't find me hard to miss.

*lliot*

*S*ix hours later, I found myself tossing and turning on an empty delivery room bed trying my best to get a couple of hours sleep before I needed to rise and check up on Dana again. The baby's pediatrician had examined Dana's new daughter. She had a touch of jaundice, but otherwise a clean bill of health. So I was overjoyed. Dana was resting well too.

I hadn't gotten much sleep this week coming down off of a three-day stint of rotation. Today was supposed to be about rest and relaxation. What could I say? Best laid plans.

I was desperate for few moments of shuteye, but sleep wouldn't come. Every time I closed my eyes, my mind drifted back to big brown doe eyes, pouty lips, and dark brown wavy curls. A pixie goddess was infiltrating my thoughts, robbing me of much needed rest.

My mind was in overdrive trying to process a boatload of new emotions stirring inside me. How was I to know that on the one day that I decided to take a day off and treat my teenage cousin to lunch in Central Park, that she was going to give birth early? She wasn't even due for three more weeks. Who knew when I scurried her into a cab rushing her to the hospital, that a luscious teary-eyed lunatic would jump into the cab with us, lapse into a full blown panic attack, and then collapse that perfect denim-clad bottom in my arms making my blood heat?

I'd had plenty of experience dealing with crazed pregnant women with raging hormones, but they had nothing on that petite stick of dynamite that fell into my arms. I probably shouldn't have snapped on her, but it took every bit of my strength to stay focused on catching Dana's baby. Jesus, that delirious bombshell wailed as much as Dana. And she wasn't even the one having the baby. What could have possibly had her so upset?

Part of me wanted to kiss those pouty lips to calm her down and put her out of misery. But I feared I was going to be forced to give her mouth-to-mouth resuscitation instead.

What was it about that woman that was awakening lustful thoughts in me, interfering with my need for sleep? Her petite frame tucked in my arms oh so nicely. She was the wholesome, healthy kind of beautiful that I found incredibly refreshing. Her mouth, breasts, and butt weren't pumped full of silicone and implants, atypical of most of the women in my social circle.

I turned over on my other side in the dark, stabbing hard at the pillow under my head. God, maybe I'd made a mistake not going home to change and to grab a couple of winks. At least at home maybe my mind wouldn't be so adrift making me feel like I was a lost ship out at sea without a rudder.

Nah. Who was I fooling? Being at home meant I'd be more like a ship tossing around on the high seas caught in the middle of the perfect storm. Going home meant dealing with my fiancée Kimber Lawson.

Torn with that choice, I did what came natural to me. I jumped in my blue scrubs, located the nearest empty hospital bed, and waited for the next opportunity to bring new life into the world. Yeah. That was the thing I loved most. It was my passion. Catching babies steadied me.

Surely, it wasn't a good sign that I didn't want to go home. I was avoiding renewing last night's argument with Kimber over why she needed another ten grand for a wedding that didn't appear to me to be much underway. Over a year had passed since we had gotten engaged and moved in together. If our post-engagement lifestyle was the precursor peek into what would be our marriage, I wasn't sure I was the right man for this job. I was starting to feel like I wasn't sharing my life's passion and joys with the right woman now.

Kimber had turned into somebody I didn't feel I knew anymore. She was cold, self-centered, and uncaring. She was a pushy twenty-eight-year-old whose only current interest seemed to be in my bank account.

Kimber routinely used our future nuptials as the excuse to tap into my finances. She made excuses whenever I suggested wedding dates. It was hard to tell that any real plans were underway, despite the fact that my bank account shrunk from enough withdrawals to finance an acceptable start for any decent wedding planner with a vision.

Not to mention, she was relentless in her demands that I buy her a new Mercedes. She claimed she couldn't be a doctor's wife without the right car to reflect the right image. I was drowning in my own sea of wrong choices.

I turned over again on my side finally feeling myself starting to drift, only to open one sleepy eye after hearing a high pitched voice outside the room, and a small hand slipped through the door jam, switching on the fluorescent lights.

"*I*'m sorry to disturb you Dr. Fischer, but you have a call at the front desk," Patty said.

Patty was one of the younger nurses on the unit. Right about now, she looked incredibly regretful for having to awaken me.

"I think it's your fiancée on the phone, sir. I told her you were resting, but she was pretty insistent," Patty said meekly, her head down and her eyes not wanting to face mine.

"Thank you Patty. Don't worry about it. I wasn't getting much sleep anyway. Really."

I tapped Patty on the shoulder, reinforcing my words that it was really okay. She exhaled, smiled, and gave me a look of relief that I'd hope would follow my words.

"No problem Dr. Fischer."

I grabbed my cellphone that I had placed on silent mode off the end table, noticing twelve missed calls from Kimber. I moved lazily, following Patty out the door to the hospital phone located on the corner of the nurse's unit desk where we each typically took outside calls.

A couple of the nurses scattered hurriedly in different directions as I moved to pick up the phone. If my facial expression was any clue, I probably looked rather ominous, and they wanted to respect my privacy. All the nurses departed except Babs, of course. Babs went to the coffee pot, poured a cup, and shoved it my hand.

Babs was one of my favorite nurses. She was middle-aged, experienced at her job, and treated me like I was her own son. She was very good at making sure that I always had whatever I needed to do my job effectively. Be it an early morning coffee, forceps for a four a.m. delivery, or late night ice cream, Babs had my back.

But, she was queen of knowing all the hospital scuttlebutt way before shit hit the fan, which meant if I didn't want my business all over the hospital, I needed to watch my words. The fact that I was even in this position at work due to Kimber's insensitivity pissed me off further. I could just about put money on the fact that whatever Kimber wanted wasn't going to rise to any real emergency. This was likely going to be a money conversation about the fact that I flew the coop last night to avoid yet another confrontation, which was why she was going to Defcon Four today.

"r. Fischer here," I said, closing my eyes and clenching my teeth.

"Elliot?"

"Yes Kimber?"

"You didn't pick up your phone, Elliot. I don't like being ignored."

"I was busy."

"I thought you were coming home after you finished lunch with the 'young and restless.' We need to finish our talk from last night. You know, the talk that we were having before you ran out the door headed to your medical sanctuary."

"My cousin is not the 'young and restless' Kimber. Her name is Dana. She went into labor. I delivered her baby today, thank you. This is my job; this is what I do. We've discussed this a hundred times before."

"Okay, so the baby's here now, but you're not."

"I'm at work, Kimber. What's the urgency?"

"I need another check for the wedding. Plus, we need to go shopping."

"Shopping is not something you need me for, Kimber."

"We need matching diamond earrings for the wedding. The one you wear in your ear is too small. Impressions are everything."

"Kimber, do you even listen to yourself? You're ridiculous."

"And I need a new car."

"Your car works perfectly fine."

"I need a new one, Elliot. What part of that did you miss last night?"

"Oh I didn't miss it. I don't plan to buy you another car. I can't talk about this here Kimber," I said, gritting my teeth.

"You either talk about this with me now, or I will talk about it there face to face with you Elliot. Either way we will talk."

"I'm at work Kimber, performing my job, something you might want to give more consideration to, frankly. Maybe you should consider volunteer work or employment."

"I've given up my career for you, Elliot, to be the perfect wife. What are you saying exactly?"

"You've done no such thing. The pageant was over two and half years ago. You haven't leveraged that opportunity into anything income-producing, other than your plans to marry me, which by all accounts is on a pace equal to taking a slow boat to China," I snapped.

"You spend more time there with your head between every other woman's vagina than you do with mine," she snapped. "I'm getting a little sick of your neglect. Come home Elliot. Write the check."

"I don't intend to have this conversation with you right now Kimber. You need to respect the fact that I'm at work," I said, raising my voice.

"Whatever," she said, taking the hint. "And, don't forget we're due at Luigi's tonight. It's their annual Halloween Party."

"I'll meet you there," I hissed.

"Meet me there? You mean you won't be coming home first? How will I know you?"

"I'll be coming as myself. I'm sure you'll be able to find me. Who are you going as Kimber?"

I had no idea why I asked that question. She might as well have been the gold-digging, pushy, make-my-life-miserable Wicked Witch of the West.

"I'll be the beautiful black mermaid in black sequins, in case you give a damn, Elliot."

"Of course I give a damn, Kimber. But you're out of control lately."

"If I didn't have to beg you for money for your own wedding, I wouldn't be out of control. We could go back to normal."

Normal. What the fuck was normal? Who was this woman? I sighed heavily, pinching my nose with my fingers, clenching my teeth and closing my eyes. Fuck it.

"I don't have time for this shit, Kimber."

I slammed the phone down on her much harder than I realized, spilling coffee, drawing attention to myself.

"I'm sorry you had to hear that Babs."

Babs looked at me out of the corner of her eye with an expression of sympathy. She was probably wondering the same thing I was wondering right now. Why in hell was I marrying this insensitive contemptuous woman that only cared about appearances and what I could give her?

"It'll all work out, Doc. If you don't mind my saying, you've got to be careful what you ask for, because you might just get it. But looking on the positive side, sometimes when we get what we don't want, it gets us that much closer to what we do want. You know what I mean?"

I nodded at Babs. But no, I didn't know what she meant. I didn't want to think about it either.

"I suppose," I nodded, feigning agreement, hoping that I didn't look as stupid as I was feeling.

"Imma say it like this Doc, 'cause I know what I just said was lost on you, you being long on intellect, but a wee bit short on common sense. What you want and what you need are entirely different things. Sometimes what you neeeeeed," she said emphasizing the word, "drops right in your lap, if you get my drift," Babs said with a wink.

Babs moved her hands out in front of her as if she was catching something in her arms.

What the hell was she talking about? I felt clueless in this mish mash called a conversation. Maybe Kimber had sucked my brain out of my head and I was going to be momentarily fucked up for a while. Before I could respond to Babs, Patty returned back to the unit desk.

"Dr. Fischer, you wanted me to remind you when Ms. Dana awoke. She's finished her lesson on how to bathe her baby and is doing a feeding right now. This might be a good time for you to check in on her."

"Thanks Patty. Hand me her chart. I'm headed to her room right now."

I was glad to have an out from that nonsensical conversation I was having with Babs. I was totally clueless to what she was saying.

"Now don't go forgetting what I said, Doctor E," Babs said, looking at me sternly as if she were underscoring her point.

I nodded silently to acknowledge that I heard her, but I sure as hell wasn't feeling like I got her drift. I didn't know anything anymore.

---

*I*sley Brothers *Fight The Power* ringtone started playing on my phone. It was a fitting ringtone for my good friend Gabriel.

Gabriel spent his early years as a physician in the Doctors Without Borders program. As such, he was now one of the best emergency room physicians in all of New York. But he was unconventional. He had no tolerance for the bureaucratic side of medicine.

Gabriel was routinely at war with the hospital's administration. They thought his methods often bordered on the unorthodox. If Gabriel thought he could get away with avoiding proper paperwork, he would. It was a conflict for the hospital because he was good at his job. But in-house counsel—namely, Dexter Esposito, Esquire—was always on his ass about how he pushed the envelope.

Dexter Esposito had it out for Gabriel and me ever since he flunked out of medical school. Unable to catch the brass ring and enter the medical profession, he went to law school instead. He later ended up here at the hospital with us, making our lives miserable at every turn. Dexter had a secret desire to be a physician. The fact that he had failed at that endeavor fed into his already humongous sense of insecurity. And when his insecurities were peaked, he looked for ways to make Gabriel and I miserable. Gabriel took advantage of every opportunity to remind that little twerp that he wasn't a physician and never will be, which only fueled Dexter's lack of confidence further.

Gabriel was exceptional at this job, but everyone had no doubt that he was a bull in a china cabinet, the epitome of unguided missile, oftentimes creating unnecessary risk management issues for the hospital. Gabriel was a child prodigy, son of the famous cardiologist Dr. Nathan DeLuca, so for all practical purposes nobody really seriously messed with him and his nonsense. He was just too damn valuable. At age sixteen, Gabriel had discovered a diagnostic test for pancreatic cancer. The fact that the hospital had snagged him had put the facility on the map, gaining it nationwide recognition.

"What's the word G?"

"Well let's see now, *Il Mio Amico*. Besides you throwing that cute little catch back into the pond?"

"What are you talking about man?"

"You know what I'm talking about *Il Mio Amico*."

"Dude, I know you're Italian and all, but aside from me not speaking the language, I hardly understand your English either."

"That beautiful woman in the cab with the dreamy eyes that were planted all over you before she collapsed into the arms of Dr. EZEEEEE," Gabriel teased.

"Man, knock it off. You think you're still out in the jungle. I've heard the stories. Here in the states, you know we draw the line between doctor and patient. And seeing how she ended up in the ER, that would make her *your* patient. Besides, I'm getting married."

"Oh no, man you got it wrong this time. That one has jumped out of the pond already."

"Damn, what kind of doctor are you man? You didn't even keep her for observation overnight?"

"Sorry E. That shithead Dexter saw to it that the powers that be came down on my head all at the same time. I had to cut the line on that little cutie. I set her loose around six o'clock."

"Damn man, was she okay?"

"Besides her being an emotional basket-case over some breakup with a man, yeah. I thought she was okay physically. Emotionally, not so much. But damn, I wouldn't have minded trying to help her mend that broken heart. A few hours in my arms, and I'd make her forget that motherfucker's name."

"Jesus man, you should have kept her for observation anyway, at least overnight."

"There's only so much fighting the power I can manage in one day. I'm in the ER saving lives. We can't all bring new life into the world E, some of us have to help to keep folks here in this earthly realm," Gabriel laughed.

I couldn't believe that Gabriel had released her so quickly.

"Whoever she was E, the big guns came out. I wasn't going to fight the power for a woman with a broken heart dude."

"What do you mean?"

"She had a bad breakup today. That fainting spell was brought on by acute stress and anxiety. Her heart is physically fine in spite of whatever asshole dude cracked it in half. Pretty little thing like that ought not to have to suffer that hard."

I felt a knot form in my throat just hearing that she was suffering from matters of the heart. I couldn't explain why I took it personal, but I didn't like the idea of her having her heart broken over some undeserving jerk.

"That was still a funky move on your part G to release her."

"You're the one that delivered a baby in front of her, barking orders at her like she was a pretend nurse."

"It was a pressing moment."

I don't know why I expected Gabriel to understand. He would have had to have been there. I don't try to tell him how to run his ER, and he doesn't try to tell me how to run my obstetrics wing. But I felt this was a different circumstance.

"Yeah, I heard about your pressing moment. She woke up out that fainting spell, babbling twenty miles and hour, about what you put her through in that cab. Where are your manners brother?" G laughed, pulling my coattails some more. "Wine and dine, brother. You put her through blood and babies."

"Me? She was the one that jumped into *my* cab, not the other way around."

"Dude, she was so scatterbrained and freaked out, I had to give her a valium. She slept for a few hours before I released her. That seemed to satisfy the folks upstairs."

"Fuck man. I can't believe you let her go. What the hell do you want anyway? I'm on my way to check on Dana and the baby."

"What's wrong E, Kimber got your Calvin's in a bunch?" Gabriel laughed. "Were you planning to come down to the ER and resuscitate that cute little package back to life?"

"Let it go G. Kimber's on my ass today. I don't need to deal with your nonsense either."

"Sorry to hear it E."

I sighed heavily, disturbed on some level that my cab mate had checked out of the hospital already. I never got to introduce myself, nor apologize for my gruffness. I hadn't said thank you.

"Now, I ain't saying she's a gold-digger," G starting singing like Kanye through the phone, "but she ain't messin' with no broke brothers."

"Fuck you man. I swear you were out in the jungle way too long. Your mind is gone, dude. I'm having a crisis here. Things are starting to get crazy. Kimber wants a new car, a huge wedding . . . money money money G."

"Dude, I already told you Kimber was a blood sucking gold-digger from the giddy-up. You just got lost in all those silicone titties swaddling your face. And she just keeps digging deep into your pockets. You're better than an ATM, man. Can I marry you?"

"Fuck you man."

"Okay dude. I'll get off your case for now. I'm gonna ride or die with you E. Whenever you get ready to get off this runaway train called Kimber, just let me know. We'll head out to Paris for a couple of months, and lay low for a while."

"Come back to reality Gabriel."

"Dude, that is my version of reality. What the hell is up with you anyway?"

I knew Gabriel was on point. I had lost my sense of humor since I had gotten engaged. I used to be fun. Now I was a basket of worries, nerves, and definitely not anywhere close to being fun anymore. And I knew why. I was drowning, trying to walk myself down the altar with a woman that didn't want me for me. She wanted me for what I could do for her. I was miserable over the thought of it.

"I've got to head home now, and hash stuff out. Kimber and I are just not on the same page these days."

"These days? Man, personally I don't like to say this because we all love who we love, but Kimber never did really strike me as anything other than a woman that wanted you for what you could give her."

"I just don't know which end is up with her and me anymore Gabe."

"Well you sure acted like you knew which end was up when you put that eye-popping ring from Tiffany's on her finger. That ring had to set you back a whole year's salary. When you go to Tiffany's dude, a woman takes a ring like that to mean forever."

"What's Tiffany's got to do with this G?"

You know, as in "Tiffany's is forever." It's like an insurance policy to a gold digger. Didn't anybody tell you that the divorce rate with gold diggers was higher than the fucking unemployment rate?"

"What should I do?"

"Cut the cord, man. Now. There's always somebody with more gold with those types. Faithful is not in their handbook. He who has the most gold wins."

"I can't man. I've come too far. I'm trying to make this work. Everybody knows marriage is work."

"Yeah, as in she's working the big "I" while you're trying to get to the "us." Dude, there's no "I" in "team." But if that's what you want, I'm here for you."

I sighed heavily through the phone, then I made a mental note to myself that I had been sighing a lot lately. That wasn't a particularly healthy sign.

"Go home and try to work it out then man. But if you need a break, I plan to grab X after work and head over to Maximillion's before we drop in at the Halloween party at Luigi's."

Our mutual friend Xavier was a personal trainer for the New York Jets. Close family and friends referred to him as X.

"Maximillion's is having Sparkles, Bubbles, and Baby Doll on stage tonight. I don't plan to miss *that* Halloween performance. Hell man, even I'm going to be frightened with all those beautiful tits and ass parading non-stop on stage in front of me. You know where to find me brother."

"Man, you know I'm working on trying to give up Maximillion's. If Kimber got wind that I was back hanging out in that gentlemen's club, you'd have to stitch my balls back on from where she cut them off."

Gabriel and I both started laughing loudly at the same time. Maximillion's was one of New York's most opulent Gentleman's Clubs. It was practically hedonistic—a very discreet club with play-mate quality dancers. It was located within walking distance of Times Square. The club boasted a two thousand bottle wine cellar with a celebrity chef steakhouse. It was a mega club, with six stages. It had well over a hundred and fifty uber hotties that held it down. Maximillion's boasted a celebrity client list second to none. Any charges hitting your credit card showed up as Michael's Steakhouse. Maximillion's was the epitome of discreet. We spent a lot of time and money there on our bad days, and lately I was having a lot of those. Gabrielle, Xavier, and I considered Maximillion's to be our escape hatch when life's pressures got too great. It was our personal hideaway from the outside world when we needed to let the steam out. It seemed upon reflection that my time spent there had increased a lot more now since my engagement with Kimber. I seem to always be pissed off, landing at Maximillion's.

"You're coming to Luigi's then?" I said.

"Do I have a choice? Who should I look for?"

"Me, myself, and I."

"Man, you are not coming as a doctor again for the third year in a row? Your shit ain't even funny anymore E. Get a life. It's Halloween, for Christ sakes."

"Yeah, and you are gonna be who this year?"

"Men in Black, baby."

"Jesus, Gabriel."

"Xavier's gonna rock his dad's old Navy pilot jumpsuit, coming as his own version of Maverick—you know, Top Gun. At least some of us are creative, motherfucker. Your coming as a damn doctor again is getting old. Matter of fact, it's getting downright frightening. Getting scared of you."

"Fine. I know who to look for then. The two clowns closest to the bar."

"Oh you're calling Xavier and me clowns now, E? It's like that?"

"Bitch, you know you and X are the bullets to my nine," I chuckled. "You're still my boy, G. I love you and X like my own brothers."

"Motherfucker you don't have brothers. *I* am your brother. Maximillion's at the top of the eight?"

"Yeah yeah yeah. I might have to sneak in," I laughed.

"Bubbles and Babydoll," Gabriel said.

"Shit man, you need to get a life, and a wife."

On a good day at Maximillion's, Gabriel and Xavier typically threw tons of cash at two Hungarian beauties, Bubbles and Babydoll. My personal favorite was Sparkles. Sparkles was a Brazilian beauty with dark brown wavy hair cascading down her back. She was a natural beauty. No hair extensions. No false eyelashes. A certified stunner. She was hot enough to make a man leave his happy home.

But in all her glory, she didn't make my heart race, like that woman that landed in the cab today. God, I couldn't keep my mind off that cute pixie and the way she looked at me before she fainted. There was no denying the strength of my attraction to her.

"Un uh . . . Marriage is not for me. You got to ride the coochie or die, E."

"You definitely don't sound like a well-bred Italian. Who are you anyway?"

"I'm your brother from another mother, E. Don't get it twisted," Gabriel laughed heartily.

"See you later man."

"You know where to find us, E."

"By the way G, the woman in the cab, who was she anyway? What was her name?"

"Hell if I know. Somebody named Julianna Becker."

"Fuck meeeeeeeee," I shouted through the phone.

I pondered momentarily whether I should tell Gabriel to come upstairs and resuscitate my ass. Was Gabriel fucking with me?

"What is your problem E? Get a grip on yourself."

I guess not. He really hadn't put two and two together. Man's working too hard.

"Becker, Gabriel. You know, *Becker*. As in Becker Obstetrical Wing. Ring a bell, motherfucker?"

"Whoooa . . . ," Gabriel said, letting out a cool whistle. "Yeah bitch, like I said . . . he who has the gold wins." He started laughing uncontrollably. "You are so fucked to the wall *Il Mio Amico*."

No, I was speechless.

 ulianna

"*H*urry up, we're going to be late," I said, shimmying my hips and trying to squeeze into the little—and tight—thigh-high green-sequined Tinkerbell dress. I slipped my feet, with green sparkly manicured toes, into a pair of gold goddess stilettos that completed my look. Logan handed me a beautiful long blonde curly wig. I placed it on my head, adorning it with tiny green sequined hair clips, accentuating the blonde hair with tiny green twinkled stars.

I glanced at myself in the full length mirror giving myself the once over. Even I had to acquiesce to Logan's choice of costumes for me. I looked like beautiful glittering green eye candy. I put my hand on my hip looking in the mirror, thinking this was as good a time as any to find out if it were true that blondes have more fun. I hoped at least for the evening, I could numb my thoughts and try to forget about the man that had stomped my heart in two.

Logan stood behind me helping me to slip into the fancy green sparkled wings. She handed me my magical wand and a bag of pink candied glitter dust.

"You did well pulling this look together Logan. Even I have to admit this is a very befitting look, perfect for the occasion."

I whipped my head around in order to give Logan the once over in her costume.

"You look freaking hot," I gasped.

"I'm a first responder," she said in her best Marilyn Monroe voice.

"You sure about that? It looks more like who's going to get to *you* first," I laughed.

Logan had on a pair of tall over-the-knee stiletto black leather boots, a black leather thigh high jumpsuit that laced up the back, and a black baseball cap that had the words SWAT written across the top in white lettering. She had a silver toy gun that looked almost real attached to a garter on her left thigh. Her naturally long blonde curls were flowing freely under her cap down to the small of her back. She applied a siren red colored lipstick to her lips, licking them slowly, then topping them off with a sparkly clear lip gloss on top. She was sporting a pair of flashy silver handcuffs that were attached to her waist, appearing ready to put some unsuspecting guy on lockdown. It was a fitting costume for Logan. She looked like a beautiful domina-trix without the whip. She was a huge control freak. And in that outfit, there was no doubt when you looked at her who was in control.

Logan slid a pair of mirrored lens aviator eyeglasses over her eyes, allowing her to see out without anyone else being able to see into them. She tossed her short chinchilla fur jacket over the back of her shoulder.

"Where's Maya?"

"C'mon, Maya, let's see what you look like, girl."

Maya exited the kitchen quickly, scarfing down a couple of my pumpkin spice cupcakes that I had recently baked for my twin niece and nephew, Miles and Milania.

"Mmm these are soooo good Jules. I hope these make it on the *Sugar Mommy* menu."

Logan and I looked at Maya. We both had huge grins on our face.

"What?" she asked with a quizzical look on her face.

I spoke first.

"Look at you Ms. LA Laker Girl."

Maya shook her hips from side to side, her mouth full of cupcake, orange icing with crumbs on the side of her check.

I dusted the crumbs and orange icing off the side of her face.

"Turn around and twirl for us Mommy," Logan said. "Let's see the goods."

Maya had on purple and gold boy shorts with a matching tank top that tied in a knot underneath her breasts, revealing a very toned midriff. *LA Lakers* was written in purple across the back of the tank top. She had on white patent leather boots, purple wristbands, and a matching purple headband securing her dark chestnut brown hair. She had a deep purple dyed-to-match tiny Tibetan lamb fur jacket in her hand. She was holding two purple and gold tinseled pom poms in one hand, and a cupcake in the other.

"Okay bitches, you wanted me to cheer you up, let's get this party started," she said, stuffing the rest of the cupcake in her mouth, shaking her pom pom filled hand.

"I'll call down and tell Silas we're on our way down."

I grabbed my white fox jacket to knock out the cold if I needed, but there was no way for me to put it on over my wings. It was just going to have to be one of those 'for show and not for go' wardrobe nights. It was hard to worry about getting cold anyway, jumping in and out of a warmed limousine.

Maya, Logan, and I reached the ground floor of Becker Towers laughing with each other about a giggling group of scary teenagers congregating in the lobby dressed like zombies. Silas was still waiting curbside in front of Becker Towers. A black Suburban was parked in front of our limousine. Another duplicate parked behind it. Two guys, each wearing dark suits and ties, with earpieces in their ears, stepped out of both cars. They stood next to their Suburbans

"Damn damn damn," I said out loud.

"Guard dogs," Logan said, walking up to the cute one with the corn colored hair, looking him up and down while flipping his tie and giggling.

I shook my head in disbelief.

"Nicky let the dogs out!" Maya exclaimed. "See what happens when you take public transportation Jules? Nicky's got the goons back on us again. Oh, I'm going to have so much fun tonight," she grinned, rubbing her hands together. "I bet you money that one's got muscular biceps and washboard abs under that look of steel."

The young bodyguard never so much as cracked a smile, despite the fact Logan hit him with her charming grin, her wavy hair bouncing as she strutted. There was no way that Logan wasn't going to toy with that one and not get some kind of rise or reaction of out him. I doubted that she was going to be denied tonight. She had transformed herself into bewitching mode.

"Yeah, I'll bet my trust fund that our fathers are in on this with Nicholas," Maya said, gesturing to Logan. "What do you think Logan?"

"Likely," she answered with a twinkle in her eye. "You think this set of body watchers can keep up with us this time?"

Logan switched her hips away from hottie protector guy, walking back in our direction.

"This so sucks with a long straw," I snapped.

"I don't know," Maya said, ignoring my complaint. "Looks like a pretty challenging group to me. Doubt that we can lose these jokers tonight, but it sure is going to be fun trying to find out."

"Right. This group looks particularly up to the job this time," I grumbled, shaking my head.

"Nicky sure knows how to keep things interesting, Jules. He makes sure Parks and Parks Protective Service has the best looking eye candy on the planet to look after us," Logan giggled. "A gal could drown herself in this deep sea of hot alpha males."

I made a loud growling sound with my teeth clenched.

"Use your words, Jules," Logan said.

"Honey, each team gets hotter than the last. I think Nicky does this to us on purpose. I have no problem staying very close to all this testosterone, never going anywhere but where I'm told," Maya whooped in laughter.

"Yeah Maya, I agree," Logan said. "I might not be going anywhere. Just stay here and rest my eyes on all these beautiful Adonis's. Mesmerfuckinrizzzzed." She cracked up laughing like a giggling schoolgirl.

I shook my head in disgust. Silas opened the door for us. The lead driver in the front Suburban put his wrist up to his mouth.

"We're on the move now with Twinkle Toes, Pretty Is, and Pretty Does," said the bald-headed leader who looked like he could be one of the New York Jets' linebackers.

I rolled my eyes and tossed some of my pink fairy dust over my shoulder in his direction. His serious façade cracked slightly, as if he almost wanted to grin, but didn't.

We piled back in the limousine quickly, grabbing the shot glasses and the tequila. This was too damn much.

First, I get my heart cracked in half today with the *not gonna marry you* axe, get barked at by Doctor Do as I Say Baby Mama Drama, and now I've got the Hot to Trot Protective Services 'all eyes are on your every move' goon squad all up in my world to complete my day.

"Guys. Remember that one time in band camp . . . when we were on spring break in England . . . ," Logan said mockingly, "and Nicky put the goon squad on us? We ran that security team all over town, losing them in the red light district. They were in a complete state of panic." Logan laughed, passing around the poured tequila shots.

I chugged my shot down first, waving my hand in a gimme motion for her to pour me another. I was disgusted that we had the extra company tonight. I firmly conceded to drown my sorrows tonight.

"Yeah," Maya giggled. "When Nicky got wind those guys lost us, he fired the entire protection team, and the replacement detail installed GPS monitors in our cell phones."

"I could have sworn some monitoring mechanism was stitched inside my Birkin bag," Logan chuckled.

"Sadly, it looks as if it's going to be that kind of party tonight again," I scoffed. "You just wait until I see my brother tonight."

*M*aya, Logan, and I strutted into Luigi's with so much confidence you would have thought we owned the place. Actually, the three of us *were* in fact wealthy enough to own the place.

I scanned the crowd, looking for my brother Nicholas. I was semi-pissed with him given that I was glued at the hip tonight with the protective services brigade. Two of our bodyguards remained outside, while two came inside with us. I looked around for Stephen and Scott Parks, founding partners of Parks and Parks Security, the firm that ran my brother's protection detail. Freaking twins, and panty-dropping fine. Stephen Parks protected Nicholas. Scott Parks protected Nicky's wife Harper. Each of Nicky's twins had their own security personnel coupled with individual nannies. I scanned the place to see which of the Parks and Parks detail was on duty, particularly the ones on my watch.

The place was crowded. I figured it would be hard for the security teams to blend in tonight, with everyone else in costume. If I found them, I'd find my brother.

Okay. So I lost my mind a bit today, jumping unknowingly into a cab where a baby was being delivered, ending up at New York's Presbyterian Hospital, fainting in the arms of Doctor Gorgeous Obnoxious Chief of Staff of the multimillion dollar Becker Obstetric Wing. Yeah, the wing my family built. I shuddered just thinking about it. But who knew? It wasn't like the world should come to an end because I took public transportation. In my mind that did not equate to my having to end up under protective freaking guard tonight.

Bingo. I spotted my brother Nicholas across the far side of the room. He couldn't be missed. Dressed as James Bond, he was the tallest, sexiest man at the bar. That six-foot muscular frame was hard to miss. Even though his dark brown hair was now starting to show some hints of grey at the edges, his killer emerald green eyes with his lush eyelashes sealed the deal that he was in my opinion the most handsome man in the room.

White tuxedo. Black bow tie. Gold cuff links in the 007 logo. A fake Walther PPK handgun lying on the top of the bar, a vodka martini in hand, likely shaken, not stirred. Those emerald green eyes were focused like a tracker on his Bond girl talking with a crowd of people across the other side of the room.

I turned my head towards the direction of his gaze. My eyes landed on the very beautiful African American woman who broke many a man's heart when she married my very Italian brother six years ago, taking herself off the New York's most eligible bachelorette market.

Harper was engaged in a conversation with another slightly younger African American beauty dressed in a black-sequined gown that tapered to a mermaid tail in the back. They looked to be somewhat familiar with each other, yet at the same time both seemingly a bit aloof.

James Bond's gaze remained fixated only on his favorite Bond Girl. Frankly, I was a little surprised he let his wife out tonight looking like she was something good to eat, my brother being madly overprotective and all. I would have loved to have been a fly on that wall to hear him whine about what she was wearing tonight. I giggled to myself at the fact that Harper had won the war. Everyone knew Harper was her own woman.

She was rocking a teeny tiny gold lame miniskirt with a black silk waistband that was fitted low to the hips, just a tad under her naval. Her naval had a sparkly diamond plopped in the middle that was glittering under the chandelier lights hanging from the ceiling. She was wearing above-the-elbow black kid leather gloves the top of which reached the gold lame halter-styled bra that was tied behind her neck.

I looked her way, noticing her big brown eyes focused only on him. She seemed particularly disinterested in whatever the beautiful black woman had to say. If I didn't know better, I would have put money on it that Harper was a bit annoyed with the woman that was trying to talk to her.

Harper smiled at Nicholas sweetly, forcing his poker face to crack, revealing his left dimple when he smiled back at her. He was looking at her as if she was the only woman in the room. There was no doubt that Nicholas Becker was in love with Harper Montgomery Becker. And, he had been that way for a very long time. I silently wished that I had what they had.

I took note of the fact that SWAT Gal and Laker Girl were drawing quite a bit of attention themselves. A server dressed as Darth Vader eased our way with a tray of Champagne flutes, which we each readily took. The dance floor was filled with a couple of Batmans, some Robins, a sailor girl dressed in hot pink, a female Snickers Bar that was dancing with a Spiderman, and a guy dressed as Dr. McDreamy. The pace of the music was starting to pick up, so I figured we had arrived at just the right time.

"Give me a minute you guys, I see my brother. I want to speak to him in private."

"Oh oh, tell Nicky I'm crushing on the new security team," Logan giggled. "Tell him he did a good job this time with the body watchers."

"Yeah Jules, tell Nicky I want to oil the bald one's head," Maya laughed out loud.

I rolled my eyes at the both of them in disgust. Maya and Logan started woo-hooing with each other like they had won the lottery. I dismissed both of their comments. Occasionally I questioned whether they were really juveniles disguised as thirty-something professional well-bred women.

I'll be back. See if you can find us a table close to the dance floor. I feel like busting a move tonight, yeah?"

"Sounds good to me Jules," Maya said. "C'mon Logan, let's find a table. Some place that will allow us to keep a good eye on Frick and Frack," she said, referring to our two bodyguards that had trailed us inside, failing at appearing invisible.

I weaved in an out of the crowded room, making my way towards my brother. I was sure he didn't realize yet it was me. Several male eyes focused on me, heads turning my direction. I slowed my steps for a minute, smiling at myself. By the time his methodical brain sorts me out, he won't like what he sees, I thought. Too bad. Call it payback for locking me in the golden cage with the goon squad tonight.

I laughed to myself watching his eyes flash at the bodyguard that is flanking me, moving discreetly when I move. Five. Four. Three. Two. One. Radar locked and loaded.

Deep emerald eyes grew wider and sharper than razor blades. Mouth dropped open. His stare teetered on mortified. Yup. It's me, Julianna, big brother. The look on his face was priceless. I stared back at him, batting my lashes as he mouthed "What the fuck?"

That big brain of his was in high gear. I wanted to break out in a fit of laughter, but I contained my smirk, taking pride in the fact I ruffled The Almighty. I kept walking, and just waited for the explosion.

*lliot*

*B*y the time I got home it was after seven o'clock, and Kimber was gone. She left a note saying she didn't feel like waiting and was going to Luigi's without me. She insisted that I meet her there instead of our going together. What the hell. It wasn't like I had much of a choice. She'd gone already.

Damn. All that effort of leaving the hospital as soon as my rounds with Dana were completed and heading straight home, only to find Kimber wasn't even here. It was hard to fathom that she wasn't even here after all the grief she gave me over the phone about my needing to be home to talk to her. No doubt Kimber was on 'let's jerk Elliot around' mode.

I felt we desperately needed to re-evaluate our relationship, and she felt I desperately needed to write checks. She decisively was upping her game since I had decided to go slow on the check writing.

This was yet again one of many things that was pissing me off with

Kimber. Everything was urgent with her. Always a fire burning, and usually I was the man on fire.

I didn't care much for her friends, so I was in no rush to get there to hang out with them. That was yet another thing I was questioning. The things we had in common were getting smaller and smaller, her friends being at the top of the list.

I reached for my phone and dialed Kimber's cell phone.

"Why aren't you home?"

"I got tired of waiting around for you. I'm on my way to Luigi's. I've got friends waiting on me there. You were taking too long."

"I thought the plan was that we were going together."

"I thought the plan was that you were coming home this afternoon."

"I told you Kimber, I was delivering Dana's baby."

"Yes, and babies are born every day, every minute, and you've got to be there to catch them, which is exactly why I'm not sure I want kids with you, only to have to raise them by myself. I will have to have a nanny, Elliot."

"What is wrong with you, woman? Are you telling me now that you don't want to have kids with me? This is new. We agreed we'd have a couple of kids after we got married."

"That was before I realized I'd have to raise them on my own."

"You knew when we got engaged this was my life, my profession."

"Oh I know. I guess I didn't consider the degree to which you wouldn't be here for me. I have needs also, Elliot," Kimber snapped.

"You're exaggerating Kimber, and you know it. I'm here right now, for example, and you are not," I insisted, raising my voice sternly. "I'm here more than you think that I am, but you see, you'd have to be here to know that."

This wasn't a good time for Kimber and I to push each other's buttons. This was a conversation we needed to have face to face. So I decided to try to de-escalate the conversation.

"Honey this isn't anything we have to talk about right now. Kids are a long way off. You need to get your career back on track first."

"What career? Who's going to have time for a career? I'll be too

51

busy having your babies, doing that whole parent teacher thing, and carting kids to soccer games, which is why I need a new car Elliot. I'm going to need help. You know a nanny, a couple of housekeepers, and a cook."

"You're taking this way too far Kimber; getting ahead of yourself."

"And I'm probably going to need a nip and a tuck here and there after punching out a couple of your kids. Maybe you can get one of your plastic surgery buddies to give you a discount."

God almighty. Who is this woman? Kimber was doing a three hundred and sixty-degree swing on me. Here I thought I had landed the perfect woman to take into my future, and all she aspired to was the life of being the trophy wife. Hell, I didn't want an empty-headed trophy wife. I wanted a woman that wanted me for me. A woman that wanted to have my kids and love every minute of a life we would build together. I wanted a woman that appreciated my passion for my work and had career objectives of her own. I didn't want a trophy wife.

Trophy wives were just that. Trophies. They were best suited for middle-aged men going through mid-life crisis. The kind of women you set up on a shelf to take up and down to look at and admire. Everyone knew that when trophy wives came down off the shelf it was ka-ching ka-ching time. Money money money. They knew how to make like the beautiful arm candy that they were: spend your money, fuck your brains out, and fake their orgasms pretending like you were good in bed. They guaranteed to make your life a living miserable hell. They lived for the shopping, the trainers, yoga and Pilates, salmon canapés, double martinis, and the charities that made them feel honorable. They were hardly good at motherhood, too incapacitated to the point that they needed someone else to raise their children. And when their looks started to go, they amped up their bitchiness scale, having already gotten their claws in you financially.

But I wasn't a middle-aged man going through mid-life crisis. I was a successful thirty-two-year-old man, looking for the right woman for the long haul until death do us part.

"Kimber, I think we should talk about our pre-nup agreements.

You haven't executed any of the contracts my attorneys have sent you, yet you're spending money like it's going out of style, with nothing to show for it. Your demands are getting to be an extreme."

"Sorry Elliot, but I don't have time to finish this discussion," she said, completely ignoring me. "I'm pulling up to Luigi's now. It's Halloween. It's a party. Some of us want to have fun tonight. Are you coming or not?"

I took a deep breath to calm myself. I was beginning to feel very unlucky in love. I glanced across the room, noticing that Kimber's little white miniature terrier, Gucci, was getting up out of its bed, staggering sleepily towards me whining for some food, and scratching on her dog bowl.

"I'll be there when I get there."

Click. She was gone.

"The way I see it Gucci, your days here are numbered."

I moved to the kitchen, opening the pantry door to find a can of that gourmet dog food that I was spending a ton of money on as well.

"Enjoy this lifestyle while you can Gucci," I said setting the dog bowl down, patting Gucci on the head, and rubbing his ear behind the Swarovski crystal dog collar, for which I'm sure I must have paid a small fortune.

---

*M*y mind was going into overdrive. I walked over to my minibar, poured myself a scotch, sat on the barstool, and placed my head in my hands. This time a year and a half ago, I thought Kimber and I were happy. Nothing about this relationship looked like the picture of happiness to me. I wanted out of these impending nuptials, and I wanted out now. This relationship was getting too dysfunctional for even my tastes. I didn't have to marry Ms. New York. I didn't have to have the most beautiful woman on my arm shot full of Botox and silicone. My pattern of moving from trophy girlfriend, rinse and repeat, to now trophy wife wasn't working. I wanted something else. Something closer to—closer to what dropped in my cab today.

Wow. She was back in my head again. I sipped the balance of my scotch and decanted myself a second pour of the amber colored liquid. Where did that thought come from again? I looked around the room, just to be sure I wasn't dreaming. I knew it was Halloween, but this was starting to get weird. I couldn't help it that her naturally beautiful panicked face kept popping into my head today, as if Cupid had been following me around all day, shooting little arrows in me. The sweet face of Julianna Becker.

I moved across the room and opened my laptop, googling Julianna Becker's name. Pictures and posts started to pop up on various Who's Who and New York's socialite pages. There she was. Fresh and beautiful in some of the photos, cute and funny in others. I loved the one of her at the Verve Cliquot Fundraiser in the Hamptons, eating cotton candy, and passing out baskets of cookies to the underprivileged kids. I smiled.

Julianna Becker was the daughter of the Maryland-based king of chicken processing, Blake Ross Becker II, and sister to Blake Ross Becker III and Nicholas Miles Becker.

Nicholas Becker was the husband to Harper Montgomery Becker. I knew them well. I had delivered Harper's twins, a boy and a girl, under emergency conditions six years ago. Shortly thereafter, her husband Nicholas donated millions of dollars, building a state of the art obstetrical wing in his name, with his wife insisting that I be the one to run the wing. I was grateful for their financial contribution and the opportunity to manage the wing in the way that reflected their family's standards of excellence.

Once a year, Nicholas and Harper threw a black tie fundraiser for the hospital to support the addition of new equipment, clinics, and other obstetrical needs to maintain that the wing remained state-of-the-art. It was a lavish event, attended by the who's who of all of New York. It was their way of contributing back to the New York Community and to thank the hospital for their extraordinary efforts to help save their babies.

I surfed the net further, noticing that Julianna Becker was frequently seen in the social pages on the arms of Oliver Banks, entrepreneur and founder of the Internet sensation social media company called "Gators." Gators was a social media outlet built for tweens that allowed them to hook up with other tweens in a safe, security monitored environment, while letting them play games and talk at the same time. Oliver was an incredibly smart man. He related to young people. He'd figured out what kids wanted in a social media environment and he exploited it. Once generation Y got wind that their parents were monopolizing Facebook, they fled and ran for cover. Oliver provided them a place to exist only with each other.

Oliver was the classic polo playboy. He was an infamous party-goer, a new money blue blood. He was often photographed at lots of horse shows, always surrounded by the crème de la crème of beautiful women, with 'pretty enough' sometimes sneaking into the mix. Julianna and Oliver were seen on many of the social pages together. I could see what she saw in him. He was a handsome guy; deep blue eyes, thick brows, light brown hair that was more blonde at the tips. It was easy to see why the women fawned over him.

I surfed a bit further, stopping on a New York Times article on Modern Love that revealed Oliver Banks had suddenly married—an elopement. Wow. Apparently quite unexpected by anyone's imagina-tion. Rumor was he wasn't the marrying type, always holding himself out as the fish that got away. He had a long trail of broken hearts in his wake.

Funny Oliver Banks should marry. *Hmpf.* Never say never. I read the brief article on the marriage, looking at the newlywed couple's pictures. And there it was. Trophy wife. Oliver must have let Julianna Becker go for the enviable trophy wife. I knew that because I recog-nized the woman he had married. She was a friend of a friend of Kimber's, cut from the same trophy wife cloth as Kimber.

I shook my head. Stupid man.

Ha. Soooo, that was the source of Julianna's heartbreak and brokenness that drove her into my cab in hysterics today. Reading the article further, I felt her pain. She had allowed herself to believe in a happily ever after with that geeky trophy wife hunter. I recognized Oliver Bank's DNA, because that was who I had become a couple of years back. I too had made that dreadful mistake of walking into Tiffany's, buying a ring to lock down a would be gold-digger trophy for a wife. What a mistake. I sighed heavily, shaking my head in dismay.

Julianna deserved so much better than him. And I deserved so much better than Kimber. Oliver had made the same mistake that I was trying to seal the deal on. The only thing saving me was that Kimber had slow-rolled our wedding planning just in time for me to come to my senses and pull my head out of my ass.

I downed the rest of my scotch. I knew what I was going to do next. I was going to take a hot shower, put on a fresh set of scrubs, and head out to Maximillion's to meet Gabriel and Xavier. If I somehow managed to extract myself out of these impending nuptials with Kimber, what did it matter that Maximillion's got on my dance card tonight?

That was going to be tonight's plan. I jumped in the shower, letting the hot water roll over me, slipping my head underneath the shower jets to soothe the muscles in the back of my neck that ached from being bent over so much of the day. My thoughts veered back uncontrollably to the beautiful petite time bomb that had jumped in my cab.

I exited the frosted shower doors, stepping on the cold marbled bathroom floor, gazing at myself in the mirror. I towel-dried myself with one of the monogrammed white fluffy towels Kimber had spent a small fortune on when she moved in with me last year. I liked these towels. I wondered if when our engagement was over these towels would be leaving with her.

I put on a fresh set of blue scrubs and a clean white physician's coat. I grabbed my stethoscope, slinging it over my neck for costume effect. I would go to Maximillion's, then head over to Luigi's with the guys and hook up with Kimber as planned. At least the *entire* Halloween night wouldn't be a complete waste of my time.

*A*s soon as I heard the MC announce Bubbles and Babydoll's arrival to the stage, I didn't have to look very far to find Gabriel and Xavier in the crowded room at Maximillion's. They were the ones sitting at the front tables closest to the stage with their eyeballs popping out of their heads.

Xavier Cook was dressed in a green jumpsuit that zipped up the front, with wing patches and pilot emblems sewn into the front left pocket and sleeves. He had on aviator sunglasses, an 8mm gauge cigar hanging out of his mouth, and a bottle of Jack Daniels sitting in front of him. He was holding a cocktail glass filled with the amber colored liquor on the rocks, his mouth wide open as Baby Doll and Bubbles twirled their beautiful Hungarian asses in front of him.

Xavier's mahogany-colored shoulder length hair was slicked neatly back into a ponytail that was cut even at the bottom. His olive skin was smooth and blemish free, giving him an exotic look reflecting his bi-racial heritage. His mother, Riley Cook, was part African American, part French Canadian, and his father, Lucas Cook, a deceased Italian Naval Officer. Every time I saw him, it felt weird seeing him with straight hair after looking at him for so many years with reddish-brown dreads.

Xavier's jumpsuit was unzipped to the chest, the sleeves rolled up, displaying his oversized muscular chest and biceps. His body looked much like the New York Jets linebackers that he worked hard to get into condition every day. He was the best personal trainer in all of New York. I needed to give some thought to having him whip me into better shape. Run me through Central Park for a few months. I maneuvered my way through the crowded club in their direction.

It was hard to miss Gabriel DeLuca either. Gabriel Deluca was the son of Italian parents. His father is the infamous cardiologist, Nathan Deluca, and his mother, legal scholar Lily DeLuca. His parents had nonstop pressure on him to continuously rise to the occasion, but Gabriel was a nonconformist at heart. He was always in a constant state of rebellion.

Gabriel was dressed in a black designer silk suit, with a white shirt, skinny black tie, black Ray Bans, and a silver neutralizer in his hand. Gabriel was true to his word. He was the epitome of Men in Black. His dark black locks were curling around his strong jaw framing his face, his skin flawless. His dark eyes were gleaming with excitement. His five o'clock shadow blended in with his dark mustache. I peered at him from across the room, realizing all he had eyes for now was the stripper Bubbles.

Bubbles was dressed as Marilyn Monroe, sashaying around the raised stage, slowly pulling off a white long gown, long white gloves, and then doing some kind of twerking move in front of him in a white scanty silver thong with white pasties on her nipples. Gabriel looked to be in a state of awe, absorbing the entire scenery, appearing as if he were on the verge of opening Pandora's box at any second now. Bubbles had her glove in her mouth, taking it off finger by finger so slowly, I thought Gabriel was going to combust.

Baby Doll slid that well-oiled ass down a pole next, dressed in a black and grey pinstriped gangster jacket with a matching black fedora, some five inch clear see through platform heels, with a mock machine gun in her hand that she was moving back and forth in between her legs, egging Gabriel into a state of lust. Gabriel was tucking hundred dollar bills in Baby Doll's G-string. Baby Doll was taking all of his money too.

I grabbed the empty plush leather chair at their table that was big enough to seat two. I was on the verge of interrupting their train of thought, when all of a sudden Sparkles hit the stage. She was dressed as a nurse, with a white nurses cap on her head, red heart shaped pasties on her nipples with the symbol of the white medical cross in the middle, and a little red with feather trim candy-colored skirt on, hardly long enough to cover her butt cheeks. She had on hot red platform heels, white stockings attached to some tiny red garters, and flaming red nail polish on her fingers, which she licked between her candy colored lips directing her attention at me as soon as I took my seat. My breath caught at the sight of her.

"Ya'll motherfuckers know I have no business being in here tonight," I said, never taking my eyes off Sparkles, watching her closely as one of the scantily clad beauties in the club brought me an empty glass with ice.

"Would you like bottle service as well, Doctor McDreamy?" the scantily clad beauty asked, noticing I was dressed in my doctor gear. I doubted she knew I was a really a doctor. She thought I was in a Halloween costume for the night.

Her chocolate brown butt was barely wrapped in the purple thong, her breasts threatening to escape her bikini top. She bent down, handing me my glass of ice, giving me a full view of her lickable chocolate breasts. I shook my head, praying to the Gods above that I wouldn't lose my mind and try to get lost and die inside those double D's.

"Bring me your best bottle of McCallen, sweetheart. You are . . . ?" I waited for her to answer.

"I'm Purple Rain," she winked, "you know, as in "Prince.""

I tucked a twenty in her G-string. "Yeah baby. Just make sure you see to it that it keeps raining purple over here tonight."

"Dr. EZ's back," Gabriel said, slapping Xavier a high five.

"Hey man, who let the dogs out tonight?" Gabriel asked in jest. "How in the hell did you get free from Kimber dude?"

"Who said I was free man? Before I could get home from the hospital this evening, Kimber was gone. When I got back to the crib there was a note on the table. Kimber said she was going to Luigi's without me. She told me to meet her there."

"Wow man, Kimber went to Luigi's without you?" Gabriel said, shaking his head.

"So I thought about it long and hard. Then decided I'd come to Maximillion's first, let some steam out, then head over to Luigi's."

"Damn E, you have no control whatsoever over Ms. New York. You are seriously losing your grip, dude," Xavier said, taking a huge swig of his whiskey.

"Who said I wanted control? My head's just not in it anymore X. Right about now, I'm trying to figure out how to find the exit ramp."

I downed my drink, lifted my glass, silently nodding at Purple Rain to bring me another.

"Whoa, that's pretty serious," Gabriel said.

"I don't mean to be talking about your woman man, but if you ask me, she was digging for gold with you. A beautiful, fine as wine digger, yes, but a gold digger nonetheless."

"Yeah, well I've really been striking out these last several years in the woman department. I thought this time was going to be different. She's turning out to be like all the other women in my past."

"That's because you keep picking these fine-ass money-grubbing stallions each time you wade in the relationship pond. I'm not trying to be disrespectful Elliot, that being your woman and all, but I told you man, you were moving too fast with that one," Xavier said. "The way I see it . . . "

Xavier reared back in his seat, at the exact moment Bubbles twirled her ass in his face, making him lose his train of thought.

"The way you see it, what?" I asked while Purple Rain switched that beautiful chocolate ass back to the table with my scotch, filling my glass.

"Ump Ummmph Ump," I said out loud. "This place ought to be outlawed. I swear to God this establishment needs to be off limits to married men."

"Which is why I'm not getting married," Gabriel said, swigging his drink, and tucking his bucks in Baby Doll's garter, pulling his neutralizer out and running it slowly up the inside of her thigh, both of them laughing together.

"You better knock it off with Baby Doll, G, before you give her your whole month's salary again," Xavier said coolly, looking over the top of his aviators at Bubbles, who was shaking her ass in his face. He tucked fifty dollars in Bubbles' bra. "We've been down this road before, my brother," he laughed. They broke up laughing, slapping each other five.

Bubbles walked over to Xavier. She did a very slow hip sliding turn of her ass in front of his face, letting him check out the goods.

"Would you like a lap dance sugar, you being the Top Gun here tonight and all?" Bubbles cooed at X. She puckered her lips at him, bending over to give him a full look at those beautiful breasts.

Fuck me. If Xavier didn't jump on that offer, I swear to God, I would have pretended like I was the "Top Gun" tonight.

"Oh yeah honey," X said, his cigar hanging out the side of his mouth. "I want you to lap me up tonight, baby. Bubble and bathe that beautiful body all over me."

Bubbles took Xavier's hand, ran her tongue over her teeth, grabbing him and moving to lead him into one of the private rooms in the VIP lounge called the Penthouse Suite.

He stood up, stretching that six-foot-three body of his upright. Xavier slid his aviators back up on his face, letting Bubbles take him by the hand. He paused long enough to take a long gulp of his drink, sat his glass down, and picked his cigar up out of the ashtray, plopping it in his mouth, saying "Gentlemen, please excuse me, I shall return shortly."

"Yeah man, knock yourself out," Gabriel said. "Dude you are not gonna have any money in the morning."

Xavier turned to Gabriel and me. "I'm a Baller baby, you best to recognize."

Fuck we were getting buzzed as shit. Gabriel and I both started laughing out loud, waving the 'fuck you man' hand at Xavier.

I looked up on the stage. Sparkles was doing a solo erotic strip dance to the Beyoncé's song "Blow."

Gabriel and I set back to enjoy the show. Purple Rain came back around. We ordered a couple of T-Bone steaks medium rare, some steak fries, and a bottle of Louis Martinis Cabernet to go with the meal. *Damn. I might order food all night just to look at Purple Rain. But* then again, one of Maximillion's chocolate fudge sundaes sounded like a good idea. *But, Purple Rain could be the cherry on top.*

Sparkles was moving her ass slow, seductively setting the stage on fire in her wake. The other patrons in the club were going crazy, realizing too that she was one of the hottest, steamiest dancers in the club. As far as I was concerned, Sparkles was *the* star of the house.

Normally, when Sparkles performed, I felt like it was only her and me when she was on stage. She'd typically left me feeling like I'd totally lost control of my mind and body. The little head would take over, blind to the big head.

But tonight, things were noticeably different. My mind was preoccupied with the arrows Cupid shot at me today in the cab. Tonight, I was preoccupied with how to get out of my upcoming nuptials, and how to get introduced to my luscious lunatic. If I could see her again, I'd work overtime to calm all those out of control nerves, heal that broken heart, and be her heart compass for the rest of her life.

Sometimes there comes a time in life when you realize that the universe conspires to align the planets in order to move in such a way to reveal to you what's really important in life. I felt like I was having that kind of moment. And then it hit me. *Maybe that was what Babs meant when she was trying to tell me about things dropping in my lap.* One thing for sure, Julianna Becker had most definitely dropped in my lap today.

"Gabriel, would you think less of me man, if I broke my engagement off with Kimber?" I asked in a thoughtful mood, chewing my delicious T-bone, the scotch taking over my loose tongue.

I hadn't even shared these thoughts with Kimber, and now I was sharing openly with Gabriel. Fuck I was high. Loose lips sink ships.

"Hell no man. If it's not right, you don't need to be doing it. Marriage is a lifetime commitment. That shit shouldn't be taken lightly."

Sparkles was dancing now to Beyoncé's *Naughty Girl*. Gabriel was acting like he was having a hard time concentrating on what I was saying, taking in Baby Doll's essence. Baby Doll was in a chair pulling water down on her body like that chick in the Flashdance movie. I thought Gabriel was going to totally lose it completely. That Hungarian princess had Gabriel all tied up into knots tonight.

"Gabriel, focus," I said, moving my two index fingers from my eyes and motioning them back to his.

I was feeling like this was a losing battle. I was losing control too. That naughty girl Sparkles was strutting her stuff with Baby Doll, both setting the stage on fire, taking Gabriel and me with them. We both threw two one hundred dollar bills their direction hoping they'd quit killing us, and move across to the other side of the stage, giving our panting hearts a break.

Xavier returned from the Penthouse Suite with Bubbles and rejoined the table.

"I hope you bitches still have some money left," X teased.

"You should shut up dude. Whatever we gave away out here, we bet you gave away double in the Penthouse Suite. Hell man, lap dances with Bubbles got to make a man dig really deep," I laughed.

Gabriel slapped me five in agreement.

"Yeah X. Betcha you dropped some serious change in the VIP room," Gabriel laughed with a raised eyebrow.

Xavier snapped his fingers together and did a little dance move to the music that was playing out loud, which so happened to be 50 Cent's "In Da Club."

"I think I'm in love, yo," Xavier crooned.

"No you're not X. You're just horny and high," Gabriel responded.

"Whatever, but I'm Top Gun tonight baby," Xavier said. "G Unit," he said out loud.

"Ya'll's asses are getting old," I said. "Ya'll need some wives."

"So they can take us to the cleaners E?" Xavier said.

"Nah, so you can graduate out of Maximillion's," I said, tossing the balance of the tab on the table.

"C'mon, let's get out of here and head to Luigi's. If I don't get there soon, there will be no more gold left to dig," I laughed.

Xavier got his Top Gun ass up, and started throwing twenties on the table to add to my tip. Gabriel got up and walked to the stage, putting more money between Baby Doll's breasts, and then tucking bucks in Purple Rain's garter on the way out, slapping her hard on her butt.

"Jesus G, you need to stay out of here for a moment. You're starting to get addicted to all these free flowing tits and asses," I said.

"Fuck you man. Let's go to Luigi's."

I heard Sparkles call my name. I turned around and watched her switch back in my direction.

"When will I see you again Doctor McDreamy?" she cooed seductively.

"Baby, I always need a good nurse at my side," I said grinning at her, tucking another hundred on the side of her G-String. "Momma's baby, Daddy's maybe," I whispered softly in her ear.

Sparkles blew me an air kiss, then flicked that gorgeous Brazilian behind around to give me the view as she switched back the other direction. I stopped dead in my tracks, momentarily contemplating whether or not I really wanted to leave.

"C'mon EZ Money," Gabriel said. "You stay here any longer and you're gonna get strummed like the money-giving fiddle that you are." He laughed again.

Gabriel, Xavier, and I headed out the door headed to Luigi's. We grabbed the first cab we could hail. I looked at my watch. It was 10 pm. Damn, I was major late. I needed to prepare myself for hell to break out on my ass. Ask me if my 'intoxicated by beautiful booty ass' gives a damn.

6

ulianna

y the time I reached my brother he was practically choking on his vodka, doing a double-take once he figured out it was me approaching him.

"What the hell Jules? I thought you were coming to this thing as Tinkerbell, not Tinker Sexy Siren," he bellowed out. "You can't walk around looking like that!"

"No?" I said, twirling around in a circle for him. "Can. Did. Am."

"And that blonde come-fuck-me wig," he exclaimed. "You need to go home and put some clothes on. You, Maya, and Logan are setting the entire room on fire. I don't like it."

I glanced over my shoulder, noticing three guys dressed as Top Gun, Men In Black, and Dr. McDreamy had entered Luigi's and were seating themselves next to our table. No doubt, that trio was trying to get close to Maya and Logan.

"If anyone finds us hot, I doubt they will be able to get anywhere near us Nicky, with those guard dogs you hired sticking to us like glue. Honestly, was that really necessary?" I pouted.

"Well if I knew you were going to go all sexy siren on me, I would have added another couple of guys to your detail."

"You know how I feel about being surrounded by security Nicholas."

"C'mon Cookie, don't be mad at me. You know I hate it when you get all pissy with me," he said, nodding at the bartender to pour him another.

Nicky grabbed a champagne off Darth Vader's tray and handed it to me. I took a huge sip. It was very chilled and very good. I took another sip, momentarily reminiscing.

Nicky always called me Cookie when he wanted to diffuse my anger. He nicknamed me that when I was a little girl, because I baked cookies when the house chefs weren't around, letting him eat the left over cookie dough. I downed my champagne and grabbed another off Darth Vader's tray, realizing my anger was quickly escaping in all of Nicky's brotherly love for me.

"Whooa . . . slow down there Cookie. The night is still young."

"I don't like being treated like a child Nicky."

"I need assurances you won't go jumping on subways, trains, and cabbies in New York Julianna," he said a bit more seriously. "Whatever you need, I can fix it for you."

"Can you fix my broken heart Nicky? There are some things even money can't buy or fix."

"I'm so sorry Cookie," he said, putting his arms around me. "I know it's hard for you to accept right now." He put his hand under my chin, pulling my face up to his and looking me in the eyes deeply. "Oliver Banks was not the man for you."

"How would you know, Nicky, what's right for me?"

"I'm a man, Cookie. Be grateful he wasn't the one."

"I want to forget about him Nicky. Meet someone new. Take my mind off the loss."

"I want you to put your mind on something more important that doesn't have to do with a man. Oliver Banks is no longer important, nor is any other man right now, for that matter. Come see me tomorrow and tell me all about your plans for *Sugar Mommy*. Let's get your business underway. Throw yourself into something more worthwhile."

I bit my lip and nodded my head in agreement, forcing the tears that were in the back of my eyes not to come down. Nicholas was never a fan of Oliver's. He never believed Oliver had my best interest at heart. Oliver proved him to be right. Oliver only had his own selfish interests at heart. Looking back, I hardly knew why he spent so many years with me at all. Maybe he was killing time.

Nicholas used to say to me, "Believe that whatever a man tells you in the moment is the truth as they know it, until that changes.' Oliver claimed he never wanted to be married, and now that had changed.

"I never seem to ever get the guy, Nicky. They always want me for their 'friend in the end', never the wife. What's wrong with me?"

"Nothing's wrong with you, Julianna. You stayed too long. But at the end of the day, it's not you, it's them."

"Easy for you to say. You're married to your soulmate."

"Sometimes, Julianna, finding your right partner is like finding a needle in the haystack. You'll know it when you see it. And then your soul won't be at peace until you have it."

Nicky momentarily re-directed his attention from me, giving his Bond Girl the once over, then glancing at her bodyguard, Scott. I suspected he was assessing whether she was in his sights.

"I suppose," I said, not feeling any more encouraged.

"You have to trust me on this Cookie."

Trust. That was a big word right now. I knew I was bright. I was talented. I might not be some runway model or Ms. New York, but I was pretty in my own way. I was lovable too. But the men I had loved hadn't married smart nor talented. They'd married beautiful, needy, and helpless. I wasn't any of those things. I was going to be a thirty-one-year-old spinster.

My brother noticed the pain that had registered across my face. I was never any good at not wearing my emotions on my sleeve.

"Cookie, I want you to have a good time tonight. Try to put that loser Banks out of your mind. Have some fun for a change."

"I'll try Nicky," I said, reaching up and kissing him on his cheek.

"And if I hear anything nutty about you and that hot-to-trot posse of yours messing with the security detail, you will hear from me," he said with a wink.

"What's wrong Nicky? You're worried we're going to end up someplace we don't belong?" I teased him, smiling to myself that I could still get his dander up after all these years.

Nicky was never going to get over how Maya, Logan, and I had deliberately lost our protection detail in the red light district of London. He still curses in three languages whenever he has cause to think back on that moment, calling that particular security detail all kinds of idiots. He could never figure out how they let three beautiful so-called inexperienced princesses run loose in London, landing their detail in the red light district and its protectees elsewhere.

Those were some of our better days. I smiled thinking about the fact that we had pulled one over on Nicky. Unfortunately for us, the first time, shame on him. The next time, shame on us. Nicky ratcheted up our security presence so tough, that was never going to happen ever again in life as far as he was concerned. That was the day he hired Parks and Parks Security. But of course, Logan and Maya took the whole matter as a challenge, not to be outdone by Nicky's minions.

"No, it's them I'm worried about. Your posse is particularly adept at turning a man out and making him forget who he is." Nicholas squinted his eyes, looking across the room at Maya and Logan.

"And if you end up anywhere you don't belong, I will fire the whole damn lot of them again, and start over with a group of Navy fucking Seals. Look at them," Nicholas said with gritted teeth, shaking his head.

I looked across the room, watching as Maya and Logan were putting down their best sexy moves on the dance floor with Men In Black and Top Gun. Top Gun had a cigar hanging out of his mouth, his hands over his head, popping his fingers, while Laker Girl was shaking that booty, wrapping those pom-poms around his ears. Swat girl was moving her body seductively, while Men in Black was holding on to her hips, moving in time to her moves. Beyoncé's *Get Me Bodied* was playing. My girls were on a serious mission tonight. I hardly knew who was going to die first, our security team or their dance partners. They were killing it.

"I know those yahoos too," Nicky said shaking his head, gulping his drink.

"Yeah Nicky, those yahoos are beyond hot," I said, licking my lips with a greedy look in my eye. "What's up with their third wheel, Dr McDreamy," I said, casually sipping my champagne. "He reminds me of a hot glazed Krispy Kreme donut. Good enough to eat," I grinned.

I could feel my brother Nicholas's body stiffen. It was like having two fathers. My own father "Big Daddy" was bad enough, insisting that I live in Becker Towers with Nicholas and his family. But I was sure living with Nicky was worse than having to live around my Dad. Nicholas was too close to my own age by comparison. The wool I could pull over "Big Daddy's" eyes was easier to get away with than Nicholas. Nicky knew most of my tricks.

But Maya and Logan were special. They had a lot more experience than I did knowing how to run game. They lived for moments for when we could slip through the gaps. They were good teachers and I was a good student.

I looked back at the yahoos Top Gun, Men In Black, and Dr. McDreamy again. I tilted my head to the side sipping my champagne, still chatting it up with Nicky.

"Not that I haven't reached my limit of doctors in my life today," I huffed thinking back again now on Gray Eyes.

Dr. McDreamy hadn't gotten back out on the dance floor. He must have been taking a break from when I saw him dancing earlier with the Snicker Bar, though I must say for some reason he looked a little more muscular than I thought earlier when I had sized him up. He couldn't have grown toned biceps that fast.

"Not for you. That one's halfway down the altar with a female hologram."

"A female hologram?"

"Yeah. All air and light. Figment of the imagination."

"Nothing wrong with marital bliss when you can find it, Nicky. Look how happy you are with Harper. Your Bond Girl is the most beautiful woman in the room, and she's in love with you. I wish I had that," I sighed, gulping my champagne while grabbing another glass from Darth Vader as he passed by.

"The right man for you is still out there Jules. Oliver wasn't that guy, trust me."

There was that word trust again. I hardly knew whom to trust anymore. I trusted Oliver, and all I got in return for my trust was a cracked heart.

I put my arms around my brother as he gave me a huge hug. I nudged my nose in the side of his neck, trying to hold back the tears again. He pulled me closer to him, wrapping his arm around my waist, comforting me.

Oliver had taken up too many of my emotions today and I wanted to forget he ever existed. I wanted to forget that I ever loved him, wasted time with him, made myself vulnerable to him. I didn't want to cry over him on Halloween night. This was a party and I wanted to get drunk, have fun, and forget he ever had a place in my life. And if I was lucky, find a new man for tonight. A placeholder until my heart healed.

---

*N*icky took another gulp of his vodka, still fixated on what was going on across the room. I watched as Stephen Parks began moving in closer proximity to Nicky. Scott Parks was moving even closer to Harper. I was nearest to my brother so I could sense his building tension, noticing that his mood had changed from fun casual to high alert. His security team was closing in quickly. I knew the pattern. I knew the dance they did when trouble was amidst.

Dr. McDreamy was at the table appearing to be having a very ugly conversation with the beautiful African American woman dressed as a black-sequined mermaid, just as Nicky's Bond Girl moved in their direction. Dr. McDreamy rose out of his seat, looking as if he were going to introduce Bond Girl, when the mermaid threw her drink in his face and hauled ass. Nicky's Bond Girl and Dr. McDreamy exchanged more words. Bond Girl handed him a napkin to wipe his face, then embraced Dr. McDreamy in a big hug, wrapping her arms around him. More words were said.

I gasped at the scene in shock. Nicky slammed his glass of vodka down on the bar, and headed like quick-fire to his Bond Girl. Stephen and Scott closed in on both he and Bond Girl, making a tight circle around them. I moved to run behind Nicky, just as my own Frick and Frack bodyguards closed in on me. We looked like cartoon characters at a movie, surrounded by some Secret Service-looking types.

Nicholas reached Harper before I could catch up, pulling his Bond Girl out of the arms of Dr. McDreamy, tucking her back underneath his arm.

"Harper baby, is everything okay?" Nicky bit out, teeth gritted.

"Everything is fine dear, right Elliot?"

I'd finally caught up with Nicholas to join this circle of madness. I was out of breath from stepping quicker than normal in my stilettos.

Before I could step fully in, Nicholas pulled me back against his body on his other side, positioning me a few steps behind him. Nicholas gave Dr. McDreamy the evil eye. I was confused as to what was going on, the music still playing loudly, my head a bit buzzed from the champagne. Logan and Maya were still breaking a sweat on the dance floor with Top Gun and Man in Black. They were all apparently clueless as to what was happening at their table.

What was happening? Hell I wasn't sure what was going on right now. All I knew was that my brother was having some kind of internal hissy fit, and the protection detail had closed ranks.

"Sorry Nicholas, I was having a moment, your wife, she was . . . "

"Telling him that I wanted to introduce him to Julianna," Harper interjected before he could finish his sentence. "Elliot's agreed to co-chair this year's fundraiser for the obstetrical wing."

Dr. McDreamy pulled his surgical mask off his mouth, and I could feel the heat rushing upward so fast that I put my hand to the side of my face. My breath hitched. I was back in the presence of Dr. EZ, not Dr. McDreamy. This was 'easy on the eyes, pain in my ass in a cab,' Dr. EZ. This doctor, I freaking knew.

"*J*ulianna, this is Dr. Elliot Fischer," Harper said. "He delivered Miles and Milania." Harper must have recognized that it was time to change the subject to keep Nicholas from going totally ballistic. Maybe I would be the one to go ballistic before my brother.

I swear I heard my brother growl under his breath. Apparently Harper did too, because she turned, giving him a look. Nicky looked past Harper, his hand still around her waist, as he quietly nodded at Stephen and Scott Parks to pull back. Stephen gave Frick and Frack the silent cue to pull back off of me.

What Dr. Elliot Fischer didn't know, was that any man that had his hands on my brother's wife was going to have hell to pay. His bodyguards had strict orders to see that such a thing never ever happened. Harper knew it too, but she was known to ignore any of Nicky's demands that she felt were unreasonable, which I suppose was why she jumped in those waters to add a bit of calm to the situation.

Elliot extended his hand to me.

"I'm sorry. I didn't recognize you. The blonde hair and all," he said, at a loss for words, and slightly off balance. "I believe we met earlier today under difficult circumstances," he said, his doctor mask falling around his neck, a shy smile forming on his lips and those beautiful gray eyes setting me on fire again.

I released a long breath that I'd been holding, not believing that twice in one day, I was back in the presence of the infamous Dr. Elliot Fischer. This was some kind of strange coincidence. Some cosmic funky occurrence. I had to tug my hand loose from Nicky to shake his hand, since my brother was beyond slow to release my hand, though part of me was glad Nicky was still holding on to me tightly. My knees were quivering like jelly. My heart was beating wildly to a drumbeat of its own. I damn sure didn't want to faint in Gray Eyes' presence again.

"It's nice to meet you," I said, a jolt of electricity passing between us as we touched hands. I smiled back at him, noticing that he was wearing a diamond earring in his left ear. I tilted my head back a bit to get a good look, thinking I hadn't noticed that diamond when I took notice of him earlier on the dance floor.

"I'm glad to see you're feeling better."

He paused, taking me in fully, and I he.

"You're the most beautiful Tinkerbell I've ever seen," he sputtered with all sincerity, tripping over his own tongue as a big smile came across his face.

Nicky growled under his breath again. I had to fight my urge not to throw my pink fairy dust on him.

I had decided earlier in the night that my pink candied fairy dust was going to be my magic potion for the night, making folks get in line and respond like I wanted them to. After all I was Tinkerbell. And Tinkerbell had magical powers.

"Thank you," I said. And you are . . . are . . . yourself?" I said, letting the words get away from me before I could pull them back.

"Bad Halloween habit," he laughed, but he was still noticeably uncomfortable.

"Another workaholic huh? I belong to that club," I smiled, trying to put him at ease.

I don't have any idea why I cared to put him at ease and let him out of his discomfort. *Here I go again, being nicer to guys than I should.* This was the same man that wouldn't let me out of a cab, holding me prisoner until I helped him deliver a baby. *What's wrong with you Jules?* Nice never gets you anywhere in a relationship. Guys don't want nice. Guys don't even want smart, or independent. No, they want Ms. New York: beautiful, needy, and helpless.

"Hopefully Jules, when you get *Sugar Mommy's* underway you'll do us the honors and head up the dessert menu for the hospital fundraiser with your delectable delights. Julianna is the best pastry chef in all of New York," Harper said to Elliot. "The world just doesn't know it yet."

"You're giving me too much credit Harper." I spoke softly, still mesmerized, turning my conflicted emotions around inside myself. Piercing gray eyes, boyfriend grief, new man anger, and alcohol was a funky combination for anyone to have to internalize on the year's scariest holiday.

"*Sugar Mommy's* is still very much in its infancy," I blushed, the heat still rushing to my face.

"I love all things sweet," Elliot whispered, his words taking on a double meaning, my blood heating at the sound of his words. "*Sugar Mommy's,* huh?" he said, looking as if he were trying the name on for size.

I twisted a curl of my blonde wig in my finger, eyeing him shyly, biting my lip, batting my eyes, still internally a bit flustered. Overwhelmed.

The one thing about Harper Montgomery Becker, she was the best businesswoman in all of New York. Before she married my brother, her company *Montgomery Consulting* was a formidable force, landing her on Forbes top 100 of the Forty under Forty. I should have known that she wouldn't let a simple thing like a Halloween Party get in the way of her missing out on a chance to do business at Luigi's tonight. But she was also the great seductress. Men fell at her feet, including my brother. I needed to remember to rip that businesswoman/seductress page out of her handbook.

"Was that your fiancée, Elliot, that I saw taking off like a lightning bolt?" Nicholas asked, his emerald eyes piercing Elliot like daggers. "You weren't going to introduce her?"

Elliot's gray eyes grew larger, his eyebrows quirking upward.

"Not our business Nicholas," Harper scolded. "Mind your manners love," she said patting him on his arm. "Elliot doesn't need any divine intervention tonight baby."

I knew my sister-in-law was referring to my brother's fetish at playing God with everyone's lives. Harper stared my brother down, pausing to give him time to contemplate himself. She narrowed her eyes at him, stepping back a bit, looking him up and down, giving him what she like to call her 'black girl stance.' She was so his perfect Bond Girl.

My brother paused, looking at her as if he'd come down out of some trance in his head.

"But of course, Kitten," he chuckled, returning her look with his famous panty-dropping smile.

"Kimber's been under a lot of stress lately," Elliot said, trying to console Nicky's concerns. "We both have," he muttered. "You know rocky road."

Eww. I didn't want to hear any more of this. It felt too intimate. Too personal.

Nicky grunted, giving him a look of caution. I hated that look. It was an unspoken man signal that said fuck off what's mine. But I was a bit confused, not knowing if this was about his Bond Girl or me. Perhaps both.

A drunken imitation of Breaking Bad Walter, dressed in a Heisenberg tee with the signature black hat approached me, grabbing my hand, asking me to dance. He had a package of blue sugar rock candy, his pretend Meth, attached to his hip. Nicholas flinched. My mouth flew open. But before I could speak, Nicholas gave Walter a look, never saying a word.

"Maybe later," Walter nodded, looking at Nicholas and deciding that dancing with me wasn't such a good idea.

"You need to get a life, Lancelot," I snapped, before I remembered where I was. Nicky looked down on my petite frame, grinning from ear to ear. He knew I was drawing an imaginary line in the sand. I only called him Lancelot when I felt he was crossing boundaries.

I was his Cookie when we were kids, and he was my Lancelot, the knight in shining armor protecting all of Camelot.

"Come now James, dance with me," Harper said seductively, making my brother forget who and where he was, scrambling his brain. "These two can take care of themselves without our help," she said, pulling him to the dance floor.

Harper strutted that gold lame miniskirt in front of him bouncing her hips from side to side. My brother untied his bow tie, and rocked his body from side to side behind her, holding both of his hands on the sides of her moving hips, rhythmically following her every move.

God my brother could dance. Somehow, somewhere in his lily-white blueblood Italian upbringing, he had learned how to bump and grind. Nicholas got really close to his Bond Girl, working his body next to her from behind, whispering sweet nothings in her ear.

Breaking Bad Walter made his way back over to me again, obviously not to be deterred by Nicky's earlier warning. A real badass that one. I really didn't want my brother to haul off the dance floor with his Bond Girl and turn him into a believer.

"Wanna dance Tink? I'll make like Peter Pan, and you can bring Wendy along," he slobbered over me, looking behind me, motioning to my girls on the dance floor.

"What part of no didn't you get earlier? Get lost and go cook some meth, asshole," Elliot barked.

Wow. I knew the sound of that bark. I'd heard it earlier this afternoon inside of a cab. It was the sound of the Big Dog. Except this time, it sounded different. Its message was not the call for help or calm. This time it sounded like a threat. It sounded like, "Go away—*mine.*"

And for a very fleeting moment, an unfamiliar feeling whizzed by me at high speed. I wanted to catch it. It was something I wanted to experience with a man of my own.

Breaking Bad Walter tucked his tail and left, totally wounded, yet convinced to split this time.

I was so glad that Maya, Logan, Top Gun, and Men in Black had decided to give the dance floor a break. I was feeling an awkward moment coming on with Elliot and me standing together by ourselves. I still wasn't sure what was up with him and the mermaid, but I had deduced from Nicky's remarks that she was his fiancée. It looked as if there was trouble brewing in paradise. Doctor

EZ must be losing his touch. But none of it was my business. I had my own problems. I had a broken heart. I looked like the picture of peace on the outside, but inside I was in pieces. I felt like Humpty Dumpty unable to put myself back together again.

"Hey Tinkerbell, when did you fly in," Top Gun said. "I must have missed you, pretty fairy, in my flyover."

I put a big wide grin on my face, having a warm fuzzy feeling that anybody noticed me.

"Julianna, these are my friends, Xavier Cook and Dr. Gabriel DeLuca," Elliot said, his stance changing. He looked irritated, eyeballing Top Gun as if he wanted to pounce on him like a panther, fingering his ear lobe that had a small diamond in the left ear.

There was that feeling again. Elliot signaling . . . *Mine.* My emotions were definitely in tune with his. No, I wasn't imagining things.

Top Gun patted him hard on the back in a friendly manner, looking satisfied that he had gotten Elliot's goat, but not really lobbing a viable threat.

"My friends call me X," Top Gun said, placing his arm around Elliot undressing me with his eyes.

Elliot squinted again, clenching his teeth. Any minute now I expected him to start pissing around me, marking me as his. He looked clearly annoyed with his own friend Xavier.

"These are Julianna's friends . . . ," Elliot began.

"Maya," Xavier said, taking the words out of his mouth.

"And Logan," Gabriel said, finishing Elliot's sentence. "Maya, Logan, this is our friend Dr. Elliot Fischer. Now that everybody knows everybody, let's say I buy a round for these beauties. What shall it be?" Gabriel said.

"Tequila," Maya, Logan, and I all said at the same time.

"Then shots it is," Xavier said. "Maya will you cheer me on?" he laughed, shooting her a seductive look.

"Tequila shots?" Gabriel said. He looked at Logan. "Do I need to worry about Swat girl cuffing me tonight? I won't promise I'll be able

77

to keep my hands to myself and off all that everything . . . umph umph umph, good God."

He moved his hands in a manner in which he was holding something, closing his eyes.

"Gabriel," Elliot snapped at him.

Logan and Maya laughed out loud. I tried to hold my laugh in, barely able to contain a small giggle, watching as Logan held her body a bit more erect, her back suddenly straightening.

"What?" Gabriel said, as if he hadn't done anything wrong. "I'm just a . . . "

"Wild and crazzzzzy guy," Xavier and Gabriel both said in drunken voices, mocking him with their best Steve Martin impression.

Darth Vader came over to the table with the tequila shots. My phone buzzed with an incoming text message.

Nicky: "Harper and I are leaving. The twins will be up early."

Me: "Okay. I'll see you tomorrow then."

Nicky: "I'll send Silas back for you guys as soon as he drops us off."

Me: "Love you Nicky. You taking my security detail with you right?"

I already knew the answer to that question but I texted it anyway. I was feeling no pain now, so I didn't mind messing with my big brother for kicks.

Nicky: "The security detail stays. We're going out the back exits so you won't see us leave."

I sent Nicky one of those emoticons with the smiley face tongue sticking out.

Me: "Love you Sir Lancelot."

Nicky: "Goodnight Cookie. Love you too."

We all nodded, passing the tequila around, and throwing our shots back. I was going to be so hung over in the morning. Oh well. I started the day asking for a certified hangover and now I was going to get it.

"Let's have a toast," Logan said.

"Yes let's," Maya said.

"Here's to broken hearts," I yelled out loud before anybody could say anything.

Everybody looked at me not knowing whether to drink their shots or remain in a state of shock. So I threw mine back first, sucked hard on the lemon, slammed my shot glass down on the table, and waited for the next pour.

All of sudden, everybody else downed their shot, slamming their empty shot glasses down on the table. Everybody except Elliot.

"Yes," Gabriel sang out loud. "To freakin' broken hearts."

Xavier howled behind him.

"Woo Hoo," X howled. "Broken hearts, baby."

Maya and Logan giggled at me, the three of us practically toppling over on each other. Now I knew why Nicky called this threesome of guys yahoos. They really were some wild and crazy guys. Some very cute wild and crazy beefcake guys.

"Please excuse me ladies, I need to make a pit stop," Elliot said, swaying a bit as he stood.

"Try not to get lost E. Wouldn't want to have Top Gun here have do another flyover."

Everyone at the table fell out laughing again. I giggled. Then I threw my pink fairy dust up in the air, most of it falling on Elliot.

I was tickled pink. Then I took in his rapidly changing facial expression. He looked surprised. Then vulnerable. Followed by a flash of heat, igniting something warm in the both of us.

 *lliot*

ood Lord. I needed to get up from this table so I could collect myself. Seeing Julianna Becker twice in one day was sending my mind and body on overload. Every time those big brown pools of chocolate peered at me, I melted. She looked beautiful, sweet, and practically edible in that Tinkerbelle costume, showing off that curvaceous body. And when she threw that pink fairy dust all over me, that was the end of me. I instantly fell under her spell. Cupid's arrow had me again.

I could envision myself taking that green bundle of sweetness in my arms, loving her, healing that broken heart, fixing all the damage that came at the hands of Oliver Banks. I desperately needed to run through Central Park for a few miles so I could beat my libido back into submission.

I pondered on how my heart skipped a beat when Harper mentioned she was a talented pastry chef. The creator behind *Sugar Mommy's.* That was a perfect branding for her. The queen of all things sweet. She was so sweet. She could be my *Sugar Mommy* every day of the week.

God, I had to reel myself back in when Xavier began flirting with her. She had that glimmer in her eye that reminded me of the first trace of morning sunlight. I saw it in her eyes as she blushed when he hinted at how beautiful she was. I wanted that look to be for me and only me. My own personal *"Sugar Mommy."* I wanted *"Sugar Mommy"* to myself. Her face, her smile, her laugh, was proof that God really did exist. I felt helpless in her presence.

I mentally slapped myself, forcing myself to remember that I was engaged to Kimber. The truth of the matter was I no longer felt I was in love with Kimber. Looking back, I doubted that I was ever really truly in love with Kimber. The fact that my brain was scrambled eggs over Julianna only underscored the truth of that fact. Still, Julianna wasn't mine. At least not yet she wasn't.

But then Cupid shot me again. Yes, I felt the sparks fly when she and I shook hands. I'd be in denial if I didn't admit my body's reaction to her. Cupid was mainlining the beautiful *Sugar Mommy* straight to my heart. It was a feeling I'd never felt with Kimber, or any other woman for that matter. And I'd had my fair share of women in life.

Something tight clenched deep around my heart when she raised her glass to toast to "broken hearts." The mere thought of another man causing her pain and breaking her heart was more than my own heart could bear. I had a deep seated need to shelter her from harm's way. I wanted to personally break Oliver Banks into tiny small pieces myself. He had put the pain in her eyes that couldn't be fully hidden under that very beautiful Tinkerbell facade. Then she threw that damn pink fairy dust over me and I was a goner.

I wanted to be the one to protect her, to keep her safe, to put her back together again. And here I was, in the middle of my own bullshit with Kimber. I had my own problems, and Julianna had unfortunately witnessed some of it tonight. How could she ever come to trust me, when she got a glimpse into my own drama-filled world tonight?

I even managed to burn some bridges with her big brother Nicholas, letting his wife Harper embraced me in a gentle hug. I thought the man was going to tear me apart right then and there limb-by-limb. Nicholas was like some crazed mountain lion protecting his own: Harper and Julianna. God, I was unknowingly making all kinds of mistakes tonight.

I seriously needed to clear my messy deck, and I needed to start with Kimber. It was bad enough that Kimber had thrown her cosmopolitan in my face, embarrassing me in front of Harper, claiming I was late. One of her male friends told her he had seen me at Maximillion's, and she wasn't having it. Whoever her little bitch male friend was, he was breaking all the man-codes. No man ever rats another man out for what goes on in a gentleman's club.

I was flabbergasted that Kimber would make such a huge scene tonight in front of a room full of influentials. So what that everyone was in costume? It didn't erase the fact that underneath those costumes were some of the most powerful people in New York, many of whom were taking note of every little nuance going on in the room. I knew better than to let the costumes fool me. Hell, I even saw one of the city's councilmen drop in with a Tony Soprano mask on, pulling it off his face once to down a whiskey.

Where was Kimber anyway? Hopefully she went to the ladies' room to cool off. Maybe she went home. Either way, this was not the proper venue for her and me to talk. Many of the folks here tonight were using this social gathering as an opportunity to network; something Kimber could have been doing for herself to propel her own career out of the doldrums. But instead she chose to act like the spoiled, bitchy trophy wife-to-be, unaware that business was being conducted, and millions of dollars were changing hands tonight.

Thank God for Harper Montgomery Becker. Harper reminded Kimber that certain behavior was considered unacceptable in this crowd, and that it would be unwise to air her dirty laundry publicly. Kimber was never one to be able to take sound advice. God forbid if anybody could ever tell her what to do. So, she called Harper a "bitch," and slung her drink. Thank God, the drink went in my direction and not at Harper.

I was embarrassed. The one woman that was helping to make my career, my wife-to-be was calling her a bitch. My hands were tied. I was my mother's child, a gentleman. I couldn't do anything but stand there and take the public humiliation of her flinging her drink in my face. A lesser man may have turned the tables on her.

I was so ashamed on behalf of Kimber. I begged Harper's forgiveness, apologizing with everything I had. Harper was not the type of woman to let something like that go. I knew she would make a mental note of it. But refined as she was, she publicly dismissed Kimber's outburst as nothing more than a tantrum from a woman that needed to grow up. She gave me a hug, and told me to forget about it. A hug that got me in deep muddy water with Julianna's brother Nicholas. Big time.

This wasn't the first time I had to deal with Nicholas Becker's zealous protection of what was his. When I was delivering his and Harper's twins, he growled and sputtered every time I had to get in between his wife's legs. I had to throw him out of the examining room on more than one occasion just to do a simple check to see how far Harper had dilated. The man performed so badly in the delivery room, he made me want to get out of the profession.

I had to set him straight and remind him I was boss in the examining room. That was my playground, not his. Nicholas wasn't the kind of man that took well to being ordered around. Especially when he thought you were getting a peek at Harper's vagina. He made it very clear that Harper, and her vagina, were for his and only his viewing. I literally had to kick him out of the maternity room. Harper was the only one that could soothe his frayed nerves, reminding him that he was in a medical environment and that I wasn't looking at her that way. She insisted he get a grip on himself and let me do my job to get his babies here safely. Poor thing, she was sweating profusely in labor having to rein her man in with a whip just to get her babies into the world, and to keep him from going berserk. I felt for her. He wasn't the kind of man that could be soothed by just any woman. She had to be incredibly special. Harper Carmichael Montgomery Becker was indeed special, and Nicholas Becker knew it. Hence, he had no intentions of letting any man into her orbit.

Harper and Nicholas Becker were practically American royalty. Nicholas, the good man that he was, later apologized to me fiercely, to the tune of building a new ten-million-dollar obstetrics wing, placing me at the helm. I guess if he ever decided to have more children, no one else but me was going to see that vagina again. But six years later, he still growled like the lion he was if any man got too close to her.

Man I really needed to get my shit together. I needed a woman that needed me for me, not for what I could give her. A woman that wanted my babies. A woman that had her own career objectives. A woman like . . . Julianna Becker.

Boom, there it was again. Cupid's arrow. Mainlining to my heart again. If this kept up I was going to be a junkie for Julianna's love. A love she hadn't even agreed to give to me. A love I hadn't worked to earn. A love I didn't deserve yet. A love I was going to one day come to deserve and own.

I shook my head, staggering down Luigi's back entrance hallway to find the men's bathroom. I slid past a couple in one of the many little alcoves in this place. This back area was like a maze, dimly lit. Either my head was buzzed or I was feeling a bit lost and confused. Actually, all of the above.

Ah . . . a face I thought I recognized. Luigi's teenage son Mario. Mario was dressed like an iPhone. He had two of his crew with him strolling in the long, dimly lit hallway. Minnie Mouse, and Captain Crunch were tagging along. I still hadn't found the men's room yet, still needing a break from my thoughts.

Mario was one of those teen geek-heads that flew under the radar, always a step ahead of trouble. As far as his father Luigi was concerned, Mario was mischief reincarnate. Mario and his geeky friends were well known in certain social media circles for hacking into their high school's database and changing their cafeteria's lunch menu by compromising inventory orders with the school's food vendors. Truly, he was a genius by anybody's definition, but what did it matter if you still had to graduate from high school.

"Hey Dr. EZ . . . ," Mario slurred. Mario had two joints in his hand, one of which that he passed to Minnie Mouse, but not before blowing smoke in my face.

I was too late in pulling my mask up over my face hoping he wouldn't recognize me. The marijuana smoke filled my nostrils, and I coughed a bit. It didn't matter that I didn't feel like talking. Mario had recognized me anyway, and was getting a kick out of the fact I was coughing back the smoke from his wacky weed.

"Mario, if I had wanted a shotgun, I would have asked for one."

"Damn, Dr. EZ, I know I'm a little buzzed right now, but seeing double wasn't on the menu tonight. Here Captain, take this blunt," he said to his friend. "I'm way too fucked up right now."

"What's up Mario," I muttered. "Looking for the restroom, man."

"Dude, you've taken quickie to a whole new level", Mario said.

"Dr. McBigDick," Minnie Mouse snickered at me.

Captain Crunch nudged her in her side to be quiet.

What did Minnie Mouse mean? Why was she calling me Dr. McBigDick?

"Fuck, I thought I just saw you in Uncle Louie's back room office with your boo, baby. Fuck me man. I'm starting to see things."

Whatever shit Mario and his crew were smoking couldn't be good. Maybe his fucking brain was fried? I knew I was buzzed from the drinks at Maximillion's, but I hadn't taken any of the tequila shots. What the fuck were these high ass kids talking about, seeing me in some back office?

"What's wrong Mario? You smoking too much of that wacky weed tonight dude?"

"What say you Minnie?" Mario said looking at his female friend, his eyes red and partially closed.

"We just saw him," Minnie giggled uncontrollably. "Maybe he's a ghost."

"Yeah, Minnie, I'm so high I'm seeing ghosts," Captain Crunch laughed. "I'm feeling like I'm on doctor remix bitches. Doctors everywhere I turn."

God, the last thing I needed to do was to have to deal with was a bunch of whacked out high school teens that needed to go home, lest

I'd be begging Gabriel to pump their stomachs tonight. What the fuck were they doing here anyway? Where were their parents?

Minnie Mouse started punching some numbers in iPhone's chest.

"I'm playing my voicemail," Minnie Mouse said, laughing. iPhone's costume starting playing tones when she punched his digits. How they made that happen was beyond me. Okay. I was a bit behind the times with respect to the digital revolution.

The next thing I heard was iPhone babbling about James Bond and his Bond Girl sliding out the back door of the establishment headed to a limousine, being chased by Her Majesty's Secret Service, but not before James Bond cursed my name royally in English and Italian after seeing me banging that "black-sequined mermaid."

I shook my head in disbelief, my head not comprehending my lying ears. My eyes widened. I was in a state of shock. The black-sequined mermaid part caught my attention.

"Can you play that voicemail again for me Minnie?" I said, playing along with her, still looking and feeling very perplexed, my buzz rapidly leaving me.

iPhone started babbling again about how he knew French, but got a little lost in translation with the Italian, except when the word "kill" was spouted a couple of times out of James Bond's mouth. iPhone claimed that as far as he could tell the word "Tinkerbell" was spoken in at least four languages that he recognized.

"I know a little Italian," Captain Crunch babbled. "And you should know Dr. McBigDick, James Bond said you were on the verge of being a "dead man."

Captain Crunch pointed his index finger in my chest. I paused, trying to decide who was the most fucked up in this picture. Them or me?

"I think Her Majesty's Secret Service is going to be looking for you dude. You best make tracks," Captain Crunch said with a straight face.

Minnie Mouse and iPhone fell out laughing so hard they were hardly able to stand on their feet. I pulled both of those laughing hyenas up by their shoulders, standing them on their feet. Shit, I needed to get away from these whacked out kids, and piss.

I gave the three of them the once over to make sure they were medically in what I considered the safe zone. Where the fuck were their parents? I did not want them to end up on Gabriel's watch tonight. Fucking kids. I'm only one man. I can't be responsible for all of them. I deal in the world of infants. Not semi-grown potheads.

"Thank you Mario," I said to iPhone and Captain Crunch. I patted them on the back. Minnie Mouse hit the red "end call" bar on iPhone. "Let's roll bitches," she said to iPhone and Captain Crunch.

I paused and shook my head, thinking some gem of wisdom might suddenly fall out and drop into my consciousness. I reminded myself that they were a bunch of pot smoking whacked out kids dressed like digital zombies. Either way, it didn't take away the feeling of dread I was having. A feeling of impending doom was overtaking me. My doom.

I placed my hand on the doorknob to Uncle Louie's office, feeling the beads of sweat that were forming on my hands. My mind was seething long before it needed to, already knowing that my emotions had to catch up with where my mental comprehension was going. The Jaws music had already begun to play its melody in my head. I just needed to turn the handle and feel the fire.

Like a good little soldier marching to the beat of the lonely hearts drumbeat, I turned the handle. I moved slowly, opening up Uncle Louie's office. And now it all became clear what crazy iPhone, Minnie Mouse, and Captain Crunch were babbling about. I was totally sober now. My buzz had taken flight. Left me in the wind. Telling me it wasn't going to stick around for drama.

You know how you see those scenes in a movie where the bartender takes a longneck beer and slides it down across of the top of the bar, but the person who's supposed to catch it misses, and that longneck crashes to the floor? That would be me right now. I'm that longneck beer crashing to the floor.

There I was. Watching myself, in my own doctor gear, fucking my own fiancée Kimber, who was moaning and groaning like I never heard her before. Except it wasn't me. It wasn't even a good version of me. It was somebody else dressed like me that was fucking my fiancée. But not me. And she was enjoying every minute of it. iPhone, Minnie Mouse, and Captain Crunch had seen it, and apparently Nicholas Becker had seen it too. It all made sense now. It was quite the sobering scene.

"C'mon baby, come for me. You know I'm better than him. Do me baby," he said pumping his dick into Kimber like a well-oiled machine in overdrive.

"Yeah baby," Kimber said, her back to him, moaning and groaning. "You're the best, love. Work it baby. I'm, I'm . . . I . . ."

He was behind her, fucking her doggie style. She couldn't see me. Her chocolate ass was grinding him frantically in a frenzy, trying to work her impending orgasm that was just about to peak.

I swear I wanted to kill the both of them with my bare hands. Her black-sequined mermaid dress was down to her knees, her latte-colored bottom curving against his dick.

I was emotionally wounded, but not blinded to the fact that Kimber's panties were ripped, halfway hanging on her body close to her knees. She was loving every minute of it.

She turned her head around, to tease him, realizing I was standing there looking at her in disbelief. Shock. We looked at each other dead on.

"Oh my God Elliot," she said babbling like the scatterbrain that she is. Her red lipstick smeared across her face, like the two-bit ho she appeared to be. "This is not what it seems," she pleaded. "I thought he was you."

The poor imitation of me had been fucking her on Uncle Louie's mahogany wood desk that was filled with pictures of Luigi's kids and family. Family values were surrounding my Ms. New York wife-to-be, who was in a back office fucking another man, like a corner prostitute.

The room's wood-paneled walls reminded me of something out of one of those old Godfather movies. The big leather chair behind the desk, leaving me with the feeling that someone important sat in it, and here my wife-to-be was sprawled off across Mr. Important's desk, with a fake doctor's dick in her ass, trying to convince *me* that he was me.

And then the very worst happened next. Dude turns around with all animosity saying, "What the fuck; first, James fucking Bond, and now you. Can't you see I'm busy? Get out of here motherfucker."

That was the point at which all sanity left me.

Kimber squirmed readily to get out from under the dude, trying to pull herself together, but not before I reached over to Mr. Important's bar filled with all kinds of liquor. I grabbed the first bottle of whiskey I could find, slamming it against his 'not so smart don't you fuck with me' head.

Kimber screamed, "Elliot!"

iPhone, Minnie Mouse, and Captain Crunch were standing in the doorway speechless from all the commotion, having witnessed this ugly scene.

I was as calm as I had been in a very long time. For once I had complete clarity. I didn't make any move to rush out the door. I didn't know if the man that looked like me was dead or not. I took note of the line of cocaine on the desk, and the traces of white powder under Kimber and my impersonator's nose. They had both been doing lines, having their own private party.

I looked at her with pain in my eyes. Who knew she would do this to me? The betrayal was killing me. Kimber refused to look at me. She was too freaked out to face me or even form a coherent sentence.

"Do me a favor Mario. Go find Men In Black. Tell him I need him right about now," I said, still holding the broken bottle in my hand. If my impersonator even so much as thought he was going to get up off the floor, I was going to make him regret that decision, making him permanently pay. Who was this guy?

"And Mario, can you do me a favor and try to be discreet," I said.

Mario nodded in agreement as if he understood. Captain Crunch and Minnie Mouse didn't move. And just in case they decided to, I said out loud to them, "Don't move."

But Kimber was moving like wildfire to pull herself together, still too afraid to move past me at this point, perhaps wondering if I was going to come for her next. I was still holding the broken bottle in my hand, staring at her like she was dirt under my feet.

"Dude, good thing the Secret Service is gone," Captain Crunch said, holding Minnie Mouse under his arm.

"I want to go home," Minnie Mouse pleaded, looking at the blood that was spilling out of Dr. Lookalike's head.

"This night's been on a remix a bit too long for me," Captain Crunch said. "Mario's father's friends tend to ratchet their shit up to a level I don't feel I'm quite ready for at fifteen."

I wasn't normally a violent person. If anything I was the proverbial gentleman. But tonight I was invoking the dignity clause. There was only so far you could push me before my sense of reason got up and walked out of the door saying 'have at it bitch.'

I wasn't any woman or any man's fool. So whichever ever one of them wanted to question me, I was putting the issue to rest tonight for once and for all.

"Damnnn, EZEEEEEE," Gabriel said as he bolted through Uncle Louie's doors. He yelled at the teenagers to take a hike, hurriedly handing them a huge wad of cash telling them to find something interesting to do with themselves and to get lost. He was waving his hand fast, shooing them on. They eagerly took the money, looking excited, glad to have the extra cash and permission to move. They ran out of that room fast. Real fast.

"What the fuck, Elliot?"

Gabriel noticed Kimber in the corner trembling like she had lost her best friend. He quickly assessed the situation.

"Who is the guy, Elliot?"

"Well he sure as hell isn't me, but he damn sure was fucking what once was mine," I seethed through my teeth.

Kimber gasped so loudly that Elliot and I both looked at her at the same time. She was rubbing her finger across her nose.

Gabriel turned that pitiful excuse of a man on the floor over, and pulled cap off his head, and mask down his face.

"Dexter fucking Esposito," Gabriel gasped. "You busted Dexter Esposito over the head?"

I looked down on the floor at Dexter Esposito, Esquire. General Counsel for the hospital. Our hospital.

"You fucked Dexter Esposito?" I shouted, turning to Kimber. "You fucking bitch of a whore!"

I backed five steps away from her in disbelief. I could hear Dexter groaning and moaning on the floor. At least the motherfucker wasn't dead.

"Leave," Gabriel shouted at Kimber.

Kimber slid her body out past Gabriel and me, staying as far away from me as she could, hugging her back to the wall to make sure she didn't get too close to me. I'm sure I was looking like a crazed man ready to snap at any minute. I started pacing the floor in short steps back and forth. Kimber staggered out of the room as fast as she could, her red bottom heels clacking against the floor as she stumbled.

Gabriel took the broken bottle out of my hand and dumped it in the nearby trashcan. Gabriel bent down over Dexter. He felt his pulse, checking his vitals. "Thank God he's gonna live, EZ. I think you just knocked him out for bit. He'll come too, but he is full of alcohol, and maybe cocaine, so it may take a few beats."

"Elliot, it's time for you to let Kimber go now. This thing with you and Kimber, it's not even healthy anymore. It's dysfunctional," he said, placing two fingers on the side of Dexter's neck, checking his pulse, looking at his watch. Gabriel took one finger and raised both eyelids, checking his pupils.

Gabriel looked at me, and I looked at him, still at a loss for words. Kimber and I had one of those toxic relationships where you knew you had stayed too long. Gabriel and I looked at each other, speaking to each other in silence, both physically nodding our heads in agreement.

*L*ucky for Dexter, Gabriel and I were real doctors. We were able to keep a check on his vitals, stop the bleeding, pack his head with some ice, and call an ambulance. The paramedics patched the knot on his head and transported him to the nearby emergency room down the street for a several stitches. I gave my number to one of the paramedics asking him to give me a status update on Dexter's condition.

Kimber left without complaint. I would deal with her when I got home. Her horrendous actions had now spilled over into my workplace. This animosity between Dexter, Gabriel, and I was beginning to go from bad to worse. I hardly knew what to expect next any more from Kimber. Having a sexual escapade with one of my own hospital's administrative heads was beyond reproach, even for her. By the time the gossipmongers at the hospital would get the news, my career might end up in jeopardy. The fact that Nicholas Becker had apparently witnessed this scene made me sick to the pit of my stomach.

Gabriel made excuses to Julianna and her friends that one of Luigi's patrons had taken ill in the back room and that I had to leave to tend to their medical needs. Gabriel said Julianna thought I was some kind of hero. The tequila shots our crews were downing helped the story along. Only Gabriel, Dexter, and I knew the truth. Oh yeah. Except for a trio of digital geek pot smoking teenagers.

Gabriel had paid the teenagers to take off, so there was nobody else who knew this story. The paramedic called me back, letting me know Dexter had a slight concussion, needed some stitches, but nothing that a few painkillers and some rest couldn't cure. He was going to definitely survive this nasty encounter.

Luigi's Halloween Party apparently went on until the wee hours of the night. I'd heard from Gabriel that by about 4 am, Julianna and her crew decided to call it a night. Gabriel and Xavier exchanged phone numbers with Maya and Logan. Julianna left with her posse.

My *Sugar Mommy* was none the wiser that all hell had broken loose on me tonight.

*exter*

I swear that douchebag Elliot Fischer almost tried to kill me.

"Mr. Esposito you're going to need some stitches," the nurse said. "The doctor will be here shortly."

"Fine," I grunted with displeasure.

Fucking six stitches in my head. I should fuck his trophy wife-to-be another time just because my damn head hurts.

Stuck here in some emergency room in the middle of the night. At least he got what was coming to him. Always strutting around this hospital like he's some hot shit peacock. All the ladies falling at his feet, calling him "Dr. Easy On The Eyes." They think because he's a doctor, he's something special. That fucker isn't special. He's just been lucky, always at the right place at the right time.

If it weren't for the fact that I was knocking boots with his fiancée, I would have pressed assault charges against him myself. He'd better thank his lucky stars that I was keeping my mouth shut. If the word had gotten out, I would have been the one to look bad. I had no plans to ruin my own reputation in the process of bringing him down. That would kind of be like cutting my nose off to spite my face. At the end of the day he got what was coming to him.

Stupid man had no idea that it was me who told Kimber that he was slinging money all over those hoes at Maximillion's. One little seed planted in her diamond studded ear that Elliot was tossing around money she could use on getting that new Benz she wanted, and the game was up.

I had heard on more than one occasion around the hospital nursing pool that Kimber was habitually wanting more money for this and that. My secretary had an ongoing pipeline to the nursing pool. Supposedly Elliot's fiancée whined enough to whoever would listen about him never being home, and spending more time at the hospital than he did with her.

Elliot had no idea that I was calling her on the phone routinely, telling her that I was her husband's friend and that I was pretty sure he wouldn't mind me checking on her to see if she needed anything. I even offered to take her to dinner, the weekend Elliot was in Westchester attending the Obstetrician's quarterly conference. That beautiful piece of ass actually took me up on my offer too. I wined and dined her so good, giving her a little snow for a pick me up, by the time dinner was over, she was giving me a blow job and letting me finger her to an orgasm on the ride home. I would have done more, but for the fact she came down with an attack of conscience, and pretended like she couldn't go all the way with me because she was engaged. So I faked the nice gentleman role, let it go, and kept calling time to time, to check in on her, playing on her vulnerability or lack thereof. And my money was on the latter. She wanted me and she wanted me bad.

After a time, I started setting up a few lunch dates here and there, giving her my Neiman Marcus card, suggesting she go buy herself one of those Birkin Bags all the ladies talked about so as to make herself feel better. I reminded that greedy little cow that she wasn't alone in her misery. That I was going to be there for her. The more I scratched her little itch, the more she came back for more. Kimber was my Ms. Jones and *yessiree* baby we have a thing going on.

By the time Doctor Kiss My Ass made it to Luigi's, Kimber's dandruff was so far up it didn't take much for her to sling her drink in his face, giving Elliot her ass to kiss. And that was one pretty good piece of ass too. One I had decided I was going to fuck from the windows to the wall tonight.

Elliot was pretty predictable. Every year at Halloween, he came as his same tired ole worn out self. I didn't expect this year to be any different. He was far from original. So, I grabbed some scrubs from the hospital laundry staff and decided to come dressed like a doctor too. I was going to do him, be him, and fuck what was his. He and Gabriel always thinking they're the men of the hour around the hospital, prancing around like they owned the place.

The hospital's CEO let Elliot and that jerk Gabriel get away with murder far too often. The CEO was constant babbling about how Elliot's mother being some renowned geneticist, and that she was so proud Elliot had chosen to go into the medical profession. I'm tired of always having to play second fiddle to Elliot's reputation and having to clean up his friend Gabriel's legal messes all the damn time. Gabriel, son of a renowned cardiologist. To hell with both of those jokers.

Bad enough that the Becker mogul gave barrels of cash to the hospital because pretty boy Dr. EZ delivered his kids. He even put a legal stipulation as a part of the hospital's endowment, that Elliot be the one to run the new wing. Who does that?

Now that Becker's kid sister managed to have a meltdown in a cab with Elliot, all that mogul had to do was drop a dime, and everyone in Administration went into overdrive to make sure that little bitch got the star quality treatment. Becker's wife even put the hospital administration on notice that little sister and doctor pretty boy would be this year's co-chairs for the annual hospital fundraiser. Hell, I wanted that job. Everybody knows that the co-chairs of the annual hospital fundraiser get to rub shoulders with all of New York's moneyed elite. Once again, Elliot is back on his high horse again.

He always got the best of everything, right down to his plans for marrying the former Ms. New York. He thinks because he was in the magazines as one of the most eligible bachelors that he's God's gift to mankind. Elliot might be the most eligible bachelor but he sucks at picking women. For the last four years I've watched him keep picking these beautiful gold-diggers. Kimber's not the first bimbo he's picked, even though she hopes to be the last. But, even I had to admit, Kimber was one fine ass piece of trophy wife. I fucked her good too, just like I owned her.

Now that Elliot knows I fucked his fiancée, I've got to up my game. I'm going to bring Elliot's stupid image crumbling down from the inside out. His wife to be, his work, and everything else that gets in my path.

It was time somebody put Elliot back in his place. And that somebody was going to be me. Come Monday, I was going to start on my mission to bring Dr. Elliot Fischer down professionally and personally. Dr. Gabriel DeLuca would be collateral damage, if he chooses to get in my way. And I do expect that clown to get in my way. Those two were two peas in a pod. What the hell. I'll bring Gabe down with him. Two for the price of one.

"Mr. Esposito. Time to stitch you up sir," the young resident doctor said. "Six stitches. It could be worse."

Yeah. Elliot was going to pay for this.

 *ulianna*

he bald-headed guard with the deep voice made sure the yahoo guys weren't coming home with us. He kept barking orders to his other cohorts when Silas pulled up to the curb of Becker Towers.

"Leader Two, we need some help here untangling Pretty Is with Men In Black. These two have handcuffed each other."

Leader One shook his head and sighed, but not really acting surprised. It was almost as if he expected something like this to happen.

Logan was sitting in the limousine on the lap of Gabriel, both handcuffed to each other, with me, Maya, and Top Gun rolling on top of each other in laughter. We were all so drunk, it was a good thing Nicky had us under protective care.

Maya and I were giggling uncontrollably, having a hard time uncuffing Logan from Gabriel. Those two were so tangled up with each other, we weren't sure we'd be able to get them apart. None of us had any manual dexterity left, and they kept kissing each other, making the task of separating them even harder.

There was no doubt that Logan wanted to get underneath that beautiful Adonis, but we gals promised ourselves when the night began, we weren't going to do any one night stands on Halloween night. We'd agreed earlier we didn't want to find scary Halloween guy in our bed the next morning. We would drink. We would flirt. We would drool, but no one-night stands tonight.

"Leader Two, they're all pretty shit faced. I need some assistance here. I've got a leash here on Twinkle Toes and Pretty Does."

The big bald-headed bodyguard yanked Maya and I out of the limousine by our hands, propping us up against the car for support, signaling his other team members for help.

"What's wrong, baldie?" I asked, running my fingertip down the side of his face, rubbing fairy dust on his shiny bald head. "You need me to help you?", I swooned.

Baldie pretty much ignored me, but he didn't take his hands off Maya and me. I wondered how it was possible that one man could possibly hold two plastered women in place at the same time.

"Wow, you are soooooooo big," I slurred, in awe of his huge muscular frame and bulging biceps.

"Big is good," Maya swooned.

Maya and I both giggled together.

"So, Jules, do blondes shrrreeeally have more fun?" Maya slurred.

I scratched my head, thinking that question was too deep to process drunk. I was ready to get out of this wig. My head was getting hot, my feet hurt, and my heart . . . I had numbed it with so much tequila all my heart lights had gone out.

Fun? Fun was being able to act out all of my bad girl fantasies with a man. I didn't even have one of those tonight to drool over.

"Hell no. Fun went to pee and then fun disappeared. You can't have fun with what you can't see." I said, shoving Maya the other way, her body leaning against mine.

"Yeah that was real weird the way Elliot disappeared. I shuu-ussspect it's that damn hypocrite oaf."

"You mean hippocratic oath, Maya," I spit out, spraying saliva in between giggles.

"Yep, that's the word Jules," Maya wobbled. "Maybe Dr. EZ comes up missing a lot?"

"I didn't want to even think about it. My best laid plan to spend the night drinking, flirting, drooling, and numbing my heart with a place-holder man, crumbled the minute we all toasted to broken hearts and the placeholder took flight. Forget him. Forget Oliver. Forget three-legged placeholders."

"Okay then it's settled. Blondes don't have more fun," Maya winked, looking back over her shoulder, grinning at Logan.

"C'mon Logan. Jesus Christ," I whined. "I need to go to the little girls' room!"

I shifted my weight from side to side like a petulant child.

"Yeah Logan, pajama party at Jules's place," Maya said.

I started laughing out loud again.

"SHHHshhh," Maya said. "Use your inside voice Jules!"

"We're outside Maya," I said looking up, checking to make sure that was true, my eyes momentarily fixated on the stars and the moon.

I was starting to sway, leaning way over to the side, and big bald Leader One guy grabbed my upper arms to prop me upright.

"Time to tuck you gals in for the evening, get these fellas home, and drop your carriage off. I need to give a report back to Guardian Angel in the morning," he said.

"I know who the Guardian Angel is . . . " I slurred.

"Yeah, he's that green-eyed cock-blocker," Maya slurred. She was barely standing on her feet, one of her white tennis shoes in her hand, and her hair a mess.

"Guardian Angel is codename for my cock-blocking brother who must have given Baldie strict orders to make sure we came home alone tonight."

Those were the last words I remember saying before my eyes drifted closed.

I turned over, pulling the covers of my soft, white, down-filled comforter up over my shoulders to stay warm, feeling my ears ringing and my head pounding. Sunlight was peeking through the white sheers that hung from my floor-to-ceiling windows.

I pounded my fluffy pillow with my fist. Oh my poor head. This is what I get. When the day began yesterday, I begged for a certified hangover. I had gotten exactly what I had asked the universe to give me. I definitely was hung-over.

My head hurt from the tequila. My heart hurt from the loss of Oliver. I closed my eyes once more, praying to God that he takes Oliver off my heart. *And please God, send me somebody new and worthy.*

I opened my eyes again, glancing across my bedroom. Maya was asleep in my oversized boudoir chair with my Cookie Monster blanket pulled over her, wearing my Cookie Monster flannel pajamas. Logan was wearing my pink ruffled baby doll nightie with my pink eye mask over her face, her long blonde hair swirling all over the pillows. She reminded me of Goldilocks.

I looked across the room, seeing my green Tinkerbell wings on the floor, my green sequined mini dress and blonde wig bundled up in a pile on top of the dresser. The last remnants of Laker Girl and Swat Girl were strewn haphazardly in the corner, never to show their wild and crazy faces again.

I looked down on myself, noticing I was back in one of Nicky's old gray Naval Academy t-shirts that I kept stuffed in my nightgown drawer. I glanced at the clock next to the picture of my mother on my night stand. I loved waking to my mother's smile, feeling like she was watching over me every day. I picked up her picture frame and kissed her picture.

"Any thoughts to share, mother, about Dr. Gray Eyes?" For some reason unbeknownst to me, every time I had thoughts of Oliver, Elliot's face would pop into my head next. I wondered if the universe was trying

to tell me something. Perhaps it was just my imagination running away with me again.

I reached down on the floor, grabbing my favorite fluffy socks that I liked wearing on my feet to keep me warm in the winter.

I suddenly remembered I was supposed to get with Nicky today to talk about my plans for launching *Sugar Mommy*. Not to mention, Harper wanted me to showcase *Sugar Mommy's* desserts at the hospital's annual fundraiser. I needed to get my act together quick. It looked bad that I wasn't up already, knocking on my brother's Penthouse doors, sharing my ideas about *Sugar Mommy's* and the fundraiser.

Hmmm. The fundraiser meant I'd have to work with Gray Eyes; Dr. Elliot Fischer is co-chair. The mere thought of such collaboration made me desperately want to be well prepared, professional, and not make a fool of myself.

Harper never gave me space to think about how I felt about taking on such a huge responsibility. Of course I would do it. I just hadn't really thought about it seriously. I knew Harper wanted my bakery venture to be a success. She wasn't going to give me a chance to think about it, get scared, back out, and say no out of fear.

I crawled out of bed stumbling, heading to the kitchen for some well desired java. I needed to put my head back on before going upstairs to the Penthouse to meet with Nicky. Logan wobbled into the kitchen area, slamming her butt on the barstool, looking beautiful as ever in my pink French lace baby-doll nightie.

"You look better in that thing than I ever have," I groaned, "maybe I should just give it to you."

Logan slid the pink satin eye mask further back on top of her head, her beautiful blonde curls dancing in the room's sunlight. She slouched over the countertop, rubbing her temples.

"Jesus Jules, my mouth feels like it's stuffed with cotton. I hope you've got that coffee underway. It was a long night," she yawned.

"Yeah, one you clearly didn't want to end, handcuffing yourself to Gabriel. Do the walk of shame now."

Logan slid off the barstool, moonwalked backwards three feet, spun around and bowed.

We both tried to laugh, but it was halfhearted since both our heads were hurting.

Logan giggled to herself, waving at me to pour her a cup of coffee. I reached in the cabinet pulling down two of my favorite "Got Milk" mugs with the chocolate Oreo cookie on the front. I slid the coffee pot out before the brew could finish, sneaking her and myself a pour.

"Who wouldn't want to be handcuffed to that beautiful body, Jules? I wanted to break our group promise, and get all up under that hot bed of testosterone last night. Gabriel is like a twelve on a scale of one to ten. He reminds me of all things beautiful, kind of like how I feel about Restoration Hardware."

"Restoration Hardware? You're comparing that man to your love of a store?," I asked in bewilderment.

Logan really truly did have her moments where she went off all charts of meaningful understanding.

"Yeah Jules. Everything is beautiful in that store. You can't help but fall in love with everything. And he's everything. He's all man. I want to get to know that cute hunk of a man a whole lot better."

"Whatever," I said, sipping my coffee, trying to put my head back on my neck. I hardly understood her analogy, but then again that was quintessential Logan Kennedy. She frequently said things that scrambled the brain.

I had to agree with Logan. If we were considering all things perfection cloaked in class, then Dr. Gabriel DeLuca wore that banner pretty well.

"So do you like Elliot?"

I paused sipping my coffee, not sure I should answer that question.

"He was staring at you all night long, as if you were the only person in the room," Logan said.

"He's engaged," I said with a tone of disappointment in my voice. "Unavailable."

"Not the way I hear it."

I raised my eyebrows up at her suggesting she continue.

"Gabriel thinks he's never going to make it down the aisle with Kimber. Apparently that marriage was doomed from the start," Logan said casually, taking a sip from her coffee mug.

"Really?" I said, the conversation peaking my interest.

"Yup. Gabriel says Elliot's fiancée makes all kinds of demands on him, that she's rude to the hospital staff, and runs through his money like it's going out of style. Apparently she has no respect for what he does. So he spends lots of time at the hospital throwing himself into the job rather than to have to go home to her."

"Well she did throw her drink in his face."

"Yeah, can you believe that woman did that in public? She has no shame Jules."

"That was pretty embarrassing. I think my sister-in-law was trying to console him, but my brother wasn't taking that whole 'let's hug it out' moment too well. Nicky isn't really feeling Elliot and his friends."

"Nicky isn't feeling any man that has the hots for you Jules. Besides you don't need his approval for who you choose to date. But whoever you do end up with, he's gonna have to have special skills to get by Nicky."

"All the men in my family have been majorly overprotective when it comes to the guys in my life. I suppose it's because I grew up without a mother. They think they know how to be momma bear, and that I'm their cub."

I shook my head, realizing I'd dealt with "Big Daddy" and my brothers Blake and Nicky interfering with my dating choices all my life. Nobody's ever been good enough for them when it came to me.

"Well so far, Nicky's been right on. Even I had to agree Oliver wasn't the right choice for you. I'm never going to like any man that hurts you Jules."

"I'm worried I'll never find anyone, Logan. Everyone I love leaves me for someone else. What's wrong with me?"

"Honey, it's not you. It's them. You're a great catch for any man with a half brain. The right one hasn't come along yet. Maybe Elliot's the one?"

"Well I can hardly do anything with a man that's halfway down the marriage aisle. Even Nicky told me to forget about it."

"I'm telling you Jules, according to Gabriel, that engagement was over before it began. Gabriel claims Elliot's never really been in love with her. That he's been going through the motions this last year and a half because he thinks it's the right thing to do. But, now he's seeing the light at the end of the tunnel and that train coming down the track is headed for his ass."

Logan sipped her coffee. I sipped mine. We both were momentarily silent.

"Where are the pastries you drunk bitches?" Maya came around the corner, joining us. "I need some sugar, *Sugar Mommy*."

Logan and I rolled our eyes at Maya. Her eyes were red and puffy. She looked like I felt. Like hell. Maya walked over to my cocktail table, towards my marble chess set. She moved her Knight, taking my Rook.

"Ah ha," Maya grinned.

"Bitch," I mumbled under my breath.

"Ya'll playing one of your marathon chess games again?" Logan squinted her nose up at the both of us.

"It appears," I said.

"What week is this?" Logan said, unenthused.

"Day ten," I groaned.

We'd had a marathon chess game going on for over a week. I could hardly believe Maya's brain could function well enough to think about such a strategic chess move. It was one of the things I loved about Maya. She could practically play chess with her eyes closed. We both loved the game.

I opened my new sub-zero fridge, pulling out a tray of cinnamon buns. I preheated my oven, grabbing a tube of icing that I made yesterday, and started making beautiful swirls on top of the buns.

A phone buzzed. All three of us jumped, picking up our phones to see which one of us was getting a call.

It was my phone. I didn't recognize the number.

"Hello?"

"Julianna Becker?" a husky familiar voice on the other end spoke.

"Huh?"

God I sound like the biggest dork walking.

"This is Doctor Elliot Fischer. Is this a good time to talk?"

"Ah . . . yeah," I said slowly.

I pointed to my phone, mouthing to Logan and Maya that Gray Eyes was on the phone. They both jumped off their barstools, joining me on both sides, pushing their ears up to the phone trying to listen. I pushed both of them away, stepping into my living room area, so as to create some personal space between them and me. I sat on the bench in front of my white Fazioli.

"I was calling to apologize for last night."

"Oh?"

"Yes, I stepped away from the table not realizing I was going to walk into a situation. One that was going to require . . . medical assistance."

"Yes, I heard from Gabriel that someone had taken a fall, and that you assisted in their medical care until the paramedics came. It was good you were there."

"Bitch you're burning the buns," Maya said out loud in the background running into the kitchen, opening the oven door to pull out the cinnamon buns. A plume of smoke filled the air. Maya was waving a potholder over the smoke alarm trying to keep it from going off.

I bit my lip, squinting my eyes closed, totally having forgotten about anything in the oven. Why do I lose my ability to think around Elliot?

"I'm sorry do you have guests? I can call back."

"No, no. It's just my girlfriends. We had a sleepover last night."

I heard the familiar computer voice come through loudly over my kitchen intercom.

"Everything okay, Ms. Jules? I sense smoke."

I waved my hand at Logan to hit the silent button on the intercom. Too late.

"It's Maya. How many times do I have to correct you Computer-Luv?" Maya yelled into the intercom at the robotic voice that was piping through the security panel. A Parks and Parks invention.

We'd named the deep male robotic voice ComputerLuv. He was a special installment put in a year ago to make sure the three of us never burnt Becker Towers down to the ground. Apparently we couldn't be trusted to cook and chew bubblegum at the same time together.

"Is there a problem, should I call back?," Elliot said amidst my chaos.

"Everything okay, Ms. Maya? I sense smoke," ComputerLuv repeated.

"Yeah, now Tech Off," Maya insisted. She was looking totally silly talking to a robot.

"Oh no, not at all," I said re-focusing my attention back on Gray Eyes.

"Yeah, I think I missed out on the fun last night," Elliot said, his lowered voice tinged with regret. "Gabriel and Xavier both said they had a great time."

There was an awkward silent pause.

"I'm looking forward to co-chairing the hospital fundraiser with you," he said sounding more upbeat.

"Yes, that. Me too. So will your fiancée be helping you with your part of the fundraiser project?"

Probably shouldn't have said that out loud.

I looked over at Logan. She was gritting her teeth, and practically stomping her feet silently trying to coax me into shutting up. Maya was shaking her head in disbelief, tossing potholders around, trying to extract the cinnamon buns from the oven, shaking her head back and forth.

"Ahem," he coughed. "No she won't. Listen, I won't keep you because I know you're busy; I wanted to call and let you know I was sorry for not returning to the table without a word."

I don't know why I said what I said. But I didn't want "His

Hotness" to think he could all of a sudden be concerned about my best interests, while walking another woman down the aisle. After Oliver Banks, I was taking my fool hat off. A man wasn't going to use me up again taking my kindness for weakness. Oh, but did I hurt his feelings? Oh God, I'm a mess. Why should I care about the feelings of man that's halfway down the wedding aisle? Shake it off Jules.

"Well, thank you for calling."

"I hope to see you soon under better circumstances," he said, sounding more professional, but upset.

"Thank you again."

Click

"*Well* you threw cold water on that hot smoldering fire," Maya said, stuffing a hot cinnamon bun in her mouth.

"Yeah Jules. What was that about? I told you he was on the outs with his fiancée, and what do you do? You off and go mention the unmentionable. This is not the route to getting a man."

"Who said I wanted man? Did I say I wanted another man?"

"YES," Maya and Logan both said in unison.

I sighed heavily, pouring myself another cup of coffee.

A heavy knock rapped on my door.

"You expecting somebody?" Logan said.

"Nope."

"I'll get it," she said, prancing to the foyer and opening the front door. My nightie made her look like she belonged on a Victoria Secret's catwalk. On me, not so much.

"Don't you think you should cover up?" Maya yelled.

"Nope, Nicky's got the body-goons outside near the elevators. Nobody of importance is getting on this floor. Jules' home takes up the whole damn floor anyway."

Logan swung open the door, blocking the doorway, leaning to the side of the door jamb with one arm held high, her long blonde hair trailing down her front covering her breasts.

---

*N*icky stood in the doorway, wearing a custom-made dark navy Italian suit, white shirt, and a presidential-looking soft blue tie. His suit jacket was draped over his shoulder, his pants riding low on his hips. His black shoes were polished to a shine.

Nicky's eyes skimmed Logan up and down, his poker face never registering a reaction. A woman could stand in front of my brother butt naked, and the only woman he could see was his wife Harper.

"You gonna stand there posing, Logan, or are you going to let me in?"

Logan made a *tsk* sound with her teeth.

"Ahh, the Guardian Angel. Good morning Nicky," she snickered.

"You mean good afternoon," he said.

Logan looked down at the watch that wasn't on her wrist.

"You're right Nicky. I'm still on Euro time."

Nicky stepped past Logan.

"Time is money, Logan," he said dismissively. "Maya," he said, acknowledging her presence.

Maya was studying the chessboard, mentally struggling to figure out her next move. Nicky took my chess move, moving the Bishop and taking Maya's Knight. Maya frowned, studying the board in disbelief.

"How'd you do that?" she said out loud.

"God knows all, Maya," Nicholas said with a straight face, slapping his leather gloves against one of his hands.

I ran over to him, kissing him on both cheeks.

"I know, I know, I was supposed to come up, but we got in real late, and well, I'm moving slow this morning Nicky. I know we had planned to talk about *Sugar Mommy's* this morning, but a gal needs time to recuperate from a day like yesterday."

Nicky sat down on my oversized loveseat, crossed his long legs, folding his well-manicured hands together on his knees.

"Would you like some coffee Nicky?" Logan said, pouring herself another cup and raising her mug.

"No thank you," he said, still dismissing the fact that Logan looked like this morning's restless sex kitten.

Maya dressed as Cookie Monster didn't get a rise out of him either. Nicky surely had emotions of steel. I slid next to him, curling my legs underneath me, moving close and resting my head on his shoulder. He patted my hair, forever being my chief comforter.

Maya was still staring at the chessboard trying to decipher Nicky's move. Logan was waiting patiently to see what was coming out of Nicky's mouth next.

"I found a spot that will be a great location for *Sugar Mommy's*. It's one of the family properties. I'd like you all to see it."

By now, Nicky understood that Maya, Logan, and I were a team. If there were big decisions to be made, it was a given that Maya and Logan were going to weigh in on things, whether he or I liked it or not. They didn't like being left out of anything that had to do with me. It was okay because the feeling was mutual. We were our own team, together for each other through thick and thin, love and heartbreak, life and death.

"How much time do you need?"

"I can look at it the first of next week."

"That works for me. I'll have Lucia call you with the details."

Lucia Falco was my brother's business partner and right arm. She was a female version of him. The Yin to his Yang in business.

"It's a good idea that you're helping me to fast track things. Now that Harper has solicited me to Co-Chair, I need to get organized."

"Yessss, the hospital fundraiser."

For some reason I got the feeling that Nicky wasn't happy about the hospital fundraiser.

"Is there a problem Nicky?"

"Not at all, Cookie. Harper and I agree you're the perfect choice this year. Elliot, that's another matter," he grumbled. "But, Harper insists he's the man for the job."

"Oh yeah, I got a call from Elliot this morning."

Nicky's poker face winced. Ah ha. A reaction. He did feel some kind of way about Elliot. He just was keeping his feelings to himself.

"What is it? Tell me."

"I questioned Harper whether Dr. Fischer is up for the task. Harper seems to think so, but then again her perspective is very different from mine. I've heard the rumors. Not sure I want Dr. EZ working so closely with my little sister. He has a reputation you know."

"He's also engaged," I said, trying to keep the pout out of my voice.

"Not for long," Logan said, sucking down a cinnamon bun. "I have it on good authority that their engagement likely won't last."

I never knew how she managed to keep all of her beautiful curves eating everything I made, calling herself my official taste tester.

"Yeah, Logan, he was looking at Jules like she was something good to eat, talking about how he loved all things "sweeeeeeet," Maya teased.

"And he called Jules this morning apologizing for leaving our table and not coming back. Somebody got hurt and needed medical attention," Logan said, spouting all my business.

She and Logan did that finger pop snap thing they do and then pointed their fingers at each other. Nicky growled under his breath like the mountain lion he was.

"More like his woman got shagged," Nicky mumbled under his breath.

"What'd you say?"

"Nothing to worry your sweet brain with Cookie. Take the weekend to chill. I expect you to be at the property first thing Monday."

"So Nicky, should we take public transportation, or do we get to have the same bodyguards this time?" Logan said, her hands on her hips, twirling a blonde lock in her finger, her perky breasts at attention.

"Yeah Nicky," who's guarding these beautiful bodies next week?" Maya asked teasingly, turning around in a circle. She looked like an uninviting red Cookie Monster, with those dark circles under her eyes.

I swore Maya and Logan loved to get Nicky's goat. His face actually turned crimson. They knew they had him now. Once they knew they had him, they were going to act out in front of him even more. It was like Nicky was some super-hot thriller racecar. They loved taking that car out for a ride and kicking the tires.

Nicky stepped close to Logan and Maya.

"Don't you two ladies have something worthwhile to do with yourselves besides getting the protective services team all hot and bothered?"

"They get hotter every assignment, Nicky. If I didn't know better, I'd say you're trying to drive us crazy," Logan said.

Maya and Logan squealed with laughter. Even I had to admit that I was amused. I pulled up from the backside of my couch, holding my hand on my head, propping it up, and watching the performance.

Nicky stepped to both of them, his six-foot frame looking down on them. "If you two continue to keep this up, I'm going to toss a couple of husbands on the team for you both. I will see to it you two trust fund babies get taken off the market so you can grow up," he sputtered. "An answered prayer."

Logan and Maya were beside themselves.

"It would take a God Almighty himself to get me married. This trust fund baby is playing the field for a while," Logan laughed, slapping Maya a high five.

"I wouldn't be so sure about that if I were you Logan," Nicky said with authority.

Logan and Maya were ignoring Nicky's words. But I wasn't. They didn't know my brother. If he got it in his head to move heaven and earth to lock them down with some husbands, they likely wouldn't know what hit them. Nicky always got what he wanted, and almost always did whatever he said he was going to do.

"You two are flying too close to the sun," I laughed.

"Honey please," Logan said. "Husbands are not on my agenda. No balls and chains for me. That would take Moses going to the mountaintop."

"Balls are cool," Maya teased.

Logan winked at Maya, giving her a thumbs up and a nod.

"You must be careful what you wish for my dear. Monday, Cookie," Nicky ordered.

And out the door my brother was gone.

Maya, Logan, and I all looked at each other.

"Was he talking to you Logan?" Maya said playfully with a fake quizzical look on her face.

"No girl, he was talking to you. I'm not getting married."

"I'm definitely not getting married," Maya said.

The both looked at me. They pointed their fingers at me, like they had information nobody knew about.

"Ahh . . . he's talking about Jules," they both started up again playfully.

"Both of you need to shut up. Marry is a dirty word in my house."

"That's right Jules."

"Ain't nobody got time for that," Maya said, standing up and doing her best 'black girl with an attitude' stance.

We fell together on the sofa, laughing.

"Oh my head, I need some ibuprofen."

My temples were throbbing, my stomach queasy, and my head achy from being hung-over.

"And some coffee," Maya said.

"And some cinnamon buns," Logan squealed.

"*Sugar Mommy's* on Monday Jules," Maya said.

"With a side of Sugar Daddy, compliments of Nicky," Logan grinned, licking the icing off her fingers.

I rolled my eyes, questioning momentarily whether Logan had come down from last night's high.

"Wow. This is really happening," I said, ignoring Logan. I'm finally going to be the queen of my own pastry business."

"We need to find you your king," Logan said.

"Do you ever not have m-a-n. on the brain Logan?"

"Every queen needs a king, Jules. You know, tooling around the castle, sweetie," Maya said.

"Preferably a naked king with only a tool belt hugging his waist," Logan added.

Logan and Maya both started high-fiving, laughing together again, enjoying Logan's joke.

"Damn right Jules. Queen takes the king," Maya smiled, walking over to the chessboard and moving her chess piece, knocking my king over. She brushed her palms together to signal our game was over. Maya was too proud of herself for beating me.

"Checkmate," Maya said.

Logan looked over Maya's shoulder. "Queen taking the king. Just like in real life, Sugar Mommy."

10

Elliot

I was glad I phoned Julianna from the hospital to apologize for my absence from the Halloween Party before coming home. She sounded annoyed. I didn't want her to be angry with me, but I couldn't fix that problem right now. I could only hope to make it up to her later. It was rude for me to have left without saying goodbye last night. I couldn't blame her for being angry with me, but I was thankful I had made the call before coming home to turn the page on the next chapter of my life. Home. Home was pure madness.

I turned the key opening the door to my home, only to walk into the whirlwind tornado called Kimber. I headed down the long hallway towards my bedroom, finding Kimber stretched upright in the bed with her arms folded across her breasts, pouting.

I raised both hands up in the air appealing to what was left of her good judgment, implying that I didn't want to hear a thing she had to say. I didn't want to argue or fight about it either. I had nothing left in me after last night's drama with Dexter. I solely wanted her to pack her shit and leave. But that was wishful thinking on my part. Kimber was not the kind of woman to make anything easy. At least not for me.

"I swear to God Elliot, I thought that was you!" Kimber screamed at me.

"The hell you did. Who knows how long you've been fucking that asshat Dexter," I said, grabbing her Louis Vuitton wheelie luggage, tossing it on the bed and throwing her clothes in it. I hurriedly moved to the closets, pulling her things down, stuffing them inside.

"Actually, now that I think about it, how long *have* you been fucking him?" I asked, pausing the packing. Waiting.

"Who were you fucking over at Maximillion's?

"Maximillion's? I was with Gabriel and Xavier at Maximillion's. And there's no fucking going on in Maximillion's. It's against the law," I said, resuming my efforts of pulling her things out of the closet, tossing them into her bag. God she had too many damn shoes.

"I'm not going anywhere."

"The hell you are. You're getting out of here. I don't want to look at you or see your face again. We're history."

Kimber was pulling things back out of her wheelie as fast as I was putting things in it.

"Don't think you can get rid of me that fast, throw me out like a piece of trash." she yelled back at me. "I've invested way too much into this relationship."

I threw her clothes up in the air at her. I stormed from the bedroom on the verge of losing all sense of self control. I wasn't a violent man. I didn't hit women. It was against everything I held sacred. But right now I didn't feel like I knew my own self. After all, I busted Dexter over the head with a bottle last night over this same unfaithful woman. Kimber was making me crazy. A surefire sign that I needed out of her space.

Last night was more that I could take. Our relationship didn't have the kind of foundation that could withstand something as horrible as this. Every time I thought about her screwing him like some sex crazed maniac, enjoying every minute, all I could do was just . . just . . .

"Grwwwwwl," I roared, my teeth clenched tightly.

Kimber followed me out of the bedroom, squeezing herself into a pair of skintight jeans in the process, throwing a clingy white furry cashmere sweater over her head, her silky black hair getting caught in the collar. She tossed on a pair of those red-bottom shoes.

"And you were doing cocaine," I bit out. "No fucking wife of mine is going to do drugs. I'm a physician for Christ sakes. Maybe that's where all my money's been going. Up your freaking nose."

"It was only a little bit of blow, and it wasn't mine, it was yours, uh . . . uh . . . I mean . . . his . . . "

I stood as close to Kimber as I could, looking down on her, lowering my voice to the closest point to calm that I could manage.

"Exactly. You know I don't do drugs. So you had to know that wasn't me you were fucking. You're a liar on top of being a whore."

Mistake. Big mistake. Things were escalating now to the ugly zone. Kimber slapped me across my face. Hard. She moved to slap me again. I grabbed both her wrists, praying to the Gods above on everything I owned to maintain what little restraint I had left. Gucci starting running in circles, barking loudly at the both of us.

"You need to leave," I said, trying to sound calm but firm, still clenching her wrists to keep her from slapping me again.

I was anything but calm. I moved away from her, heading towards my wet bar. I picked up the bottle of Jack Daniels, pouring myself three fingers, my face still stinging from Kimber's slap.

"And where am I supposed to go Elliot? I live here too."

"I'll put you up in a hotel, or you can go to your parents. Matter of fact, that's a good idea. Go the fuck home."

"Don't think for one minute Elliot Emmanuel Fisher that my father is going to stand for you throwing me out on my ass like this. Especially when I tell him it was my own fiancée that I was making love to, mister."

"You're a liar and you know it."

"I'm Daddy's girl. He'll believe anything I tell him."

"You need to accept the fact that we're done."

"Daddy's got money invested in this wedding too, Elliot. You think he's gonna take this sitting down do you? That you're wasting his money over a little lover's spat?"

Damn. Kimber was crazier than I thought. Kimber's father was Jefferson Lawson. Jefferson Lawson was Chief of Staff for Senator Clayton Lawrence Montgomery. Senator Montgomery was father to Harper Montgomery Becker, wife to Nicholas Becker. This picture was going on a downhill slide at high speed, but I needed to hold my ground. Still, it was hard to quiet my mind with all the ramifications that this breakup would hold.

"This is not a lover's spat. This is the end. I'm not going to marry you, Kimber."

"Oh yes you will. My daddy's got hundreds of thousands of dollars invested in this wedding."

"What money? I'm the only one paying massive amounts money on this wedding. As far as I can tell you've done absolutely nothing with my money or your Daddy's."

"My father's been paying for things too," she snapped. "Women don't tell men every wedding detail Elliot. Details are things brides deal with, not grooms. Besides, how would you know? You're so wrapped up in delivering babies, how would you know anything?"

Kimber was crazy as a loony tune if she thought she was going to get me to believe her dad's been shelling out thousands of dollars on wedding planning. Surely she didn't think I was that gullible.

"Get your stuff and get out. You make me sick to my stomach."

Kimber went back to the bedroom, grabbing her Louis Vuitton wheelie, her Birken bag, and her short chinchilla fur jacket. I sat on the sofa, nursing my drink with my head in hands, wondering how all of this could be happening to me. Last night. Dexter. Her. This.

"I'm not done with you, Elliot."

"Color me done, Kimber. I'll send the rest of your things to your folks' house."

Kimber stood in front of me, her head turned the opposite direction, her hand held out. Ahhhhh, the money hand. I knew it well. How could I forget there was a greedy, raging bitch underneath all that beauty.

I pulled several Benjamins out of my pocket, slapping them in her palm. It was enough for her to take a very long cab ride to the end of Long Island and back. Maybe by the time she reached her daddy's house, I will have emotionally braced myself for the next round of fallout.

Bam.

Kimber slammed the door and was gone. I sat alone in my home for the first time in a long time.

Mostly in disbelief, but relieved.

"*Well* damn, man. Think of it this way. You dodged a bullet this time. Don't let this happen again. Pick a better woman next time," Gabriel said.

"Like you can talk."

"I wasn't the one getting married. I like to keep it that way. I'm still sowing my oats."

"You couldn't tell it by the way Xavier revealed you had yourself all locked up in cuffs with Swat Girl."

"I know man. That Logan. She's something special. But this isn't about me. Getting yourself all primed for marriage with Kimber would have been a huge mistake," Gabriel said as we walked through the hospital's cafeteria line, grabbing bowls of fruit and ice cream.

"Well I made it through the weekend without hearing from her. So far so good. I hope to keep it that way. At least no one from the hospital was at Luigi's besides us. If this gets out it would be disturbing. I pride myself on keeping my reputation untarnished."

"No man. I covered all the bases for you on that one. I even kept your story straight with Julianna. She looked a little bummed you didn't make it back to the table, but she thought your actions of rendering medical attention were heroic," Gabriel said with a wink.

"I appreciate you holding it down for me man. I'm hoping to keep this breakup quiet. It will be bad enough when Kimber's dad gets the word. That man is like a bull in a china closet."

"Yeah, well there's no amount of bull that's going to make you marry that gold-digging daughter of his. Not if I can help it."

"It's over, man. I'm done. Besides, believe it or not, I'd really like to get to know Julianna better. Maybe I'll get my chance since her sister-in-law Harper has appointed us co-chairs for the annual hospital fundraiser this year."

I redirected my attention away from Gabriel, noticing a bunch of the nurses congregating at the coffee and fountain station whispering, looking as if their ears were on fire.

"Wonder what's up with them?" I asked.

"I'm not sure. But that little redhead really holds it down in a crisis down in ER. Cute too. Special."

I shook my head.

"I thought you said Logan was special. They all can't be special, Gabe."

Then I heard a familiar voice behind me. Babs was in a huff.

"What's up with them Babs?"

"I'll tell you what's up Dr. EZ. It's all over the hospital this morning that you and Ms. Kimber broke up. Real sorry to hear it, though I didn't think she was the one, if you get my drift."

Gabriel and I looked at each other, perplexed and puzzled. How in the world did this get out?

"Seems Mister Esposito was on the phone with your ex this mornin'. Let it slip with one of those new gals in the Ivory Tower that you and Ms. Kimber hit the skids. When word got around that you were free and single, your stock blew up so fast it crashed through the glass ceiling," Babs chuckled.

"Damn Babs, isn't anything a secret around here?" I shook my head in disgust.

"Only secret left is what happened so major ya'll called off the engagement. You wanna talk it out?"

"No I do not want to talk it out. Not with you. Not with anyone. I wish that folks around here would just mind their own business for once."

"I'm here if you need me Dr. EZ," Babs hummed, headed out the cafeteria, turning her back and waving her hand in the air.

Gabriel shook his head, pointing to a table near the window for us to sit. It was far away from the group of nurses, each of which were looking at me like I was on an auction block up for bid, and they were bidding.

"Fuck man. That Dexter is the stupidest idiot walking the planet earth. No wonder that dumb asshole punched out of medical school. He's definitely not the smartest crackerjack in the box. Three days have hardly passed since I cracked him over the head, and he's on his usual roll already. Diarrhea of the mouth."

"Ah huh. He left out the part about him being the cause of your breakup, seeing how he was screwing Kimber."

"He did me a favor, man. He just didn't know it. I was on my way out anyway. He sped up the train in the tunnel that was coming at me. If I had any feelings left for her I would give a damn, but I don't. The fact is, this news floating around the hospital complicates my life even further."

"The way I see it, it's a nice complication to have. All tits and ass coming at you every day," Gabriel said, grinning like he was telling some joke that I got.

The fact of the matter was, I needed the nursing staff to focus on the business of medicine, not the business of slipping a ring on my finger, or theirs, for that matter. My thoughts were centered elsewhere. Mostly on the lovely Julianna Becker.

I wanted a nice wholesome woman so that I could start fresh. A woman that wanted me for me. A woman that didn't need me for my money. A woman that had an inner beauty, and not some superficial mannequin of woman. If this breakup had taught me anything, it was that my focus on what I thought I needed in a woman had been wrong all these years.

abriel was so busy talking about how much fun we were going to have being able to go to Maximillion's without worrying about some woman looking over my shoulder, that neither of us noticed Dexter walking towards our direction. His lunch tray was filled with fried chicken and French fries.

I put a scoop of orange ice cream sherbet in my mouth, swallowing hard. I reminded myself that I was a professional. That I'm in my workplace. That he's General Counsel of the hospital. And to expect a provocation, but by all means keep my cool and not try to kill this motherfucker all over again.

Gabriel and I managed to stop talking and eating at the exact same time, bracing ourselves for a sleazeball moment.

"Mind if I join you, fellas?" Dexter smirked, his beady eyes peering through his black horn-rimmed glasses.

"Yes we do mind," Gabriel snapped back. "Unless you want some more stitches on the right side of your head to match the ones on your left side, I'd suggest you keep it moving."

"Thank you, Gabriel. I always count on your hospitality, jackass," he said, setting his tray down on the table, sliding in the empty seat across from Gabriel.

Gabriel stood up with a fierce look in his eye, standing over Dexter, practically ready to pound him. I grabbed Gabriel's wrist so as to restrain him, steeling myself, mentally sending vibes to Gabriel to keep his cool. The last thing we needed was a brawl in the hospital cafeteria between the Chief of Emergency Services, the Chief of Obstetrics, and the General Counsel. That would definitely make Channel Six's evening news. Gabriel managed to sit himself down under my pleading gaze.

Then I reminded myself to behave, noticing my hand had involuntarily closed tight in a fist around my fork. Dexter didn't seem to be the least bit intimidated, despite the fact that Gabriel looked like a racer itching to come out of the starter's block, waiting to hear the bang. I was a close second.

"What do you want Dexter?"

"This is business."

Dexter stuffed a French fry in his mouth, and bit into the side of his chicken leg. He took his napkin, wiping the grease off his fingers, chicken crumbs falling out of his dark black mustache. He pulled a couple of pain killers out of a medicine bottle he had in his jacket pocket, threw them in his mouth, chasing them down with his lemon-laced ice water. He took his index finger, pushing his black horned rim glasses back up the bridge of his nose, then ran his fingers through his curly black hair. His olive colored skin reflected off the light coming though the window.

"Then you should come up to the 4th floor. We're on our lunch break. Gabriel and I have a strict rule. Lunch means no business, and last we checked, you weren't invited."

I managed to give Dexter a long hard stare. I got why Kimber was attracted to him. I had no doubt women found his strong Hispanic features quite attractive. Even I had to admit he was a fairly handsome guy.

But still, I was seething that Dexter chose lunchtime to aggravate us. I got very few breaks around here, and hardly any sleep. Mealtime was the one moment that I liked to savor. Spending it in the face of Dexter Esposito, the same man that fucked my fiancée, made me plain angry and nauseous.

"You admitted a patient to the hospital after she had a baby in a cab. Dana Bridges. You remember the name?"

"So?"

"So she's uninsured. We've got rules around here on how many uninsured patients we can take in a quarter as charity. You should have dropped her off at the City Hospital down the street. Now you've forced me to have to make an exception report on the matter for next month's board meeting."

"Go fuck yourself Dexter," Gabriel said, visibly cringing.

"That little chickadee and her baby cost the hospital fifty thousand dollars for a three day stay. The Pedi coats say the baby had a touch of jaundice."

Dexter licked one of his fingers then squeezed a pile of ketchup on his plate, dipping his French fry in it and still chomping.

"That chickadee that you were referring to is family. Last I checked hospital policy, family members of hospital staff are guaranteed admission regardless of their ability to pay. Or do I need to go get the hospital policy manual and . . ."

"And stuff it down your throat," Gabriel said, continuing my sentence before I could finish.

"Hmm. I suppose you do have a point, Dr. Fischer. Who knew Ms. Bridges was family?" Dexter said, realizing his little plan was unraveling.

"I did."

"Guess you got me on that one."

"Yeah well here's another hospital rule that you might want to think about. There's a hospital policy against employees engaging in unlawful substance," I said, staring Dexter down with a vengeance. "I doubt that there are certain little pieces of information you would want to get in the hospital gossip mill—the one you managed to turn the handle and open up the spout on this morning."

Dexter's face turned an ashy color. He hadn't figured that I knew about the cocaine that he and Kimber were doing at the Halloween Party. He was so quick to put my broken engagement on the gossip hotline, he completely forgot that his little tété-a-tété with Kimber came with a cost to *his* reputation as well. He hadn't contemplated his own recreational drug use exposure and the implications on his professional career. *Yeah Buddy. Shit rolls downhill.*

"Yeah, Dexter. Who do you think cleaned up your little white messes before the ambulance came while you were knocked out unconscious? Maybe you should think a little harder about who you decide to go off and try to fuck around here," Gabriel said dangerously.

I thought Dexter was going to choke on his chicken bone. He had no idea that Gabriel and I had the goods on him. He damn sure didn't know we'd made sure Mario had taken his picture with his little pile of cocaine while he was unconscious. I had Mario email the photos to my Gmail account minutes before the medics arrived.

A well-dressed woman in a grey suit walked over to the table, interrupting what surely was going to be a bloodbath showdown in the hospital's cafeteria if Dexter stayed in our presence any longer. I recognized her face from the Ivory Tower pool.

"Sorry to interrupt you, Mr. Esposito. You're wanted in the CEO's office, sir. The budget meetings are starting earlier than planned."

"Thank you Melissa," Dexter said, giving her backside the once over as she turned and headed out of the cafeteria.

"Well Doctors Fisher and DeLuca, it was a pleasure having lunch with you. It appears you've carefully managed to have a legitimate 'out' this time, Dr. Fischer. But you should remember, I'm keeping a good eye on the both of you. If you two cross the line around here, I'll be the first one you see on the other side." He pointed his finger first at me and then at Gabriel.

"Fuck you dickface," Gabriel said, looking totally unremorseful for his lack of decorum in the workplace. "You best worry about the eyes we're keeping on you, motherfucker."

And with that, Dexter stood and left the table, leaving what was left of his greasy chicken and French fries behind. Gabriel and I were momentarily silent, both trying to force our anger down ten degrees.

"He seriously has it out for us G."

"Who cares?"

"We should."

"He's a bad warrior," Gabriel continued. "The first rule of warfare: never telegraph your moves to the enemy. He just put us on notice that he plans to attack. Told you he was a dumb ass crackerjack."

"I've lost my appetite."

"Me too. I prefer the company of my patients any day over the company of that clown," Gabriel said. "And most of them are ill. Maybe we should have Xavier get a couple of his linebacker friends to send him a message."

"If he keeps his shenanigans up, I'm going to send him my own message."

Gabriel and I headed across the other side of the cafeteria, dumping our dirty dish trays in the tray bin, exiting the cafeteria.

Gabriel and I said our good-byes, him taking the elevator to the ground floor, and me going up to the fourth floor. We agreed to catch up with each other a little later.

Like clockwork, my thoughts went back to Julianna. I needed to reach out to her personally so I could inform her that my marital engagement was off. I wanted her to hear it from me first, rather than hearing this news from folks around the hospital who were going to be plus-ing and minus-ing their own additions to the story. The last thing I needed was her coming up to the Becker Wing and getting an earful that would leave her with a bad taste in her mouth, now that Kimber and I were done.

I stepped off the elevator just in time. One of the patients that had been in labor for twelve hours was ready to give birth. I was glad to have the distraction so as to take my mind off my problems. Between Kimber and Dexter, I felt like I'd been immersed in a pool of madness for the last thirty-six hours. Delivering a baby brought me joy. Babies were new, fresh, and unscathed by the ugliness of the world.

Nurse Patty pushed a chart in my hands.

"Mrs. Bennett is ready, Dr. Fischer," she said, as I opened the hospital room door.

Her husband was holding Mrs. Bennett's hand, looking anxious like all new fathers do. I smiled at both of the expectant parents, pulling my stool up to the stirrups. I widened her legs so I could see.

"Okay Mrs. Bennett. I want to you to take a deep breath, and when I tell you, I want you to push."

"Okay," she groaned, nodding her head up and down extra fast.

Thirty minutes later their son arrived. A bit of a quarterback that one. A solid nine pounds. His mom and dad were overwhelmed with joy. I watched as the new father wiped a tear from his eye, proud that his firstborn was a boy. Daddy couldn't stop thanking me enough.

I smiled, knowing that when I caught that little fella, I wanted one just like him. *One for Julianna and me.*

God. Cupid was alive and well, back shooting little arrows at me again.

11

*J*ulianna

*F*our days later, there was one thing that couldn't be denied. The property that my brother Nicholas had envisioned for *Sugar Mommy Pastries* was absolutely perfect. The back of the house area for the kitchen was clean, spacious, and most of all ideal for the floorplan that I had envisioned for the equipment that I would need. Maya and Logan both agreed with me, the front of the house area was properly sized for a retail space, with room enough for a seating area for customers that could be designed in such a way so as to create the feel of an elegant French Bistro.

The property was conveniently located within a thirty-minute travel distance in traffic to Becker Towers, and conveniently located next door to Jimmy Choo's on Fifth Avenue. The way I figured it, once you got tired of trying on all the beautiful shoes, you could stop in at *Sugar Mommy's* for a coffee, a French pastry, wind down, and go back for more shoes. The St. Regis was next door on the other side of me. I would get the foot traffic from both The St. Regis, and Jimmy Choo's. I could market my pastries to the St. Regis patrons through my plans to enfold a side catering business within the pastry shop.

I loved the fact that I was squeezed in the middle between better and best. The location couldn't have been any more perfect. Nicky was satisfied that his choice of property selection met my, Maya, and Logan's approval. He had that look that he wore on his face, when he was on his mode that "God knows all." Everyone knew he saw himself as the God of all things Becker and then some. This was right up his alley that I was happy with his choice of property selection for my new pastry shop. *Sugar Mommy's* was actually coming into existence.

Nicky and I had a one-on-one, while Maya and Logan looked the place over. I spent a couple of hours going over my business plan with my brother. He was a financial whiz, so if there were any holes in my thought processes, he would catch them first. I was glad I had spent the whole weekend, before today's meeting, getting my ducks lined up in a row. I had to rise to the occasion, and act like the Becker that I was bred to be when it came to business discussions with him. I was not going to let my big brother down. He had so much faith in me, so I rose out of the ashes like a phoenix bird. When I finished going over my business plan, I was sure he was pleased.

"It's perfect, Nicky. When can I move in?"

"Whenever you want. It's all in the family, Cookie. Your wish is your command. You're a Becker. This is what Becker's do. Knock yourself out. I know you can do this, Cookie."

It was nice to have a private moment with my brother. He was my biggest advocate, reminding me that I was very capable of launching a successful business. With Nicholas and Harper at my side, there was no way I could fail.

"I want to get started right away."

"No problem. We'll need to get the property manager to send over the paperwork so you can execute the lease agreement. You'll need to get a tax I.D. number, create a Limited Liability Corporation for tax purposes, open the appropriate bank accounts, hire staff, etc. Call the office. I'll have one of the family accountants assigned to work out the logistics with you, and I'll call Blake to do the legal eagle stuff for you."

"Thanks Nicky. If I push things along, I can see myself up and running by the end of the month."

Blake Ross Becker III, was our older brother. He was legal counsel for the family business. Our family seemed to have its own little hierarchy. Blake saw himself as my father's watchdog over Nicky. Nicky saw himself as the watchdog over me. My father "Big Daddy" was watchdog over everyone, despite the fact that he didn't feel he needed anyone looking over his shoulder. After my mother passed, no one fulfilled that role for him.

Nicky and Blake were closer to each other than Blake and I. I supposed that had to do with the differences in age, as my brother Blake was two years older than Nicky. Blake didn't devote too much time with me when we were growing up. He was mostly consumed with learning the family business, seeing himself as heir to the Becker throne. Nicky and I hardly cared about such matters, but my brother Blake lived and thrived on it. The thought of our spending our lives dealing with a chicken processing empire made us both nauseous.

"I think we should throw a big launch party, Jules," Maya said, walking around in the front area, taking pictures with her camera of the unfinished space.

"Yeah Jules, we could have a nighttime pastry shop launch party. Make it kind of like a Champagne cocktail opening with desserts. We could bring in a small keyboard. I could play soft music for you," Logan added.

"Oh that sounds like a wonderful idea. Lets go over to Sequoia's and talk it out."

Sequoia's was one of our favorite hot spots located in the Time Warner Center. We considered it the best watering hole in town for the young upwardly mobile. We called it our private place to see and be seen. Sequoia's was a contemporary membership-only restaurant that specialized in gourmet sliders, tapas, and sushi. The entrees were small, gourmet, and highly specialized. The beef sliders were made from the best Kobe beef in the country, the vegetables were sourced locally, the fish flown in fresh every day from Maine, and the pastries prepared by a renowned French pastry chef. I loved the rapidly changing pastry menu so I could try out new things. It helped me in my own business to keep my perspective fresh.

No money was ever exchanged in Sequoia's. It was the best, private, white tablecloth restaurant in town to eat well, conduct business, and not have to worry about who was connecting the dots with whom. No paparazzi were allowed within fifty feet of the place. So if you wanted privacy to discuss business, this was the place.

"Going to Sequoia's sounds like my cue to leave now," Nicky said, kissing me on the top of my forehead. "Party planning is not my forte, Cookie. You'll have to do that without me."

Nicky whipped his phone out, dialing Silas to meet him out front. He was leaving us to ourselves for the afternoon. Or at least we thought he was leaving us to ourselves for the afternoon. Nicky made another call as he walked out the front door of what would be my new pastry shop.

"Yes please, Stephen. That will be fine. Oh and Stephen, I need a "heaven sent" package for Cool and the Gang. Okay, Cookie, I'll see you later back at the Towers," he called back to me.

"Okay, Nicky. I promised I'd make some Thanksgiving turkey cookies with Miles and Milania. So I'll see you back at the Penthouse a little later." I tossed a wave back at him and turned to Maya and Logan. "Let's hurry over to Sequoia's. Maybe we can beat the afternoon lunch crowd," I said.

I rushed, grabbing my lamb's hair bag and wrap-around cashmere coat. It was cold outside. The temperature had been dropping rapidly these last few days.

"Yeah Jules. Nicky's gone. We can sneak a cab this time," Maya said, grabbing her things, totally as excited as me. She grabbed her cute little military style jacket, and her bright red scarf, carefully wrapping it around her neck.

"C'mon Logan, Maya said. "Let's find a cabbie. Nicky won't mind if it's the three of us together."

"Don't plan on it," Logan said, picking up her leather jacket, slinging it over her short mini skirt.

Maya opened the door first, walking out into the brisk cold November air as we followed on her heels. Her mouth flew open so wide you could have flown a Boeing triple seven through it. A long black super stretch limousine was outside. A black Suburban in the front, a black Suburban in the black.

Leader One was back. He was standing by the black Suburban in the front, surrounded by the best looking protective service eye candy in all of New York. My mouth flew open too, making room for the second triple seven to fly through it.

"Yeah baby," Logan said, high stepping it through the door, moving past Maya and I who were still stuck on stupid. Logan's head lifted a tad bit higher. She strutted over to the dark-haired, drop-dead-gorgeous, make-you-want-to-melt-like-a-vanilla-ice-cream-cone-on-a-scorching-hot-day bodyguard. "Now, this is what's known as "Heaven Sent," she said out loud, looking back over her shoulder at us. She looked like a kid lost in a candy store.

Logan stood in front of the man, looking him up and down like he was a delicious lollipop in her favorite flavor that she needed to lick. His face was blank. Serious. Invincible. Dark Ray-Ban's were covering that beautiful smooth face.

"You and I are going to have so much fun," Logan said in her best sultry Marilyn Monroe-like voice, flipping his tie like she did all the rest of our bodyguards. "Oh good Lord. Nicky has really stepped up the game this time."

"I cannot believe it," I gasped out loud.

"Sure you can," Maya snickered.

"Jules, Nicky's really trying to marry us off. Who could resist all this? I'm not even going to try," Logan said. "Forget the cab, Maya."

"That's the point Logan. Remember?"

I was fuming. I fucking was going to kill my brother. This was totally out of control. He seriously was trying to marry my best friends off, showering them with fucking educated, protect-their-bodies hot guys. Oh how I wanted to scream. This crossed the line of fair play. But then again, my brother was not one to play fair. He was in it to win it.

"Hell to the no," I said, coming to a complete stop. Stomping my foot, pissed again, that my brother had us back under guard for the day.

"You and Maya can resist," I said, reminding them that Nicky was messing with them. "Maya, Logan, control yourself," I demanded.

"Oh no not me," Maya said. "That Nicky, he really knows what a woman wants, and I want all of this. All of it, Goddammit," Maya said, like a woman who had lost her mind. "Sorry Jules, but you're on your own."

Yep. She really had lost her mind.

"Maya!" I shouted.

Maya acted like she didn't hear a word I said.

"Logan, get a hold of yourself. This has Nicky written all over it. Get a grip."

Logan and Maya were slapping each other high fives, like I was speaking a foreign language. I shook my head. Logan and Maya were walking right into the Nicky's "I'm going to marry you off" trap. If Maya and Logan were off the market, he figured I would soon follow in their footsteps. Nicky loved a challenge. For him, this was like playing a game of high stakes poker. It could be lives or money at stake, but Nicky would not lose. He was a winner. Harper Montgomery, now Ms. Nicholas Becker was living proof of that. Maya and Logan were succumbing, subject to be his pawns today. They couldn't see it. Or didn't want to see it. But I knew better. That was *My* brother after all.

Maya couldn't take her eyes off the tall, lean, African American wearing the cool blue tinted Aviators. He was wearing a well-pressed black suit that hung on him so well, any woman with eyes would surely do a double-take. He looked like a chocolate kiss that could melt in your mouth. If it weren't for the fact that Maya was looking like she had died and gone to heaven, I might have considered the possibility of getting my swirl on.

"Leader One, I'll take the lead on Pretty Does", the African American hunk spoke, his eyes fixated dead on Maya like a predator.

"Roger that," Leader One replied.

"The rest of you can take Pretty Is," he said, referring to Logan. "That one requires extra work. Hold on to your handcuffs," he commanded.

"I'll keep a third eye on Twinkle Toes," Leader One said, squinting. He gave me his stern "be on your best behavior look."

I tossed my hair back, rolling my eyes at him. I was going to personally figure out a way to cut Leader One's balls off. Silas opened the door.

"Good to see you again Ms. Jules."

"Silas, do you always do everything my brother says?"

"When it comes to you Ms. Jules, pretty much. He's just looking out for you."

"I'm not a baby you know. I'm a grown ass woman."

"You're also a Becker. In the business world he plays in, he doesn't want anything to happen to you. He's lived through that already."

I knew Silas was referring to the incident that happened with Harper six years ago, due to Nicky's business dealings with his Angel Investment company, *Milk Money*. Because of it, Nicky was hard pressed never to change his mind about my needing a security detail, but that didn't mean I had to like it.

"Take us to Sequoia's please Silas."

This was a battle I wasn't going to win today. And likely not the war either.

"At your pleasure, Ms. Julianna."

My good mood had suddenly left me. I was back to my reality. Why couldn't Nicky treat me like the adult that I was? I hated being carted around all the time like a little kid. I wanted to feel normal. Take a subway. A train. A cab. A commercial plane, for Christ sakes. I was tired of private planes, limos, and yachts. I closed my eyes and shuddered. Maya and Logan, on the other hand, loved the life of the rich and famous. They loved the royal treatment. And, Nicky was practically blinding them with beautiful guys, convenience, and all the trappings of wealth for which they were so accustomed. He definitely knew what he was doing. I better understood how and why he became successful. Perhaps I needed to spend more time with his wife Harper. She was his check and change. I needed more lessons in how to check my brother.

"It's not so totally bad Jules, we can take a cab the next time," Maya said.

"Or we could do lunch and run this team ragged all over Atlantic City," Logan said with all sincerity. I knew she was just trying to make me feel better.

"Atlantic City? That would be new and different for a change," I said.

"Yeah we could hit the casinos and play some Baccarat," Logan offered.

"No. Today is about business, remember," Maya said. "Today is about getting *Sugar Mommy's* on the top."

"Yeah, Jules, did you check out that little blonde haired guy in the second suburban in the back? Yeah baby, *Sugar Mommy* on top of that," Logan said.

Logan looked at me, I looked at Maya, Maya looked at her, and we all looked back at each other and then fell out laughing.

"What. What?" Logan said, tears running down her eyes in laughter. "There's more than one way to take *Sugar Mommy* to the top, Maya."

The exchange between us lifted my mood.

"Maybe Nicky's trying to cheer me up from the loss of Oliver. Maybe he thinks if I looked at some hot guys every day, I'll start to feel better."

"Well do you?" Maya asked.

"I can't deny it. I do feel a little better," I giggled.

"Hell yeah, who wouldn't feel better? You could be like Cleopatra, surrounded by all those beautiful Mark Anthony's."

"Or maybe this is intended to be a distraction from Elliot. I get the impression he's not too high on Lord Becker's list," I said, making fun of Nicky's alter ego.

"I tell you what. Every time I lay eyes on cute, fine, sexy, and the delicious riding in front and behind us, all I can say is there truly is a God. And his name is Nicholas Becker," Logan squealed.

"You guys are no help. When my brother gets through manipulating the two of you, we won't be able to go anywhere on our own, nor will you want to. He's messing with your head Logan. You too Maya."

I grabbed a bottle of Champagne off the limousine mini bar and looked at my watch. It was two o'clock.

"Right about now I deem the moment Happy Hour."

"Happy Hour," Logan and Maya both said at the same time.

I poured myself a glass of Champagne still in a state of disgust. Maya and Logan clinked their flutes. They were on Cloud Nine. Nicholas had made their day.

"Cool and the Gang on the move," Leader One came across Silas's radio.

I growled out loud and quickly closed the privacy window, shutting Silas out of my space. I tried not to think about Bald Eagle and his merry band of beefcakes riding in the lead Suburban in front of us and the Suburban holding up the rear.

I huffed to myself, sighing heavily. I took a sip of my Champagne, not believing this bullshit. The only thing that was going to be "on the move" as far as I was concerned was my brother. Who said he could be any good at picking a man for my friends or me?

---

*T*hirty minutes later, our limousine pulled up to Sequoia's and Silas opened our door.

Leader One screeched his tires up in front of us like we were the freaking Secretary of State, late for a United Nations gathering. The second black Suburban behind us, also coming to a screaming halt.

I was cursing my brother under my breath because he had to make a show of everything. People on the sidewalk were looking at us as if we were dignitaries. Maya and Logan were lapping it up, but I was hardly pleased. Under normal circumstances, Maya and Logan would have been on my side of the fence, trying to figure out how to get rid of these lackeys, but Nicky had raised the stakes. These lackeys were fucking irresistible. Maya and Logan forgot what team they played on. They were acting like the million dollar girls that they were, except their brains had been seared by all that male heat. They had lost all of their good judgment. I remember the day when we used to take pride in figuring out ways to get rid of bodyguards, not attaching ourselves to them. Of course they never looked quite this good.

I hated that Logan had challenged my brother with all her talk about not wanting to be married. She had thrown down the gauntlet and Nicky had no intention of losing. One of us was going to be married. I just wasn't sure which one. Nicky couldn't resist a good challenge. It was sport to him. And after all, "God does answer prayer," he would say. Nicky would deliver. Maya and Logan didn't know it because they were lost in a man fog, not being able to see the forest for the trees. One of them was going to walk down the aisle.

The three of us exited, stepping on the mini red carpet. Sequoia's was good for little details like that, making its guests feel special.

"Hello Ms. Becker," the doorman spoke loudly. "Ms. Matthews, Ms. Kennedy," he said, acknowledging us.

Sequoia's was a private members-only club that kept a recognizable list of its members. They made sure that their members felt like they were the most important people in the establishment. They were trained to know each member on sight.

"Hey Joshua," we all chimed in at once to the doorman.

"I'll be right here when you're ready to leave Ms. Jules," Silas said.

I nodded in silent agreement.

Maya's bodyguard spoke, his voice deep and melodic.

"I'll be in the corner over there if you need me," he said, his towering frame looking down on her.

Maya was still off her game. She was speechless while she gaped at him as if he were the last man on earth.

"And your name is. . .?" I asked.

"Craig. Craig Meyers."

"Nice to meet you, Craig Meyers,"

At least I had a name for Maya, since she was incapable of getting his name for herself. The way I figured, if Maya needed any more detail on Mr. Superfine, I could go upstairs to the eighty-sixth floor to Nicky's Penthouse, sneak into the Becker security terminals, wade through all things Parks & Parks Security and get the goods on Mr. Craig Meyers. I glanced in Maya's direction. She was still catatonic.

"This is my friend, Maya. Maya Matthews, Craig."

"Hi Maya," he said in his best Morris Chestnut voice.

Maya was done. Color her a freakin' goner. Her mental acuity had taken off and left the room. I kicked her foot to ease a polite reply out of her catatonic mouth.

"Nice to meet you Craig."

The Maître d' walked us through the restaurant across the polished hardwood floors that were reflecting off the high chandeliered ceiling, showing us to our crisp, white tablecloth-draped table. I followed behind Logan, who was moving through the well-dressed crowd with ease and grace. Logan was the kind of woman that when she walked in a room, heads turned. And they did. She could hardly be ignored, denied, left out, or dismissed.

I reminded myself yet again that she . . . we . . . could own the place, despite the fact I wanted to pretend that I was common. But I wasn't common. My brother alone was worth over a half a billion dollars. My family, three times that. For the rest of my life, and the life of several generations after me, Becker's would want for nothing. No matter how much I wanted to run from the money, the money was going to run after me. It was hard accepting that I couldn't run from who I was. I suppose Nicky was trying to get me to accept that.

I looked around at the folks who raced to our side to make us comfortable. It wasn't because we were smart, beautiful, or had something they thought we had to offer. It was because my friends and I were filthy fucking rich.

And then for the first time in my life it hit me.

I wanted a man, somebody that wanted me for *me*. Not for what I was worth monetarily, but for what and who I was. I needed him to love me, not because I was rich, beautiful, or fit in the mold of something he thought his family could accept as the acceptable wife. I wanted him to love me for my faults, my complications, my idiosyncrasies, my good, my bad, my flaws, until death do us part.

That was the mistake I had made with Oliver Banks. He wanted me for my family name. Combine our wealth he used to say. My family was old money. Oliver was new money. He wanted to merge assets. Oliver didn't really ever want me for me. And in the end, he didn't even want me for my money.

"Your usual table, Ms. Becker?" the hostess asked.

"Yes please."

The hostess directed us to the table that was reserved for members of my family. It was the best table in the house. My father saw to that everywhere our family traveled.

"Thank you," I said, as she seated the three of us.

We took our usual seats, ordering a Stags Leap California Cabernet Sauvignon.

"So let's talk about the *Sugar Mommy* launch," Maya began first. "I've got some sketches I've created to set the place up like a French bistro. I was thinking some soft pastel colors for the walls. I figured some white wrought-iron tables, with both tall and short barstools that surrounded by the glass cases that showcase your finest pastries."

"That sounds very French," Logan said. "I think it's perfect."

"Maybe some of those pastel and white checked tablecloths," Maya said.

The server brought over a tray of mini sourdough breadsticks with an herb-laced dipping oil. We each grabbed a hot breadstick, dipping the tips in the oil and munching.

"You guys have managed to practically test sample everything I've planned for the menu, so I don't think I'll have to focus too much on the pastry choices."

"Well you need to pick your vendors for the equipment," Maya said. "I took some photos in case you need to show the vendors the space and determine what equipment will fit in the back of the house."

"And you need a staff. I'll help you interview," Logan said. "I'm really good at that stuff. I used to hire musicians in London all the time. I'm a good judge of people."

"This is great," I said, feeling more comfortable that my plans were coming together. "Maybe we can pull this off by the end of the month."

"That will take us right up to the first week of December," Maya said. We could have a Christmas themed opening. How perfect is that? We could send out invitations to all the beautiful people we know."

You mean beautiful male people," I laughed shaking my head.

"Speaking of which," Logan said, "beautiful male people abound, flanked by beautiful male people," she said softly, her breath hitching.

"What?" I asked.

"Don't look now Jules."

Maya and I raised our heads from the breadsticks.

"Wild and crazy guys at ten o'clock," she said.

Gray Eyes was entering the restaurant, accompanied by his friends Dr. Gabriel Deluca and Xavier Cook. Who knew they had a membership to our spot? And to think Maya, Logan, and I thought Sequoia's was our own special place. Not. One or all of those three Yahoo's—as Nicky called them—were rolling in dough. The plot was thickening. Perhaps they were trust fund babies in disguise. You didn't get into Sequoia's unless you were filthy dirty sexy money rich. My eyebrows raised. Logan looked at me. I shook my head and nodded. I didn't have the answers. Logan was thinking the same thing I was thinking. Who or which of them was rolling in dough? Maya literally woke up out of her daze.

"What the fuck?"

"Chill Maya," I said quietly.

Craig Meyer's body went on high alert in the corner of the room. He was sitting at the bar, trying to look as if he were blending into the woodwork watching over Maya, but he was doing a pitiful job. I, for one, could spot him out of crowd. He looked like a fish out of water with his elegant suit, earpiece in his ear, looking like he had bodyguard written all over him. Nonetheless, that handsome fish was totally focused on Maya.

The Yahoo threesome walked together across the room headed to the table nearest to ours.

What the hell were these three doing at Sequoia's?

"What are they doing here?" Maya whispered, as if reading my thoughts, trying to keep her voice low.

"Okay, so let's regroup. I need a moment. That fine ass hunk of a man I handcuffed myself to is in the house," Logan snickered.

I couldn't tell if she was happy or not.

"Logan is this a good thing or a bad thing?" I figured I'd ask and put it on the table. Get this over.

"It's all good baby. All six-foot-three of it is all Mmm Mmm good."

Now why wasn't I surprised? I should have known better than to ask. We were talking about Gabriel DeLuca after all. And this was *my* friend Logan, the man-eater.

"But what do you think they are doing here?" Maya asked.

"Obviously the same reason we are here. Business. It's not like we have the corner market on this place, you know," I said, trying hard to take the shock and awe out of my voice.

Maya, Logan, and I watched as Elliot, Gabriel, and Xavier took a seat at a table near ours, huddled in a corner with their heads together.

"Maybe they don't see us," Logan said.

"They see us. Craig Meyers sees them too," Maya said with a huge cheesy grin.

Maya liked the fact that my brother put that gorgeous hunk of a black man on the "All things Maya" security detail. I figured Nicky was going to pick her off first. It made sense. Logan would be the hardest nut to crack. Maya was going to be his first pillar to fall.

I studied Craig Meyers from across the room. His chocolate brown skin glittered under the afternoon light peeking through the window. I decided he was a goner. He didn't stand a chance in the face of my bestie, the very beautiful Maya Matthews. Maya was like a hot fudge sundae. Caramel-colored, sweet, cherry stained lips, and totally hot. My brother was going to pick my posse off one at a time, starting with the easiest knock off first. Maya Matthews. Touché Nicholas.

139

Thank God Logan was a hard core die hard. She meant what she said. She wasn't getting married. She would hold her ground. But my brother was old school. He played to win. Logan might think she didn't want a husband, but Nicky was relentless. Nicky had the ability to wipe her off the playing field before she knew what hit her. But trust me. It would be 'battle royale' between her and Nicky. Logan didn't fall in love easy. That was something I did. I was the one who always fell in love head first, brain later. But I wasn't going down that same path again. I would be different the next time on love's merry-go-round. Oliver had cracked my heart, and I wasn't going to fall in love with just anybody again. The next man I would fall in love with next was going to love me for me, not for what I was worth. Nicky might think he was going to pick off Maya or Logan, but I was determined I was going to be the last hold-out to go down a marriage aisle until it was absolutely right. The next time it would be me who got what she wanted.

Elliot, Gabriel, and Xavier sat at the table very near ours. I thought for a minute they had failed to see us. Nope. Elliot spotted me and was headed to our table.

"Incoming," Maya said.

"Thanks for the heads up," I said, not realizing before she said it that Elliot was practically at our table. This was the first time I got to see Elliot when he wasn't dressed in baby fluid, a white coat, or blue scrubs. Dressed in a tan cashmere button-down sweater and dark grey flannel pants, he looked good enough for me to beg my posse to tie a bow around him and place him under my Christmas tree. His gray eyes were nailing me to my seat, daring me to move.

"Hey Julianna, Good to see you. You're looking beautiful—as always."

"Hi Elliot. Surprised to see you here."

He smiled a gigantic smile that filled his face, his eyes dancing with delight.

"My family has a membership. I take advantage of it from time to time."

Now I was curious. Elliot was loaded. Who were Elliot's parents?

"Umm," I nodded in agreement.

"Hey Maya. Logan."

They both nodded.

"Hey Elliot," Maya spoke first.

"Well look what the cat drug in," Logan said teasingly to Dr. Gray Eyes. His eyes hadn't yet left mine. He had grown a slight stubble on his face since I'd seen him last. A five o'clock shadow that made him look even more adorable than before. His eyes were boring into my soul with a fierceness.

"Have you been here long?" I asked, pretending not to be affected.

"No, we just arrived. You mind if we join you ladies?"

"Not at all," Logan said energetically.

"Please join us," Maya said before I could speak.

Good God, a feeling of nervous exhilaration was washing over me.

Elliot motioned to the hostess and they had a brief conversation. Before I knew it, we were being moved to a circular booth that was large enough for all six of us. Elliot sat next to me, close to one end. Gabriel sat next to Logan in the middle. Xavier and Maya sat next to each other at the other end of the booth. Craig had changed his location too, moving a tad bit closer to all of us, appearing uneasy at having to watch Maya sitting next to another man. His facial expression and demeanor had changed from casual ease to stoic and stern.

"So what brings you beautiful ladies out this afternoon?" Xavier asked.

"We had some business to conduct, so we thought we'd sneak in for a burger and fries," I spoke first.

"Jules is opening *Sugar Mommy's* next month," Maya chipped up, not giving me a chance to dispute her comments. "You know, her new pastry business."

"Yeah," Logan added. "We're here planning a launch party opening for the first week of December," she said, looking totally starry-eyed at Gabriel.

Gabriel put his arm around the back of the booth over Logan's shoulders, leaning his body in close to her, wrapping his finger around one of her loose blonde strands. Even though Logan was talking to the whole group, she was only looking at him.

"I'd love to help you out, Julianna, if you need some extra hands. I've got some spare time now that my engagement is off."

Elliot grabbed my hand, holding it in his, his thumb stroking my palm, igniting that familiar something that always seemed to pass between us, sending thrills up my spine. I took a sip of my wine hoping he hadn't noticed that the air had left my lungs. Elliot was a free man? No strings attached? Free? Free for whomever? Free for me?

My heart did a backflip that felt like a small hiccup. Oh my God. My mind was racing a thousand miles a minute going into overdrive. I wasn't supposed to be getting ahead of myself. Maybe this was a momentary breakup. Couples do that, you know. God knows Oliver and I had a ton of breakups. Maybe Elliot and his fiancée would get back together. What the hell was he saying exactly?

"You're no longer getting married?" I asked quizzically.

Maya was staring Elliot down hard. Even Logan momentarily shifted her eyes from Gabriel to him. He had my girls' attention. They didn't do bullshit; their bullshit meters had clicked on.

"No, we're done. We're over. Finished."

Elliot sipped a bit of the lemon-laced water in front of him. His expression changed. He was looking at me with pleading eyes, hoping I would accept this newfound information as gospel.

"Oh. Okay," I mumbled. I hardly knew what else to say.

The pretty server re-appeared. She was beaming at Elliot, tipping her head in a flirtatious manner, interrupting, asking to take our order, batting her long lashes at him. I didn't know what had come over me. It must have been the green-eyed monster on my shoulder because I didn't like the way she looked at him, not one bit.

I looked away from her and him pretending as if I were studying the menu that I knew by heart. I frequented this restaurant, but today I couldn't seem to manage a coherent thought about what to eat.

"She's going to have the Kobe sliders with a side of onion rings," Elliot said, grinning, taking his hand and placing it on top of mine.

Instant electricity drew me closer to him again. Pulling me slowly into his quiet charismatic web. Tingles pricked me under my skin. He must have felt it too, as I heard him take a deep breath, in and out.

"I'll have the calamari. And the Greek salad with chicken."

Logan and Gabriel couldn't seem to form a collective response between them either, googling at each other like two star struck lovers in high school.

"Bring him the French onion soup, the chicken nachos, and she'll have the Kobe sliders too, with French fries," Elliot said, ordering for Logan and Gabriel.

"Does that sound good to you man?"

Gabriel nodded in agreement, but still never taking his eyes off Logan. She definitely hadn't unglued her peepers from him.

Maya looked at me, avoiding Craig's serious gaze. I could tell Maya and I were both at a loss for words. Maybe she was still in shock too, over the news that Elliot was no longer getting married. Or maybe it was the fact that Logan had let Elliot order for her as well.

Flirty server girl reluctantly turned her attention to Maya and Xavier, just as I was about to give her the evil eye. Elliot sat the menu down, brushing his hand up against mine, igniting the current again that was passing through us. I felt a blush sear across my face.

"I'll have the fish tacos and she'll have the fish tacos. And we'll have another bottle of the cabernet the ladies ordered earlier," Xavier said, picking up the bottle and checking out the label. "Make that two bottles."

I could almost hear the wheels turning in Craig Meyers' head. I'd lay bets that he was gritting his teeth. Maya bent her head down a bit, looking over the top of her glasses in his direction. Craig was one unhappy camper, but Maya wasn't the kind of woman that needed his approval. This was really starting to get interesting. Not to mention different kinds of tension was floating in the air on a lot of levels. Elliot seemed nervous about spilling his engagement news. I wanted flirty girl to go away. Another man ordering food for Maya wasn't going down well with Craig Meyers. And, Maya had that "you don't know me well enough to be running me" look on her face. At least not yet. But Craig must have been oblivious to her look, because he seemed like he was stone's throw away from wanting to pulverize the Yahoos.

Whoa. But, I didn't want Craig to kill Elliot. I had dibs on Elliot. *Elliot was mine.* Oh God, did I just think that to myself? I am so screwed up. I was supposed to be looking for a temporary place-holder, not getting cuckoo for coco puffs over Elliot.

"So Xavier, do you enjoy being the personal trainer for the Jets?" Maya asked, twirling her fork nervously over an empty plate.

"Yeah, I love helping the team perform at their absolute best. Their body is how they make their livelihood, so it's important to me that each team member stays in tip top shape."

"You sound very dedicated to them. So do you do private sessions?" I asked innocently. "Maya and I hate the gym, don't we Maya?"

Oh God that sounded like it came out wrong. I threaded my fingers together, squinting, feeling like my nerves were getting the better of me.

"I sometimes do private sessions for special friends, Julianna," Xavier winked.

I felt Elliot's body tense next to mine. This so came out wrong.

"Your body looks pretty perfect, if you ask me, Maya," Xavier whispered softly her direction.

I peeked out the corner of my eye. Elliot had cocked his head to the side at Xavier. Craig had moved like a stealth fighter, closer to our table. He'd mumbled something in his earpiece, but he wasn't close enough for me to make it out.

"I don't know, we're pretty undisciplined when it comes to exercise, Right Logan?" I nudge her verbally, trying to get her to engage with the rest of us and to take the pressure off of me.

"Yup."

That was all I could manage to get out of Logan by way of a response. She and Gabriel were undressing each other with their eyes. He was still twirling one of her blonde curls in his finger and she had started to lick the gloss on her lips. I decided to just forget about including her in the conversation. I redirected my attention back to Gray Eyes.

Maya and Xavier seemed to be having their own conversation about workouts.

"I'd love to take you up on your offer of help, Elliot."

"Good, we can make a date to talk about things. Just you and me. Without our posses," he said in a soft whisper, looking around at his guys and my gals. "I'll take you out on the town. You can let me sample your dessert menu afterwards. I promise I'll give you really good feedback," he said, his gray eyes glistening.

"I'd like that," I said, feeling the blush creep across my face again.

Whoa. The only thing that needed sampling was him, now that he was a free man. Freedom never ever looked so good. For the first time, I realized Elliot had the cutest, most inviting lips. He must have kept them hid under that surgical mask. They looked soft. Kissable. And just maybe I'd get a chance to taste them real soon. After all, nurse Babs did say the best way to get over a man was to get under a new one. I snickered to myself at the mere thought of that idea.

 *lliot*

ow. What were the chances that Gabriel, Xavier, and I decided to grab a bite to eat and run into Julianna and her friends at Sequoia's? Not everyone could get in here, which was why it was our first choice of places to eat today. I guess the wine was out of the bottle now. I knew Julianna's family came from money, but what Julianna didn't know was so did mine. One thing is for sure: Julianna wouldn't have to worry about wanting me for my money. She had enough of her own. The thought of money and wealth not having to be the centerpiece of my relationship was refreshing.

Now that I knew Julianna was here, nothing was going to stop me from letting her know that I was no longer engaged. This felt like a stroke of good fortune. She could hear it from me first, before the news traveled around the hospital gossip train like wildfire, or worse yet hit the society pages. Then I was going to ask her out on a date.

It didn't take long for Gabriel, Xavier, and I to get the ladies to agree that we could join them and to get situated. I took the lead

146

ordering food for everyone. I hoped Julianna liked a take charge man, because that was who I was. She was an independent woman, but even independent women needed a man to support them. I wanted to be that man. I wanted her to feel like she was in safe hands with me. I hoped she felt that too when I put my hand on hers, not giving a thought to the female server that was working overtime to get my undivided attention.

We both felt the jolt of electricity that passed through me to her when I touched her hand. I touched her hand at the right time too. I needed to quell what looked like a flash of anger, or perhaps a tinge of jealousy that was crossing her face. Julianna need never have to worry about me looking at another woman, ever. She was the only woman I could see.

It didn't take me long to let it out that I was no longer engaged to Kimber Lawson. I wasn't sure if she believed me or not, but I could tell that my information came as good news. I took advantage of the moment too, refusing to let any grass grow too long under my feet. Hence, I offered to help her sample the desserts for the launch of her new pastry business *Sugar Mommy's*. I definitely wanted to taste her dessert menu all right. If her pastries were any near sweet as her, I was going to make the lovely Julianna Becker mine, helping her in any way I could to build her brand.

I hadn't forgot how much she'd been hurting from the loss of her relationship with Oliver Banks. I was going to work my hardest to erase all thoughts of Oliver from her memory. Whatever it was going to take to heal that broken heart, making her forget his existence, I was going to do it. And I was going to start now. I wanted that sweet *Sugar Mommy* for myself.

I loved the fact that she wasn't the typical overly vain spoiled rich girl. She wasn't a silicone injected brainless trophy wife straight off some "real housewife" episode either. Julianna was anything but. She was a business-minded woman with goals. She was naturally beautiful inside and out. Just sitting here next to her without Kimber's wedding noose around my neck left me feeling happy, ecstatic, and exhilarated.

*J*ulianna's eyes lit up when the food arrived.

"Is everything to your satisfaction sir?" the female server asked, mooning over me, placing her hand on my shoulder.

"Julianna are you happy with your food honey?"

"Yes, thank you," Julianna mumbled back at me, dipping her French fry in a mound of ketchup.

The way she licked the ketchup all around her French fry caused a warm heat to pool in my belly. My pint-sized princess was a tiny little package of big temptation. I totally lost my thoughts watching her, almost forgetting to tell the young female server we were pleased with our meal. But I didn't have to. Our server looked totally annoyed, letting out an audible sigh at Julianna, then quickly scurried off. If I didn't know better I would have sworn Julianna had mad cat woman skills, letting our server know that it was she, not her, who had my attention. I smiled at Julianna studying her closely as she lifted the red wine to her lips.

Gabriel and Logan hadn't stopped eye fucking each other. There must have been something in these French fries. Gabriel was dipping Logan's French fry in ketchup feeding it to her himself. Gabriel and Logan looked like a scene straight out of the Roman Empire, him being Caligula, her being his Livia. Both taking turns feeding each other in a smorgasbord of food and lust. All I could do was shake my head at those two.

"I'm really loving the fish tacos," Maya said, thanking Xavier. "This was a healthy choice, unlike that cow my gals are pigging out on. I won't have to work fish tacos off."

"Trust me not to do harm to that beautiful body of yours," Xavier said, dipping a tortilla chip into his salsa, bring the chip up to her lips, letting her have a taste.

"Mmmm. So good," Maya moaned.

It didn't take long for Xavier and I to figure out that the couple of suits that were scattered nearby in the room belonged to Julianna and her gals. We knew that from taking one look at the good looking African American guy in the suit standing at attention. His facial expression had tensed up from watching Maya and Xavier. We knew who thought they belonged to whom in this room. The tension with those guys was so thick you could cut it with a knife. Bodyguard dude must have really had a case for Maya. I knew that look. It was the same mind blowing look I would have had on my face if any man had his arm around a woman I wanted.

Both Xavier and I caught the look, but Xavier seemed indifferent to it. Gabriel must have caught wind of his change in facial expression too, because he began speaking about the guy in Italian with Logan. Logan responded to Gabriel in Italian saying something about a mission with a Guardian Angel. My Italian wasn't as good as theirs, so I could only catch bits and pieces of their conversation. They both laughed heartily together.

It wasn't unusual for Gabriel to slip in and out of Italian, especially if he had someone else to speak the language with him. He mostly spoke the language when he was with family, trying to impress a woman, conceal a secret, or in a spurt of anger. It was one of those old family habits that was going to die hard with him.

The thing I knew that the suit didn't know was that Xavier was a born flirt. A lady's man. Not one to be put on lockdown by any one woman. He was a man for all seasons. Xavier wasn't the kind of guy to settle down anytime soon. What the guy in the suit didn't know was that Xavier wasn't a real threat. He just looked like he was. But I knew that sometimes things were never what they appeared. I suspected that if a good looking bodyguard wanted Maya, Xavier was going to help that fire along, and make him work for her.

We were all enjoying our meal, each having our own individual conversations making small talk when an unrecognizable voice called out.

"Julianna, is that you?" the man said.

I gave him a brief once-over. He reminded me of a California surfer dude turned businessman in a suit type. Blonde hair. Fit.

Tanned. Handsome. Nothing less than what I would have expected in a man who might be found to be on the arm of Julianna Becker.

Julianna raised her head from her meal, looking past me, registering shock on her face. I felt her body tense up immediately. Her face turned pale. Gabriel and Xavier cut their conversations short with Maya and Logan, also sensing a male threat had just hit their radar. The question was, a threat to whom? It didn't take long for us to figure out who. Me.

I immediately recognized him from his pictures on the Internet. He was walking towards our table at a fairly quick pace. I didn't like the idea of him interrupting our group's happy time—not one bit. He had already cracked Julianna's heart once. I suppose now he wanted to show his face again and rub her nose in it. She'd hardly had any chance to heal yet. Immediately I wanted to protect her shattered heart. Put up a shield in front of her so his words wouldn't penetrate her.

Maybe he wanted to do that thing guys do: "be friends." Which translates into man speak for 'he's not done yet.' Not really. Well I had news for him. Oliver Banks had kicked Julianna to the curb, so off with his head. That was *my* man speak for 'there's a new sheriff in town, his name is Dr. Elliot Fischer, and buddy you're done.' She's mine now.

---

*J*ulianna squirmed uncomfortably in her seat. I put my hand on her knee so as to calm her, setting my fork down, placing my left arm around the back of the booth, hopefully letting Oliver the Asshole get the message. I did not want him to not mistake the fact that she was with me. Men fully understood non-verbal signals, and we were well versed in how to give them to each other. I positioned my body in such a way that I wanted to make it perfectly clear that she was with me now. What could he possibly want with her?

"Well Julianna, I see it didn't take long for you to land on your feet," he said snidely, staring at me and putting two and two together.

Smart fucking man. That was just the message I wanted him to get. I also didn't like the tone of voice he was using with her. Guess this meant this was going to be a war. My brain went on automatic, setting itself to lock and load. Male threat on the horizon.

"Maya, Logan." He nodded at them with an obvious sense of familiarity, though I got the impression that there was no love lost between them.

"This is my . . . " Julianna paused, not sure how to identify me.

"New man," I said, pulling her closer to me. "And you must be Oliver Banks, the very newly married ex," I goaded him. "I've heard all about you."

I felt Julianna's body tense some more. We both knew that we hadn't spoken a word between us about Oliver, but he sure as hell didn't have to know that. Besides, I was staking claim to her as of now. "I'm so happy to meet the man that let this beautiful gem go so I could thank him. Thank you man."

Oliver turned beet red in the face. Insecurity flashed across his face.

"Oliver, this is Dr. Elliot Fischer, and his friend Dr. Gabriel DeLuca, and Xavier Cook," Julianna muttered.

"So is this the bloke that was two timing Julianna? Man you need to stop by the ER and let me examine your head. You might possibly have a tumor or something up there," Gabriel incited him.

That was the one thing I loved about Gabriel. He always could be counted on to have my back, and I his. Xavier too.

"Yeah who wouldn't be happy with a girl like Julianna. She's got everything, the beauty, the style, the grace," Xavier added, winking at her.

Maya, Logan, and Xavier all starting giggling under their breath. Julianna kept a straight face, eyeing Oliver warily. I think part of her wanted to let out a small chuckle of her own, happy that the guys were taking up for her with another guy. For a second I thought she was smothering a grin. I watched the blush creep on Julianna's face.

She was in an emotional state somewhere between the intersection of amusement, anger, and surprise. But then I saw a flash of pain flicker across her face. It wouldn't have surprised me any if she wasn't internally registering a lot of different emotions. I wanted to be sympathetic to her and whatever she felt she was going through.

What Julianna didn't know was that I would have taken up for her with or without her friends or mine. She really was going to be mine. I'd be damned if I let her go in order for him to try to morph her into his mistress or something. I had no intentions of letting her go for any other man for that matter. I wasn't going to be her rebound man either. I intended to play for keeps. It wasn't lost on me that she was vulnerable. I suspected she may have had deeper feelings for him than I ever had for Kimber. I hardly knew for sure, not having had some one-on-one personal time to talk it out with her.

"So what can we do you for man? Something you wanted to say to Julianna?" I asked dryly.

Oliver looked irritated. He was caught off guard. Perhaps he was too full of himself to think that Julianna could have possibly moved on from him as quickly as he had moved on from her behind her back. Served him right. Guys like him always miscalculated. They always made the mistake of thinking that they were the "one and only."

"Ahh . . . ahhh, never-mind," he said, mumbling something unintelligible.

Oliver looked annoyed. As far as I was concerned, there was nothing more to say to Julianna. He was married. She was available. Oliver wasn't likely to undo his marriage anytime soon, so what was there left to say? If Julianna agreed to be my woman, I was damn sure going to make sure he wasn't going to be some leftover wannabe tooling around in the wings, waiting for the next man to drop her so he could take advantage of her in the name of "friendship." I was a man, and I knew the games men played. I knew that trick. Played that card a couple of times in my past myself.

"It was good to see you again Julianna," Oliver said in a huff.

Julianna smiled a weak smile at him. I put a grin on my face; happy he was taking off, getting out of her space.

He paused for an uncomfortable beat before departing from our table. And with that, Oliver Banks was gone. I watched him as he walked towards the other side of the room. He shook another man's hand, saying a few words, patting him on the shoulder. He turned our direction, looking back over his shoulder once again at Julianna, and then was out the door.

Maya and Logan looked at Julianna, as if they were trying to check in with her, gauging her mood. You know, those silent looks with unspoken words that girlfriends give each other all the time.

Gabriel asked one of the male servers passing by to open the second bottle of wine and to bring fresh glasses for all of us. The server poured each of us a glass.

"To new beginnings," I said earnestly, lifting my glass to toast, hoping to reassure Julianna.

"Salute," Gabriel said.

"Cheers," Maya and Logan said.

"To new beginnings," Julianna said with a flush in her face and a softness in her eyes, clicking her glass to mine.

"You're an amazing woman," I said.

"And, you're an interesting man," she said.

Then Julianna leaned into me, planting a soft kiss on my cheek.

I hope that wasn't a 'let's be friends' kiss, because Cupid was back to shooting his arrows at me again. Because I was falling deep and fast. I wanted us to more than friends. I wanted her to be mine.

lliot

Three and a half weeks had passed since I'd seen Julianna and her girlfriends at Sequoia's. I'd spoken with her over the phone every day, both of us having exchanged phone numbers before we left the restaurant. She'd been busy getting new equipment installed at _Sugar Mommy's_ and I'd been managing to catch her in between sleep and delivering babies. She was excited about how well things were progressing with the launch of _Sugar Mommy's_. Maya and Logan had been helping her with the shop decor and party planning for the launch.

Our phone conversations were sometimes brief, me often catching her at the pastry shop between vendor deliveries, and her meeting with accountants and lawyers. At other times we'd both gone on for hours in the evenings, both talking at length when my shifts were over and her business concluded. We used our time apart to learn as much as we could from each other about each other.

I finally let her in on the fact that my father was the well-known commercial real estate mogul, Elliot Lanister, and my mother Carmen Fischer Lanister, the Noble Laureate geneticist. Because both my parents were famous, and I had wanted maximum obscurity, I'd taken my mother's name as my surname, my mother being mostly well known in the scientific community only. It was my way of flying under the radar as much as I could, although I would lay bets that her brother Nicholas and her sister-in-law Harper perhaps knew the truth of my parentage. There wasn't much her brother Nicholas didn't know.

Julianna thought I was lucky to have figured out a way to manage my obscurity complaining that the faster she ran away from the Becker name, the more it chased her down. While she hadn't made a complete surrender to her family's notoriety, she knew she was losing that battle. I teased her a lot telling her not to worry because one day I was going to give her my name. That earned me a cute giggle out of her. I loved hearing her laugh.

The more I came to know Julianna the more I was falling for her. I think I really did want to give her my name. I loved everything about her.

Our nightly telephone calls were filled with laughter, new insights, and occasional back and forth on our giving each other business and investment advice. We both shared so much in common, our love for chess, skiing, boating, and books. We even liked some of the same authors, both sharing a love for Jude E. McNamara's thriller, *The Heart of A Helmsman*. When we weren't having marathon talks at night, thoughts of Julianna haunted my thinking during the day. She was under my skin and in my head.

But tonight was the big night. Tonight I was taking Julianna out on our first real date. Alone.

I wanted this workday to be over soon. I was going to catch Mr. and Ms. Wilson's baby that I hoped would come within the next hour. They were having a little boy. I'd had already rubbed Mom's belly, telling the little man in my last examination that I had a date with the most amazing woman I'd met in a long time, and man to man it was important that he be prompt getting himself here. He kicked his mother real hard too, she screamed, cursing her husband and me under her breath, so I figured little dude and I had an agreement. I was going to lay here on this gurney, rest and wait on the little man. Then I'd help him into the world, express my thanks to him for his timeliness, check on mom, shake dad's hand, then I'd hurry home, shower, change, and be on my way. If little man came swiftly like I'd asked, I'd be out of here by two o'clock at the latest.

It was Friday night, the twenty-second of November. I thought I'd stop by the jeweler and pick up a little something for Julianna. It would be my gift to her to celebrate the launch of her new pastry shop. I was going to wine her, dine her, and take her dancing. We were going to have a fun night together. Julianna promised to take me back to *Sugar Mommy's* afterwards for pastries and coffee.

It was hardly like me to fall head over heels for a woman so fast, but Julianna was different. She wasn't the kind of woman I typically spent time cozying up to, but that was exactly why I knew we would work. Because of her, I wasn't the man I used to be. She was authentic, unpretentious, and certainly didn't need me for my money.

I heard a knock on the hospital door. Someone had found my hiding place again. Babs stuck her head through the opening. Damn, I couldn't hide anything from that woman.

"Little man's right on schedule Dr. EZ."

"Thank you Babs," I said, opening my eyes wide, nodding my head, and picking up my watch to check the time. "That's great news," I said, closing my eyes. "His mom's been in labor for sixteen hours. I'm sure she's ready to get this show on the road."

A ten-pound baby boy coming through the birth canal at high speed was just what the doctor ordered. Little man had a head start on male bonding.

"If he comes a little early, you'll have enough time to get home and make yourself pretty for your date tonight."

How in the hell did the queen of the hospital grapevine know I had a date? Was there nothing sacred around this place?

"Babs," I exclaimed out loud. "How did you . . . "

"Don't sweat it, Dr. EZ. It'll be our little secret," she said. "The florist called. They wanted to confirm delivery of those flowers you had sent over to that new pastry shop. . . . Sugar Shack . . . Sugar Cone . . . Sugar . . . something," she said waving her hand and entering the room, grabbing some clean sheets off the steel rack in the corner of the room.

"I didn't want to wake you, seeing how you need your rest and all . . . " Babs said, her back turned to me. "The florist wanted to read your card back just to make sure you had the message right, "Looking forward to seeing my favorite *Sugar Sumthin* tonight."

God I can't believe this place. I pinched the bridge of my nose with two fingers, willing myself not to raise my blood pressure up over this information.

"So you know me, Dr. Ez, I told them it sounded fine, and that they should add a smiley face at the end, that being a cute touch and all."

Damn. One thing I am not is a "smiley face" man. Julianna's going to likely think I'm some girly, touchy feely kind of nerd guy. I hope she doesn't get the wrong impression and think I'm the wimpy type. Please Lord don't let her show that card to her brother Nicholas. He'll yank my man card for sure.

"You gotta problem with that Dr. EZ?" Babs asked, turning her head around, looking over her shoulder at me, putting her hand on her hip.

I knew that gesture. That was her 'don't tell me what to do' gesture. I swear this woman thinks that I'm her son and she's my mom, playing watchdog over me and my affairs. It's a good thing I know she means well, always trying to dot my i's and cross my t's behind my back. I sucked down my momentary dismay. I love Babs dearly in my own way. I know she loves me back, but sometimes she gets on my last nerve.

"What would I do without you Babs," I mumbled.

I don't know why I thought she was going to let me off the hook either, but it was a good try.

"Say what?" she asked, putting her hand up against the back of her ear.

"I said . . . I don't know what I would do without you, woman." I grinned wide at her.

"That's right," she said with all authority. "Now get your butt up and go catch that little running back. His dad seems to think his little man's going to follow in his father's footsteps."

"I'll be right there."

I leaned up from the side of the gurney, stretching my arms wide, happiness filling my heart for the evening to come.

My phone buzzed. "Fight the Power" was playing on my cellphone. Gabriel's name came across my Caller ID.

"Hey Man, what's up?"

"You're what's up man. Tonight's date night with Julianna."

Well at least Gabriel knew that because I told him, and not because he gleaned that information on the hospital grapevine.

"Heard you sent flowers today. Nice touch."

Now *that* he couldn't have known. Fuck.

"And you know this how?" I sighed audibly.

"How do you think brother? Those nurses on your floor are always in your Kool-Aid now that they know you're a free man. They are going into overdrive trying to figure out who's the lucky gal. You know me man, my name is West. I'm not in that mess," Gabriel laughed.

Gabriel got a kick out of the fact that the nursing pool stayed on high alert when it came to my relationship affairs. And they told him everything, using what they knew about me in order to get close to him. He secretly loved it. I really was going to have to figure out ways to keep my personal life off this hospital grapevine. I did not want Julianna's and my business made public for everyone to latch onto every piece of gossip, nurturing it until it turned into some kind of full blown scandal hitting the high society pages.

"Yeah dude, I can't talk now. I've got a bundle to catch first before I can't get out the door. Then I plan to go home, dress, and swing by Becker Towers to pick up my sweet little *"Sugar Mommy."*

I left off the part about stopping at the jewelers.

"And sweet she is. You're a lucky man if you can pull this one off. Take your time. Go slow. She's fragile right now, that one."

"I plan to be on my best behavior man. Not going to blow this up."

"Listen man, before you go, I could have sworn I saw Kimber today coming through the Emergency Room doors, taking the elevator up to the Ivory Tower. I don't know man, maybe I was seeing things. I was busy dealing with some critically ill patients that had come in with monoxide poisoning. It's wintertime, man. Everybody improvising, killing themselves."

"Kimber? Are you sure? What could she want around here at the hospital? She isn't sick is she?"

"That evil bitch is a lot of things, but sick isn't one of them. She was dressed to kill. Besides I was too busy trying to keep this elderly man off the cooling rack to give Kimber too much attention."

"She always dresses to kill. Maybe you were mistaken, Gabe?"

"Hardly. That killer body switching through our halls is hard to miss, but I could be wrong. I had to yell at a couple of the male residents to stay in their lane. Focus on saving lives. But I'll go out on a limb and place the bet this has something to do with Dexter."

"Well those two are a likely pair. Two peas in a swamp pond. Either way, not my problem. I've moved on, remember."

"Yeah man, and I'm all for it. But don't lose sight of the fact that Dexter's gunning for us. I don't trust him or Kimber at this point. Both of them being in the hospital at the same time makes my blood curl. She's lethal and he's a . . . "

"A stupid crackerjack. That's all he is Gabe. Forget him and her."

"I'm just saying man, don't lose your vision here."

"I hate to cut you off G, but I gotta catch up with this ten pound running back. See you later."

"Man, Don't do anything tonight I wouldn't do."

I laughed. "Well that's leaves a lot of room for me. You'll do just about anything."

Gabriel laughed his wicked laugh and hung up. I stuffed my phone in my jacket pocket scurrying at a fast pace to catch my little man.

An hour later, I was out of the hospital and standing in the middle of Tiffany's looking for something nice for Julianna.

Looking up and down the glass cases, I searched with the help of my personal shopper until I found the perfect gift to give Julianna for her grand opening of *Sugar Mommy's*. It was a very beautiful Kaleidoscope Key Pendant in round brilliant diamonds on a sixteen-inch platinum chain. It expressed best how I felt about her. Every time she wore it, I wanted her to be reminded that she held the key to my heart. I hoped she would wear it the night of her grand opening, which was only a few weeks away if everything stayed on schedule.

"I'll have it gift wrapped for you right away Dr. Fischer if that's okay," Lindsay, my personnel shopper said, taking the necklace off the black velvet mat in front of me.

"I'll be right back sir. It's a lovely piece any woman would love. Feel free to have a glass of Champagne while I wrap this for you."

"Thanks, Lindsay. I think so too."

Now all I had to do was to head home, catch a couple of winks so that I'd be rested, shower, and then head over to Becker Towers. I relished catching a couple of winks in my own bed instead of on top of a hospital gurney for a change.

I gulped my Champagne down, just as Maya Matthews walked down the staircase from Tiffany's second floor level. I took a final swig of my Champagne, setting my flute on the small end table, freeing up my hands quickly as she approached me. I moved to embrace her.

"I thought that was you," Maya said. "Happy holidays Elliot. It's so good to see you again," she said, kissing me European style on both cheeks with air kisses. Maya was an incredibly beautiful black woman. She reminded me of one of those women that if I had a sister, I'd want her to be like Maya. Pretty. Funny. Smart. Loyal. Hot.

She clutched several small Tiffany packages in her hand, and a Nikon camera with a big lens was hanging around her neck.

"What brings you here today?"

"Julianna," I smiled, as Lindsay walked up, discreetly handing me my little blue shopping bag, and returning my American Express Black Card.

"Oh, that's so exciting," Maya giggled. "I trust you got my girl something nice?"

"The key to my heart," I winked. "A little something for her to wear to the grand opening. So please don't go spilling the beans ahead of time. You didn't see me here."

"My lips are sealed," Maya said, making a closed sign with her hands against her lips.

"And what brings you here?" I asked, helping her with her packages.

"Ahh . . . friends and family. Some early gift shopping for my Mom," she said.

I held the door open for her as we headed outside into the cold, grabbing some of the packages from her to carry.

"I had a shoot earlier with a couple of kids and a Turkey," she smiled. "A Thanksgiving family thing. Actually a tradition."

"It's hard to believe this year has flown by so fast," I pondered.

"The Christmas crowd seems to be showing itself a bit early this year," she said.

A light dust of snow was beginning to fall. It was twenty-eight degrees outside. The wind chill was even colder and the sun was beaming bright. I loved the fact that it was cold. It meant I'd have an excuse to cuddle Julianna under my arm to keep her warm. I'd planned the perfect date night for us.

A black stretch limousine awaited Maya by the curb at the front door of Tiffany's.

"Can I give you a lift?" she offered.

"No thanks. I think I'll walk. My home's only a few blocks away, but thank you anyway."

I pulled my coat together, turning the collar up, wrapping my scarf around my neck to ward off the chill that was starting to whip through the air as the temperature seemed to be dropping.

"No problem," she smiled. "I'll be on pins and needles waiting to hear the outcome of your date with Jules. You make sure you show her a good time, or I'll come looking for you," she said feigning a threat.

At least I thought she was feigning. But then again, the way gals were these days, that threat may have been real. God knows all the stories I've heard from Gabriel about the guys he's had to stitch up in the emergency room from some crazed woman cracking them upside the head with a spiked heel. I shook that thought straight out of my head.

I moved to open the limousine door for Maya, but the handsome African American body watcher that I recognized from Sequoia's stepped in front of me, non-verbally suggesting that he had her door. I'm sure he remembered my friends and me too. I sensed there was going to be no love lost between us. I didn't blame him. After all, it was my friend Xavier that was all over the woman I was sure he wanted to make his. I handed him Maya's packages, his hot breath billowing out in the cold air reminding me of a dragon.

"Elliot, this is Craig Meyers. Craig this is Dr. Elliot Fischer," Maya said, sensing the tension between us and making an effort to quash it.

"Hey man, nice to meet you," I said, hoping he'd silently agree we didn't have to be enemies. But, he refused to let his guard down any, so I shoved the rest of Maya's packages in his hand.

I rub my hands together, allowing my fingers to adjust to the abrupt change in temperature as I momentarily contemplated what she saw in him.

"Here you go brother. What can I say? They love to shop until they drop."

Craig grunted, walking towards the front of the limousine jumping in the passenger's seat up front.

"What can I say?" Maya asked with a sly grin on her face. "I love carnivals, and that's one ride I want to take," she said.

"Too much information," I laughed, shaking my head while tucking her coat inside and closing her door. We both waved good-bye.

Wow. Maya Matthews liked playing with dragons, I laughed to myself.

---

*F*ifteen minutes later I was home, dropping the little blue Tiffany's bag on the kitchen counter, stripping out of my denim jeans and polo shirt. I headed to my bedroom.

I stripped down to my boxers, moving to light my bedroom fireplace to warm the room a bit. I turned on my Bose. The artist Joe was singing "All The Things (Your Man Won't Do)." I thought about Julianna, Oliver, and the broken heart I intended to mend.

I glanced at my Rolex. I could still catch a couple of winks before having to shower and dress for our date. I tumbled across my bed enjoying the music, my eyes dry and heavy, trying to slip off into a state of slumber when I head the door to my condo open. Someone was walking inside my home.

What the hell. I grabbed my Yankees slugger bat from the corner, headed down the long hallway past my guest room and entered back into the living area. I was half naked in nothing but my blue Egyptian pinstriped cotton boxers, ready to beat the hell out of whoever was breaking into my home.

I appeared in the main living area, raised bat in hand, only to find Kimber standing front and center in my living area. She looked as startled as I felt, I suppose not expecting me to be home.

"What the hell?"

"I still have a key," she said dismissively, her look of surprise having left her face. "I came for some of my things I left here."

It took me a moment to process the fact that I was so pissed the day our engagement ended, that I hadn't gotten my key back from Kimber. Nor had I changed the locks. I'd also forgotten to alert my building's security that she should no longer have access to my home.

My housekeeper had packed Kimber's things after our breakup. I was certain all her things had been shipped to her folks' place on Long Island. What else had I missed? Everything was gone.

"That's a load of crap Kimber," I mumbled, setting the bat down on the couch, grateful a burglar hadn't broken into my home. My heartbeat was slowing down from its rapid pace from the realization that a stranger hadn't invaded my home. But that didn't mean I wasn't still under some kind of threat of attack. I moved about cautiously.

"You forgot my Blu-ray collection," she hissed in a snit. "I want them back."

Was she kidding? Her Blu-ray collection was less than fifteen videos, none of which were current. I was the one that brought all the movies in this relationship. This was more of Kimber's games to get back in my face front and center. It wasn't lost on me that Gabriel mentioned Kimber was at the hospital earlier today. She was up to her dirty tricks.

"Leave the key," I spoke forcing myself to stay calm. "Don't think you can run in and out of my home anytime you want."

Kimber slammed her key ring on the marble kitchen countertop next to where I had set the Tiffany's bag with Julianna's necklace inside. Kimber's key ring was a heavy silver Bloomingdale's B, with a bunch of keys hanging off it.

"You take your key off my ring. I don't want to break my nails," she said, curling her fingers back glancing down at her nails, never looking up at me.

"Get what you came for and get out."

I snatched the key ring out of her hand, pulling my key off the ring, returning her key ring back to the countertop.

Kimber sauntered over to the media rack where we kept our movies, and started pulling out videos. At this point I really didn't care what she took. She could take all the movies. I just wanted her out of my home.

Kimber began stacking videos in a nice little neat stack, lining them up in groups of five.

"I spoke to Dexter today. You didn't waste any time letting any grass grow under your feet. Dexter tells me that it's all over the hospital that you're pursuing someone else. Who is she?"

"Last I checked Dexter was your "fuck buddy," so for the record, my life and who's in it is none of your business or his."

"Maybe you've been seeing someone all along. Maybe that was why you were so quick to give up on our relationship."

"You were fucking my co-worker Kimber. Go to hell," I snapped. "You played me for the fool that I was in the relationship."

"Don't think for one minute I'm giving you the engagement ring back. Dexter says since you were the one that broke the engagement off, the law says I get to keep the ring."

Fuck me. Whatever made her think I wanted her or the ring back? That gold-digger hat never seems to come off that beautiful air-filled head. I wanted nothing to do with her, or any reminders of her, rings or otherwise.

"Why in the hell do you have to discuss our business with Dexter Esposito anyway? He's my peer."

How did I ever think this self-centered, self-indulgent, cruel, heartless woman could ever have been my wife? She was a raving bitch under all that beauty. What in the world was I thinking?

"He cares about what happens to me, Elliot."

"I don't care about what happens to you or that ring Kimber, all of which has nothing to do with Dexter."

"Plan to hear from my father any day now. He wants you to reimburse him for the wedding losses."

"Are you kidding me? There were no real wedding losses. You didn't even pick a date. There are no save the date cards, no vendors, bridal gowns, nothing. As far as I'm concerned, my money went on your back and up your nose."

I was fuming. I needed to get Kimber out of my place. She was fucking up my mood. I didn't want to be all out of sorts when I went out on my date with Julianna. I could tell by the look on her face that her thoughts were racing a mile a minute, stirring something up in that black cauldron of a brain of hers.

Kimber looked my half naked body up and down, staring at the opening of my crumpled boxers. I reached down on the side chair, grabbed my jeans, putting them on quickly. I knew that look on her face. That was her seductive look. Kimber was effortlessly desirable, but now she just plain pissed me off. The last thing I needed was an erection to give her any ideas that she had any control or hold over me sexually or otherwise. My big head dared my little head to rise. I clenched my teeth, narrowing my eyes at her for even trying to attempt to look at me that way. Perhaps Kimber couldn't help herself.

"I need a bag for these Blu-rays," she hissed, her arms folded across her breast, her head tilted up in the air.

"Hold on let me get you something."

I returned to my bedroom, pulling a Hugo Boss shopping bag down off the top shelf of my closet. She could throw them in the bag, then get the hell out of my home. It would have been another fight had I given her anything less than a "status" bag to carry down the streets of Manhattan, God forbid.

I grabbed my grey Ralph Lauren cable-knit sweater, slipping it over my head. I threw my black suede Ugg moccasins on my feet.

I returned to the living area, stopping dead in my tracks. A feeling of shock ran through me. Kimber was gone. The blu-rays were gone. And so was Julianna's fifteen-thousand-dollar platinum necklace in the Tiffany's bag. The key to my heart in the little blue bag was gone, and the key to my home was still laying on the marble countertop.

Oh fuck me. No, Kimber didn't run off with Julianna's present. I grabbed my key, stuffing it into my pocket. I opened my door at the same moment I saw Kimber, Tiffany bag in hand, headed down in the elevator, doors moving to a close.

"Kimber, come back here," I shouted.

Kimber threw me the middle finger as the elevator doors shut. I ran to the end of the hallway, ramming open the stairwell door, taking the stairs four at a time. I was jumping down the stairs as fast as I could. It would be hard to beat the elevator from the twentieth floor. I reached the bottom of the stairs opening the door to the lobby. I could see Kimber running out the double door in her brown shearling leather coat, leather pants, hobo bag, and my blue Tiffany's bag in her hand. Kimber was running down the pavement fast in those red bottom heels of hers, bumping into the holiday pedestrians, practically knocking over several moms with baby strollers. There was no way she was going to come into my home, steal Julianna's gift and get away with it. I was going to kill this wench for sure.

I ran as fast as I could behind her, slipping, sliding, trying to be mindful of knocking over elderly pedestrians and kids. Kimber darted across the busy traffic, slipping in between several cabbies and a couple of town cars. Horns were honking, blaring loudly at the both of us, but I stayed on her trail. I lunged at her almost in arms reach, only to hear the screeching of tires braking hard, a couple of cabbies trying to avoid hitting me in the process.

"You crazy dumb shit idiot," the cab driver yelled at me, cars screeching to a halt to keep from hitting him in the rear.

I fell across the top of his cab, making a hard thud. I felt the pain shoot across my back from landing on top of his grill. But there was no way I was going to let her get away. I slid off the hood of the cab, making sure I kept Kimber in my line of sight.

Kimber turned the corner sharply headed East. Once she turned the corner I lost sight of her. It was freezing cold, but sweat was beading up on the top of my forehead from having run out my own home with no coat to chase after Kimber in the falling snow.

I stopped weaving in and out of traffic, stepping back on the sidewalk. I looked both directions up and down the street. I was panting hard, totally out of breath. Who would believe I ran three miles a couple of days a week on my treadmill the way I was gasping like a sixty-year-old obese man on the Biggest Loser. Jeez-us. It wasn't like I was carrying any extra pounds on my body. I prided myself on being in shape. Maybe I was spending too much time in the hospital. Maybe I needed to get in the gym more often and let Xavier whip me around some more. No way I should be panting this hard. Perhaps the cold weather and my rising anxiety level were getting the best of me.

I couldn't see Kimber anywhere. But in a stroke of good luck I saw a man holding the door open for a frazzled woman, running inside Lutz's, the corner deli. I caught a glimpse of my little blue bag going through the door. I sprinted like a mad man towards Lutz's deli doors close on her heels.

---

*W*hen I opened the door shortly behind her, Kimber started screaming out loud for help.

"Help, that man is trying to attack me," she screamed pointing her ring filled index finger at me.

"Get back here Kimber," I yelled, my voice out of breath. I was still panting hard. My back hurt from the fall on top of the cab. I scrambled her direction. A couple of guys got up out of their booths, grabbing me by both arms in an attempt to restrain me.

"Don't listen to her," I yelled. "Get your hands off me! She's a lying thieving bitch."

"Somebody call the police," Kimber shouted.

Before I knew it, Kimber ducked behind the man in the dark shirt, tan pants, and leather jacket that was sitting at a booth in the far corner. Damn. I recognized him. It was Dexter fucking Esposito.

"This has nothing to do with you, Dex," I said, struggling to pull the other two guys that were holding me back off of me. I pushed one of the guys hard. He flew across one of the empty tables. Several women in the crowded deli let out screams. I must have looked like a crazy man.

"You're a royal shithead, Elliot," Dexter said. "I warned you to stop fucking with me."

"Fuck you, you little asswipe."

"I'm not going to let you harass a woman. Pick on somebody your own size motherfucker."

"I swear I'll . . . "

"You'll what?" Dexter shouted, stepping close to me.

Before I knew it, my arms were restrained again by the one oversized big man still holding onto me, and Dexter punched me square in the face.

"Ugh," I moaned, as blood spurted from my nose.

Dazed, I pulled away from the man, swung at Dexter but missed. He landed yet another blow to the side of my face and then in the gut. My face felt like it had been trampled by an elephant. Air left my lungs and none seemed to come in them. The big man grabbed my hands again, as Dexter landed another blow to my abdomen, and then my head. The room started to go dim, right before blackness took over.

The next thing I knew I was handcuffed inside a NYPD neighboring precinct with New York's finest looking at me from behind lock bars surrounded by sleazy assholes. A medical attendant yelled out at the other uniformed men "If he's not dead, he'll live."

He threw a handful of gauze at me to wipe the blood that was seeping out of my nose and face.

I was livid. All I could think about sitting there in handcuffs was imagining Dexter Esposito's head impaled on a spike in the middle of Times Square. I paced the floor of the holding area like a caged tiger, wondering how I was going to salvage my reputation with the hospital staff and worse yet, how was I going to ever work next to Dexter again without killing him.

How I was going to explain this to Julianna. She wouldn't want a man that she thought was capable of attacking a woman. Kimber made it clear to anyone who would listen in that deli that I had attacked her and was coming for more. And Dexter . . . he looked like the hero in the crowd. All of it was a trap, and I had walked right into it.

Six hours later, I was being released from a holding cell, my eye blackened, my face badly bruised, my ribs hurting like hell, and my spirits low from having missed my date with Julianna.

"*J*'m your lawyer, John Matthews, Esquire," the very soft spoken, well dressed fifty-something African American man said.

He shook my hand.

"I've been hired to represent you. Untangle you from this messy business. You can get your personal effects and then you're free to go, Dr. Fischer," he said calmly.

"Matthews . . . Matthews . . . your name sounds familiar"

"I'm Maya Matthew's uncle. I understand you two may know of each other. I'm one of the three Matthews with the firm of Matthews, Matthews & Matthews.

"Maya's uncle?"

"The firm is owned by Maya's Mom, Dad, and me. Maya's mother is my sister-in-law."

I nodded. I realized Matthews, Matthews & Matthews were *the* best litigators of *the* largest African American owned law firm in all of New York. I hadn't occurred to me that Maya Matthews was *this* Matthews, but it made sense. Julianna's circle of friends would hardly be anything less, and here I was locked up in jail like local riffraff.

"I love my niece dearly. I haven't quite decided yet about her friends," he said peering over the top of his eyeglasses giving me a good hard look.

"Maya's a good friend of a friend."

"Seems like your "friend" is more than a "friend," seeing how you're chasing down little blue bags, nearly getting yourself run over by a cab, and practically beat to death inside a deli."

"I didn't say she wasn't special," my voice gruff yet stern.

"Yup," he said waiting for the clerk to hand him a stack of forms.

I took a minute to study the man. Maya's uncle looked like the pinnacle of prominence. Well dressed, sharp nose, well-manicured hands, alert eyes, calm demeanor. He struck me as a man that might have been a shark in disguise underneath his calm demeanor and Armani.

"You should see a doctor. Get that cut over your eye looked at as soon as possible," he said, signing release papers with the court clerk.

He stood close to me, speaking in a low tone out of earshot of wandering ears.

"Who knew I was here?" I said, walking to the barred window to collect my things.

"Harper Montgomery Becker."

I could feel my face registering shock. John Matthews never changed his poised expression.

"That's who retained my services. Apparently Harper's husband's driver Silas ducked into that deli at the same time you were getting your lights knocked out. He called Ms. Becker and here I am," he said still signing several slips of paper. "Must be your lucky day, you dodging this bullet and all."

The clerk at the window passed me a large envelope with my belongings. I caught a reflection of myself against the nearby silver water fountain. My jeans had a slight rip in them, my Ralph Lauren cable knit sweater had noticeable dry bloodstains on the collar.

"You need to check to see if everything is there," the Court Clerk said to me in an uncaring fashion.

"Matthews, I want to press charges for assault, robbery, and anything else," I began to quibble, suddenly getting back in touch with my anger.

I wanted revenge on Kimber and Dexter.

"That won't be necessary. My job is to fix this situation so that it goes away quickly and quietly, never to veer its ugly head again."

"Situation? This isn't a situation. This is a crime."

"Not anymore son. This is a situation that has been handled. Put to bed. Gone away. You mustn't lose sight of who you are, and who your ex-fiancée is for that matter."

"What's that got to do with anything?" I bit out.

"It's got everything to do with the fact that the people who care about you and those who care about her have enough money between them to start world war three over your little breakup. Your ex-fiancée's father, Jefferson Lawson, is Chief of Staff for Senator Clayton Montgomery."

"I'm very well aware of that. I was engaged to his daughter."

"Senator Montgomery is Harper Montgomery Becker's father. Harper Montgomery Becker is wife to Nicholas Becker, Elliot," he said, looking as if he were giving me a moment to put two and two together. "Need I remind you?"

I sighed heavily feeling much like the mushroom that had been shitted on in the dark.

"Nobody, but nobody, wants to read about this on Page Six in the morning. I've been paid handsomely to make sure this "situation" goes away. Now open the bag son. Everything that belongs to you should be there."

I sat down on the hard wood bench nearest me. I dumped the contents of the envelope, watching everything fall out of the brown manila envelope. My Rolex, my contacts, my keys, my wallet, and to my surprise, the little blue Tiffany's bag, still carefully gift wrapped in the blue box with the white ribbon carefully tied.

I exhaled loudly.

"What . . . How did this happen?" I said, looking up at Matthews in disbelief.

John Matthews patted me on the back in a display of comfort.

"Small miracles my boy. I'm in the business of fixing situations. Think of me as Oliver Pope. Scandal averted."

He shook his head chuckling at his own joke, none of this at all funny to me.

"How can this be? She stole this from me," I said, surprised.

I must have sounded totally naive to him.

"It's like this, son: once Harper Montgomery Becker decides you're her friend, you have a friend for life. And you, my friend, are her friend. Embrace it. Ms. Harper doesn't take too kindly to anybody, male or female, screwing around with her friends."

This felt like a lot for me to process all of a sudden. I decided to change the subject and come back to that thought later when I could contemplate the events of this day in peace.

"How much do I owe you? I'm perfectly capable of paying your legal fees myself," I huffed.

"Not necessary, Dr. Fischer. I stay on a retainer for Mrs. Becker for moments like these, and trust me I love every minute of it. Never a boring moment, working for that woman. I don't know who's the craziest, her or that over possessive zealous husband of hers," he chuckled. "That family sure knows how to make my day, I tell you that."

"Well thank you, John," I said awkwardly, still trying to hit my own pause button so as to delay processing everything that happened today and happening now. Kimber stealing Julianna's gift, Dexter beating the crap out of me, jail, Harper, U.S. Senators, and the list seem to go on and on. I wasn't even the one that was guilty here.

"It's not me you have to thank. I'm just doing my job."

I put on my Rolex first and I put my contacts in my eyes next. My eyes were dry. My contacts felt uncomfortable, but I preferred seeing over the discomfort in my eyes. I took another hard look at John Matthews. He was pretty close to my initial assessment of him from what I'd seen without my eyes in place. I placed my hand up to my jaw, opening my mouth as wide as I could. I couldn't open it very wide without pain. My nose was killing me. And to think, the day had gone so well. And now Kimber and that clown Dexter had totally ruined my well-planned evening.

I glanced down at my watch. It was well after midnight. All I could think about was the fact that somebody was going to pay for ruining my night with Julianna.

"I called your friends. They're waiting outside for you. That crazy doctor friend of yours hasn't stopped cursing since I called him, and that other guy that trains the Jets, he's been pacing back and forth, pounding his fist in his palm, sprinting around the block a few times unable to sit still. I recommend one of you physicians prescribe that young man some Xanax."

"That would be Xavier," I mumbled. "I'm sure Gabriel has a third eye on him. We're kind of used to having to talk Xavier back off the ledge."

John Matthews patted me on the back. "Let's get out of this place son. The less time I spend in the trenches of this cesspool, the better."

"Harper Montgomery Becker, huh?" I said out loud, before I realized it.

"Not a woman I would dare to go up against. Threats have been made tonight. That woman takes no prisoners. Now that she's married to Nicholas Becker, that's a power couple that is downright lethal. She's wealthy in her own right without his millions. Story goes Harper and Nicholas used to have a longstanding battle with each other. Kind of like the War of the Roses. But love does cure all, now doesn't it?"

"I wouldn't know," I grumbled.

"Well you should acquaint yourself with it soon son. It's the real thing, especially when it drops in your lap," he chuckled.

I was perplexed yet again. That was the second time this month those words were said to me. First from Babs, and now lawyer John. A strange coincidence.

"What exactly do you mean?"

"Julianna Becker, my boy. A man of your stature shouldn't be running down the streets of New York like a hooligan for just any ole woman. I'm fully aware of what and who's at stake here. Just don't fuck it up."

John patted me on the back again, as if I were his son. I winced from the pain in my back. Speaking of "sons," I hoped like hell my parents didn't get wind of this nonsense. I owed a boatload of thanks to Harper for pulling my ass out of some very deep waters this time. This could have been a career ending moment. I could have lost Julianna forever, behind this madness with Kimber and Dexter. Those two were surely trying to ruin my reputation and my career. The Chief of Obstetrics being arrested would not look good in hospital land. This was information that needed to stay out of the hands of the folks in the Ivory Tower.

Lawyer John and I walked down the precinct steps, just as Gabriel and Xavier both ran up to me. Actually, John walked, and I limped.

"Ahh . . . E, I told you to keep your guard up," Gabriel said, grabbing my chin, turning my face side to side to look at my black eye, swollen nose, and bruised face.

Gabriel looked at me with disgust, as if I were the puny kid that got beat on the playground by the bully because my protector wasn't around. That was hardly the case. But it didn't change the fact that he looked at me that way anyway. I suppose my heart should have been warmed that he cared that much for me. But it wasn't like I was some chump. Some huge incredible hunk had restrained my arms while a sleazeball beat the crap out of me.

"C'mon, man. I've got a car waiting. Let's get you home to heal," Xavier said. "You need to get your head out of all those vaginas every day, and come down to the gym and learn how to box. Or some martial arts. Yeah, some martial arts," Xavier said, contemplating choices in his head.

Jesus, now Xavier was acting like I was some weakling. I hated these two had even got wind of the fact that I had gotten my ass beat this afternoon. Not only had my body taking a beating, now my feelings were bruised on top of my physical pain.

"Dr. Fischer, I'll leave you to your friends," John Matthews said, shaking his head in dismay. I suspected he thought the three of us were lost causes, but that couldn't have been further from the truth. We were actually rising stars, at the top of our game. We just didn't wear our egos on our shirtsleeve, hence not many people knew how incredibly talented we were individually or otherwise.

"Here's my card. Let's hope you won't be needing it again anytime soon."

John gave a once over look to Gabriel and Xavier.

"Overgrown frat boys," he mumbled under his breath.

I was glad I was the only one close enough to hear him. I couldn't deal with another conflict tonight. All three of us might have taken him on for that comment.

John waved his hand in the air, facing north up the street. A black sedan pulled up, screeching to a halt in front of the three of us. John got in the back seat and was gone.

I felt myself shiver. It was freezing cold, and I realized for the first time that I had no coat.

"My SUV is parked ten feet up the street, E. Let's get you out of here."

"Take me to Julianna's. I need to explain. Give me your phone, X."

"Hell no," Gabriel countered. "I sent her a text already. I told her you got mugged. I sent Logan a text too, in case Julianna didn't recognize my number. I held it down for you EZ. I think it's all good on the *Sugar Mommy* front."

"I still need to see her. I need to speak to her, explain."

"Shit man, have you looked at yourself?" Xavier asked. "You can't see her right now. Have you looked at yourself?" he repeated. "Maybe that blow to the head gave you brain fog or something. You need to examine him, Gabe."

"Let's run you by the ER, examine you, make sure you don't have a concussion, then get you home," Gabriel agreed.

"Yeah man, you can call her later. Or better yet, webcam her or something," Xavier said. "Who goes and sees a woman looking like you do?" he grumbled. "You trying to give us a bad name."

"Fine," I said, totally not in the mood for an argument.

Xavier jumped behind the wheel. I got in the back, and Gabriel took the front seat. The last thing I wanted was to go back to the hospital. Somebody might see me, and the rumor mill would fire up again. But I couldn't argue with the fact that I needed medical attention. Better to be safe than sorry. They say doctors make the worst patients, and yes we were right up there with lawyers making the worst witnesses.

"That goddamn Kimber and Dexter," Gabriel said out loud pounding his hand against the dashboard.

"Let it go for now," Xavier said, steering his SUV out into the nighttime traffic.

"This scene is so bad, I'm going to need to hit the VIP room at Maximillion's tomorrow just to calm myself down," Xavier said.

"Yeah, man I'm going to need a lap dance," Gabriel said. "That will help to keep me from going up to the Ivory Tower and beating the shit of Dexter."

"Health and healing does not reside in Maximillion's," I moaned.

"Says who?" Gabriel and Xavier both said almost in concert.

We all started laughing at ourselves at the same time, except I hurt when I laughed.

"Ohhhhhh, I need a Percocet," I grunted, putting my hand over my head.

My head and ribs were hurting, but not nearly as bad as my heart. I was in pain over the thought of having stood Julianna up tonight. This felt so funky. I wasn't sure how she was going to handle this. We'd waited a three weeks for this date, and here I was standing her up. This was not a good start. Not in the least bit. She might not want to have anything to do with me after this. But if that were the case, I was going to win her over. I was certain. My mind was made up. There was no one that was going to keep me away from Julianna. Not Dexter, not Kimber. No one. She was mine.

14

 *exter*

"Fuck we almost had Elliot," I hissed. "I thought for sure when you texted me from his place, that we were home free. I knew grabbing that Tiffany's bag would send him running out the door after you. It was such a great set up."

"Set up? Set up? No, you set *me* up. I'm the only person that got set up!"

"No I didn't."

Okay. So I had my moments. But setting Kimber up wasn't one of them. That was never in my plan.

"When I told you to grab it, I knew full well Elliot would come looking for you and follow you right into my clutches. It really was a good plan, Kimber."

"Who says?" Kimber shuffled in her seat, not completely convinced.

"Punching Elliot in the face was payback for him cracking me over the head Halloween night. Getting him locked up was even better.

That was icing on the cake. I had hoped he'd be tied in red tape, legal fees, and bad press for days. Enough to ruin his reputation at the hospital," I stammered. "Instead, he's out free like a bird."

"Well you thought fucking wrong," Kimber winced.

"Who knew he had access to the most powerful law firm in New York? I'm still trying to figure out how that happened," I stammered.

"I did, you stupid little no nothing attorney. Your idiotic little plan backfired. I was about to be charged with breaking and entering, robbery, assault, and God knows what else," Kimber said grumpily. "My father had to pull strings and call in chips all over town."

Man, Kimber was a force to be reckoned with. No wonder Elliot got his ass out of that marital trap, and fast. I could tell Kimber was not happy. This woman was like Mount St. Helen. She might explode any minute now.

"He had the nerve to be buying somebody some jewelry from Tiffany's? I had to beg on my hands and knees just to get him to buy us both bigger diamond earrings for the wedding. He kept rejecting the idea, yet within a few weeks of our being done he's buying expensive jewelry? For who?" Kimber whined.

"I could find out for you if you want?" I said thinking this might keep her engaged in the battle a bit longer. Maybe I could play on her curiosity.

"Who cares? If it's not for me, then what does it even matter," she snorted. "Daddy made me give it back anyway."

I sensed Kimber was at the end of her rope. I was starting to feel like I was losing control of her. I had a done a good job so far of keeping her under my thumb, but now things were getting hot and heavy. Kimber wanted no part of my plans to bring Elliot Fischer to his knees. I needed Kimber to stay on board with my plan for a little bit longer. She was ready to forget this madness and move on.

"I'm a lawyer, baby. I told you I wasn't going to let anything happen to you," I said, walking over to her, trying to convince her that she and I still had the upper hand.

I needed Kimber to get to an inner place of calm. But, damn, she was insulting me. She didn't think for one minute that I had the goods. As far as she was concerned, I couldn't protect her from the reach of Elliot. But Kimber was wrong. I had an inside track to his work related activities. Dr. Elliot Fischer wasn't big enough to keep me from getting what was mine.

I began rubbing my finger down the side of her cheek, trailing it further down to the crevice of her breasts, running my finger across her white angora sweater that was complementing her brown mocha colored skin.

Her nipples were getting hard just from the touch of my finger running down the middle of her chest bone. I ran my finger inside her bra, fingering her chocolate brown nipples until they both turned hard like little pebbles. I knew she was angry. But, she was also extremely excited. Kimber loved attention, so I decided to play her like the fiddle that she was. I listened for her breath to hitch, while she vacillated between her anger and her sexual tension.

Kimber started to succumb to my advances, but then she pivoted once again. She was so freaking unpredictable.

"Tell that to my father, you asshole. Somebody called him and threatened him with charges against me. Now he plans to eat the thousands of dollars in wedding expenses that I told him I had. He wants no part of getting on Elliot's bad side at this point, and he definitely doesn't want me to marry him now. I had other plans for the money I told my father I needed. And, now your little plan bungled that."

"You're his daughter for Christ sakes!" I shouted, not fully understanding this particular father daughter relationship. "Why the hell won't he give the money back? The daddy is the one that pays for the wedding!"

All of this chaos was to my own peril. Kimber was done with Elliot. She may have been done with trying to please her Chief of Staff father, but I wasn't done with her. I was going to work at manipulating her to stay in the game with Elliot. I needed her to not lose her focus and keep her mind on being Elliot's wife. The fact that she was unable to convince her dad to give her money to reimburse Elliot for the wedding expenses was a problem. I was hoping to use Kimber to latch on to some of that money. It was going to be like taking candy from a baby. Now everybody was having an attack of conscious. Ugh.

"You stupid fuck. My father works for Senator Clayton Lawrence Montgomery. He can't afford to draw bad political press. He thinks this engagement has become a liability. And don't think that I didn't have to make up a story about you Dexter, to pull your ass out of the sling tonight. I told my father that you were consoling me over the breakup, and that we met at the deli to talk, and you came to my aid as my protector."

"Well that was a good story. It was true too," I said, hoping to get her to see me in the role as her protector. Hopefully, that would mean Kimber would continue to trust me. If I could keep Kimber relying on me, then I could control her to my liking. Dumping her down the road would be easy.

"There's no changing my father's mind. You're immaterial to him, Dexter."

"What in the hell does that mean Kimber? Immaterial?"

"It means, I don't know about you, but I have to be done with this marriage bullshit to Elliot. Besides, I'm starting to get bored with this whole marriage thing anyway," Kimber huffed. "Daddy says I have bigger fish to fry."

"Bigger fish to fry?"

Damn. Kimber and her damn Daddy. Elliot must have been stupid as hell to want to marry this airhead. She could hardly last for the long haul. She failed to see the big picture. Her utility to me was starting to hit the zero mark. Perhaps it was time for me to cut Kimber loose and go it alone. Kimber was starting to feel like an anchor holding me down. But that didn't mean I still wasn't going to screw that beautiful brown chocolate booty into tomorrow. She was beautiful. Delectable. Desirable. But not much there between the ears.

I reached in my desk drawer and pulled out small tin of cocaine. I dipped my pinky into it, and put a bit under her nose. And then mine. Kimber's eyes got wide. Her legs parted like clockwork. I unzipped my pants, pulling my erection out that had come to attention. I reached my hands past that flurry angora white sweater and grabbed her breasts. I put my head down on her hard pebbles, and gave the girls the attention they'd been begging for all night. She moaned out loud as my tongue caressed her breasts.

"Are you cold baby?" I said, noticing Kimber was shivering. "I'll warm you up."

"Umm," she moaned, inviting me in further.

I grabbed an afghan off the sofa my mother had crocheted. I laid it out on the floor in front of the fireplace. Kimber was a delicate creature. She needed special attention, this one. I laid her out on the floor spread eagle, and threw an extra log in the fireplace. I moved to my bar, and poured her some brandy in snifters for the both of us, to chase down the line of coke we both shared.

And then I pulled that tight little black leather skirt off those beautiful chocolate hips, tugging her fire engine red panties with the lace ribbon bows on both sides down those long tall legs that went on forever, tossing them over to the side. Then I put my tongue on her mound, reminding her why we were in this together.

I wasn't done with Kimber. And I damn sure didn't need her to be done with me. Daddy Jefferson was going to have to wait until I was done with his baby girl before he got ideas in his head about "bigger fish to fry." He might as well have turned the heat up a notch. I still had use for his daughter. I was going to continue to manipulate her, and then I was going to continue to fuck her into oblivion. Then, and only then, would I send her back to him on her knees, reminding him who was the biggest fish in Kimber's universe. Perhaps all those Lawson's, Kimber included, needed a reminder lesson in who runs the world.

15

Julianna

"Oh my God Gabriel, I'm so sorry to hear Elliot got mugged. I've been waiting here for hours, pacing the floor wondering what was happening with him and if he was standing me up."

I glanced at the flowers on my kitchen countertop that I'd received from Elliot this afternoon and realized that idea didn't make much sense. His card with the flowers had the cutest little smiley face. My heart was warmed every time I rested my eyes on the beautiful flowers, taking in the wonderful floral scent, re-reading his heartfelt card to myself over and over again.

"Not at all Julianna. He got beat up pretty badly. Xavier and I took him by the emergency room. I gave him a thorough exam. He's going to be fine, but bed rest is what he needs right now," Gabriel said.

Gabriel spoke in his professional physician's voice. It was weird hearing him for the first time sounding so serious. When Gabriel was around Elliot, he was playful, jovial, hardly ever to be taken seriously. I tended to forget that he was a medical professional, he was often so loose and free. But tonight Gabriel was all business. He sounded like a . . . like a doctor. This felt so strange, as I was accustomed to him being a cut-up.

"Oh this is so upsetting. Is there anything I can do? Surely there is something I can do?" I pleaded. "Can I see him?"

"I'm sure he'd love to see you. But I must warn you, he's pretty battered. It will take a couple of weeks for his bruises to heal completely."

"Did they find out who did this to him? Did they want money? Oh my God, I feel so bad."

I could feel myself talking a mile a minute in Gabriel's ear. I was holding back my own tears. I wanted to sob. But I needed to be strong. The last thing Elliot needed was for me to turn into some wimpy woman who couldn't hold up under pressure. Most men I'd been in relationship with never expected me to be the strong one in a crisis. But I was stronger than anyone thought I was. Particularly, Oliver, and maybe even Nicky for that matter. I knew how to rise to the occasion when required. After all, I was raised without a mother, and that in itself made me stronger than most women. Unfortunately, not many people knew that about me. They assumed I was fragile and needed protecting. But wrong. I was very capable of taking care of myself, and frankly those that I cared about . . and I cared about Elliot.

Did I just think that? Did I really care about Elliot? Well of course. I would care about any person that had been mugged in the streets of New York. It's a normal reaction. Even though we hadn't discussed the status of our relationship, I got the feeling we were going to be headed down that path soon.

"Whatever was taken, was retrieved," Gabriel continued. "Nothing of value was permanently lost. Perhaps Elliot's pride at this point," Gabriel's tone sounded as if he were assessing his words carefully.

"Well I'm going to call my driver and head over to his place immediately."

"Well you should know, I've administered him a pretty big dose of pain killers for the night. He's going to be out of it for a while. Maybe you want to consider touching base with him in the morning," Gabriel said, his voice still professional.

"No, I'm going to him now. He needs me," I insisted. "He shouldn't be alone."

"Okay, well I'm at his place now. We'll wait for you. You can relieve Xavier and me from the night shift. Pick up where we're leaving off, so to speak. You can watch over him through the night, and I'll check with you again in the morning."

"Okay, then it's settled. I'll see you in a few. Thank you for calling me, Gabriel."

I was genuinely grateful that Gabriel had phoned me. It helped knowing that Elliot hadn't stood me up. After all the betrayal that I had been through with Oliver, I really didn't want unnecessary baggage in my next relationship. I wanted my next relationship to be built on trust and open communication.

"I'm doing what I know you do for me Jules if the situation was reversed."

"Absolutely. See you soon. Good-bye."

Shortly after midnight I arrived at Elliot's home.

---

*E*lliot was knocked out for the night when I arrived, which was good because it gave me time to adjust to his physical appearance. Gabriel warned me that his face looked like—well it looked like he'd been in the ring with Floyd Mayweather. Those beautiful lips had multiple cuts on them. His nose and eyes were black and blue. He had a deep cut above his left eye. Gabriel gave me strict instructions not to touch Elliot's rib cage too hard because they were beyond sore. Gabriel had wrapped his rib cage in tape so that his bruised ribs, one of which was fractured, would heal quicker. The good news was he hadn't lost any teeth, didn't have a concussion, and his smooth hands that caught all those beautiful babies every day were absent any serious cuts or scrapes.

"It's not as bad as it looks," Gabriel said, looking at my shocked face as I first laid eyes on Elliot sprawled out in his bed. "Initially I didn't think it was a good idea for you to see him like this, but X and I decided that you being here would actually be good for him."

"Are you sure you're going to be okay?" Xavier spoke next. "I feel kind of guilty leaving you by yourself."

"Oh I'm not alone," I said softly, feeling like an overgrown child; much like I felt when under Nicky's cautious watch.

"My security detail is right outside the door. As long as I'm here, a couple of guys will be here. If I need anything, they're an open door away," I sighed.

"Oh cool," Xavier said with a wicked laugh. "Another chance for me to rock Craig Meyer's world again."

Xavier rubbed the palm of his hands together in jest, like he was starting a fire.

"Knock it off X. You know that man's got eyes for Maya. You're not the 'settle down with one woman' type of man anyway. You're giving that guy heartburn. Bad enough I had to stitch up EZ. You want to be next? Why the hell do you want to mess with that guy for anyway?" Gabriel said.

"Because I can."

Xavier clenched his fingers together, stretching his arms out in front of him as if to crack his knuckles, rotating his neck, his dark ponytail flipping from side to side. I noticed the tattoo inked on his huge bicep. It was a design of two crossed naval swords with the words "Rockin Wingman" blazed across the middle. I wondered about its significance. I was sure it meant something personal to him. As he passed in front of me, I caught a whiff of his scent, Clinique's Happy cologne for men. It was fitting too. Xavier struck me as a jovial kind of guy.

Gabriel shook his head at Xavier, rolling his eyes up in his head.

"Maya's a beautiful woman, let Craig work for it. Isn't that right Julianna?" Xavier asked teasingly. He stretched his hands above his head next.

"I wouldn't know. It's not like I get any awards lately for knowing anything about matters of the heart," I answered with another deep sigh.

"Well you're here helping us out with Elliot, so as far as I'm concerned your heart is just fine," Gabriel said.

"You know Jules, broken hearts are my specialty," Xavier teased flirtatiously. I could help you with that."

I grinned at Xavier, pretty much thinking he was lucky Elliot was knocked out on meds, missing out on this flirtatious discussion, but I wasn't surprised that Gabriel had Elliot's back.

"You're such a man whore Xavier," Gabriel hissed at him. "Elliot would kick your ass right about now."

"Just keeping the rest of you guys on your toes, my brother."

The three of us all laughed out loud together. We paused our laughter as Gabriel's phone began playing Beyoncé's *Naughty Girl*. Xavier and I were all ears. A slight grin spread across Gabriel's face. He answered the phone in sexy Italian. Xavier flagged his hand at him. We both figured Logan was on the other end of the line.

Minutes later, Gabriel and Xavier were out the door, instructing me to put the locks on the door from the inside. I could hear Xavier outside the door razing Craig. Maya was going to love this story. But it was so late; I was going to have to wait until the morning to call her. All I wanted was to get some sleep, but I was so wound up, I wasn't sure how that was going to happen, my not being in my own home, with a hot man in the other room.

I opted for the couch instead of the guest bedroom, so I could hear Elliot's call if he needed me. I tossed and turned on the couch for over an hour, before finally tearing off my jeans, throwing on one of Elliot's t-shirts and crawling into the bed with him. I figured I'd be up before him in the morning, so he'd never notice my sleeping next to him. The warmth of his body was calming, helping me to drift off to sleep.

*N*o one would have believed that four days later I was still at Elliot's apartment, nursing him back to health. No one except Maya and Logan. They were both incredibly supportive. They were helping me with the launch plans, helping out with details at the new pastry shop while I worked from the remote location of Elliot's home. Things were coming together at the pastry shop. Equipment was flowing in, my staff was hired and on board. The interior decorator was carrying out my final changes.

Elliot's home was elegant, sophisticated, and warm. I wondered how much of his decorum was his touch versus Kimber's. Either way, someone had very good taste in furnishings. His place had sky high ceilings with huge floor to ceiling windows that that allowed the sunlight to flood the large living area in the daytime, and moonlit spectacular views of the Manhattan skyline at night. His kitchen was adorned with black granite countertops framing the eating space with tall black leather barstools and sunflower-filled vases.

I'd set up a makeshift desk at Elliot's dining room table, not wanting to disturb anything in his home office. Maya, Logan and I talked on Skype, covering all the details from the food, guest list, music, and holiday decorations. Things were shaping up rather fast. I scanned a couple of the legal contracts with some of the vendors over to my brother Blake for review. Unlike Nicky, Blake had his head up daddy's business so he hardly cared much about my ventures, but still gave my legal documents his full attention.

Gabriel made arrangements with the hospital CEO for Elliot to take time off from work on sick leave. I was happy to hear that news since the temperature outside had dropped dramatically the last several days. It wouldn't have done Elliot any good to be outside, nor was I in any big hurry to be out in the cold either. Craig came inside occasionally, just long enough to put some logs in the fireplace and to stoke the fire for me. He said very few words to me, if any. He took more time stoking the logs in the fireplace when he knew I was talking on Skype to Maya. I was certain he was smitten with Maya, and liked hearing her voice, catching a glimpse of her on my laptop. I told Maya I thought it was kind of cute, up until the moment that she reminded me that Craig was probably making a daily report to Nicky about my whereabouts. But I didn't care. I only cared that Elliot was getting better.

I fed Elliot several times a day, alternating between tomato and chicken soups that I managed to make fresh from scratch. His kitchen was well stocked. I enjoyed working with so many fresh ingredients. I forced Elliot to sip hot herbal teas in-between the periods that he was partially awake and coherent. For the most part he remained drowsy. He was so out of it from the medications that Gabriel had given him, I wondered sometimes if he even knew I was there.

Caring for him emotionally was a mix of pleasure and pain. I hand bathed Elliot daily. It was an emotionally difficult task. Bathing those beautiful broad shoulders and rock hard abs took everything I had to stay in control. He was an angelic gift of hotness from the heavens above.

My inner slut raised her head daily, forcing me to vacillate between jumping his bones or running out the door as if a lightning bolt had struck me. Elliot was totally sex on a stick. It was a good thing those beautiful gray eyes remained mostly closed or else I would have been undone altogether, losing all sense of control. I didn't do well in the presence of a man whose physical aura left me so incredibly speechless and powerless.

Gabriel came by each day to examine Elliot, administering a couple of different meds. Gabriel mentioned that he'd given Elliot enough painkillers to immobilize a horse, which explained why I often sensed he was practically catatonic. Gabriel felt that immobilizing Elliot for several days would accelerate his healing. He insisted it the only way to keep Elliot out of the hospital to allow time for his body to heal. He knew Elliot was a big workaholic, and would never take time off on his own to properly heal. He eventually began decreasing his dosage in the days to follow, as Elliot was healing properly as he had hoped.

A couple of times Xavier stopped by to check to see if I needed anything, always thanking me for keeping watch over him. No doubt,

Elliot and his friends had the resources to hire a private duty nurse to care for him. But I was sure they loved the fact that it was me that had stepped up to the plate to care for him.

Elliot was in and out of it. Even though Gabriel had reduced his meds, he still seemed heavily sedated. I kept his television running in his bedroom, changing the channel from the NFL football, soap operas to CNN, not knowing enough about what his tastes were in media. Occasionally, I turned on the Food Channel and ate my meals in the bed with him, talking more to myself about my favorite television chefs, and how I would cook him whatever was being made on television at the time. Once, he got some silly grin on his face, mumbling words that I couldn't make out, but I liked to think that meant he was in agreement with me.

In between nursing him, bathing him, and a bit of television, I managed to keep my efforts on track with my vendors, staying on target with my plans to keep the launch party of *Sugar Mommy* on schedule for an early December opening. The last thing I wanted to hear was my brother Nicholas thinking I couldn't manage a simple launch party for the opening of my own pastry shop. I kept busy. I even had baking ingredients hand delivered to Elliot's so I could stick to my promise of making Nicky's twins Turkey cookies, which I sent over to them by courier. I kept a dozen or so around for Elliot and myself.

I later discovered from Nicky's wife Harper that their twins had the measles, so their whole household was in an uproar. While I cringed at the thought of the twins being sick, I could just imagine that my brother was fully acting out over it, the thought of which tickled me just a tiny bit. Even though each twin had their own nanny to care for them, plus their Mom, I had no doubt he was making everyone around him miserable, doting on them to ensure they had anything and everything. I was glad Nicky had something else to focus his attention on other than me for a change. It allowed me free rein to focus on Elliot and my pastry business without hearing Nicky's mouth about my caring for Elliot.

Logan and Maya were overjoyed about my staying at Elliot's,

Logan insisting that I send them a selfie of Elliot, so all three of us could fawn over the fact of how hot he was even in sickness. I declined to take the picture, wanting to respect Elliot's privacy. I didn't want anyone to see him at his lowest point, a hottie in sickness or otherwise. For now, he was mine alone to drool over.

In our brief moments of boredom, Maya, Logan, and I Googled his parents, discovering his famous Noble Laureate mother was Swedish American, his mogul father of African American-Seminole decent. That explained the contrast of his light brown skin with the mesmerizing gray eyes

At night I laid in bed next to Elliot, clothed in his Georgetown University t-shirt, and his hiking socks. His bed was spacious enough for me to keep my distance in case he woke up wondering what I was doing in his bed. But, no matter how hard I tried to keep my distance, every morning I found myself waking up with Elliot spooning me, his strong arms tucking me neatly up under him. I felt protected and safe in his arms. Comforted.

---

*I*t wasn't until day six, Thanksgiving morning, when I entered Elliot's bedroom to check on him, my hot steaming morning coffee in hand, that things changed. It was barely eight in the morning, so I was caught off guard when a pair of beautiful pewter-colored eyes whizzed through my body past the surface, curling a path straight to my core. For the first time in a week, my breath caught in my throat.

"How long have you been here Julianna?" Elliot said, those beautiful gray eyes boring deep into my soul again.

"Almost a week," I said, all of a sudden feeling vulnerable in his navy blue and white "Got Baby" t-shirt with nothing else on under it. Instinctively, I tugged on his t-shirt so as to pull the hem of the shirt down to cover my knees, realizing it was a futile effort. My feet were bare. I dropped my eyes down, noticing the slight chip of red toenail polish that had come off my big toe. I was certain I had bed-head that I lazily hadn't dealt with when I'd brushed my teeth earlier.

"Today is Thanksgiving," I muttered, noticing that my voice sounded like the scratching sound against a blackboard.

Elliot's eyes, clear as a whistle now, looked me up and down, his gaze taking me in head to toe, running the full length of my body. A hot feeling of warmth swept over me in a glorious wave. God I needed some bottoms on quick. Was I stupid enough to think he'd stay in a medical stupor forever? That I could run around his home half naked? I had been so caught up in nursing him back to health, playing nursemaid, knee deep in my work that it never occurred to me that he was in a temporary state for which he would one day awaken. Oh sweet Jesus, I was surely going to pass out from embarrassment any minute now.

"A week," Elliot said out loud, repeating after me, contemplating the time in his head. "My patients?"

"Gabriel called the hospital CEO and had you put on sick leave. You were mugged," I said innocently, still not sure how he felt about me standing in his bedroom with one of his coffee mugs in my hand, half naked.

My feet felt like they were frozen in a block of ice, and I wasn't sure where this conversation was going. I wanted to run, but had lost my ability to move under his gaze.

"Oh . . . yes . . . the jewelry . . . Kimber . . . Dexter," he said as if all of a sudden remembering things that were coming back to him in a mental rush. "I remember now."

"What?" I said confused.

What did Kimber's jewelry have to do with him being mugged and robbed? Maybe Elliot wasn't ready to enter reality just yet. Perhaps he was having repercussions from the blows to the head. I wondered if I needed to call Gabriel to let him know he was fully awake. But it was Thanksgiving Day. Gabriel was probably with his family. Which was someplace where I would have needed to be myself, but for the breakout of measles at my brother's house with the twins. My father, my oldest brother Blake, and his family had taken off in Daddy's private Lear headed to Europe for the holiday.

Elliot shook his head as if he were dusting his thoughts off.

"May I have a sip of your coffee?" he said, patting his hand on the bed, inviting me to sit next to him. I felt my cheeks flushing.

I paused for several beats, still feeling vulnerable, not knowing whether to move or what to do next.

"Please."

I tucked both hands around the coffee mug, moving to sit next to Elliot on the bed, crawling in next to him. Elliot took the coffee from my hand. He took a big gulp, inhaling the Guatemalan aroma that was penetrating his nostrils. He handed the mug back to me. I took a sip, neither of us saying anything to each other.

"Julianna, I don't want anything to be between us. I had hoped to tell you some of what I wanted to tell you now on our date, so that we could have a fresh healthy start, without secrets," he said, squinting as if sucking in air to breathe was uncomfortable.

Elliot set the coffee mug down, grabbed my hand, pulling me closer to him. I was anxious, not sure what he was going to say, not knowing whether or not I wanted to hear it either. He held my hand in his tightly, as if he thought I might take off and run. My heart was beating so fast it was probably a good guess on his part that I might be subject to take flight any minute.

"On Halloween night, when I was forced to duck out on you and your friends, it was largely because I found my fiancée Kimber having a sexual tryst with one of my co-workers from the hospital dressed in costume looking like me."

My mouth flew open and I gasped out loud, but said nothing, covering my hand over my mouth. My mind raced back a month to Halloween night, thinking of the subtle differences in things I thought I missed in Elliot's appearance that really actually were someone else. The thought of it was simply mind boggling.

"My co-worker Dexter Esposito and Kimber were having an affair behind my back. Finding that out ultimately led to the end of my engagement. Frankly, I had planned to end it anyway. That whole ugly scene Halloween night only accelerated the breakup."

"So you weren't helping someone that was hurt?"

"Yes and no. It was me who hurt Dexter. It was me who also tended to his care."

I had heard the name Dexter Esposito tossed around at the hospital fundraisers, but I didn't know specifically who he was. I was vaguely aware that he worked in the legal department of the hospital. My mind was racing a mile a minute, while Elliot continued to talk.

"To make a long story short, this little scene with Kimber and Dexter has made my workplace relationship with Dexter that much more difficult. Dexter's been out to harm Gabriel and me at the hospital for some time now, only this time he used Kimber as his weapon."

"Oh my God, Elliot. I'm sorry this happened, but what does this have to do with anything?"

"On the day of our date, Kimber came here under the ruse of needing to pick up some things she left after our breakup. Some videos actually. I momentarily left her alone in here to grab a bag for her to carry them. When I did, she took something that belonged to me and ran."

"Why did she . . . ."

"Wait, I really need to get this out okay?" he said shaking his head.

I wondered what Kimber had taken from Elliot, but I sensed I shouldn't ask, recognizing that he wasn't ready to open up about it. It sounded personal.

"I followed her out of this building, chasing her several blocks through the streets. She darted into a deli. Dexter was waiting for her —well for me too, for that matter. Dexter proceeded to physically beat me while some other large goons restrained my hands, thinking of course that I was after Kimber to do her harm."

"Good Lord," I said out loud, gasping again, my hand back over my mouth.

"I couldn't protect myself. Certainly I would never do any woman any physical harm. I hope you believe me when I say that. It was all a trap that I fell right into frankly, but I would never harm a woman, ever. I just wanted what was mine back."

My mouth remained covered with my hand, not sure that I knew what to say next, so I remained silent. I nodded at him to hand me the coffee mug, so I could sip some more, forcing myself to listen and to not ask questions before he finished his thoughts.

It made me sad that Elliot had been assaulted with no way to protect himself. Kimber really sounded like a piece of work. Beyond her obvious beauty, I wondered what he even saw in her. She didn't seem like a nice person.

"I was taken to the nearest precinct, held for several hours before your brother's wife arranged for my release."

"Harper? What's she got to do with this, and how does she know about this?" I asked, my mind now going into overdrive, realizing that it was possible that Nicky knew this story too.

I moved to stand up on my feet, but Elliot pulled me back down swiftly to a seating position next to him. It was bad enough Nicky thought Elliot and his friends were a bunch of yahoos as it was, but this news was going to really fuel his fire. And to think I was the last to know. Was it possible Harper may not have shared this information with her husband? No one in my family had said a word to me about any of this. It's been six days.

"Your sister-in-law sent Maya's uncle, John Matthews, from the Matthews Law Firm to secure my release. According to John, Harper's driver was coincidentally in that deli and supposedly saw the whole encounter. Talk about being at the right place at the right time," Elliot said with disbelief. "What are the odds?"

Oh sweet Jesus. Is nothing sacred? This means Silas knows about this incident too. I'm the only one in the dark. Why hadn't anyone shared this with me?

But then I realized for the most part I had kept my phone powered down while here, except in the moments I reached out to Maya and Logan to work. Nicky and Harper had been overwhelmed with sick twins. Perhaps no one in my family had yet found a free moment to fill me in on this incident.

"Julianna, the fact of the matter is, Kimber and Dexter meant to do harm to me any way they could. I suspect she's angry that I've broken the engagement, and he's out to ruin my professional reputation. Dexter's been jealous of both Gabriel and I ever since he flunked out of medical school. It's just that his tactics to harm us have reached an all-time low."

Elliot grabbed my free hand, standing us both up, walking me with him into his master bathroom, the marble floor cold under my feet. I wrapped my free arm around his waist in case he needed to lean his weight against me, not sure of his strength. Did he need to pee? I didn't need to see this, did I? This duty had normally been taken on by Gabriel and Xavier these last few days. But I kept moving with him, not to deny my inner slut from a peek at that beautiful body and all.

I caught a glimpse of myself in the mirror. I looked disheveled. I instinctively pushed my hands in my hair so as to calm my bed-head, but I knew my efforts were futile. I forced myself to resign to the fact that it is what it is. I'm not a superwoman or a Barbie doll. This is all there is.

"I'm usually more together," I said, feeling an insecurity void calling out deep within me having to explain my appearance. But I could kick myself for even going to that place.

Elliot smiled a warm smile, but did not respond. Those gray eyes scanned over my body yet again, taking in my full essence. I felt a pang of self-consciousness. I felt inadequate.

He reached for his toothbrush that was lying next to mine. I hoped he didn't mind that I had set my toiletries up in his bathroom using the other his and hers double sink.

Maya had gone by my place earlier in the week to grab a few of my necessities, sending them to me by way of Craig. I had taken over half of Elliot's bathroom space, liking the feeling of closeness to him. I felt self-conscious about the fact I had invaded his personal space. I searched his face for a reaction, but he hardly seemed to mind.

Elliot brushed his teeth. When finished, he grabbed the coffee mug from my hand and took another sip. I took a sip behind him. I liked and relished the fact we were sharing coffee together. I watched in silence as he turned the heads of the massage jets on in the shower. The bathroom filled with steam. Elliot began slowly ripping the white tape off his ribs, his skin still slightly purple and blue, his face scrunching up in pain.

"Are you sure you should be doing that?" I asked.

"Do you think we should call a doctor and see?" Elliot chuckled at me.

"Oh, you've got jokes, now?" I said, slightly amused that he was poking fun at me.

I pouted my lips, folding my arms across my breasts, certain I had a petulant look on my face.

"I'm teasing you, Julianna. It's okay. Really I'm fine," he winced, pulling more tape off his ribs.

My heart clenched from thinking about all that Elliot had gone through at work, not to mention his dysfunctional relationship with Kimber. Thank God, those two didn't marry. And Dexter, he sounded like a real douchebag. My eyes teared up from thinking about it and I wasn't even the one who had to live through it. I suddenly realized that I had unconsciously groaned out loud. Elliot sensed my internal discomfort.

"I would understand it, Julianna, if you didn't want anything to do with me right now. I'm fresh off a broken engagement with a high maintenance drama queen. That might scare any good woman into taking to the hills. But I must warn you, I have no intentions of letting you get away from me," he said ripping the last bit of tape off himself, his eyes squinting in the mirror.

"I'm glad you shared the truth of what happened to you. I like the fact that we aren't keeping secrets between us."

I tilted my head back to meet his gaze, looking up at his six-foot frame, taking a deep breath and stepping back away from him two paces. The shower steam in the air had nothing on the heat passing between us.

Elliot stepped forward two paces, closing the gap between us. I backed up two steps more, banging my head against his bathroom wall.

Elliot leaned closer to me, lowering his voice, saying "Good, because I don't want anything to come between us. I don't want to be your rebound man, Julianna. I want to be more."

"And I want more," I whispered back, matching his same sense of intensity. His energy was drawing me in to the point I was unable to pull out of his orbit.

"Julianna, I have something for you," he said, as if debating whether it was safe to go forward.

I'm sure I looked at Elliot with a deep sense of curiosity. Elliot moved momentarily into the bedroom for a minute and then back into the bathroom where he left me. He was holding a blue Tiffany's shopping bag in his hand.

"Here baby, I was saving this for a more important moment, your launch party exactly. But frankly there is no more important moment than right now."

I looked in the bag and pulled out a little blue box dressed in white satin ribbon. I pulled the string, opening it. It was a silver platinum diamond studded key on a long matching chain.

"The key to my heart Julianna," Elliot said.

I was taken aback. Elliot had literally and symbolically given me the key to his heart. I felt special. The moment was special. A moment I dearly wanted to preserve. Elliot was gifting his heart to my care. I grinned a wide grin. My heart was turning backflips.

Wow, can somebody wrap this man up and put him up under my Christmas tree? I couldn't believe he had opened himself up to me like this. I realized I no longer wanted a temporary placeholder in my life. I wanted Elliot.

Elliot's gray eyes darkened as he grinned his slow sexy smile. I felt my nipples get hard under his t-shirt. His eyes traveled downward to my puckered nipples. My skin was beginning to flush. Gray Eyes were heating up my skin again with that look of his. Elliot stepped closer to me, placing both his hands on the wall, pinning me in his space.

"And now that you've promised to cook me all those delectable dishes from the Food Network show, I really don't intend to let you get away from me," he said, switching from serious to playful.

"You heard that?" I said, my face flushed with embarrassment.

"All closed eyes aren't asleep Julianna."

Elliot had an amused yet watchful look on his face.

I raised an eyebrow with a smirk before saying, "So you intend not to let me get away, huh?"

"That would be accurate," Elliot said, stepping his body closer to mine, his naked chest practically touching my breasts.

He tilted his head and grinned, his eyes focusing on my lips.

"Can we start with that turkey dish first?" he said, his voice all deep and sugary, triggering every button on my arousal meter and skyrocketing my desire for him through the roof.

My body was on fire, every nerve tingling, my lips needing to be touched by his. Elliot seemed just as desperate to taste me too. He dropped his lips to mine, my tongue willingly following his as it tangled with my own. He tasted sweet and minty from his spearmint toothpaste. I was sure I was going to go up in flames. Gray Eyes was going to be the death of me.

We kissed until we were both panting and breathless. The steam from the shower jets had nothing on us.

"You taste so good," Elliot moaned. "You've been sponge bathing me all week. It was a form of torture, frankly. I think I'm well enough to shower on my own now," Elliot said. "But, I would love it if you would join me."

I buried my head in Elliot's chest until my breathing evened out. Elliot was running his hands up and down my arms, planting soft tender kisses on my cheek and neck. His kisses were gentle, but filled with hunger. I opened the glass shower door by its gold handle, turning the water on and stepping inside, letting the hot water run down the front of his t-shirt that I was wearing. Elliot laughed out loud.

"I guess I should have been more specific, darling."

"Yes you should have," I laughed, the water soaking me, plastering his wet shirt against my breasts.

Elliot stepped inside. I put my head under the hot water, raising my arms for him. Elliot pulled his t-shirt off me, and I pulled his plaid boxers off of him. I sighed in happiness as he poured shampoo in his large hands and began lathering my hair. I tilted my head back for Elliot. He kissed me softly yet again.

"You know what else I would love?" Elliot said.

I shook my head. "No what else would you love?" I grinned.

"You." He smiled.

And I smiled right back at him, the hot water pouring down on the both of us.

16

E lliot

*J*ulianna's wide-eyed innocence did me in every time
those big brown sugar eyes were giving me that look. It
was that hungry 'I want you, and I need your cock inside
me' look. When she joined me in the shower, I couldn't resist raising
both my hands, cupping her face, laying tender kisses on her lips and
neck. I ran my finger down her breastbone looking at where the platinum key pendant, the key to my heart, fell against her soft creamy
skin. It was a perfect moment, the key to my heart wrapped around
Julianna's neck. Perfectly positioned. *You got me Cupid. I'm hers for the
taking.*

As the hot steamy water streamed down the both us, Julianna put
her arms around my neck, trying hard to avoid my bruised rib cage. I
ran my fingers through her dark wet slick hair, on her head and in
between her legs. I began pulling her closer to me, my hand steadying
her in the small of her back. I knew in that moment that she was the

one——the woman I needed be with forever. I had already written her name on my soul. Julianna wanted me for me, not for any ulterior financial purpose, unlike Kimber. She had come to care for me in my time of need, and now it was my turn to care for her.

I kissed her hard, my hands cupping her breasts, then moving slowly down to her hips. I was desperate to get inside her. Her hot tongue blazed a trail of liquid heat to my groin. I moaned into her mouth, my body responding to her with hardness. I was hard. Hot and hard, my tongue plunging in her mouth deeply, longing for more.

Everything about her turned me on. I lathered her body with soap first, then mine, holding her under the massage jets in my arms, rinsing us both off. I grabbed the white fluffy towel off the rack, towel drying the both of us carefully. She shared the towel patting my ribs softly, watching my face for any signs of pain. I turned her around, towel drying her backside, my arousal reigniting again as I dried her off.

"You're so beautiful," I said turning her around, whispering in her ear, planting soft kisses again on her lips and neck.

I led her back to my oversized bed, pulling the comforter back, tucking her underneath to keep her warm. I opened the drawer of my end table, reaching for a condom. I tore it open with my teeth, pausing for her permission. Julianna took the condom out of my hand and slipped it over my erection oh so slowly, teasing me, rubbing her hands down my shaft.

My fingers traveled over her body, exploring her perfect curves. Her breasts jiggled as I flicked my tongue over her nipples caressing those beautiful globes. I ran my hand over her hips as my finger slid against her mound, the moisture inviting me inside. I kissed her lips at the same time I slipped my middle finger inside, watching as her body trembled beneath me.

I needed to calm down, feeling myself losing control over my urges the more I touched her. I wanted this to be good for her. I wanted to see that come inside me look in her eyes again. I was as hungry for her as she was for me. She pulled her lips from mine.

"Please Elliot. I need you inside me. Now."

I opened Julianna's legs wide with my knee, drawing my eyes over her gorgeous, willing body that was urging me on. Her fingers wrapped around my cock, her fingers framing the place where she wanted me. I buried myself deep inside her. In and out, slowly.

Julianna began whispering my name, my name melting over her tongue like sweet hot chocolate. I rode her sweet spot with my hardness, striving for an orgasm, feeling her muscles tightening around my erection. She shifted her hips under me, and I palmed her butt, cupping my hands under her to pull her closer to me. Her curves moved in sync with mine, and I tongued her mouth, owning it until she let out a throaty groan. She was close to climaxing. I mentally readied myself for the blast of heat that was coming next.

"Say my name. Let me hear it baby," I said, her eyes closed, her facial expression reflecting sheer bliss.

"Elliot. Elliot. Elliot," she whispered softly first, then louder, then louder again.

I groaned a primal sound as she grabbed my hips, pulling me deeper. I pulled closer to her, feeling the pounding of her heart blending with mine. My fingers found her clitoris, all slippery and wet, massaging it gently in tiny small circles, applying just the right amount of pressure.

"God I can't get enough of you," I moaned.

I turned over, taking her with me, her body on top now riding me. A mess of emotions raced through me as I wrestled for control. I held on to her tightly, letting her have her way with me. I held on to her hips and let her ride me, my strokes long and deep. Our rhythmic pace picking up to a fierce frenzy. *How I loved my beautiful Sugar Mommy on top. Mine, all mine.*

I let out a primal growl at the same time she let out a scream, both of us climaxing together. She whimpered in pleasure. An odd feeling of intimacy buzzed around the both of us, almost as if bonding us forever.

Julianna fell into my arms, exhausted. I held her close, not letting her go.

"You're everything I want and need," I whispered into her ear. "You can fuck me within an inch of my life and so help me God I will fall down to my hands and knees and beg you for more."

Julianna breathed heavily, catching her breath as the moment calmed.

"If you keep killing me softly like this, I won't be around for you to beg me for anything."

She was panting with exhaustion, still lying on top of me. I rubbed the middle of her back, as her dark silky hair swept down it in glorious waves. It was official. *I was crazy in love with Julianna Becker.*

And I smiled.

---

*F*or the rest of the afternoon, Julianna and I had a hard time getting out of bed. She massaged and rubbed my rib cage down in warm baby oil, while I kissed and caressed her breasts in return, rubbing them in oil. She was constantly worrying that I was going to over-exert myself. Even though my bruises had faded a ton, they were still a reminder to her that my recovery was still underway. But there was no such thing as my over-exerting myself. I couldn't get enough of her.

Our entangled bodies were wrapped around each other like vines. Julianna sighed into the pillow, rolling deeper into the blanket. It was time for me to take care of her. I buried myself in those long dark curls that free flowed down her shoulders, cascading in beautiful waves. We spooned, cuddled, and made love again. And again.

In between our non-stop lovemaking, we settled for cold turkey sandwiches, potato salad, chocolate cake with berries and Pinot Noir for our Thanksgiving dinner. We both loved the fact that we had inadvertently managed to avoid the big lavish traditional family holiday meals that bored both of us to tears. We loved sharing this one on one time together. Our little dinner was so much more intimate.

We ate in bed, Julianna feeding me berries, and me spooning chocolate cake and vanilla ice cream in her mouth. This was so much better than the date I had planned. Feeding Julianna in bed was one of the things I could take off my bucket list.

We resumed talking, cuddling, caressing, and spooning after our no frills food fest. I opened wine while Julianna told me all about how much she had progressed with the launch opening plans for *Sugar Mommy*. I told her all about my college days with Gabe and Xavier. She giggled through all my crazy stories while I relished making her laugh. The sound of her laughed splashed over my core, dousing me with warmth and happiness. *My Tinkerbell had mesmerized me with her fairy dust. Cupid's arrows were at it again.* We talked for hours about our families, and her European pastry training. We made love, we slept, we woke up and made love again, each wanting more. We were wild and loud.

"Elliot, you're going to have to stop making me scream so loud if you don't want my security team outside to bust your doors down," she giggled.

"Nah baby, it's me that's gonna need rescuing," I laughed. "Not you," I said, slapping my hand against her naked butt.

We both starting laughing wildly, the wine starting to make her even more gigglier.

While I knew Julianna made that remark in jest, I fully took her comment seriously. That was a fun fact I hadn't contemplated, and definitely something I was going to have to start getting used to fast if I was going to remain in her orbit. Her brother Nicholas was a powerful man who was not going to have his younger sister walk the earth without a team of guards surrounding her, regardless of my presence or not. Nicholas had been through a terrorizing ordeal because of his business dealings a few years back that put his wife at risk. According to Julianna there was no changing his mind about her security or any other members of his family.

Julianna was special. She was special to her family. She was special to me.

y the end of the Thanksgiving afternoon as early evening approached, Julianna's body was practically boneless but sated.

"You need to take a bath and soak," I hinted.

"I like that idea," she said.

I turned on the Jacuzzi jets in my oversized tub, pouring in some lavender bubble bath leftover from Kimber. I ran her a hot bath so she could soak her body.

"Why don't you join me?" she offered.

"I need to call the hospital, check in with my answering service so as to start to plugging back into the patients I've missed over the last week."

"I understand," she said solemnly.

"I don't plan to work today, but I at least want to know the extent of my workload going forward."

Julianna nodded in agreement. I lay across my bed, reviewing notes on my laptop of some patient files, listening to Julianna sing with earphones in her ears to the sounds of some country music song "Here for the Party." She could hardly carry a tune, but I loved hearing her sing anyway. It was quite maddening, but cute.

I lifted up one of my pillows smelling her scent that was already familiar to me. I loved the way she smelled. I liked the fact that there were reminders of hers, strewn in and around my space. I liked running across little things of hers, hair ties, her toothbrush, her jewelry——things reminding me of her presence.

I threw on a fresh faded t-shirt and some jeans, resting my laptop on my thighs, my bare feet tapping one foot against the other to the beat of Julianna's shrilled singing.

My moment of solitude was disrupted by Julianna's phone ringing on my nightstand. A nutty sounding ringtone with some wild and crazy guy's voice rang out saying "Don't answer that phone" as Oliver Bank's name scrolled across the screen.

What was Oliver doing still calling Julianna? I stared at her phone deciding whether to invade her privacy and answer it, compelled to tell him to go screw himself. I suppose he didn't get the message from our meet-and-greet at Sequoia's that she had a new man. He was probably using the whole Thanksgiving holiday occasion as his excuse to call. He was married. He needed to move on fast.

But before I could act, a dialogue box on Facetime popped up on my laptop. It was from *@Geekdomcom*. Ahh little . . . Mario. My own private online vigilante. I clicked the answer button, my mind still preoccupied with thoughts of Oliver calling Julianna.

Mario was looking a lot more sober than when I saw him last. Only today he had a red and green streak running through the top of his spiked blonde hair. I rolled my eyes up in my head. Today's youth. What could I say? I hadn't heard from him since the Halloween party. Maybe he was forwarding Dexter's cocaine pics for me to store in my Dropbox.

"Hey Dr. EZ Gobble gobble dude."

"Hey Mario, Happy Turkey Day to you too. How goes it?"

"Not so bad. School's out for a minute. So I'm riding in your lane for a beat to keep the boredom down."

Oh this was going to be interesting. Mario being bored meant he and his tech head friends typically entertained themselves by hacking into other folks' computers. Hopefully that did not mean mine.

"Yeah and how might I be keeping your life exciting?" I said.

"Attaching some pics of your body double's snow moments for your files."

"Thanks, I was on the lookout for those."

I opened my Gmail account to look for the attachment of pics. No surprises there. Dexter's cocaine pile sat on the table in the back office of Luigi's on Halloween. I really didn't want to go down memory lane with Mario if I didn't have to frankly. But I was grateful to have the pictures of Dexter's cocaine use memorialized in several photographs. I put the part of Kimber snorting it out of my mind.

"Dr. EZ, for the record, your body double's been busy."

"How so," I ask, knowing that Mario likely tripped upon something interesting in his quest for personal entertainment.

That's the downside of giving a geek-head like Mario a specific assignment. Geeks tend not to stay in their lane. Their curiosity knows no bounds. You give them an inch, they take a mile.

"Well it appears your body double is a social media hound. @IllegalPapi likes to tweet with @KimmyKazi if you know what I mean."

I was slow to catch up with Mario as always. But one thing for sure this had something to do with Dexter and Kimber when I heard him use the words body double and Kimmy in the same sentence.

"Yeah . . . and . . . " I mumbled, glancing up hearing Julianna singing and splashing around in the tub still.

"Well they're Facebook friends with @OllieGator, head honcho at Gators."

"Yeah, who's Olliegator," I said, still not connecting the dots.

"Oliver Theodore Banks, bitch," he snapped. "What the fuck?" he said, looking at me like I had idiot written across my forehead. "Gators bitch, *the head geek in charge* man."

Then it hit me. Oliver Banks, CEO of Gators, *the* Oliver Banks. Julianna's heartbreaker. The man who rang her phone two minutes ago.

"Oh my God. Oliver Banks?" I repeated.

"Knock knock bitch, you home bro?" Mario squealed.

"Yeah Mario, the lights are on now."

My faculties automatically went on high alert. What does Oliver Banks have to do with anything related to Dexter and me?

"Well I took some liberties on your behalf. Hope you don't mind. But it seems @OllieGator wants to drop some large bank with @IllegalPapi in exchange for arranging some meet and greet to talk to some shorty called Jules."

Oh fuck. Oliver is paying money, donation money to talk to *MY* Julianna? In private, as in without me around? Oh hell no.

I looked up across my bedroom to make sure Julianna hadn't come out of the tub. My paranoia was outside of its box. I didn't want Julianna to catch me having this chat about her ex, especially since I had no idea that Oliver even knew Dexter. I pondered whether I needed to minimize the dialogue on my laptop box so she couldn't see who I was chatting with, but I *had* to continue this chat. I needed to know more about Oliver paying money to talk to Julianna and why he was so hard pressed to talk to her. He was married after all. Why hadn't he moved on?

"What about the Shorty?" I spoke in a hushed tone to Mario, pretending like I didn't know Julianna.

"Like I said, He's making plans with @illegalpapi to arrange a private moment with Shorty. He's offering to drop 10K for a private session. Thirty minutes of her time, EZ. Calling it a donation to some hospital fundraiser."

"Are you sure?" I asked, my mind still in a state of disbelief.

"I feel ya, dog. That's over three hundred big ones a minute. He must have sumthin' real special to say to that boo at those prices."

"What the fuck," I said out loud, squirming in the bed, my body filling with tension as I stared at Mario's face on my laptop, and scratching the top of my head. Mario pushed a big wad of Bazooka bubblegum in his mouth and started to chew. I had no idea why Oliver would need to pay to talk to Julianna. The whole thing seemed stupid to me. Mario must have been reading my thoughts based on what he said next.

"Apparently Shorty's been avoiding his calls, and she's got body watchers around her 24/7, on orders by some brother not to let @Olliegator get within fifty feet of her," Mario said.

Thank God for brothers. Nicholas Becker wasn't going to let anybody get close to his little sister for too long. I was surprised he let her stay with me for as long as she had without disruption. Mario popped the piece of bubblegum in his mouth, blowing a large bubble in my face at the screen that popped when he finished his sentence.

Damn. That sleazeball Dexter is accepting ten thousand dollars from Oliver Banks to arrange a private moment with Julianna. I couldn't tell by this conversation whether Dexter knew Julianna and I were seeing each other or not. That would be bad news if he did. Both of these sleazeballs needed to get out of my woman's world. Oliver and Dexter. Oliver was not getting a private moment with *my* woman.

And Dexter definitely was not going to facilitate that meeting. Not if I could help it. Not now. Not never. All I wanted was a peaceful loving relationship with Julianna. I certainly didn't need all of this drama.

I heard a noise, turning, watching as Julianna exited my bathroom, looking semi-wet and edible. She was towel-drying her long dark curly hair with one of my white fluffy towels wrapped around those beautiful breasts and small waist. I sighed out loud wanting nothing more than to devour her some more.

I told Mario I needed to go, pretending in front of Julianna that it was business as usual. I thanked Mario for the information, simultaneously sending him a chat text message to keep me posted should any new information turn up. I typed that I'd be gifting him a game card that he could use on *Gators*. Mario typed back a smiley face with a notation that said "Try Again Dr. EZ."

What was I thinking? Mario likely didn't need a game card to play games. He had the power to hack into any site he wanted in order to play games, but I was hoping that I'd be providing him encouragement to play honestly. I said good-bye, slamming the top of my laptop down with a bang at the same time Julianna stepped out of the bathroom.

"Hey baby," I said, hoping Julianna didn't pick up on the fact that my anxiety level had ratcheted up a notch.

I took a couple of deep breaths so as to slow my heart rate down. Standing there in front of me like the angel that she was, I was compelled to forget that we both needed to get back into our work groove, wanting to pull her into my arms to make love to her all over again. She stared at me with that hungry look in her eyes.

"What?"

"Nothing."

"Tell me," I said, egging that hungry look in her eyes on further.

"I love that smattering of hair on your chest that runs straight down to your naval like a happy trail. It's a huge turn-on," she said, her head cocked to the side, her lips pouty and still swollen while she towel dried her head.

I looked down at myself noticing my old faded gray t-shirt had risen slightly above my low rider jeans. I debated internally whether I was going to rip my t-shirt off my body and take her all over again, but my thoughts were interrupted before I could decide my next move.

*lliot*

*T*he doorbell chimed repeatedly as if someone was desperate to get inside. We both look surprised, neither of us expecting guests.

"Are you expecting company?" Julianna asked softly.

God she was so damn sweet. She was as sweet as those cookies she had made earlier for our turkey dinner dessert.

"Nope," I say honestly, but a bit confused. It's Thanksgiving evening. Most people are home. "Of course it could be somebody from your posse or mine," I smiled, figuring her girls were trying to get her attention on Thanksgiving night.

"Yours perhaps, but not mine," Julianna laughed. "Shall we make a bet," she giggled casually.

"Bet," I said. "Your posse, you spend the night here, my posse, we sleep at your place."

"You're on," she laughed, "but it is time for me to get back to my own home for a change you know."

"Bet, I'll get the door, knowing I'll just love any excuse to keep you around my home for another night."

Julianna grinned a wide grin at me, moving quickly, wiggling her cute little butt into her jeans, grabbing my t-shirt off the chaise lounge. I paused, giving her a moment to put it on, in no rush to open the door. When I did, Craig Meyers and two of Julianna's security people were blocking the doorway, working hard to pin down some flailing caramel-colored arms. I knew those arms. Fuck. Shit. Damn. It was Kimber. She was working hard, attempting to shove her body past Craig and his men. Any fool trying to penetrate Craig and his minions was working against the impossible. Any idiot could see that would be the equivalent of going up against a tank with a Tonka toy. Kimber obviously didn't get the memo because she was flailing about, waving her arms, not taking no for an answer.

"Kimber," I snapped.

"Elliot, who are these people? Tell them to get their dirty paws off me," she shouted, hurling a slew of curses.

"It's okay," I said, wondering what in the hell did Kimber want. Why the hell was she here?

Kimber stepped through the doorway as I ushered her inside. She gave Craig Meyers the once over. His jaw tightened, his eyebrows flinched, and his mulish expression cracked, his normal game-face a tad bit off. I shook my head at him in disgust, but I understood. It was hard for most men not to react to Kimber. She had the kind of assets she knew how to work. Kimber was the kind of beauty that could turn heads of steel. She and everyone else knew it too.

Kimber tossed her head of soft dark goddess curls back over her shoulders, acting like she belonged here and how dare this stranger interfere. She was carrying a container in her hand marked Tuscan Italian Soup from the local deli around the corner. My favorite.

Craig was having a hard time concealing that he too was affected by her beauty. I pursed my lips, shaking my head at him with look of disappointment, signaling to him that he was slightly off his game. But surprisingly, Craig wasn't having it. He slammed her hard against my doorjamb, running his big palm under the inside of her hem up her thigh, under her tiny leather skirt, both her arms plastered over her head with one of his hands, his eyes pinned on hers, daring her to move. In was in that moment when he released her that I knew just how lethal of a woman Kimber could be. On the outside looking in, I realized how I had been manipulated into succumbing to her spell.

Craig flinched as Kimber planted those big brown eyes on him, her breath hitching as she licked her lips slowly with her tongue. Thank God Craig only had Julianna's best interest at heart. He gritted his teeth as he spit out a hiss, exhaling a breath. His head on this thick neck jerked, almost as if he were shaking his thoughts off. I was certain his blood must have been rushing down from the big head to the little head before racing back to the command center. Craig released Kimber's body, and his hand swept down from up under Kimber's thigh convinced that she had no weapon of destruction underneath her pretty skirt. What Craig didn't know was that Kimber was the weapon of destruction. She just hadn't detonated herself on him yet.

He moved himself aside in my foyer before letting her make a full entry into my home. Kimber gave Craig her best 'I'm going to fuck you hard' look, making it clear she was going to completely unhinge every bone in his body for her personal enjoyment. It was the same look that put me under her spell two years ago. But I was no longer spellbound.

True to form, Kimber momentarily toyed with Craig for what must have been her own personal kicks, but he was not her real target for the night. I was. Craig muttered unintelligible words under his breath, while Julianna rolled her eyes at him.

"I came to apologize," Kimber said, pushing past both Craig and me. "I didn't want you to be hurt and alone on Thanksgiving night," she said, licking the glossy lipstick on her lips, pulling out of her jeans pocket a fresh tube of the deep red lip color she always wore called Vixen, refreshing her lipstick again.

Kimber turned to look over her shoulder, giving Craig the once over, her eyes searching his body up and down letting him know that she, not he, was the one in charge. I watched as Craig shifted his weight from one foot to the other moving to step back outside the door. I wondered if the "Dragon" could hold it together under all that pressure.

Jesus, who could believe this nonsense? Kimber acted as if the fact that I'd been hurt had nothing to do with her. It had everything to do with her, and I damn sure preferred aloneness to her company.

Kimber flung her short ranch mink jacket off, tossing it on the barstool, setting the hot soup down on the countertop. She wiped the spilled juice that was dripping from her hand on the backside of her skinny-legged denim jeans. She brushed the front of her black turtle-neck sweater that was pulled down long over her hips off, as if it might have had something on it. And then my eyes fell on her neck, at the same moment that Julianna entered the living area looking puzzled at both Kimber and me.

"But I see you've managed to occupy yourself in my absence," Kimber said looking hard at Julianna, her eyes narrowing, but giving nothing else away.

"You're not absent Kimber. You and I are done. You're no longer relevant to my life remember?" I growled.

Kimber gave Julianna the once over, raising her hand to her own necklace, and clutching it. The same Tiffany Platinum Key necklace that I had purchased for Julianna, and had given to her. Yes. Another key, exactly like Julianna's key to my heart, was dangling around Kimber's neck.

My body clenched in disbelief. No, this fucking wench did not have on *that* necklace.

"I came by to apologize," Kimber cooed. "I brought you your favorite soup, but I had no idea you had company, baby."

Kimber truly looked surprised.

I cringed at the thought of her calling me baby in front of Julianna. There was no need for any terms of endearment to be spoken between us.

"Why would you know that Kimber? We're not friends," I bit out. "We're not anything to each other anymore, remember?"

I gritted my teeth, staring at her like the enemy she was. I wanted to strangle Kimber.

I mentally dusted the cobwebs off in my brain, reminding myself that this was the most important feature about trophy gals. They lived to earn their freaking titles. They don't get to be called trophies for nothing. They got the title because these bitches are always out for the kill——the win. And, they never lose, hence they fully believed that they were indeed the trophies. These women were in a league of all of their own.

"I never intended for you to get beat up by those guys," she said re-directing her attention from me, looking occasionally towards Julianna, who by the way was looking like a panther ready to pounce.

"You expect me to believe that?" I growled louder. "That was every bit a setup. You know it and I know it. You and Dexter."

The last thing I needed was an apology from Kimber. My brain was still stuck on the necklace wrapped around Kimber's neck. It was everything I had not to wrap that pendant around her neck and strangle her. I wondered whose Black Card had she given a workout in order to afford *that* necklace. What man had she ignited next?

How was I ever going to explain this to Julianna? I couldn't. The fact that Kimber was wearing the exact same key pendant I had given Julianna moments earlier that she now wore around her neck, was totally embarrassing.

"I'm not that easy to throw away Elliot," she whined, her voice suddenly high, shrill, and filled with a sense of desperation I hadn't heard before.

Was this one of her command performances? If not, it sure as hell looked like it. One thing Kimber wasn't, was desperate. Intuitively I knew not to trust in this new emotion she was exhibiting. Helpless didn't become Kimber.

"The hell you are," I shouted, losing my sense of control.

"And who might you be?" Kimber said, ignoring me, looking Julianna up and down as if she were the hired help. Kimber pivoted quickly off desperation mode, moving from zero to bitch, now on threat mode.

"Your worst nightmare," Julianna spit out, stepping in between

Kimber and me.

Whoa. Where did that come from? A new side of Julianna was revealing itself in front of me. I liked it. She had no intention of being intimidated by Kimber's skanky behavior. Even though Kimber and Julianna had never been formally introduced, Julianna must have had some sense of who she was, or at least detected a threat when she saw one. Not that Kimber would ever be a threat to Julianna by my standards. I grabbed Julianna's hand, pulling her back behind me. This wasn't her fight.

A knock rang out at my door, interrupting what was fast becoming the start of World War Kimber, distracting me from imminent plans to throw her out on that pretty little ass. Jesus, who could it be now? Somebody better be having a baby. Our wonderful bliss-filled holiday moment was beginning to turn into a freaking nightmare. Kimber always brought out the worst in me. Actually in everybody. I was just the last to know it.

I swung open the door exasperated, yelling "What is it now motherfucker?" mistakenly thinking it was Craig Meyers.

I was sure my face registered shock. Nicholas Becker stood in my doorway. My timing with *Mr. God of all things Julianna* still managed to suck. Everyone close to Nicholas Becker knew he had a fetish of playing God with everyone's life. His family was no exception.

Dressed in an elegant dark navy wool cashmere blend topcoat, a crisp blue shirt, grey tie, navy and green tartan plaid cashmere scarf double wrapped around his neck, black leather gloves clenched in his hand, Nicholas looked ever so menacing from the top of his head to the bottom of his Ferragamo's.

"May I come in Fischer?" Nicholas said in a low voice, his eyes locking in on Julianna's, his gaze unwavering. Julianna was still on panther mode focused on Kimber.

"Please come in . . . please," I repeated.

Here we go. First drama time with Kimber, and now God himself has shown up. Nicholas looked back over his shoulder, nodding, waving his glove filled hand at Craig, closing the door behind him.

I pulled Julianna close to my side, rubbing my hand down the side of her arm to calm her. Hell I needed calming. Nicholas's eyes shot to me like daggers staring at my hands wrapped around Julianna, while Kimber's attention had re-directed to Nicholas, her facial expression filled with heated desire.

"Aren't you going to make introductions Elliot? Where are your manners, love?" Kimber said focusing her attention now on Nicholas, twirling that damn necklace in her hand.

The muscle in Nicholas's jaw clenched as he regarded her.

"Nicholas Becker this is my ex-fiancée Kimber Lawson."

Jesus, that glamazon called Kimber could smell money a mile away. And Nicholas Becker had a shit boatload of it. I swear I heard Julianna hiss under her breath. I could feel the muscles in her arms tensing as I held her close. The tension in the air was so thick you could cut it with a knife.

"Oh yesssss, Jefferson Lawson's daughter," Nicholas said. "How could I forget? Your father works for my wife's father, Senator Clayton Montgomery," Nicholas said, his emerald green eyes revealing a slight flicker of anger passing through them. "Chief of Staff, right?"

Suddenly the headlights turned on in Kimber's empty brain. I saw the expression on her face change as the realization hit her. She was beginning to put two and two together. No way she was going to get on the wrong side of this equation. Pissing off the Senator's son-in-law might suddenly lead to her daddy dearest not having a job. Kimber was a lot of things, but stupid in the face of money she was not.

"Well . . . ah . . . yeah . . . that's right," Kimber stuttered. "I heard Elliot hadn't been feeling well, and I was in the neighborhood, so I decided to drop by with some of his favorite soup."

"Really? How kind of you," he said. "Coincidentally, I too happened to be in the neighborhood. Thought I'd give my lovely sister here a lift home," Nicholas said, his smile not reaching his eyes.

"Yes, Kimber this is Nicholas's sister, Julianna Becker," I bit out. "My girlfriend."

I paused not filling in the silence in the room, hoping my words would slowly sink in for all parties in the room. Kimber, Nicholas . . . Julianna.

Kimber was caught off guard, looking angry enough to send herself into a seizure, her purse dropping to the floor, the contents of which spilling at her feet and mine.

I dropped down to the floor the same time she did to help her pick up the contents of her purse. Vixen lipstick, red lip shaped mirror, money clip, brush, EPT test stick. EPT test stick?

Jesus Christ, Kimber had an early pregnancy test stick in her purse? Kimber snatched her things up, shoving them quickly into her clutch. I suppose at the pace at which she was moving she was hoping no one had else had noticed either. But I for sure noticed. I was in the business of knowing all about those little sticks. I looked at them every day. I had pregnancy stick radar. Those very important little sticks either revealed joy or pain, depending on your point of view.

My eyes honed in on Kimber's like lasers as she looked away from me dismissively as if nothing had happened. I caught a hint of shame flash across her face.

Julianna's body shifted as I rose to my feet the same time as Kimber. Nicholas tore me a look that pierced my soul like a Samurai's sword cutting through silk. I couldn't blame him. If it were my sister, I would have protected her at all costs too under similar circumstances. Appearances were everything. And this scene looked like a hot mess straight out of segment of one of those Real Housewives show that Julianna watched while I was ill. A freshly broken engagement, my old fiancée showing up with drama, my new woman on caretaker mode, me unable to show a clean break, the appearance of which implied that I was putting his little sister at risk for heartbreak. And worst of all, an early pregnancy test stick marked positive.

I wasn't sure if Nicholas or Julianna saw it, but I sure as hell did. This was so fucked up on so many levels. But, I got it. I got where Nicholas was coming from for sure. But I was determined. Determined to make my claim to what was mine. Everybody in the room needed to get with the program as far as I was concerned. Julianna was my everything. I didn't want to lose her, but a pregnancy stick in Kimber's purse was complicating matters beyond my ability to control what was happening in this moment. Good God, I hoped Kimber wasn't here to tell me that *I* was going to be a father.

I focused my attention on Julianna. Her face was as white as a sheet. My gut churned as a wave of fear swept over me. Yes. She had definitely seen that fucking white stick. The angry expression on her face told me everything that she must have been feeling. How fast could she slit throats and chop off balls. The look on her face was so icy, I was certain my hand grabbed the boys to make sure they were still there.

"It seems my wife Harper has handpicked the two hardest working people in New York to chair the hospital's annual black tie fundraiser this year, but even workaholics need a break, isn't that right Julianna?"

"Of course. A break is just what the doctored ordered," Julianna snapped, her chocolate brown eyes still spitting bullets at Kimber, and now me. Nicholas moved towards Julianna pulling his sister close to his side like a cool assassin readying himself to lock and load.

"Silly me, I should have called first," Kimber said. "I didn't realize Elliot had company," she said nonchalantly, grabbing her fur coat, pulling it over her shoulders, slipping it on, wrapping the leather trimmed tie at her waist.

Thank God Kimber was open to leaving. But then it occurred to me so was Julianna. Julianna was moving around my place at warp speed, gathering things, and her own coat as well. She and Nicholas were riding the same vibration, reading each other's mind, albeit no words passing between them. They were moving almost in rhythm with each other. And me, I was somewhat clueless.

Oh Fuck. Was my woman leaving me before I could even talk to her and clear the air? I didn't want her to think I was okay with Kimber being here in my apartment and she not, coupled with the fact that her brother had arrived to extract her from my space as if I was some kind of disease she needed to avoid. Julianna was gathering her work papers, packing her clothes, all while Kimber was moving closer to my side, edging her way into my personal space.

Julianna's phone rang with that familiar ringtone alerting me that douchebag Oliver was ringing her phone yet again. Her face turned red as she hit the top button of her phone, throwing the call into voicemail, then hurriedly stuffing her phone into the pocket of Nicholas's topcoat. I watched, feeling powerless as Julianna stuffed the last few papers of her business documents into her black leather Tumi backpack. She moved over to the wet bar. Kimber was the one standing next to me now.

This scene was getting incredibly awkward. I stepped two steps to the side so as to create some distance between Kimber and me. Fully aware of the appearance of things, this picture looked horrid.

"It's time I get back to my own place," Julianna mumbled, directing her comment to me, but her eyes speaking volumes silently to her brother Nicholas.

"Good-bye Elliot."

"Jules, I . . ."

"Shall we?" Nicholas said, holding my front door open for her, interrupting me, daring me on some level to stop her exit.

Julianna nodded in agreement, stepping out of my home and into the foyer as Craig and his black suited minions awaited for Nicholas to pass in front of them. Julianna's phone starting ringing again with the sucky ringtone again in Nicholas's pocket. Oliver must have been desperate to talk to Julianna. I watched in shock as Nicholas threw Julianna's phone on the ground, crushing it with the back of his heel. Nicholas facial expression looked to be a stone's throw away from wanting to crush me and anyone else that got in his way under his heel.

"Get her a new one," Nicholas barked at Craig.

God that made me so happy. I was on the brink of wanting to tackle Nicholas myself, pull that damn phone of hers out of his pocket and throw it against the wall, smashing it into a thousand pieces. Nicholas had done it for me. Oliver wasn't getting Julianna back. She was *my* woman now. But I sure didn't get the feeling Nicholas saw it that way. He was definitely not behaving like a man that was playing on *my* team.

Nicholas and Julianna exited my home with lightning speed, faster than I could collect my own thoughts. This scene had gotten out of control so fast I wasn't sure which end was up anymore. I glanced at Craig. He'd turned his wrist upright to his lips mouthing "Guardian Angel to the Towers please."

One of the other guards further ahead pressed his hand to his earpiece acknowledging Craig with a "ten-four on Guardian Angel."

Hmpf, Guardian Angel? That was an understatement. Guardian Angel looked more like Death Angel. His unspoken message was clear. If any of you lunatics get near my little sister again, I will bring you down myself.

I had no doubt that Nicholas's paranoia about me had risen multiple degrees up the Richter scale. His people hovered over Julianna as if they were guarding Fort Knox. I sighed loudly in frustration watching as the Becker bodyguard entourage and its charges were gone within a split of a second.

And then it dawned on me. Like Oliver, I too had no way to contact Julianna. Her phone was smashed. I'd have to wait for Julianna to reach out to me or seek her out in person myself.

J turned my attention back to Kimber who was dressed in coat and scarf to leave but hadn't.

"Well it didn't take you long to move on Elliot, letting that woman play nursemaid with you all holiday. I guess you won't be needing my help," Kimber hissed, her mood changing from her original fake show of concern, back to the bitchy woman I had come to know. Yes, indeed. The real Kimber was back.

"That woman is my new girlfriend, Kimber. You'd be wise to remember that unless you expect your Daddy dearest to be out of his lucrative position. If you even give so much as a thought to messing with her, your life will get complicated extremely quick. And seeing how you have expensive taste and all, I doubt you'd be too happy if Daddy's money train dries up on you."

"Are you threatening me Elliot? You'd be wise to remember that you too have problems in your little patch of paradise. For the record, I heard her ringtone too. Someone else is blowing up your girlfriend's phone vying for her attention," Kimber snarled.

I gritted my teeth hating the fact that Kimber had caught on to that too. But I was less concerned about what she thought and more interested in that pregnancy stick that had fallen out of her glittery looking red clutch.

"Us gals tend to know these things," she said rubbing salt in my already open wound. "So you can just fuck that shit dot com, Elliot. I doubt you're going to get your happily ever after like you think you are," she snapped. "Especially since you've managed to rob me of mine."

Lord what was I thinking? Kimber was a lot of things, but she wasn't totally stupid. I couldn't deny that her words didn't have a ring of truth to them. The mere thought that her words could be true made me crazy.

"Well I certainly wouldn't have gotten a happy ever after with you Kimber."

"Like Daddy says, I've got bigger fish to fry Elliot. I only wanted to apologize for your injuries. I wanted to let you know that I can't be with you anymore. You do need to move on. I wouldn't want you to have hope that I'd be coming back to you, because I'm not."

Was this woman completely nuts? Did she not realize that I was the one that broke off our engagement? What in the hell was she saying? Does she call herself breaking up with me? We broke up already. I broke our engagement off. What the fuck is wrong with this lunatic woman? My mouth flew open in disbelief.

"Kimber, I realize you've been playing me for the fool for a long time now with Dexter. Perhaps you've lost control of him—the situation—and want to make amends. I get that. But get this. It's too little too late. Why are you really here anyway?"

"I need your help Elliot. I'm pregnant."

I sensed my face had to have turned completely ash grey in a flash of fear. No doubt Kimber saw the fear in my eyes too. I saw it reflected in the look she was giving me.

"Oh don't worry Elliot. It's not yours. It's Dexter's baby. I haven't told him yet, or anyone for that matter. Only you. I don't want to have his baby or anyone else's baby right now for that matter."

"Well then what's any of this got to do with me? Is that your real reason for being here, screwing up my holiday?"

"I need your help. I want to abort."

"Abort? I don't deal in abortions Kimber. I bring life into the world, not take it out. You should know that about me by now."

Lord, this woman hardly knew who I was. I worked hard every day to help make beautiful bundles of joy arrive in this world safely. While I didn't judge women who had to make that choice, it wasn't something that made up a part of my professional career. She had to know that.

"That's pretty much what I expected to hear from you Elliot. But I know you've got physician friends that can handle this little problem for me. I need a referral that's all."

Man, I was so wrong about this woman. And to think I was planning to make her my wife. Kimber was as cold as they come. She only cared about herself and no one else.

"Have you spoken to Dexter? Don't you think he should have a say in this?"

I didn't like Dexter. But I felt as a man, if it were my baby a woman was considering aborting, I would want to know.

"It is what it is. What he doesn't know won't hurt him. No way I'm strapping myself to him for the rest of my life over some crumb snatcher. Are you going to help me or not Elliot?" she spit out with a fierceness.

I left the room, coming back with a business card that I handed to Kimber. It was a clinic that was run by one of my colleagues that I knew could help Kimber.

"Here. Take this. He's the best in the business," I grumbled. "I think you should consider other options Kimber."

Kimber took the card and put it in her clutch, a look of shame coming across her face. Some part of me felt sorry for her. Even though we both knew our relationship was done, I still didn't want Kimber to feel like she had no other options left other than an abortion. I was struggling trying to behave as a friend, engaging this discussion further at my own risk.

"Kimber I'm sorry you've having to go through this. Really I am."

"Well, if you had been better to me in our relationship Elliot, I suppose none of this would have ever happened."

What the fuck. Kimber did not just blame me for getting pregnant by Dexter. She truly was a piece of work. My blood was starting to boil all over again. She twirled her finger nervously around that fucking necklace again.

"What the hell are you doing with *that* necklace on?"

"Oh this little thing? You always did have good taste Elliot. I saw the one you bought for your little playmate. I liked it. Decided I needed one of my own, that's all."

I looked at Kimber as if she had two heads. She had stolen Julianna's necklace from me a week ago. Now she was wearing one exactly like it. How did I miss the fact all these years that Kimber suffered from some kind of neurotic narcissistic psychosis?

"What? You think you're the only man in New York to buy a woman nice things, Elliot?"

Kimber was like a rabid dog. She would turn on me quick, ungrateful for whatever goodness or olive branch I would extend. She was selfish. It was always about what she wanted, what she needed. Never about anyone else.

"You truly are a piece of work," I said, shaking my head in disgust.

For a moment I was really feeling sorry for her. I didn't want to be her husband, but I did want the best for her. I wanted her to find happiness. Just as long as it wasn't with me.

"And you're a certifiable asshole that doesn't know how to sustain a relationship with a beautiful woman like me."

Kimber tossed her black locks over the side of her shoulder, her breasts pushed out as if she were proud of herself. Today was a win-

win for her. She had peeped my sense of insecurity around who was calling Julianna, provoked my outrage over Julianna's necklace, and drove me off the cliff emotionally over the possibility of a pregnancy. She knew me better than I gave her credit. She had succeeded in pushing me over the edge with all her twisted schemes stirring the pot, in the name of a faux apology, while intentionally creating disharmony between Julianna and me. She had fully manipulated me.

I grabbed her by her elbow and started dragging her to the door. She jerked her arm out of my clutch, moving towards the door on her own steam.

"Is that the story you're going to write Kimber, because if so, this is the part where you get the hell out of my home and don't let the door hit you in your ass on the way out," I hissed.

Kimber opened the door, stepped outside into the hallway, turned around and blew me a kiss.

"You know Elliot, I do try hard to be friends with you, but you make it near too impossible. You don't know how to please a woman like me. I get it."

"With friends like you Kimber, who needs enemies?"

"Thanks for the referral. Good-bye Dickhead," Kimber said, as she passed through my doorway.

I walked to the door and slammed it behind her, still wondering what tornado had blown through my home within the last hour, shattering everything I held precious to pieces. The stress of the last hour was getting to me. My ribs were starting to hurt again.

I needed to get back to work. Back to what I loved. Back to the babies. And more importantly, back to Julianna.

I walked over to my wet bar to pour myself a scotch, downing three fingers in one big gulp. My eyes locked on the glimmer of sparkle twinkling on top of my wet bar. I needed another scotch to quell the pain that was shooting through my heart. The only visible evidence left of Julianna lay before my eyes.

Julianna's key to my heart, lying on top of my bar. The pit of my stomach felt gutted. My heart was shredded. The moment felt as if someone had stabbed me to my core.

ulianna

icholas and I rode back to Becker Towers in silence. I couldn't decide who was seething the most, him or me? Every time I thought about Kimber appearing, wearing the exact same necklace that Elliot had given me, coupled with a used early pregnancy test stick falling out of her clutch, it made me want to kill somebody. But who, I was unsure. Elliot? Kimber? Both?

It was hard not to deny that skanky Kimber wanted Elliot back, but worse she was trying to make a play for my brother. She didn't know Nicholas was totally dedicated, madly in love with his wife, not that a woman like her even cared. Other women don't know that vying for his attention was a waste of time. Nicholas had given up his well-known playboy ways the day he married Harper. The only other woman that held his attention beyond his wife was his business partner, and that was business.

I had no doubts that this evening's whole scene had pissed my brother off. He looked like I felt. In a fucking foul mood. The fact that Kimber still wanted Elliot all while making a play for my brother had me pretty much seeing red too. And to think Elliot announced to my brother that I was his "girlfriend." He could have at least said it to me in private first. You know, discuss the meaning of it. I had a say in this too. Exclusivity was a big milestone in any relationship. But one thing that was certain, Kimber having Elliot's baby was going to be the end of me as "girlfriend," or anything else for that matter.

And Oliver, he freaking wouldn't leave me alone. There was some truth to the fact that "the never go away" Oliver Theodore Banks was the perfect example of wanting to have his cake and eat it too. He was ringing my phone multiple times a day trying to keep his options open. Why wouldn't he leave me be?

I thought my life was starting to make sense. Instead it was getting more complicated than ever. I was glad Nicholas reminded me to get back to what was important, —my business. I suppose that was why he showed up at Elliot's. *Sugar Mommy* needed my undivided attention.

I stared out the window silently, taking a deep breath trying to make sense of that scene at Elliot's. Surely, Kimber was there to tell him he was going to be a daddy. I could see it now. New York's own renowned Baby Doctor is the next Baby Daddy with Baby Mama Drama spread out on Page Six. I needed to steer clear of them both so as not to get caught up in the fallout. Association would hurt my business.

And that explains my brother's untimely appearance. Nicholas was one step ahead of the game as always. Protecting me. Protecting his family. He was nobody's idiot. He was the imperial Chessmaster, always three steps ahead of everyone else in the game of life. *Thank God for my brother.*

And to think Kimber had on the same fucking necklace he'd given me, twirling it in my face like I was her sloppy seconds. The mere thought that Elliot hadn't thought to give me something uniquely different from her was disturbing. Perhaps every woman in New York had a key to Elliot's heart. I felt like the fool once again. First Oliver, now Elliot. I was being played again like a fiddle. Except this time, it was at the hands of the infamous Dr. EZ.

My brother shifted in his seat, sighing loudly. He knew I was upset, fuming in silence. Nicholas was my confidant, my protector since the day I was born so I was going to wait for him to speak first. It was the unspoken code that we both abided by since we were kids whenever we faced difficult situations. Nicholas always went first.

"You love him?"

"Yes. No. I don't know. I'm confused. That whole scene . . . "

I shook my head in disgust. More mad at myself than anything. Embarrassed. That last place I wanted to be was to get played by yet another man. I allowed myself to be vulnerable. The price of vulnerability was that I was getting my heart cracked in half again. I was pitiful.

I was still reeling from the loss of Oliver, trying to heal, and now this. I could feel the tears welling up behind my eyes, despite my best efforts to hold it together. I pulled the collar of my jacket closer together, not wanting to look down at myself still wearing his gray "Got Baby" t-shirt.

"Harper says he's a good man," Nicholas said, turning towards me, grabbing my hand in his and handing me his well pressed white and blue monogrammed handkerchief.

"And what do you say?"

"I say very few men are good enough for my sister. Fischer has good qualities. It's hard to hate the man who's responsible for bringing Miles and Milania into the world under such difficult circumstances."

"He lives for the babies," I mumbled.

"That makes him a good doctor, not necessarily a good boyfriend."

"He'll want his own babies one day," I said, thinking about the fact that my own mother died in childbirth getting me here.

Newborn babies scared me. I panicked around them. I was ill equipped. And, now I'd gone off and done the worst thing possible. I'd fallen in love with New York's most sought out available renowned baby catcher.

"And he'll see to it that they arrive safely, I'm sure," Nicholas said, not giving anything away. "I cannot deny I have him to thank for the twins. He would do no less for his own, I'm sure."

I couldn't have this conversation. I didn't want to talk about babies anymore.

"Why didn't you tell me he was arrested? That Harper helped secure his release?"

"I feel differently about Elliot and that rogue of yahoos he calls his friends. My wife and Elliot bonded during her pregnancy through a medical emergency to get the twins here. I try to respect their relationship for her sake. No need to win the battle and lose the war with my wife."

I nodded in silent agreement.

"But if Elliot can't protect himself, he sure as hell can't protect you. The mere thought of you being harmed in any way gives me grief."

My brother was a hyper vigilant overprotective taskmaster when it came to his family. If it were up to him, I'd remain inside the golden cage forever, never to be set free to fly, all under the guise that I needed protecting.

"If I let anything happen to you, you know as well as I do, I would never forgive myself. Not to mention Big Daddy would rake me over the coals personally."

"You and Big Daddy both suffer from the same disease called 'Daddy's little girl syndrome'," I huffed. "I'm not a little girl anymore."

"We both love you. When you have kids of your own you'll be better equipped to understand."

"Yeah, well remind me to make a note in my journal to be sure to give my niece Milania a personal lesson when she grows up in how to evade you over-possessive Becker men."

"It's not so bad Cookie. Accept the fact. You were born into a very high profile family, that's all. It comes with certain obligations."

A pregnant pause passed between us. Nicky was giving me a moment to process his words. It was hard to argue with him. I couldn't discount that our family hadn't been under the threat of harm in past years. His concerns were real. Hardly imagined. But that didn't mean I liked having to live inside the golden cage. And then there was the fact of my possibly having kids. Kids of my own. Could I get through all that would come with having kids of my own? Surely. Deep down, I knew if I were carrying the baby of the man that I loved, that loved me back fully, anything was possible.

My thoughts drifted back to Elliot again. Nicky must have been reading my thoughts. After a few minutes, he spoke.

"You know this relationship you're developing with Elliot, it's not what I think that's important Cookie. I only want for your happiness dear. I only want you to be careful. I don't want to see you hurting again that's all."

"This was such a great week turned nightmare. We were bonding so well. I was happier than I had been in a long time. But then things got out of control so fast. I don't know Nicky. What do you think I should do now?"

My brother paused as if contemplating his words carefully.

"He struck me as a man that was done with his past—Kimber, I mean."

"You think?" I asked with genuine interest.

"I'm a man. I can say that. I know these things," he said with a confidence that suggested that I take his words as the gospel.

I nodded, gathering my courage to embrace the elephant in the limo.

"You obviously didn't see that pregnancy stick that flew out of her purse."

"I don't miss much Cookie. But take it from me based on personal experience; sometimes things are not what they appear. These matters can't be sorted out in the heat of emotion, try as we may."

Wow that was strange. Not what I expected Nicky to admit out loud, but I knew he was drawing on his own personal experiences.

"What do you suggest I do?" I repeated.

"Stick to the plan. Focus on getting through the launch of *Sugar Mommy,* and the hospital fundraiser. Matters of the heart will sort themselves out over time. Trust me."

I reached over, wrapping my arms around my brother's neck just as Silas pulled up to the curb of Becker Towers. Nicky kissed me on the cheek. He wiped the tear off my cheek with his thumb. He didn't do tears well. And I needed not to cry in front of him, lest I triggered that God complex in him to start personally fixing my life for me.

I needed to suck it up. This was my own fault. I had no one to blame but myself, opening myself up so fast to love again. Why did I have to always be the one in the relationship to fall in love with the man first, before he fell in love with me. I wanted to kick my own butt for my continued repeat performance on love's stage.

Nicky must have thought I was rebounding but wasn't going to say it. But I wasn't rebounding. I truly loved Elliot. Just like I loved every other man that I had loved that hadn't loved me back. But this felt different. This time I had really believed Elliot loved me back. Was I wrong yet again?

Nicky's phone began buzzing like crazy. Someone was blowing up his phone. He sighed out loud glancing at his text messages. A look of annoyance flashed across his face.

"It's that gang of yours," he sighed. Maya and Logan. "I suppose they think I'm your messenger now or something," he said indignantly.

"You smashed my phone, so you have to pay the price," I said, feigning indifference. Secretly, I was overjoyed that Maya and Logan were on the lookout for me. When a man gets finished cracking your heart, you will always have your girls. And my girls were like blood-hounds. They could smell asshole heartcrackers a mile away.

I grabbed Nicky's phone out of his hand before he could resist, texting Maya and Logan that they needed to hurry to Becker Towers A.S.A.P. I needed emotional support and a game plan to deal with this nightmare called my love life.

Silas opened the limo doors shortly after we pulled to a stop. Nicholas got out first, grabbing my hand, pulling me out. A blast of cold arctic air hit me in the face. It was freezing, much like my heart was starting to feel towards Elliot.

Craig pulled up to the curb behind us. He moved quickly to get out of the black suburban, blowing his hot breath on his hands to warm them. He reached in his coat pocket and handed Nicholas a new phone, stomping the ground to get the cold out of his feet. I wanted them to hurry. It was far too cold for me. I could hardly feel my fingers and I knew that phone was for me.

I rolled my eyes to the top of my head at Craig. On a different day I would have been pleased. But I already knew this phone was fully equipped with the latest greatest GPS locators allowing my brother to find me anywhere in the northern hemisphere. No, actually anywhere in the world.

"Here Cookie. You can play with "hot" and "bothered" on this new one. I'll take mine back now," he said grabbing his phone out of my hands, pushing a brand new iPhone into mine, my fingers feeling numb from the cold.

I knew he was joking on Logan and Maya.

"Must I?" I pouted.

"You can't hide from the real world forever, Cookie."

"What you really mean is, I can't hide from you," I bitched.

"Cookie, it's time to get back in the game. Get your piece of the Big Apple," he pleaded.

"Why should I, you already own the Apple."

"As do you," he laughed, tugging me into his side, kissing me in the cold on the top of my forehead.

Besides being cold and numb, I started mentally kicking myself again, thinking if only I hadn't blindly jumped in Elliot's cab, I'd be sparing myself a splattered heart right about now.

My new phone rang. I slid my finger across the screen to the unlock position. It was Maya and Logan on three-way. I walked inside the double doors of Becker Towers as the doorman Rick held the doors open for me. Nicky and Craig followed. The warmth inside the lobby felt good.

"Good evening Mr. Becker. Welcome home Ms. Jules," Rick said, tipping his hat.

"Rick," Nicholas said, acknowledging him with a nod.

I nodded with my new phone up to my ear, still connecting my three-way call with Maya and Logan not realizing the speakerphone was still engaged. Nicholas, Craig, and I stepped onto the open elevator doors while Craig put the codes in for the 75th floor, mine, and then for the Penthouse, Nicky's floor.

"Jules, Logan and I are headed over there pronto. We'll bring the tequila. We want the entire scoop. Was it a good cock ride or what honey?" Logan laughed.

"Yeah Jules. We want details," Maya chipped up.

I immediately took Logan off the speakerphone as the elevator rose to my floor. Craig coughed out loud. I suppose he needed to suppress the snicker he looked to be holding in that beautiful rock solid jaw of his. Nicky was turning beet red. Too much information for my brother.

"Yeah, it was indeed a ride all right," I replied haughtily in the earpiece. "Can't talk. Got the peanut gallery nearby," I hinted. I was going to have to shore myself up some more to get this story out without tears in front of Maya and Logan.

"I swear somebody needs to take Logan off the market fast before she sets all of Manhattan on fire," my brother bristled. "She reminds me of my Harper back in the early days. She simply refuses to color inside the lines, that one. And Maya, always managing to leave a bunch of male wannabes in her wake," he continued.

Nicholas turned his head towards Craig, soliciting agreement.

"Pretty Does is a whole helluva lot of beautiful woman sir," Craig said, making a muscular groan, drawing in a deep breath but not revealing any cracks in his armor.

I glanced up to the top of the elevator ceiling, begging for this elevator ride to end.

"Well it's time for the entire three ring circus act to grow up and settle down," Nicky said, popping his black leather gloves in the palm of his hand.

Thank God the elevator stopped on my floor because I could feel my brother winding up again about Logan, Maya, and I needing to settle down and get married. All of it being totally ironic especially coming from him. It wasn't that long ago when Big Daddy rode my brother's ass hard about his need to get married, insisting that he knock off his playboy ways. Nicky was resistant to the idea, living his life on his yacht with playboy bunnies, supermodels, and every glamazon flavor of the month from here to Switzerland. If he couldn't have Harper, he didn't want anyone. Now I got a glimpse into what that feeling must have felt like. Now I could relate. Just like he didn't want any woman, I didn't want any man. I wanted Elliot.

"I'll be up to see Harper and the twins tomorrow Nicky. Bye Craig. Maya sends you her best," I winked, my phone still up to my ear.

I could see Craig flinch, caught off guard, right as I jumped off the elevator at the same time the elevator doors were beginning to close.

"Craig's not going anywhere," my brother spat out. "He's coming with you. I'm sending him back down." The elevator doors closed.

Well I guess that was settled. I felt like I had taken one step forward and two steps backwards. Love and freedom had flown the coop at the exact same time. I'd be back under guard real soon. At least Maya would be happy. Another chance for her to melt into the arms of that chocolate kiss of man called Craig.

---

*D*espite the fact I was melancholy and feeling like I had been on an emotional rollercoaster filled with highs and lows over the last week, it felt good to be home back in my own space. At least here in my own home I could fall apart into a thousand pieces without having to explain myself to anyone. Logan and Maya would understand. They would be there for me. I could count on my girlfriends not to betray my heart.

I glanced down at my new phone, unpacking my laptop from my backpack, setting it on my cream granite kitchen countertop. I needed to dock my new phone to download my personal and business contacts from the Cloud. I could feel my eyes beginning to swim in tears again. I had no doubt, the next few weeks were going to be rough. I already knew what was coming next because I had been at this emotional place once too often. When was I ever going to learn?

I turned the phone around in my hand giving it a once over. This one was white and gold. Not bad I suppose. I was thankful Craig hadn't placed it in some hideous survivor case that would conceal the beauty of the phone's design. But that could be a bad thing, now that I was living on the edge ready to pitch it and everything else at somebody's head. My brother shared my distaste for concealing the beauty of a phone's design with some ugly case that was a snub to whoever must have put in godless hours to perfect its beauty.

Tears began to fall slowly down my cheeks despite my massive efforts to hold them back. I watched in silence as the blue dialogue bar moved slowly across my laptop screen making the transfer of my contacts. Somewhere deep in my heart I came to grips with the fact that it was going to be a struggle to get my groove back post Elliot.

Memories of lying in Elliot's arms tortured my every thought, bringing with it a pang of grief that gripped my heart. Inhaling a deep breath, I headed to my kitchen, opening the French doors of my sub-zero fridge and pulled a bottle of chilled Chardonnay out of the wine bin. I grabbed a bottle with a screw top, not wanting to aggravate myself a moment longer to deal with a corkscrew. I pulled a wine glass down from the overhead wine rack hanging from the kitchen ceiling. I poured an ounce in the glass, swirling it to aerate it, taking in the wine's nose, before sipping. Apples, pear, and oak infiltrated my nostrils as I pondered alone my unfolding predicament to come in the next few days. My predicament? How to get through my days and nights after those beautiful gray eyes?

I could still visualize the tortured expression on Elliot's face as I had gathered my things abruptly to get out of his space. The mere thought of it gripped my heart like a vise. I had barely let out a goodbye before scampering out his door.

I took a huge sip of wine to quell my nerves. I wanted to numb the pain in my chest. What was Elliot doing? Was he making up with Kimber? Had he managed to keep his hands in Kimber's little cookie jar all along, getting her pregnant, even while making a play for me? God, the mere thought of me being played like the fool was tearing me up in pieces.

Way to go Julianna. If you keep thinking about those two, you're going to open the floodgate of tears again, and that won't serve you. Do something with yourself. Try to keep this flood of emotions in check. Bake some cookies or something. It's good for your soul. It's good for your business. You didn't get the nickname "Cookie" for nothing. Go test drive some new recipes for Sugar Mommy's or you'll fall into the depths of depression. You've got to fight this. All hope is not gone. Falling into the abyss won't serve you or your new brand. You're going to build an empire, remember. Stay focused.

I gulped another large swig of the Chardonnay, topped my glass again, and headed towards my office down the long hall in my home. I threw myself into my large oversized almond colored leather chair where I often spent ungodly hours creating my new recipes.

Tears pooled in my eyes as I try to fight the feelings of loss. I powered up my MacBook, opening up the digital files in Dropbox where I kept my favorite pastry recipes in the Cloud. I thumbed through the digital files with no real mission. Suddenly, I had an epiphany.

Wow. I had enough recipes here to create a *Sugar Mommy* Cookbook. Perhaps a cookbook for kids would be nice. I could let Miles and Milania test sample my recipes. I made myself a note, forcing myself to think about anything as a distraction from my mind slipping back into all thoughts of Elliot. I blinked back my own tears as I continue to scour my catalog of recipes, my soul feeling that familiar emotion of having been beaten down once again.

I needed to bake. The routine motions of baking with soothe my soul. Baking would distract me from my own thoughts, not that I felt like eating. There it was. My mint brownie recipe. Mint brownies were going to be my recipe of choice tonight. Maybe I'd even spike the first batch with some crème de menthe. Sorry kiddies, *Sugar Mommy's* not really feeling kid friendly recipes tonight. My heart was hurting so I needed to go all out hard.

I grabbed a tissue, blew my nose, and wiped my eyes. I twirled around in my chair, staring upwards and looking at the blank ceiling, feeling numb like a rock. I needed to endure this heartache. Would I see Elliot again soon? How would I feel? I was determined not to fall into my old patterns after a broken heart. Wake, eat, sleep, cry, drink, bed, rinse and repeat. No, this time I was going to be stronger, tougher, impenetrable, and formidable. I wasn't going to let the men that come into my life drive me crazy.

I forced myself to get up. I tracked back towards my kitchen, preheating my Viking stove, pulling down mixing bowls, flour, chocolate bits, and pouring more wine to soothe me while I baked. I turned the music on my Bose player that was piped throughout my entire home with my favorite playlist: Toni Braxton's "He Wasn't Man Enough For Me." That was my 'Oliver' mantra, but it might as well be my mantra for Elliot at this point. Better yet my M.A.N. mantra. They all sucked as far as I was concerned.

I poured myself another glass of wine, just as my door buzzer started chiming wildly.

"Let us in bitch, it's beyond cold out here," Logan commanded.

Maya and Logan. Yessssssss. My reinforcements had arrived.

19

J ulianna

J kicked off my shoes, paddling barefoot to the door, opening it quickly, totally not expecting Logan to be in what used to be my pink sheer nightie coupled with a floor length white mink coat, blond locks flowing down her breasts. She had diamond bracelet cuffs on both wrists.

Maya, on the other hand, was dressed in black skinny-legged leather pants cropped above the ankle with a white Rolling Stone midriff shirt, the one with the red tongue hanging down. She had on a dyed-to-match black long-haired fox fur jacket, with a matching black hat on her head that had the word SWAG written on it in gold. She totally looked like this month's best dressed rocker chick. Hot fuchsia lipstick adorned her perfect lips. Maya was slinging the Cuervo bottle in one hand, with one slender arm crooked around Craig's neck.

Ahhh. Craig was back.

Maya was giggling like the cat that had swallowed the mouse. I didn't doubt for one minute that Nicky had sent Craig back in my direction to hang outside my door tonight for my safekeeping. Maybe he thought I was a bit too despondent and would hurt myself. Seemed to be such a waste of time, considering he could have just watched out for me on Parks and Park's monitors upstairs. But Craig's interest in Maya probably had everything to do with the fact that the "chocolate kiss" was standing outside my door tonight as opposed to catering to my emotional state of well-being.

I took one look at those two wrapped around each other. Yup, Maya was the Cat. And, Craig was definitely the Mouse. I gave Craig a look that seriously questioned my concerns about who here was in control. Him or Maya? No one could have convinced me otherwise that Maya had Craig wrapped around her little finger. The question on the floor was, whether that was the case the other way around?

I grinned from ear to ear looking at both my friends, my own wine glass in hand. And then I without a warning, I busted out loud in tears.

"Oh good Lord," Logan yelped. "Whatever did that man do to you baby?"

"Yeah Jules, what the hell? You're blowing my buzz," Maya said, letting go of Craig, directing all of her attention to me.

Logan pushed her way inside, ignoring Maya and Craig. Logan's stilettos clacked on my marble floor. The moment took on a tone of seriousness with my gals focused only on me. Craig grunted under his breath from Maya re-directing her attention to me. Maya whispered something in Craig's ear. Craig stepped backwards outside the door again.

"I'll be right outside," Craig mumbled, his face turning tense. His guard dog game face was back in place as he closed the door.

"Shot glasses," Logan spat out. "Let's hear it Jules. Spill the beans."

"I smell cookies," Maya said.

"Brownies," I mumbled through my tears, a bit ashamed of my outburst. But, oh well, it was my girls, and it was okay to let them in on the fact that I was upset. That's what besties do. They hold you down when the men treat you like crap.

"Don't burn them this time Jules," Maya insisted. "I don't want to fight all night with ComputerLuv."

Logan shuddered at Maya, ignoring her demand.

"Try to be nice Maya," Logan ordered. "Can't you see Jules is hurting?"

Maya let Logan put her on guilty mode for her harmless outburst. She put her arms around me, giving me a big hug so as to console me in my grief.

I proceeded for the next thirty minutes to fill Logan and Maya in on all that had happened over the last several days in between mint brownies and tequila shots. I shared with them my days and nights with Elliot and how wonderful things were progressing with us—up until the time Kimber and Nicky showed up. Then all hell broke loose and not in a good way.

"You couldn't have known things were going to end up this way Jules," Maya said, trying her best to comfort me though my tears as I finished bringing them up to date on the whole week's saga.

"Maybe I shouldn't have put my heart out there on the line so quickly," I sighed. "I thought I wanted a placeholder. I didn't realize I'd actually develop feelings so fast."

"You just need a plan now Jules. We always have plan when a man strings us along leaving us lost in the sauce," Maya said thoughtfully.

The three of made our way to my living area, sitting on the floor with oversized pillows behind our backs. It was like old times back in Europe when we had our own private pajama parties in Logan's loft. How I missed those days where the sting of a broken heart from a fleeting fling didn't seem to hurt quite as hard.

Perhaps time and age had softened my heart. Now when a bona-fide heartcracker slipped through the ranks, I definitely felt it in a major way. I would not miss the lesson the next time around, though.

I threw back a tequila shot, waiting for who was going to speak first with the grand plan on how to untangle my mess otherwise known as Elliot.

"I think we should grab our Can-Am Spyders with our matching helmets and go dirt biking in the Dirty South. Let off some steam,"

Logan said. "Dirty and cute. Miley Cyrus got nothing on us, girl-friends."

"We did that last holiday remember," Maya said. "God knows how much I love those South Carolina southern gentlemen, but this time we need to go big or go home," she pondered, pouring each of us another tequila shot.

"Okay, then we take the Can-Am Spyders to the A.T.L. Hot—would be a nice distraction right about now," Logan replied, not giving up on her idea so easily.

"We could hijack Nicky's Challenger 300 and head for the UK," I said, thinking we could take the fastest jet in my brother's fleet and make for London.

Nobody wanted to be gone more than me. Leaving town sounded like a good idea.

"We could buy next year's Jimmy Choo's. You know, have a real European soiree. Spend the holiday in London."

"Borrrrrring," Maya and Logan said at the same time.

"No, Jules. We need a man plan. If you and Elliot are seriously meant to be together, the last thing you need to be is out of sight out of mind," Logan said.

"I would have to agree with that Jules," Maya said co-signing everything that came out of Logan's mouth like it was gospel, pouring herself another shot. "We have to stick around to protect your interests."

"Did you forget he could be having a baby? What the hell is wrong with you two?"

"I'm really not feeling this baby business Jules," Logan said.

"Why the hell not? Do you know something I don't know?"

"Inside track roadie."

"What inside track?" Maya asked.

"If it doesn't come out of Gabriel's mouth, it's not necessarily so," Logan said, as if she was now the authority of all things Elliot and Gabriel. "And I know everything that comes out of Gabriel's luscious mouth," she said wide-eyed, grinning hugely.

Maya shook her head in disgust, rolling her eyes up in her head at

Logan. I laughed at Logan's unadulterated confidence that came with all things Gabriel—or any man actually.

Logan and Gabriel had managed to stay in touch with each other every since they met. They were definitely building on something. Too many phone calls and text messages passing between them for it to be otherwise. Logan hadn't owned it yet that there was something happening between her and Gabriel.

"If Kimber was having Elliot's baby, Gabriel would be beside himself. He hates that woman for his friend almost as much as we do. I really don't think that's what's going down here. Call it women's intuition," Logan surmised.

"Okay, so the plan is we stick around for the rest of the holiday?" Maya said. "And do what?"

"I've got the perfect plan ladies," Logan said with a wicked look of devilment in her eyes.

"Yeah what?" Maya said.

"Yeah tell us," Logan.

"Well this calls for some serious 'pull out all the stops' action, gals."

Maya and I studied Logan. We knew that look. Logan said nutty things that routinely scrambled my and Maya's brains, but for a moment we both felt she might be on to something this time.

Logan reached in her little pink clutch and pulled out a blunt.

"Time to fire up and get serious ladies. We need a plan," Logan giggled. She pulled out her pink Hello Kitty lighter and fired up the blunt. She took a huge pull on it, passing it to Maya who then passed it on to me. I took a pull, dragging hard. I handed it back to Logan, who was letting a stream of smoke flow out of her mouth. I moved quickly across the room to crack the patio doors leading to my balcony so as to let the fumes escape. A cold blast of brisk wind hit my body. But instead of feeling the cold chill, I instantaneously felt the warm glow course throughout my body. My throat burned in a good way. Damn, I love New York.

"You know I love your view of New York," Maya said, red-eyed, her head tipped back on the big pillow as she blew smoke rings in the air. She passed the joint Logan's direction.

"Okay ladies, I think we're acting out now, right?" Logan slurred.

"Hell yeah," I said. "Acting out does have its enjoyable moments," I laughed, full of the giggles now. "This might just be my best performance, bitches," I said, dragging on the blunt and taking another deep pull.

"Yeah girl, now tell me again what was the problem we were trying to solve? I forgot," Maya said, sounding tongue-tied.

Logan and I looked at each other like Maya was crazy and both fell out laughing, tumbling to the side all over each other.

"We were coming up with a plan on how to forget a man, remember?"

"Oh yeah," Maya laughed. "Just as long as it isn't that hunk of beefy chocolate outside your door Jules."

"Jesus Maya, get a grip. "We're solving Jules' problem tonight," she said, putting the blunt on a roach clip, wobbling to the side as she passed it to Maya.

What the hell. I wanted to forget. I wanted to forget Elliot, wanted to forget Oliver, wanted to forget love. I just fucking wanted to forget it all.

"I think I'm really fucked up," I slurred with a laugh.

"What the fuck was in that joint Logan?"

"Hell if I know," somebody said. "Hawaiian."

"Don't ya'll start acting like lightweights on me," Maya said.

"You should talk Maya. You're so high you forgot we were on a mission," Logan giggled, while starting to choke on residual smoke that still hung in her lungs.

It had been a long time since I had gotten high. I sipped a huge gulp of my drink, spilling tequila on my coffee table. I ached for Elliot. I didn't want to think about him. I didn't want to cry again. But I missed him already.

"Yeah Logan, what is in this joint? Maya is sounding like he has lost her ability to communicate," I giggled.

Maya took another hit, amplifying the glow on her face, and laughing.

"What the hell are you laughing at?" Logan said to Maya.

"You," Maya laughed. "And whatever you do, don't open the door, or else the heat I'm feeling right now, I'll do my best to melt that hunk of chocolate outside it. Matter of fact maybe I'll be the one to open that door." She stopped giggling for a minute as if pondering her own thoughts.

"Don't you dare open it," Logan said her fingers texting on her smartphone. "He'll tell Nicky we're up to no good."

"Says the one texting dirty messages right now," Maya chuckled. "I'll bet my new Manolo's you're having phone sex with 'Doctor Feel Me Up' right now as we speak," she teased.

I knew Maya was referring to Gabriel. I didn't want to think about the two of them potentially having a hot night with Craig or Gabriel. It only made me want and miss Elliot even more. This was so fucked up. Definitely I was fucked up. Fuck I didn't need to think about men. I needed pizza.

My attention diverted to the song that was playing on my intercom system. Feeling every beat of the music, I honed in on the fact that we were listening to some old school Christopher Cross remixed version of that 80's song called *Spinning*. Lord knows my head was truly spinning. Hell yeah I was spinning in a good way, trying to forget Elliot.

Maya grabbed the remote, changing the music to Iggy's *Fancy*. Maya started moving her body and nodding her head on the two and four beat. She started shouting "Who Dat Who Dat," out loud. I grabbed my phone, putting the song in my contacts beside her name for her ringtone. Next time she calls me I'm gonna answer "Who Dat."

I needed food. The munchies were starting to come down on me.

All of a sudden out of the clear, Logan jumped to her feet as if she had an awakening, startling Maya and me at the same time.

"I've got it bitches, I fucking got it!" she yelled out loud.

"Pizza!" I shouted. "Let's make a pizza in my new Viking stove."

Part of me wasn't sure if that was a good idea or not. We were so high, we might be at risk for burning the Towers down, but for ComputerLuv interceding. If we got close to burning the place down,

ComputerLuv would rat us out and the doors to my home would be kicked down pretty fast by my giant body watchers.

"Yeah I've got the munchies," Maya said. "Pizza sounds good." She rushed in the kitchen to turn the oven on.

"Is that you, Ms. Jules?" ComputerLuv all of a sudden awakened on high alert.

"Hell no. How many times do I have to tell you, It's me, Maya."

Maya was back to fighting again with ComputerLuv through the intercom. By now, I was certain ComputerLuv and Maya had a love/hate relationship.

"Not pizza bitches," Logan stood, ignoring Maya and the robotic voice garnering Maya's attention.

I was high. I wasn't sure what was coming out of Logan's mouth next, or if I'd even be able to comprehend it. Maya and ComputerLuv were fogging my thoughts with their constant non-stop back and forth, going nowhere. You would have thought Maya thought ComputerLuv was real.

"A freaking engagement party," she shouted, eyes wide.

"An engagement? Whose engagement?" I slurred in a foggy haze.

"Yours," Logan said.

"We're going to plan a fake engagement to get the man," Logan yelled.

I looked at Maya and picked up the joint in the ashtray.

"Bitch is high, alright," I sneered. "I'm not getting married." I laughed out loud.

"Of course you're not going to get married, but that doesn't mean these assholes don't think that you are. You're going to be the fish that got away," Logan said, smiling to herself as if she just had some huge epiphany.

"What the fuck, Logan, too many doobies for you bitch," Maya grumbled.

Logan flung her long blonde hair over her shoulders.

"In case you didn't realize, I am the bitch that got away. I left Elliot there with Kimber!" I shouted.

"In other words we don't have a plan then," Maya said, looking first at me and then at Logan.

We each looked at each other as if the other one had the answer. Then all three of us broke up laughing, falling over the top of each other.

"This so sucks with a long straw," Logan said.

"Your fault," Maya said quickly. "It's the weed. We're incapacitated. Our minds aren't functioning. We need a plan."

"Absence makes the heart grow fonder," Logan said nonchalantly, getting up, opening the fridge to find something to munch on. My pink negligee was swaying with her hips.

"I vote we hit the road."

"Out of sight, out of mind," Maya said, following her to the fridge and looking over her shoulder.

They both sounded like they were slurring their words or either their lips were moving in slow motion. I couldn't tell if something was wrong with the way they were talking or the way I was hearing. Either way, I was down with the idea that eating some food was a good idea. I was starting to feel a little paranoid. That was one thing that I hated about getting high, was the feeling of paranoia. It never failed that when I got high, that I started to feel like I needed to be watching my back more closely. I felt paranoid in my own home. Why, I do not know. It wasn't like Elliot was going to come busting through my doors like a white knight at any moment now.

"Goodnight Ms. Jules," ComputerLuv spurted out.

ComputerLuv was letting me know that he and my oven simultaneously had turned themselves off for lack of attention. No pizza. No heat. No Computerluv.

Maya and Logan came back from the kitchen with stale potato chips, raw carrots, guacamole, and onion dip. I didn't want to ruin their buzz by telling them I hadn't gone food shopping in over a week since I'd been living out of Elliot's home. I was content to eat the mint brownies. But this crap they brought back out of the fridge was making me disgusted. Okay, so let the record show I'm a pastry chef, but this is totally not on my list of foods that comforted me. No way in hell did I want to eat this.

"I got it. I got it. I got it," Logan said with all confidence, ignoring the frown on my face and my nose turned up about their pitiful food run.

"Then spill it woman," Maya said, getting impatient crunching a potato chip loudly in her mouth.

Maya was like Mikey. She'd eat anything right about now. At this point, even I realized we were all too high and too fucked up to come up with any ideas to help me out of my situation. I needed to count this night as a good ending with no real resolution.

Yeah my heart was hurting, but I was surrounded in love by my two best friends. So at the end of the day it wasn't all bad, and my life wasn't over. I had a business to launch in less than ten days. That was all that mattered. Whatever would become of Elliot and me, was all up to the universe. I would shore myself up. I would be confident and let go without of Elliot absent all the pain and drama I'd taken myself through over Oliver. I would grow from this experience with Elliot. For the first time in my life, I was going to go forward minus the personal devastation and rise.

"I'm gonna rise," I shouted out loud to Logan and Maya.

"Yes, we are on the rise," Logan said, raising her glass in the air.

"I'll will rise! Maya Angelou right?" Maya said.

"No," I said, looking at them as if they were clueless. "I will rise," I repeated.

They looked back at me like I was the clueless one.

Hell, we were all clueless. Clueless felt good. I liked being clueless. It meant I didn't have to think. I didn't have to feel. Hmm. Clueless was a cool emotion. I needed to do clueless more often.

"Let's drink to clueless," I laughed out loud.

Maya and Logan looked at each other, perplexed like I had grown a second head. I threw back another tequila shot.

One thing I knew for sure, the three things that weren't going to rise tomorrow, but would definitely be clueless, were Logan, Maya, and me. I tossed back my shot glass, and grinned widely.

Logan and Maya followed like good little soldiers with their shots, slamming their glasses down hard on the coffee table, not to be left out.

The hot tequila ran down my chest and for a moment we were all quiet, awaiting our next big bright idea to surface. I started to feel hot. I couldn't say it out loud, but I was missing Elliot. I was getting nostalgic. I was in love with Elliot. I didn't want what we were building to end.

"Let's flash Stephen," Logan said.

"Yeah Jules, let's flash Stephen," Maya said.

"Damn, aren't you guys tired of flashing Stephen and his guys? We do this silly stunt every holiday."

It wasn't totally a bad idea. I needed to do something silly to free myself from my thoughts of all things Elliot that were rippling through my body causing me emotional pain.

"Hell no," Maya said. "We gotta keep with tradition."

"Besides, you know how much it pisses Nicky off," Logan said.

"Yeah Jules, c'mon. We gotta keep with tradition."

"You guys are getting too old for this nonsense."

"Exactly," Logan said, hi-fiving Maya who was clearly in agreement.

"C'mon Jules," for old time's sake," Maya goaded.

"Fine fine fine," I said.

It never failed. Once a year, Maya, Logan, and I got drunk and flashed the security cameras hoping that my brother would be so repulsed he would pull them out of my home. But it never worked.

"Okay, then Maya, you get in the middle again," I said.

"Yeah Maya, reverse Oreo Cookie, white black white," Logan said.

"Ready?" I said.

"Yeah," Logan said.

"Hell yeah," Maya said.

The three of us ran over the corner where we knew my brother had planted a camera in the ceiling slightly left of the balcony terrace. We each turned our backs to the camera, Logan on one end, Maya in the middle, and me on the other end.

We all three turned around, pulled our bikini briefs down, turned our bums to the camera and shook them. Then we cracked up laughing, falling all over the floor.

"God we do this every year. Haven't you guys outgrown this stunt yet?" I said.

"Nope," Maya said.

"I added a new twist this year to spice things up," Logan said.

Maya and I looked at each other with curiosity.

"Look," Logan said.

Logan raised the hem of her pink nightie up for us to take a peek.

"You bitch," Maya said out loud laughing. "You scandalous bitch," she said again. "I want one too."

Logan grinned her beautiful smile as if she had won the lottery.

"What?" I said, legitimately clueless now.

"Logan's got a new tattoo."

I raised the hem of Logan's nightie with her permission. She had a new tattoo.

I felt out laughing in stitches.

Logan had a new tattoo on her right bun that read, *"Not all those who wander are lost,"* spelled out in Italian. Script font.

It was perfect. So totally Logan.

"I want one too!" I yelled.

Maya was laughing so hard tears were running down her face. I was doubled over in laughter as Logan got upon a chair with a paper towel, wiping the camera, blowing kisses, and teasing her boobs in my low coat pink nightie, then turning around and flipping her buns into the camera.

The three of us were laughing like crazy people. Maybe Stephen and his minions wouldn't see us on the tape until the morning if we were lucky. I looked down at the Cartier on my wrist. It was one o'clock in the morning.

One thing for sure; Maya, Logan, and I were known for stirring the pot, keeping everyone around us on their toes. We figured since we had to put up with the extra security we would keep life adventurous for the watch-keepers. But this moment in time was beyond the pale by even my standards.

The last twenty-four hours felt like being on an emotional roller coaster of highs and lows with no way to get off. But, it felt good to laugh and not to have to connect with my pain. My gals were a much needed diversion. That was why I loved them. They never let me be down.

I had managed to get through my Thanksgiving Day, emotionally singed but still in one piece, with a bit of high on top. Tomorrow would come soon enough. I probably wouldn't have a plan. But we'd have each other.

I would pay for this fun filled diversion tomorrow. A huge hangover would arrive. My pain would be back. But what wouldn't be back was the 'treat Julianna like the old shoe'. That gal would be gone.

"How much do you think it would cost to get Logan's tattoo artist to show up here and give us a copy of her tattoo?" I asked, my brain fogged with Hawaiian weed.

"Who said money is no object?" Maya slurred. "Money doesn't spend itself."

We all three ran to the phone while Logan placed the call to her favorite tattoo artist, "*Inky's Manhattan Blue.*" She was the best tattoo artist in all of Manhattan.

Two hours, several shots and a couple of joints later, Maya, Logan, and I all had the same tattoo drilled on our asses.

Not All Those Who Wander Are Lost" spelled out in Italian script.

And, there it was. Note to self.

20

*D*exter

"I bet it killed Elliot seeing that necklace around your neck," I said, chuckling to myself, loving that Kimber was sporting a copy of the same Tiffany necklace we managed to grab off Elliot days earlier.

I knew buying that necklace and wrapping it around Kimber's neck would piss Elliot off to the high heavens. It was my way of letting him know; he wasn't so special after all. Okay, so my necklace was an imitation knock-off, but neither he nor Kimber needed to know that. Far be it for me to spend that kind of money on a necklace for any woman, Kimber or otherwise. But I managed to achieve the same desired effect with a knockoff. Piss Elliot off to the high heavens. The icing on the cake was that his new girlfriend had on the same necklace too. I couldn't have planned the moment better. I only regretted not being able to see the expression on his face as he hit the "oh my god no mat." Dexter Two, Elliot, Zero.

"To the hunter goes the spoils," Kimber laughed out loud, tucking herself under my armpit as we both sat together, sipping Merlot in my oversized stuffed chair for two, quietly watching the wood in my fireplace crackling. It was Thanksgiving evening. A night to chill, and give thanks. Yeah, a special thanks for all the misery we were causing Elliot.

"You deserve it baby. Elliot never treated you the way he should have, leaving you alone all the time, working all those long hours. You need attention too," I said, twirling a lock of her dark black hair through my finger, running my thumb against her fake Tiffany necklace.

"If only you could have been a fly on the wall, and seen the look on his girlfriend's face when I let that pregnancy stick fall out of my purse."

"Oh that had to be priceless," I said, exuding my best Cheshire cat smile.

"Yeah, I had my very pregnant sister-in-law piss on that stick for me. No way am I messing up this beautiful body with a baby, but it was nice to flip the script and let Elliot's new woman think I was having his baby."

"Oh hell yeah," I said, clinking my glass up against Kimber's. "That should put the bullet in that relationship. Color those two done." I smiled wickedly.

"She ran out of his home so fast, she beat me out the door," Kimber said with glee. "She looked devastated. Her brother, not so much."

"Her brother? You didn't mention anything about a brother."

Kimber ignored me like I hadn't asked her anything. She kept spouting on like a faucet that wouldn't shut off.

"I even practiced my acting skills, making him think that I was in need of an abortion."

"Your body is way too beautiful, baby, to mess it up with some stretch marks. I like it the way it is. Perfect, toned, and beautiful."

Kimber grinned from ear to ear. Some days I debated whose ego was the largest between us, hers or mine. It would take a very rich man making all kinds of promises to get Kimber to have a baby. But

Kimber ran in the right circles, so that wouldn't be too hard for her to manifest if she put her mind to it.

But then again, I'm kind of surprised Elliot even fell for our little trick. It made me wonder did he really know Kimber at all. I took a huge gulp of my wine and pondered that thought for a bit.

I was pretty sure Elliot's new woman was finished with him now that she thinks he's got baby mama drama headed his way. He won't be able to keep any women. And when I finish with him, he won't be able to keep his job either.

"You did pretend like the baby was his, right?"

"Not exactly."

"What do you mean not exactly?"

Here we go.

It was hard as hell as always getting this chicken head to play by the rules. She thought too much. For once I would love it if Kimber could just stay on the fucking script. She was always good for a surprise, always deviating from the plan.

"Well I kind of told him the baby was *yours*."

"Mine? Are you crazy?" I said, spurting red wine out my mouth, thankful I'd miss my new shirt. "Why in the hell would you do something stupid like that?"

"Because I didn't want to be bothered with him pestering me for days about having a baby. Elliot doesn't believe in abortions. You failed to consider that little fact while you were conjuring up your big scheme," Kimber spouted as if she had the biggest brain in the room. "I had to improvise."

"What the hell does that have to do with the price of tea in China?" I shouted.

"It has everything to do with it Dexter," Kimber said, getting up out of the chair, pouring herself another glass of wine.

I got up behind her and poured myself another glass as well. We were standing facing each other eye to eye now like we were in some kind of standoff. I hoped she kept drinking her wine. I didn't want Kimber to get any bright ideas like throwing her wine in my face. Kimber had her moments where she could be extremely touchy. I damn sure didn't want red wine on my new Brooks Brothers shirt.

"You want to explain it to me," I said, through gritted teeth, hoping I at least appeared to be holding my composure.

"If Elliot thought I was carrying his baby, he would want me to keep it. If he thought I was carrying *your* baby, then he would leave me alone. I've got plans for myself, and they don't include Dr. Elliot Fischer stalking my world over trying to convince me to have a baby that hasn't even been conceived. You get it Dexter?"

"No, can't say that I do Kimber. You deviated from the plan for personal reasons without discussing this with me in advance. We had a plan remember. If you had led him to believe the baby was his, then you . . . we . . . could have gotten money from him, then faked a miscarriage or something else later. Why can't you ever stick to the plan?"

"I'm not the one that cares about Elliot or his money. I told you a long time ago, I'm getting bored with this little game of yours Dexter. Daddy says I have bigger fish to fry. I am a former Ms. New York," she said tossing her hair back over her shoulder.

Years from now, Kimber was going to still be holding on to the fact that she was a former Ms. New York, despite the fact that she hadn't done anything for herself since, other than look beautiful. I knew full well what she was doing. She was holding herself out for the man with the deepest pockets willing to pay the highest bid for the woman that wore the tiara to treat her like the queen that she thought she was.

"What exactly do you call yourself doing with me Kimber, warming me up, while you keep other men in the batter's box? Is that what our relationship has come to?" I asked, my eyes narrowing, faking it if as if I really gave a damn.

"Elliot is a waste of my time. I'm only in this little game of yours still because of you. Because you were nice to me when Elliot wasn't," Kimber purred. "But I have to keep my options open, Dexter."

Kimber needed to think she was the one in charge in this relationship, that it was *I* that needed her, when really it was *she* that needed *me* all along. But neither her heart nor her brain could comprehend such matters.

"Keep your options open?" I said, with raised eyebrows.

Kimber starting fingering my tie and gave me her best 'fuck me' look. For a minute, I almost forgot that we were in the middle of a very important discussion on a major point of contention. Kimber had that way with men. She could actually make you forget your own name. I needed to get this conversation back on track.

"So tell me Kimber, how was telling Elliot that the baby was mine going to achieve anything at all the way you see it?"

"Well, regardless of who the baby daddy is, the whole matter creates a problem on the home front of his new relationship. You being the father means I don't have to deal with him on the daily. Nobody says you have to believe that the baby is yours anyway, because there is no baby."

"What makes you think I want anyone to believe I'm having a baby out of wedlock? I have a reputation to protect around the hospital, Kimber. That is not something that I would do or flaunt."

"Oh so you would fuck a woman, get her pregnant, and leave her holding the bag with a baby, Dexter?" Kimber said, raising her voice.

"I didn't say that, Kimber. You're talking hypotheticals now. All I'm saying is that I wouldn't get a woman pregnant and not be a husband. Why are we talking about this? This conversation is starting to get stupid," I said, throwing my hand up in the air in exasperation.

"Oh you're calling me stupid now, Dexter?" Kimber said, her expression starting to look more like she was worked up and pissed.

Anger and frustration warred on her face while she decided whether to sling her drink on me or not. She pulled her shoulders back, showing off her beautiful breasts. I stepped back away from her in case she decided to toss the wine. Getting through to Kimber was like talking to a rock. Just because she was destined to be some man's trophy wife didn't mean she was trick-less. Kimber had an uncanny way of changing the subject. Twisting words to fit her needs.

"No, I'm saying that I'm a man of authority at the hospital. I'm Chief Counsel. I have to maintain certain impressions and decorum.

Getting a woman pregnant and not being married would not be a move that *I* would make. It would jeopardize my career. The only career that needs jeopardizing around here is Elliot's. You have potentially created a problem for me now," I tried to say as gently as I could, realizing Kimber had fire in her eyes.

Dealing with Kimber came with complications. Her brain wasn't ever big enough to handle big picture matters. Surely I gave her way too much room to maneuver on her own with my latest scheme of dropping a prego stick at Elliot's feet.

"Well, seeing how I'm not the one pregnant, you shouldn't have a problem seeing your way out of this little mess you've created," Kimber spat back at me.

"Mess *I've* created?"

No, Kimber didn't go there. She was actually going to blame me for her change in the script. Seriously?

"Yes, mess *you've* created. I could care less at this point about a baby, and who and what Elliot or anyone else thinks about it. As long as it's not my problem. I'm not the one really pregnant."

"But you've made it my problem." I gritted my teeth.

"So sue me," Kimber said, reaching in her pocket and pulling out a small mint tin, filled with cocaine.

"Bump, baby?" Kimber asked coolly, rubbing white powder on her gums, then taking a huge swig of her Merlot. She dipped her little finger in the tin again, rubbing it across her lips.

"Kiss and make up?"

I grinned back at Kimber like a man lost in a whorehouse. This woman was going to be the death of me. Surely she was a manslayer in disguise. All beauty, no brains, and the best piece of ass on the planet.

I kissed Kimber on the lips, my cock starting to get hard like a rock.

"So Kimber, Elliot's new girlfriend?"

"Yes," she said sucking on my lower lip, running her hand across my pants leg, getting a good feel of my need beckoning her.

"What did you say her name was?"

Kimber unzipped my pants, and I moaned loudly, my cock in her hand, twitching, ready and willing.

"Julianna. Sister to Nicholas Becker," she said, bending down, putting her entire mouth over my cock.

"Oh fuck me!" I yelled at the top of my lungs.

"Yes baby," Kimber moaned with excitement.

"No, fuck me," I said again loudly.

Kimber moaned louder and sucked me louder. Maybe it was the coke, maybe she was the beautiful buffoon, but either way, she didn't get it. Kimber didn't realize what was really going on in my head. And what was going on in my head had nothing to do with the fact that she was sucking my dick off, trying to kill me.

She didn't get it. But, I got it. Yes. Kimber was going to be the death of me.

I needed to kick Kimber to the curb. Disassociate myself fast. But I needed to keep her around at least until after the hospital fundraiser.

Shit. Elliot with Julianna Becker. Nicholas Becker's sister. This was too close for comfort.

If my dealings regarding Nicholas's sister ever got out, I would have no career left. I was fucked now, in more ways than one.

Kimber was killing me with her mouth, sucking on my cock really hard now. And if Kimber didn't kill me right about now, Nicholas Becker would be killing me later.

Nicholas Becker would chop what would be left of my balls off for fucking over his little sister if my involvement in this scheme ever got out. How was I to know Elliot was seeing Nicholas Becker's sister? The stakes were getting higher.

I dipped my finger into Kimber's tin full of coke, rubbing it on my gums and under my nose in a state of panic. Then I pulled her off my cock, turned her around, and desperately tried to fuck all of my negative thoughts and fears out on her.

What did it matter that Kimber had bigger fish to fry? I needed to get myself out of the frying pan.

$\mathcal{E}$*lliot*

$\mathcal{M}$y personal funk monkey had finally settled over me and taken over. The Thanksgiving holiday had come and gone. It had been a week since I'd last seen Julianna. Her energy still filled my home. I couldn't stand to be in my own home anymore, so I spent every waking minute at the hospital. I welcomed the thought of babies being born, so I could keep my mind off all things Julianna. I took as many extra shifts as I could to keep from going home. My colleagues loved the fact that they got a bit of extra time at home with their families. I was their best friend this holiday. I got lots of thanks and pats on the back. It was a good outcome for all involved. At least here at the hospital I didn't have to connect with the memories of Julianna that seemed to be everywhere in my home. Not even the fact that I was forced to eat more in the hospital cafeteria wasn't enough to drive me home.

I missed my woman. I had no way to contact her, now that her old phone was smashed to pieces. Her necklace, the key to my heart, was still lying on my wet bar countertop right where she left it. Even I had to agree it had lost its significance once Kimber had the same necklace wrapped around her scrawny neck. I needed to return the damn thing to Tiffany's. The whole thing was a good memory gone badly. It had lost its significance.

But today would offer new hope. Today, maybe I'd get to see her since this was the day the fundraiser committee would be meeting to discuss the upcoming black tie fundraiser.

Thank God Harper put Julianna and I on that committee together. Only three more hours to go, and I would get to see her. Maybe I'd even get to pull her aside privately to plead my case for why she and I should be together. I would get her new number. I didn't want this business between Kimber and me to come between Julianna and me.

I was determined to connect with her, to comfort her, to feel her warmth, her essence. Julianna belonged to me and to no other. I couldn't help myself. She was mine. I wanted her for me, and me alone. I didn't need much to be happy, but I needed her. I was going to come clean with her and let her know everything that I'd been feeling over the last week. I wanted her to know how much I missed her. I wanted our relationship back on track.

I felt sick to the pit of my stomach at the thought of our having even spent the last week apart. I pushed my food around on my plate unable to eat. Loneliness permeated my space. I wondered how long it would take for Gabriel to notice I had completely lost it.

"Look man, you've got to pull out of this funk you've been in all week. Snap out of it," Gabriel pleaded as he sat down in the chair next to me, joining my table.

"I know this cafeteria food sucks, but at least pretend like you give a damn for my sake. You're ruining your reputation. You're not looking so easy on the eyes these days, Dr. EZ. You're getting dark circles and bags under your eyes."

"Double shifts," I brooded.

"You did it to yourself, acting like you can't be in your own damn home," Gabriel grunted.

"Have you heard any news from Logan? How is she?" I asked.

I was good at pulling any little tidbits about Julianna that I could get from Gabriel who was still in touch with Logan.

"Well the launch of *Sugar Mommy's* is imminent. From what I hear, she's thrown herself into the *Sugar Mommy* opening that's coming up this weekend. The opening sounds like it's going to be the who's who affair of the month."

I shook my head in disgust. Was I so easy to forget? Was Julianna moving on without me? I hadn't even got a call or so much as an invite at this point.

"Things got so out of hand so fast Thanksgiving night," I said, my thoughts trailing off.

"Ah yeah, Kimber being pregnant. I would call that getting out of hand in a major fucking way dude," Gabriel said, grabbing the piece of un-eaten sourdough bread off my plate. I slid the croutons in my salad to the side of my plate in case he wanted those too.

"It's not my baby. Therefore, it's not my problem," I grumbled, looking around the cafeteria to make sure that Babs and her gang of rumormongers were nowhere in earshot.

Gabriel bent his head forward towards me, dropping his voice down to a whisper.

"The problem here EZ, is that Julianna doesn't know that. She thinks Kimber's baby is yours," he whispered in a low tone. "You need to come clean and tell her."

"So she did in fact see that EPT stick?" I said, confirming my earlier suspicions.

"Hell yeah she saw that stick. She and her moneybag brother both saw that baby stick," Gabriel said licking a crumb off his finger. "That's all Logan talks about."

"And what did you say?" I said, still in a state of shock that Julianna saw that early pregnancy test that had fallen out of Kimber's purse.

"Deny. Deny. Deny. What the hell else did you expect me to say? I know that baby's not yours. The whole idea of it is so ridiculous, seeing how Kimber was doing Dexter for weeks and not you."

I'd done the math over and over in my head. No way that baby could have been mine.

"Tell me about it, that two timing whore."

"Not to mention this whole matter between you and Julianna is getting in the way of my getting intimate with Logan. My balls are starting to turn blue solely on the strength of having to defend your baby mama drama. Logan's got me on a long leash as if I'm the one who's not to be trusted."

"Well there might be a bit of truth in that."

"It's not like I'm dead yet. A man has to sift through the haystack to find the needle, yo."

"You know that's not my baby," I said again, repeating myself, intentionally ignoring Gabriel's woes over Logan.

I had my own problems.

"Yeah I know it. But try to run that up the flagpole with Logan, Maya, and Julianna. I can't even get to first base with Logan anymore. Your baggage is starting to spill over into my ability to get the booty."

"So go get a few lap dances down at Maximillion's. Work it out on Bubbles and Baby Doll."

"Not the same EZ. That Logan, she's one in a million, a dreamsicle, that one," Gabriel said, mouthing a low wolf whistle.

"Don't tell me you're starting to catch feelin's man?" I stopped pushing my fork around my plate and focused my gaze on Gabriel with particular interest.

"You should talk, Elliot. You're the one in love."

"What the hell do you know about being in love, Gabriel?"

Though I knew deep down I was in love with Julianna, I wasn't going to admit it out loud to anyone before I at least told Julianna how I felt.

"I imagine it feels pretty much how you look right now, that's what. A man lost without his compass."

I closed my eyes and ran my hand across the top of my head.

"But frankly, you might as well be dead to her. At least as far as her brother is concerned," Gabriel said nonchalantly.

"Oh man, this is worse than I thought. No way I lose my relationship with Julianna over a baby that's not even mine. That's Dexter's baby for Christ sakes," I hissed. "Assuming Kimber hasn't aborted by now."

"Oh and that whole necklace business. Do you know how painful that was for me to hear that story over and over and over with Logan? Logan is starting to sound like a broken record going on and on about Kimber and that damn necklace."

"That Kimber is a certifiable bitch," I grunted.

"Wherever did you find that woman anyway, E? 1-800-Go-Fuck Yourself?" Gabriel complained.

"I know man. It's my own fault. I did it to myself at the end of the day."

"Indeed you did my brother, but I'll always have your back. You can count on me to pull you through these troubled waters. Matters of the lady's hearts are my specialty."

"Good Lord, this means I'm going down with the ship and don't even know it. If you're the answer to my problems, I'm surely in trouble," I laughed.

"Well at least I got a laugh out of you finally. You've been sulking all week. Even Xavier is starting to get concerned about you. He keeps calling me to see if you've snapped out of it yet. You haven't been answering your phone."

"So the opening of *Sugar Mommy's* is this weekend, huh?"

"Yeah, well, you're welcome to come to the launch party as my plus one man," Gabriel offered.

Funny, though I couldn't tell for sure if he was serious or not.

"*I*ncoming Assface at two o'clock," Gabriel said, as I noticed Dexter headed our way.

Both Gabriel and I straightened our backs a little stiffer to brace ourselves as Dexter made his way towards our table. I took several deep breaths. The last thing I wanted to do right now was to listen to Dexter.

Dexter grabbed a cafeteria chair from the table across from us, sitting it at the end of the table while Gabriel and I remained seated across from each other.

"What do you want Dexter?" Gabriel spit out at him.

"Yo, fellas," I come in peace," Dexter said. "I realize you two non-pluses think you're better than everyone else around here. I see the way you guys look down your nose at me constantly but that's neither here nor there," Dexter shrugged, pushing his black horn-rimmed glasses back up to the bridge of his nose. Dexter's tray had a slice of pizza on it that he had sprinkled extra helpings of parmesan cheese on the top. I looked down at my own plate of tuna salad and tomato, reminding myself that he was a walking heart attack waiting to happen.

"What do you want, Dexter?" I said, pretty much wanting to know what his next play was going to be to warrant this untimely visit.

I glanced at my watch, pretending I had somewhere more urgent to be. Anywhere but here having a conversation with Dexter was preferable to me at this point.

"Here's the deal, Elliot. As you know the hospital fundraiser for the Becker Wing is fast approaching. The committee meeting is in a couple of hours. I've gotten out of the gate early to come up with a plan to collect some extra donations from a few of our high end sponsors."

"Yeah, what plan might that be?" I said, feigning interest.

I've suggested we have an auction in exchange for a date night with some of the female nurses and committee members. You know, kind of like bidding on a date night."

"Oh, really? Doesn't the committee have to approve of this idea?" I said.

"Well, I've already run the concept by Harper Montgomery Becker. She loves the idea," Dexter said reaching for my glass of water to drink it as if it were his own.

Gabriel grabbed my glass and shifted it to the left of my fork shooting him a look of disdain, daring him to reach for it again.

So this was what Mario must have meant. This was Dexter's plan to set up Oliver with Julianna. With the exception that any money changing hands may never get past Dexter's pockets and rightfully into the hospital coffers.

"I plan to bring the concept up this afternoon at the meeting. I'm pretty sure we'll have a consensus. I wanted to give you a heads up in advance."

"You wanted to give Elliot a heads up in advance," Gabriel gritted out. "How kind of you," he snorted.

"You know you need to pay more attention to what goes on in that place you call an Emergency Room rather than twiddling your thumbs into the affairs of hospital administrative business, Gabe. If it weren't for you and your kind wasting hospital resources on some of your cockamamie mis-adventures down in the ER, maybe we wouldn't have to keep doing these fundraisers to keep the hospital state of the art," Dexter shot back at Gabriel.

Gabriel suddenly grabbed Dexter by his necktie, practically choking the air out of his mouth.

"You little shit, you better hope you never end up in my ER while I'm on duty," Gabriel said, while slamming Dexter back in his seat, brushing his hands off on Dexter's shirt.

"You're wearing out your welcome here, Dexter. You've said your piece, now move on," I grunted.

I needed Dexter to get up and leave our table before the three of us made a spectacle of ourselves. This scene was rapidly turning into the moment from hell headed straight to the abyss.

"By the way Elliot, this fundraiser being a black tie affair and all, I wanted you to know that I'll be attending the gala this year with your ex-fiancée Kimber. Folks are liable to be talking, seeing how she used to be engaged to you," he said, looking all smug, puffing his chest out.

"Nobody cares Dexter," Gabriel spit out at him.

"Well I care," Dexter spat back. "I want Kimber to be comfortable.

Elliot's moved on and so has Kimber." Dexter directed his comments to Gabriel, and then eyeballed me for a response.

"Not a problem Dexter. Keep it moving," I said.

Deep down I hoped the whole matter wouldn't prove to be embarrassing. The last thing I wanted was for Julianna to have to be in a room with Kimber yet again. I hated it when my personal life got mixed up with my professional life. I had worked so hard through the years to keep both of my personal and business fronts separate. This is what I get for daring to marry a woman who needed to have a high profile. Not to mention she had latched herself onto my arch enemy co-worker of all people. Kimber was starting to function like a big fish in a small pond. She had plenty of reasons to step outside of my workplace social circle, but no, that wasn't good enough for her. She had to position herself on my work-place playground and milk the shit for all it was worth, as if she didn't have a social circle before meeting me. This was cruel and unusual punishment.

"No hard feelings, Elliot. Seeing how the best man here won the woman and all. That would be me, get it?"

Dexter started to laugh wickedly, shaking me out of my thoughts. It was everything I had to keep Kimber's confidences and not mention that the only way Dexter could ever get a woman like Kimber and keep her, would be to knock her up. I bit my tongue, reminding myself that loose lips sink ships.

"Elliot's moved on," Gabriel said. "You're late to the party. Nobody gives a shit about you or Kimber. Have at it."

"Funny, that's not the way I hear it," Dexter chuckled. "The way I hear it, everyone else has moved on from Elliot."

That was it. That was the last freaking straw. I balled my fist up, rearing backwards out of my chair right at the moment Gabriel yanked me forward by my stethoscope, nodding his head no.

Dexter pulled his chair back from the table out of my reach, nodded his farewell, and slid off into the cafeteria like the snake that he was.

I could feel the beads of sweat starting to form on the edge of my nose. That was my body's signal that my anxiety level was high. I was close to losing my own sense of control.

"Forget that douchebag," Gabriel said, realizing my state of angst, patting me on my shoulder so as to calm me down. Now we know which way he's going to come at you."

"Yeah, that motherfucker is always one to hide behind a woman's skirt. He throws the rock and hides the hand. I'll bet money he's behind Kimber coming to my place on Thanksgiving. Can't he ever man up for himself?" I squawked. "Always sending a woman to do his dirty work."

I balled my napkin up and threw it inside my plate, signaling that this pitiful meal was over.

"Well at least we know which way the winds are going to blow," Gabriel said, resigning himself to what was coming next.

"Yeah, Oliver's planning to make a play for Julianna, Kimber will be in cahoots with Dexter, coming along for the ride as his fundraiser date, possibly pregnant or possibility not? And me? I'll be assed out if I don't go after what's mine."

"Exactly," Gabriel said.

I looked at the clock on the wall in the obstetrical wing lobby. It was finally three-o'clock. I had caught two babies in the morning, and another one after that God awful visitation with Dexter who had managed to infiltrate my lunch with Gabriel.

My stethoscope bounced around my neck, bobbling against my chest as I made my way to the Becker Obstetrical Wing. I walked briskly past Babs who'd grabbed a clipboard with an empty note pad on it, shoving it in my hands.

"Dr. Fischer, you're gonna need this for that important meeting with those money people," she said shoving a pen in my hand.

"Thank you Babs."

"Don't mention it," she smiled looking halfway between satisfied and worried.

I took the clipboard Babs handed me. I needed something in my hands to occupy me by taking notes or better yet, to beat that wimp Dexter over the head with it.

"I'll be in the conference room for about an hour if anyone needs me," I grumbled to Babs.

"I know where to find you Dr. EZ," Babs said with an air of confidence. "If anybody needs you Dr. EZ , they got to come through me."

I nodded in agreement. Babs had my back. Somehow the two of us were tied at the hips. She knew when I needed space, and when I needed to be found. She hovered over me like a bear caring for her cub. Part of me was grateful that nobody was going to fuck with me, unless they came through Babs first. The other part worried that I had no real sense of privacy.

I smiled affectionately at her, totally appreciating all her efforts to look out for me. I suppose every doctor needed a Babs in their world. Life was complicated as it was, without having to look over one's shoulder twenty-four and seven.

I entered the stairwell, taking the steps two at a time to the fifth floor. I could hear a barrage of voices coming down the hallway leading to the conference room. I peered through the door's oblong window to see if I could get a glimpse of her. There she was. Sitting erect. Picture perfect. My Julianna.

Her dark locks toppled over her shoulder, flowing down a white leather dress, adorned with a platinum and crystal lariat necklace. She had some sparkly silver eye shadow on her saucy brown eyes, and large diamond earring posts in her ears. She looked like a beautiful princess in winter white. My woman was beautiful. And I missed her.

I entered the room, acknowledging the other committee members, shaking hands, pausing to spend a few moments with a couple of the board members I hadn't seen in a while. Harper approached me warmly, hugging me in her warm embrace.

"Elliot, it's good to see you again, but I must say you're looking fatigued, my dear."

I kissed her on the cheek, looking around the room and over my shoulder in a quick moment of insecurity. I wanted to make sure her husband was nowhere around to murder me for hugging his wife again.

"You're a sight for sore eyes as always Harper," I said warmly. "I've been doing double shifts all holiday. I suppose the wear is taking its toll."

"Well get some rest Elliot, and soon. The committee needs you to be firing on all cylinders," she said with a look of concern.

I nodded in agreement, squeezing Harper's hand. I gently guided her towards the corner of the room out of earshot of the other committee members.

"By the way, I never got a chance to thank you for sending Matthews my way. I appreciate your looking out for me. That was kind of you."

"Don't mention it," Harper said. "We're friends. I was happy to send some much needed legal help your way."

My eyes drifted from Harper's gaze toward Julianna.

"She's putting up a good front, but she misses you too," Harper whispered in my ear.

Thank God, somebody in the Becker family was on my side

I glanced in Julianna's direction. She looked stoic and expressionless.

"I've missed her," I whispered under my breath to Harper.

It had been almost a week since I'd seen Julianna, but it felt like a lifetime. She had dropped into my world quite unexpectedly, managing to turn my world upside down. I could barely eat, sleep, drink, or think without her. I needed her in my life.

"I have no doubt the sentiment is mutual," Harper replied. "Give her time."

I walked behind Julianna's chair, gently putting my hand on her shoulder, touching her softly as I moved to take my own seat. Yeah baby. I haven't forgotten you. You will always be mine. You may be out of sight, but never out of my mind.

"Julianna," I said calmly, her expression turning slightly anxious in nature.

"Dr. Fischer," she said, acknowledging my greeting.

Oh I was back to being Dr. Fischer now. That wasn't going to work for me at all. We were past that phase. We were lovers. I wasn't going back to being Dr. Fischer. No sirreee.

The rest of the committee members joined the room, rounding the table to take their seats. Dexter made sure he sat himself directly to the right of Harper in the seat closest to her, she being at the head of the table. I sat directly across from Julianna. I wanted to rest my eyes on her. I wanted her to look back at me.

Harper clinked her spoon against her water glass so as to get the room's attention.

"Before we get down to business, I want to thank everyone for coming today," Harper said. "Things are moving rapidly with the fundraiser and we've had a lot of great ideas for this year's fundraiser."

Thirty minutes passed quickly as Harper went through the bulk of the meeting's agenda. She had a done a good job of moving the pace of the meeting along, not wasting a room full of professional's time. I zoned out on most of what she was saying, fixated on Julianna, who was working overtime not to look at me. I knew that by the way she squirmed in her seat to keep from looking at me.

"But before we close," I heard Harper say, "Dexter Esposito has a new plan this year for us to add a date night auction with male and female volunteers from the nursing staff and fundraising committee members."

"That's a great idea," I heard one of the elder committee members agree.

"Yes, it is," said another.

There was a consensus around the room that the auction would be a given. I sighed inwardly, hating the fact that Dexter was the instigator behind this so-called wonderful idea. I would have laid odds that he hadn't thought that up on his own. It sounded more like the work of Oliver Banks if you ask me. Dexter was never that creative.

"It is a great idea indeed, and our own Julianna Becker has volunteered as the committee member's person to bid herself off as one of the single females for the date night auction. Several of the single male doctors will be bidding themselves out to some lucky ladies was well," Harper continued.

"Wonderful," Dexter said, looking like he was ready to do back-flips. "No one can accuse us of not being equal opportunity auction-eers." He smiled that shit eating grin that I wanted to wipe off his face.

Everyone in the room applauded for Julianna, and congratulated Dexter on his so-called dumb ass idea. I tapped my pen nervously against my clipboard putting a half smile on my face. I hated the whole idea, and damn sure wasn't going to applaud for Dexter, but I didn't want to offend Harper's sensibilities since she was obviously on board with the whole idea.

"Why Harper, every man in the room will love to get in on the bidding process for a chance to date the very lovely Julianna Becker," Dexter said, brown-nosing up to Harper, then cutting his gaze my direction, his beady eyes twinkling with devious amusement.

Harper nodded and smiled in acknowledgement. Me? I growled under my breath. Something primal stirred within me. My stomach clenched in a knot. Dexter's feigned compliment fully cloaked in deceit awakened the animal in me that wanted nothing more to be unrestrained and unleashed on Dexter.

I could feel the fire in my own eyes. I agonized whether to tear Dexter to shreds right here and now. I was itching to pounce on him, paying whatever price it may cost me, even at the expense of losing my professional standing in the community, my career and everything else I held dear.

Brow furrowing, I sighed out loud, vacillating between my yearning to touch Julianna and my desire to castrate Dexter. For the first time throughout this whole meeting, Julianna actually raised her eyes to look at me. Her look relaxed me, her proximity to me providing me a much needed sense of calm, distracting me from my anger.

There was no way in hell I was going to let my woman ride off on some fake date Oliver and Dexter had conjured up in the name of a fundraiser auction event. There wasn't enough money in the world, Oliver's or otherwise, to get between Julianna and me.

Julianna had no idea what was coming, and I sure as hell couldn't tell her, since the only reason I even knew of Dexter's plan for her to get with Oliver was through Mario's hack job.

"We have several male and female nurses who have agreed, so we have ten volunteers now in all," Harper smiled.

"And with that I think we'll close today's meeting. Thank you all for coming," Harper said. "It was a good meeting folks. Meeting adjourned."

*lliot*

A rush of noise and small talk ensued as the room's occupants moved about in a flurry across the room. Dexter moved to get Harper's attention. I got up out of my seat to move towards Julianna before she could leave the room. I would not let her get away from me this time without hearing me out.

I moved around the table and caught Julianna by her forearm, as the other occupants in the room moved about nosily. She had risen from her seat, working hard to avoid eye contact with me.

"We need to talk," I whispered.

"Nothing to say," she said in a low voice, piling her papers one on top of the other nervously, still not looking me in the eyes.

I leaned in close to her, my ear to her ear, both of us standing in front of the large windows that ran the length of the conference room walls.

"Baby, there is a lot left to say."

"I'm not your "Baby," Dr. Fischer. Seems you're the one having babies," Julianna huffed.

I grabbed Julianna's forearm, pulling her close to me.

"The only babies I'm going to be having are going to be with you," I snarled, feeling like my brow was frowned with frustration.

I was annoyed. She was annoyed. But the passion between us was so tangible you could practically taste and touch it. I felt it. She felt it. I took a deep breath, exhaling loudly. The phone in my breast pocket sounded off. Julianna stepped backwards, out of my grip, folding her arms over her chest.

"I'm not done with this conversation," I said in a low whisper. "Text me your new number. We need to talk."

Julianna looked at me as if I were crazy to be giving her directions.

"Now," I spat out, my voice slightly raised above a whisper.

I didn't like giving Julianna orders, but this was serious. I was serious. I needed her full attention. We could discuss it later.

"Fine," Julianna said in a whispered huff, texting me her number. "But don't think because you have my number that means I plan to talk to you."

"I owe you an explanation," I insisted. "We need to make some time for each other baby."

"I don't have time for games Elliot," she went on, her fingers texting me her new number. "*Sugar Mommy's* is opening his weekend. I'm preoccupied."

"Yeah, and not so much as a personal invite to me. I had to hear about the launch from Gabriel of all people. How the hell do you think that makes me feel?"

I could feel my own annoyance coming through in my voice. None of it was what I wanted to convey in this moment.

"Hopefully left out," she spit out.

"Baby," I pleaded. "You don't really mean that?"

Both our anxiety levels had risen. I wanted to de-escalate our conversation down a notch, but I wasn't feeling like I was having any real luck.

"And I should care about how you, Kimber, and your new baby

should feel, why?" she said, her voice a bit raised, as she looked around the conference room to see if anyone else was listening.

I opened my mouth to reply, just as Babs ducked her head in to the conference room to say I was needed for an emergency C-section that had come in through Gabriel's emergency room.

"We need you in Emergency, Dr. EZ."

I cursed under my breath in frustration, momentarily ignoring Babs.

"What do I have to do? Be Gabriel's plus one in order to get into my own woman's launch party?" I spit back in a moment of desperation.

Man, I couldn't believe I said that out loud. Julianna's eyes glistened with interest. She raised her eyebrow—I thought with a bit of amusement. But then she looked pissed again as if some evil thought ran across her brain. And, then there was *that* look again. I had a love/hate relationship with *that* look. I loved the way she gave me that look of raw hunger and need. And I hated that she pulled that one out of her bag of feminine wiles when I was in no position to do anything about it. I had to fight off my urge to throw her across the conference room table and bury myself deep into her until she screamed my name.

"Your own woman? Really now? The way I see it, you seemed to maintain more than one woman at a time; it's getting hard for me to keep up," she hissed.

"Baby you know that's not true," I begged.

"Tell that to the next key holder Elliot."

Oh did that one hurt. And I didn't have a comeback. I had no idea how Kimber ended up with the same necklace I had given Julianna, but I could just imagine.

"I don't like the idea of you auctioning yourself off," I snapped, forcing a change in the subject, recognizing I was losing this battle.

"It's for a good cause. Why wouldn't a Becker want to raise money for the Becker Wing? she snapped back at me, her eyes narrowing. "It's my family obligation."

I caught a subtle whiff of her cologne that floated through my nostrils, thinking she looked really hot when she was pissed off. Maybe we could have makeup sex, this being our first fight and all.

"Then I'll be sure to make it my obligation you remain with family."

Yeah babe, you can't see it yet, but you and I are on the road to being family. Husband and wife family.

A look of befuddlement passed across her face. I stared her down, giving her a moment to process my words, my own thoughts contemplating the two of us having a wonderful future together.

"Are we done here Elliot?" Julianna said, jolting me out of my haze, not giving me a moment to collect my thoughts and speak.

I was at a loss for words, having lost my train of thought on the present moment.

"I thought so," she stammered. She reached in her bag, shoving an engraved invitation with my name on it in my hand. It was a personal invitation to the *Sugar Mommy* Launch Party with my name on it.

So she wasn't trying to exclude me from her opening after all. She wanted me there as much as I wanted to be there. Her eyes met mine causing my cock to twitch. Images of taking her on the conference room table began flooding my brain again.

"You're welcome to bring your own plus one if you like Elliot. Perhaps Kimber?" she glared at me, her cute nose flaring with jealously.

Damn. Here we go again, back on this treadmill to nowhere. I was confused, pissed, aroused, and dumbfounded all at the same time. Julianna had no reason on earth to be jealous of Kimber or any other woman for that matter. I was hers and she was mine. What was it going to take for me to get this point across to her?

Julianna turned away from me, swinging the conference room door open, leaving me in her wake. Her hips shimmied in that skintight white leather dress that was hugging her beautiful curves all in the right places. If she called herself giving me her ass to kiss, I was certainly on board with that plan. God I did love this woman.

"Oh, no, we're not done here," I said, my brain kicking back in gear. "To hell if we're done," I said, stomping out of the conference room steady on her heels, realizing she was leaving me again. I was hardly through the double doors of the conference room before I realized that our conversation hadn't gone so well. Julianna jumped on the elevator headed down. I watched the double doors to the elevator close. I wasn't done with this conversation. One thing for sure, Julianna Becker would hear from me. At least I knew the score. I was a little angry, she was a lot angry, but she and I were far from done.

J made my way down to the emergency room in a huff, hearing my name being paged again over the hospital loud-speaker. Julianna had my brain and emotions all scrambled together in ways I couldn't explain. I had to redirect by focus fast in order to deal with the young eighteen-year-old pregnant woman who had been in a car accident. This baby was going to have to come by emergency cesarean section, two months early. Today's preemie for the day.

"I think the mother is critical, Dr. E," Patty spouted. "I'm having a hard time containing her husband in the waiting room. He's babbling about his lack of insurance and that he can't pay for any procedures," Patty said worriedly. "She's having a girl."

"We don't have time to transfer her to City Hospital," I say. "It's now or never. Forget about him. We'll have to sort it out later," I command.

"He's lost his job," Patty sighed.

"This baby doesn't care about that. She's got to come out now, so we need to focus here, Patty," I repeated.

"I don't know, Dr. E. Baby Daddy doesn't seem too stable to me."

"Neither am I at this point."

Patty looked at me with a mix of emotions flashing across her face. She hardly knew what I meant. How was she to know that I was a bundle of confusion, anger, and totally discomforted over my conversation with Julianna. I needed to collect myself and calm Patty down.

"You're a good nurse, Patty. You're going to be a great nurse one day. Focus," I demanded.

"Okay Dr. E. All I'm saying is that, the man out there in the waiting room really looks like he belongs up on the sixth floor in the psych ward if you ask me."

Before I could digest Patty's words, I heard the hospital intercom ring out throughout the entire hospital that the entire facility was on lockdown.

Fuck. This can't be good. This shit only happens when some lunatic is running free through the facility disrupting the natural order of things. I didn't have time for this. The mother in front of me was losing blood faster than I could stop the internal bleeding all while her baby was struggling for life.

"Call Dr. DeLuca Patty. Please tell him he's needed in Operating Room Six in the Becker Wing immediately. And while you're at it, page Babs please for assistance."

Things was going to hell in a hand basket fast in my OR.

I could hear Patty carrying out my commands. An anesthesiologist and a couple of the resident doctors made their entry in the operating room quickly. My patient's blood pressure was dropping fast. The baby's heartbeat was getting irregular.

Gabriel bolted through the door, having scrubbed in quickly, entering the operating room at the same time one of Bab's nurses arrived to assist. He was carrying a black folder filled with the patient's charts, setting it down, moving quickly while tying a white mask around his blue capped head.

"Whatcha need E?" Gabriel shouted, his clean hands at a ninety-degree angle in the air.

"I got a bleeder here, Gabe. Give me an assist, while I get Lil' Momma here out the womb," I insisted.

Patty scurried around the operating room in a focused state, moving double-time, prepping the incubator at warp speed. She was doing a fine job. I was proud of her. She really was going to make a great nurse supervisor one day.

Patty rushed to my side handing me scalpels, attending to my surgical needs. I reminded myself and Patty that everything was in control. We weren't going to lose the mother or the baby. Whatever was going on elsewhere in the hospital, we were all in control in this room. We were going to focus on both mother and baby, getting them through this emergency surgery safely. I wasn't going to lose them on my watch. That was all that mattered to me. I recited those facts out loud in order to keep everyone calm in the operating room. That was right up and until Mr. Madman husband entered my operating room brandishing a gun, waving it wildly at everyone in the room, his hand on Bab's throat.

*I*n all my years of practicing medicine, all I really cared about was getting the babies here safely. The one thing about babies, they were so innocent and beautiful when they were born. So wondrous. Who knew they might grow up to curse you out, take drugs, and turn out to be nut cases brandishing a gun at somebody's throat in the very operating room you delivered them in years ago. I relished the moment when they were first born, fresh, new, and innocent. Long before life had a chance to make its mark on them.

"Put that gun down man, and let the nurse go," I yelled. "I know you're skittish, but we need to get this baby here safely."

"You don't care about me or my kid," the panicked soon-to-be-father said. His hand was shaking feverishly. His dark eyes were wild. He looked to be in a state of full blown hysteria. Maybe he was on drugs or something. I shuddered to think this display of crazy was brought on by the lack of insurance. These were terrible times when lives had to be threatened over the lack of health care insurance. I momentarily wondered if I needed to re-think my profession.

Gabriel and I looked at each silently. Patty froze in her place. Gabriel kept his hand on the bleeder he was helping to suture on the mom's arm while I extracted the baby by cesarean section.

Gabriel began speaking to him in Spanish.

"Cálmate Amigo," Gabriel demanded insisting the man calm down.

"Those people downstairs tried to send us away. Leave my baby and wife dying because I lost my job and don't have any insurance," he bit out, his gun still pressed against Bab's throat. "Mi epsousa. Mi bebé," father shouted, beads of sweat pouring from his dark olive colored skin.

I looked up over my surgical mask at him. He was a young buck. Scared. Afraid. Feeling alone. Out of control. He couldn't have been more than nineteen or twenty.

"Look man, your baby's coming within the next few minutes. You want to be a part of her life. This decision you're making right now, holding that gun against the throat of the one woman I need to get your baby here safely isn't helpful. Don't do this man. This is not the time," I said, my hands shaking from the adrenaline that was coursing through my body. "Let go of my nurse," I said motioning my scalpel-filled hand at Babs.

I could see SWAT team members through the glass window, shuffling outside the operating room positioning themselves. One of the SWAT team snipers had a perfect shot, his gun aimed at the hysterical husband.

I didn't want him to die. I didn't want to bring life into the world at the exact same moment someone else was taking it out. I did not want the police to kill this baby's father. He had a new daughter to meet. I didn't want him dead. He was too young and inexperienced in life to die.

"There she is," Gabriel said, solely focused on the job at hand.

I nodded at Gabriel.

"C'mon baby girl, come to Big Poppa," I said, sliding her out of her mother's abdomen.

The father dropped his gun no longer aiming it wildly, pushing Babs my direction, falling on his knees in uncontrollable tears, his gun still pressed tightly in his hand.

I handed the baby to Patty. I needed to focus on not losing the mother. I needed to get her closed up quickly to prevent any more internal bleeding. Suddenly we all heard the sounds of the newborn's cry.

The new father was in a state of disbelief, hearing the sounds of his baby girl. He looked at his child, glanced outside the window of the operating room door, seeing that he was fully surrounded with no way out. Before I could say something, he was pointing the gun at his own head.

"Please don't," Babs yelled at him.

Gabriel and I looked at him, and then each other, knowing we had a full blown crisis on our hands.

"No, Mi Amigo," Gabriel pleaded. "Por favor!"

I could see NYPD SWAT members outside the double doors, all guns pointed our direction.

Babs walked towards the distressed father. Beads of sweat began to fall from my forehead, bubbling up on my nose next.

"Babs please," I said as calmly as I could, not wanting her to do anything stupid.

If this man pulled the trigger and harmed Babs, I couldn't promise I would hold it together. Maybe I'd be the one to kill somebody today. I was functioning on a thin thread as it was, coupled with an overdose of adrenaline from the day's events.

Babs took hold of the man's hand.

"Give it to me," she pleaded. "You have so much to live for now."

The baby's father dropped the gun to the floor. He was crying uncontrollably. Babs held him in her arms and hugged him. She kicked his gun to the other side of the room.

I motioned for the Swat Team to stay outside the Operating Room, daring them to come inside. I didn't need anyone else contaminating my sterile environment. One lunatic father was enough for the day.

Patty was still clinging to the baby, proud of having brought life into her little lungs. The baby was crying loudly.

"Now now little one," Patty said nervously.

I knew in my heart of hearts this entire situation was out of Patty's realm of experience.

Babs rushed to her side, helping Patty with the newborn while Gabriel and I finished preparing the mother for recovery. Both mother and daughter were going to pull through their horrendous accident.

Despite my directives, the Swat Team rushed the operating room doors, grabbing the father, handcuffing him, taking him into custody.

Patty handed me the baby. I cuddled the newborn amidst my own bittersweet emotions flooding me, given my inability to customarily hand her off to her mother who was still too critical to share in her new bundle of joy.

"Your Mommy's going to be fine," I said cuddling the newborn both nurses had cleaned and weighed. She was slightly under five pounds.

You're going to be fine too, baby girl," I said as I placed her gently into the incubator next to me. "Daddy's got issues, but I'm sure it will all work out. But, he got to see you being born."

Babs stepped closed to my side, tilting her head against my shoulder, her eyes tearful. I knew she was afraid. And, so was I. But we were in the moment together as always, each having the other's back.

"God damn, you people in obstetrics make me want to go back to the Rain Forest. Helluva lot safer," Gabriel said, connecting IV's up to the baby's mother.

"You did good, Dr. E," Babs said, ignoring Gabriel and signaling the other attendants to help her roll the mother to recovery.

"And so did you Babs," I said, hugging her into my chest. "So did you."

"You can take her to the NIC unit now, Patty," I instructed.

I could feel myself getting emotional. My voice was cracking.

"I got this Dr. E," Patty acknowledged sounding completely confident and in control. I smiled, thinking about how Patty was turning into one very skilled nurse.

Gabriel and I looked at each and then embraced with a hug.

"Man its days like this that take me back to my stint with Doctors Without Borders."

Like me, Gabriel was feeling the rush of adrenaline and excitement.

"Like old times, E."

"I wouldn't know, but I'm sure you're going to tell me."

"Yeah man, I got stories for days," Gabriel laughed, whipping the rubber gloves off his hand, tossing them in the trash receptacle.

My thoughts faded back to Julianna as I watched Patty and the new mommy leave delivery.

I was physically wiped out. I wanted my own precious little newborn in my arms that was coded with Julianna's and my DNA. I wanted to the pleasure of making a baby with her, growing old, and looking back on our lives fifty years from now, sipping brandy, talking about how our grandkids looked like us.

I scampered out of the operating room to get out of my scrubs, shower and dress. The fact that the hospital had been on temporary lockdown was buzzing all over the hospital. Teams of local newspersons had arrived. The local press was infiltrating the hospital by the dozens, asking for comments from the hospital administrators. Camera crews were stationed outside the hospital doors. Dexter Esposito was coming inside the building, rounding the corner down the hallway, headed my direction having overseen statements given to the press by the hospital's public affairs office.

I wanted no part of the hysteria. None of it was important to me. The only thing that was important to me was Julianna. I needed to know if she was safe.

"Dexter," I shouted.

"What is it Dr. Fischer? I hardly have time for you right now," he said, walking at a fast paced towards the elevators. Dexter's hands were filled with had a stack of press releases.

"I need to know if Harper and Julianna are safe?"

The double doors of the elevator opened, and Dexter jumped on, ignoring me as if I were speaking in a foreign language. I jumped on the elevator behind him, right as the doors closed.

"I said I need to know if Harper and Julianna are safe?" I asked again, grabbing Dexter by his suit collar, forcing him to drop his papers on the elevator floor while backing him into the elevator corner.

I had reached my limit with Dexter. I was stressed, exhausted, and damn sure didn't feel like playing games with him. I slammed my hand against the red emergency stop button, hitting it hard, bringing our elevator to a sudden halt.

"Get off me Dr. Fischer or else I'll bring you up before the Board."

"Answer me, jackass," I ground out, my hands tightening further on his collar, pulling him closer to my face.

"Of course they are all right," Dexter said, pushing me back off of him, breaking my connection with his collar and brushing himself off. "They have bodyguards, you idiot."

"Oh yeah," I stammered, letting go of his person.

I sighed loudly with relief. I didn't want to reveal to Dexter my care and concern for Julianna, but it was too late. He was the keeper of the information and I needed to know she was safe.

"Have you gone mad? Everything's not about you Elliot. If you put your hands on me again, I'll have you charged with assault. This is a workplace for heaven's sake."

I slammed my hand back against the red emergency button, causing our elevator to jerk back into motion upward.

"You've done that once already, remember. Only this time there will be no one around to save you from me like the last time.'"

The double doors of the elevator opened. I jumped off before allowing Dexter an audience to say anything more to me. Dexter remained on the elevator headed back up to the Ivory Tower.

"You're gonna regret this Fischer," he barked as the elevator doors closed behind me.

---

*T*hank God, Julianna and Harper had managed to make it out of the hospital safely, before all hell broke loose. It was a miracle that no lives were lost at the end of the day.

The mere fact that I had her new number made my heart happy. Her giving me the invitation was even better. This was progress. As far as I was concerned, Julianna wasn't totally done with me either. Some part of her must have wanted to see me as much as I needed to see and talk to her.

For the first time in over a week I actually wanted to get back to my own home. My mind was frazzled from lack of sleep, our first fight, and worst of all learning that she had volunteered to unknowingly be in a rigged auction date with contrived by Oliver and Dexter for the hospital fundraiser. I was going to be fucked six ways to Sunday if that ever went down on my watch. I wanted to rest, and to talk to her in private without having to look over my shoulder for fear someone would be hearing our words.

I had been so tormented from living the last week without her I thought my head was going to explode. But after seeing her today, being in the same room with her again, I knew for certain that I wasn't going to go another week without her. I had a renewed sense of confidence.

There was no way I was going to miss her launch party opening. This was Julianna's dream business. I wanted to be right there with her in the moment, sharing the joyous experience with her. I needed to end this mis-understanding between us about Kimber's baby before things got any further out of hand. I wanted our relationship back on track before the fundraiser. I needed my energy to figure out a way to thwart Oliver's plans to date Julianna under some pretense of raising money for the hospital.

My phone buzzed, pulling me out of my thoughts. *The Halls of Montezuma* was playing.

It was Xavier

"Elliot, it's X."

"Hey man, what's up."

"I'm around the corner from the hospital. I heard about the hospital lockdown. I wasn't sure if I had to come infiltrate the place and rescue you and Gabe."

"We're fine really," I said. "Health insurance, or shall I say, the lack thereof, got between a man and his baby. But thanks for checking."

"I thought I'd give you lift home. I want to catch up, see if your six pack has turn to flab. Gabe tells me you've fallen in love, and have gone off the side of the cliff. I haven't heard from you all week."

"Sorry man. It's been a tough week. Julianna taking care of me was the best thing to happen to me in a long while, and before I knew it, the drama with Kimber had started up again, and poof Julianna was gone."

"So go get your woman, man. Do what you do, my brother."

"That's the plan X, that's the plan. But it's not only her. I fear I'm on the wrong side of the fence with her brother Nicholas as well. He actually showed up on my doorstep dragging her out of my home."

"Damn, man. That can't be good, being on the bad side of family and all," Xavier said, letting out a slow whistle.

I felt a wave of sadness come over me, reliving the loss of Julianna over a week ago, but I quickly pushed that feeling out of my mind. I wasn't going to lose the love of my life now that I found her.

"Yeah tell me about it. I managed to be knee deep in shit, all because of Kimber and Dexter. This is not how I like to roll."

I brought Xavier up to speed on everything that had happened today with Gabe and my confrontation with Dexter, Mario's hack job, the fundraiser meeting regarding the auction, and my conversation with Julianna.

"Well you're off to a new found start E, you got her digits today, that's progress," Xavier said through the phone. "You didn't get killed trying to bring another baby into the world. I say it was a very good day."

I walked through the double doors of the hospital, phone still up to my ear listening to him. Xavier's Lexus was parked in the hospital standing area. I slid my phone to the off position, tucking it in my pocket. I jumped in the front seat of his car.

"Jesus man, you look like shit," X said, with a look of surprise. "When have you slept last?"

"It's been awhile," I said, wishing he would change the subject. I knew I looked like hell. The only person that hadn't said it in the last twenty-four hours was Julianna. But that didn't mean she wasn't thinking it.

"Whatever the plan is man, you're not going to get that pint sized princess back looking like shit. You need some rest, dude."

I shut my eyes and laid back against the headrest, wishing I could fall asleep, but knowing full well my mind and body weren't going to rest until I had a chance to speak to Julianna in private.

Moments later, Xavier was opening his car door, shaking my shoulder.

"Wake up E, you're home man."

I must have dozed off and didn't realize it. I was glad that X was the one driving, otherwise I'd be lying is some ditch right now. I had seriously burnt the candle at both ends this time. Stick a fork in me. I was done. I was suffering from exhaustion.

"You need some rest E, or else all that time off spent healing in the arms of Tinkerbell is going to be all for naught."

"Yeah man, even I have to admit I need rest. Thanks for the lift, X."

I managed to stumble my way back into my home, letting myself in, opening the door and throwing myself across my bed, my head hitting my pillow. I inhaled the smell deeply.

Julianna's scent still infiltrated my pillow. Damn.

 _ulianna_

he first week of December was practically gone. In three more weeks it would be Christmas, which meant the New Year was right around the corner. The launch party for _Sugar Mommy's_ was fast approaching. I only had two days left to make sure everything was absolutely perfect before Saturday night. I could feel my nervous energy rising.

Logan and Maya were helping me put the finishing touches on the decor. All my staff were in place. Equipment was installed. Invitations had gone out. RSVP's had been properly returned. I wanted everything to be flawless. My first introduction into the New York business community was riding on this launch. I didn't want to be the one in my family to taint the family name with a launch failure. Especially since I was a young woman entrepreneur among a family of genius businessmen. Everything had to unfold perfectly.

I'd managed to stay clear of my brother Nicholas as much as

possible over the last week, taking advantage of the fact that I truly was too busy for chitchat. I'd gotten a text message from my brother Blake earlier in the week, teasing me that my girlfriends and I were trying to give Nicky a heart attack.

I never did hear the end of Nicky's non-stop rampage about Logan, Maya, and I flashing our butts at the security cameras. Nicky was so pissed, he cursed through my speakerphone in Italian for so long I could hear his wife Harper in the background, threatening to cut off his sexual privileges for a month. She reminded him that he was behaving emotionally, forgetting what it was like to be a young person having a few kicks.

Nicholas insisted that his sister's ass on display for all to see was where he drew the line in the sand. Then he went on and on again, cursing some more in Italian. I closed my eyes, listening on my speakerphone at him carrying on for what felt like hours, even though it was only minutes.

I tuned out the parts about Logan and Maya being bad influences on me, my mind coming to attention when parts of his flurry of curses sounded as if he were going to have our fathers cut our credit lines if we didn't grow up and start acting like the well-bred women we were trained to be.

My brother loved me, and would never do such a heinous act, but I momentarily contemplated the fact that maybe my gals and I had pushed the envelope too far this time. We *were* pretty high, showing our asses, sporting our new tattoos. I giggled to myself, thinking how much fun we had that night conspiring to come up with a plan to deal with Elliot that never materialized. But we paid heavily for it the next couple of days in hangovers.

No doubt, I was getting older. But so was my brother, which meant his tolerance for our bullshit was waning. A wife and kids had grown him up. I decided he'd forgotten what he used to do at my age.

It was hard for me to get a word in edgewise, though I tried on several occasions to interrupt his tirade. No doubt, Maya, Logan and I were pretty stoned that night. It was hard for me to explain anything to Nicholas that made sense, so I put on my big girl panties, let him rant, and took the well-deserved verbal lashing in stride.

When he got to the part about the new tattoos, he switched languages. He'd moved on to French curses. I couldn't help but love him. By the time he was finished throwing his fit, he was yelling "fuck this shit," in English.

Poor Harper. I felt bad that she had to deal with my brother's funk for however long it was going to take him to come down from his anger with us. At least I lived eleven floors underneath him and didn't have to deal with him on the day to day. That was why she was the wife. Wives had to deal with their husbands' tirades. Better her than me. I was just the sister whose girlfriends were making every effort to cheer me up.

I looked at myself in the mirror, brushing my hair, wondering how I'd get out of the dog house with my brother by Saturday night. I put my brush down, thinking he'd have to get over it soon or later. Being a Becker wasn't as hot as folks thought it was. I envied other young woman who had their personal freedom, because they didn't have to carry around a family name that was fodder for the psychos to slander or kidnap. The good news was I'd made an internal change. After this business with Oliver and Elliot, I was no longer going to be the gal that could be readily put aside and taken for granted. I was coming into my own, and in a major way. The world was going to have to take note of me sooner or later. And as far as I was concerned the sooner the better. *Sugar Mommy's* was opening in two days. I was off to a running start—with or without a man. And the way things were looking, I was going to be without.

Elliot looked the worse for wear the day of the hospital lockdown, so I could only imagine what he must have been going through since. It was all over the local news how Elliot and Gabriel managed to maintain a sense of calm, save the lives of a mother and baby, and avoid being shot to death by a distraught father and husband. A mad man brandishing a handgun in his operating room was a lot for him to handle, but I'd been going through a lot myself too.

The last few days, I had gone from being worried sick, to relieved, to pissed, to sad, and back to worried sick all over again. I couldn't take it anymore. The circle of Elliot, Kimber, babies, and gun threats were wearing me out. I wanted off the highs and lows of the gray-eyed thrill ride known as Dr. Elliot Fischer.

All that talk in the hospital conference room with Elliot hadn't changed much between us. I still hadn't spoken to him, despite his insistence that he needed to speak to me. I had received several texts from Elliot saying it was urgent that he speak to me. He had resorted to blowing up my phone as well, but I'd been making it a habit of pushing his repeated calls into my voicemail. I focused my attention on the opening, refusing to listen to his numerous voicemails. I must have had ten messages from him. But I didn't want to get any more upset than I already was at this point.

---

*M*aya's ringtone *Fancy* by Iggy Azalea began playing loudly. I grabbed my phone.

"Who Dat? What's up?"

"You're what's up Jules," she said, ignoring my joke. "Your man has resorted to calling me now because you won't answer your phone."

"Who, Elliot?"

"Unless there's some other man whose mind you've managed to have blown. Yes, Jules, Elliot."

"Why's he calling you?"

"Because he wants to see you Jules. And he sounds heartbroken. You didn't hear this from me because I promised, fingers crossed behind my back Jules, not to say anything. But Logan was right. That's not his baby Kimber is having. He has no intention of losing his relationship with you over Kimber's drama."

"It's a good thing you crossed your fingers woman. Otherwise your ass would be grass and I'd be the lawnmower."

"You know my loyalty is to you and not Elliot, Jules. I needed to hear what he had to say, so I could call you and tell you what the tea leaves were saying."

We both fell out laughing at ourselves.

"But I ain't mad at you, Jules. I've got no problem with you making him work for it."

"I've been busy with the *Sugar Mommy* opening. I didn't want to get on any more emotional treadmills for a while, Maya. You're doing the photography Saturday night, right?" I said, trying to change the conversation from Elliot. I didn't have a plan on how I was going to handle Elliot, and I wasn't ready to commit to any plan of action with Maya at this moment.

"That's the plan Jules. I'll be sure to get some good shots so that you'll get plenty of media coverage afterwards. Everything's going to be perfect Jules, not to worry."

I was startled out of my thoughts with Maya by the sound of the intercom buzzing in my apartment from the concierge's desk, ringing loudly.

"My doorbell's ringing Maya. I'll check you later."

"Okay Jules. Talk to you later babe."

I ended my phone call with Maya to see who was at my door.

"Yes Rick?" I said, releasing the intercom button.

"Ms. Becker, You have a delivery. Shall I send the delivery person up?"

"Yes please."

I knew Craig was outside my door. He would screen whoever was there. One of the venders for *Sugar Mommy* has probably gotten confused on the delivery location.

I opened the door. Predictably, Craig was standing outside my door, giving a young teen a pat-down, signing a delivery sheet and tipping him generously. Craig looked aggravated, his brow furrowed tightly as the young teen gave a loud whistle for two of his other compadres to proceed into my home carrying dozens of beautiful vases filled with pink roses in their hands. Craig properly inspected each vase individually, as if there were a bomb inside them or something. I shook my head in frustration feeling Craig was overreacting.

"Is there a card?"

"Yes ma'am," the young teen said, handing me a piece of beautiful pink stationery. He and his friends continued to place the vases anywhere they could find a space in my home.

"Somebody's really got case for you," the young teen teased.

I could feel the blush heating my face over this overt display of extravagance. Inwardly I was overjoyed with glee, knowing deep down that this must be Elliot's way of cracking the ice that had settled over my heart. Craig was staring at me as if he were owed an explanation as to who they were from after his hard work of inspecting each vase, and helping to find a suitable location. Craig was glaring at me with a look of expectation.

I swear Craig was starting to feel like one of the girls in a weird kind of way. It had to be hard for him watching me on the gray-eyed emotional rollercoaster, and much like my brother Nicholas, be totally powerless to do anything about it. I held the card up to my nose, smelling the lovely lavender scent on the card, grinning internally but trying to maintain my poker face. I read the card privately.

Julianna,

Because of you, I know what love is. Placing you now in the circle of love that blooms in my heart for you every day. Ever Thine. Ever Mine. Ever Yours,

Love Elliot.

"Dr. Fischer," I said out loud to Craig. "They're from Elliot."

Craig nodded in acquiescence with a look of satisfaction on his face.

"Well done. Balls to the wall," Craig muttered out loud. I grinned, no longer being able to hold back my excitement. Craig looked pleased that I had a smile on my face again.

"So it appears," I responded, nodding my head in agreement.

Craig nodded, opened my door and was gone again.

I fisted my hand up in the air, pulling my elbow down sharply giving myself a mental high five in my head.

Elliot hadn't given up on our relationship, despite the fact I'd been refusing to speak to him. I was vacillating between feeling guilty and overjoyed. I didn't understand how we could be together if he were having a baby. But based on my conversation with Maya, apparently

Elliot's not going to be a father. But it was time now for me hear what he had to say. I needed to hear this admission again with my own ears. Because deep down, I didn't want us to be done either.

I looked around my home filled with a sea of beautiful roses in different shades of pink. It felt like a piece of Hawaii had landed in my living room in the dead of the winter and I was ecstatic. I totally loved it. I searched endlessly for my phone so I could call Elliot and thank him.

*M*y intercom buzzed again before I was able to find my phone. I was flustered I couldn't find it. I was sure it was Craig calling from the foyer, making sure I was dressed. I suspect my brother had come down out of his Penthouse to check on me, but I was curious why he hadn't just used his key. I swung open the double doors, hardly able to wait to see Nicky's face when he saw the sea of pink filling my home.

"Hey gorgeous." Gray Eyes was peering down on me, taking me in from head to toe, his tone deep and husky.

I was certain I was doing a horrible job of concealing the shocked expression on my face. Elliot was the last person I'd expected to be standing in my doorway.

"Come in Elliot. I wasn't expecting company. I've been looking for my phone so I could call you and thank you for all this," I gasped, waving my hands out to my side referring to the state of my living room. "The flowers are beautiful."

Elliot unraveled his red cashmere scarf from around his neck, seeking my permission with his eyes to take off his black leather bomber jacket. He handed me his jacket, and I nervously picked a spot on the back of my kitchen barstool to drape his jacket. He was wearing tight jeans and a black t-shirt that wore like a second skin, accentuating his beautiful biceps and tight abs. He looked so sexy in his casual dress. I had a strong urge to put my arms around his neck. I wanted to kiss those beautiful inviting lips.

"Julianna?"

A rush of heated desire ran through me as I heard him say my name. I wanted to get him naked on a bed of those pink roses. I wanted to feel his touch all over me. I had a deep urge to feel his body next to mine, but I constrained myself. He was obviously here to talk. And, we're long overdue for *the talk*.

"Yes Elliot," I replied almost in a whisper.

Elliot took two long strides towards me. I took one step backwards.

"You've been pushing my calls into your voicemail. Avoiding me," he said, stepping closer into my space. I planted my feet this time.

I felt the butterflies form in my stomach. He was standing so close to me, we could practically touch. I could feel the heat radiating between our two bodies.

"Why Juliana? Haven't you wanted to hear my explanation for what happened with Kimber to ruin our Thanksgiving night? I've wanted to put this behind us for so long."

"I think an early pregnancy stick falling out of Kimber's purse was explanation enough. Or did you think I missed that?"

Well now the cat was out of the bag. It was time to deal with the proverbial elephant in the room. I would finally hear the truth from Elliot. Good Lord, I was back on the emotional rollercoaster again. In a state of ecstasy thirty minutes ago riding on a high, and now holding my breath in anticipation of a possible dip and a turn headed to a new low. I wasn't sure I could handle whatever information was coming at me next. Maya had tipped his hand, but what if she were mistaken? I wasn't ready for bad news.

"I'm not the father of Kimber's baby. I've been trying to tell you this for days. I haven't been with Kimber, or any other woman, for that matter. I've only been with you."

I heard myself sigh out loud in relief.

"You are all that I need and want," Elliot said, his fingers reaching up, catching a curl of my hair in his hands, twirling it.

Elliot's eyes never left mine as he waited for me to absorb his words. My thoughts scattered throughout my brain at high speed. I wondered why Kimber would show up at his home if not to tell him she was pregnant with his baby? Elliot read my thoughts, answering my unspoken question before I could speak it.

"She wanted an abortion. I don't deal in abortions."

I knew Elliot was telling the truth. His eyes didn't lie. He would never let any woman abort his child. Kimber or otherwise. Elliot lived and breathed for the babies. It didn't take a degree in rocket science to know that. To know that was to know Elliot.

"My God Elliot, I never even considered that it couldn't be yours. I'm sorry for not giving you the benefit of the doubt."

"Kimber can be vicious. She figures if she can't have me, no one else can either. Even if she's pregnant by someone else."

I felt guilty for how quick I jumped to the conclusion that Kimber waving an EPT stick meant that Elliot had to be the father. My brother was right. Sometimes things aren't always what they appear. I had shut Elliot out unnecessarily without regard for his feelings. I dropped my head down, feeling pretty shitty, a case of guilt preventing me from holding my gaze to his. Elliot's fingers slid off my curls, caressing the side of my cheek. He lifted my chin, forcing me to look at him. While I was curious to know who the father was, I knew Elliot wouldn't betray Kimber's privacy to discuss the details any further. I decided I didn't want to talk about Kimber anymore so I deflected to change the subject.

"I loved the flowers Elliot. Such a nice surprise."

I had no idea how I was going to keep all of these roses. I was going to have to check in with Logan and Maya on how best to handle all these flowers, but I wasn't going to share that concern with Elliot. It was so thoughtful of him. I wanted to relish the moment.

"I wanted to make sure you knew how I felt, how much I missed you baby."

"I missed you too," I said sheepishly. My thoughts were still racing. This was a lot to take in after the chaotic week we'd had.

"There's another matter we need to discuss Julianna."

"Oh?"

"Yes."

Elliot walked over to his leather jacket, reaching towards the inside pocket. He pulled out a blue velvet box tied with a pink satin ribbon.

"I wanted you to have something special to wear for the launch of *Sugar Mommy's*. A token of my affection for you. Once I gave you the key to my heart. I was embarrassed when Kimber arrived wearing the same necklace. I have no idea how she managed to have on the same necklace she'd stolen from me earlier."

"We don't have to talk about this Elliot."

"Oh but we do. Julianna, I need you to know my intentions," he said, his voice low and calm.

"I thought maybe you'd gave the key to your heart necklace to all the women in your life, so I left it. I didn't want to be part of that. I'd given up on loving you. I want to be special in a man's eyes."

I could see the pained look that flickered across Elliot's face in almost a nanosecond.

"You are special to me Julianna. You are so special, baby; I won't be caught in that position with you ever again."

"No?" I quizzed him a bit sarcastically, looking at him as if he were like all the rest that had come before him.

"No," he said sternly, not appreciating my sarcasm. Elliot placed the blue velvet box in my hand, wrapping his own hands around mine. I recognized the insignia. The box was from Harry Winston's, the Diamond Maker King himself. My thoughts were swirling in my head much like the butterflies in my stomach. I willed myself to remain calm, and to relax.

"Sweetheart, I had this custom made especially for you. Because you see, contrary to your opinion, you are indeed very special to me."

My eyes widened. I slowly tugged the pink satin ribbon from around the box. I was going to have to remember to tell Craig that he was right. Elliot's gone all out this time.

I lifted the lid on the beautiful velvet case. Holy balls to the walls. I wobbled a bit and Elliot grabbed my elbow to steady me. I ran my fingertip around the sparkly diamonds. My eyes beheld the most beautiful choker designed as a zipper, the necklace pavé-set throughout with brilliant cut diamonds. The pulley was modeled with a dangling cupcake set with tapered baguette pink diamonds mounted in a platinum setting. It was flawless.

"Holy balls to the wall," I said out loud.

"Do you like it Julianna?"

"Bejeezus Elliot it's beautiful," I said, feeling the tears welling up in the back of my eyes.

"Good baby, because it's the first piece in the Julianna *Sugar Mommy* Couture Collection, designed especially with you in mind. I plan to add to this collection every special moment between us that I can."

I search Elliot's face as I try to find my words. It took a lot for most men to overwhelm me, but in this moment I was speechless. I'd never felt more special in any other time in my life.

"Will you wear this for me at the *Sugar Mommy* launch opening Julianna?"

"Does this make me your cupcake Elliot?" I laugh, injecting some playful humor so as to lighten our moment. I'm nervous. I'm in shock. I'm enamored. I'm on cloud nine. I'm falling in love.

"This very much makes you my cupcake; my woman, my lover, and anything else you want or need me to be."

"You know you're forcing me to have to walk around under guard, every time I wear this necklace Elliot."

I'm still trying to keep the mood light in fear that I may pass out any moment now in disbelief.

"The only thing I want to guard baby, is your heart."

I looked into Elliot's gray eyes knowing he meant every word. I gave him a huge grin. I reached for the delicate choker, my hands shaking. Elliot helped to put it around my neck, snapping the lobster claw into place. It was exquisite.

Elliot leveled his eyes at me, giving me a soft kiss on the lips. I reached up, wrapping my arms around his neck, pulling my body close to his. I kissed his lips, prodding my tongue in his mouth, happy that he opened for me, tangling his tongue with mine.

"Am I forgiven Julianna?"

"Absolutely," I whispered, my voice softening.

"Good. Because the only babies I'm going to have are going to be yours."

"You sound pretty sure of yourself Dr. Fischer."

"Don't worry baby. I'm going to make it my mission to make a believer out of you yet," Elliot laughed, snapping one of the heads of a pink rose off, planting it behind my ear.

"My mother died in childbirth having me," I whispered. "The thought of having babies scares me."

I can't believe I've voiced my vulnerability, my fears, out loud. I've never said this to any man I've dated, but I felt compelled to say it to Elliot. It felt safe to say out loud.

"Julianna, I'll never lose you or any children we may have together. I swear to you sweetheart, on everything I own."

"I'm subject to have panic attacks around newborn babies," I said, hoping Elliot would take me seriously.

"As am I," he said, dismissing my concerns.

"I'm so serious Dr. Fischer."

"As am I," he said with all sincerity.

"Newborn babies racing to get here make me nuts," he said in a comforting manner. "The fact that the babies we would make together are eager to get to us, makes me crazy."

It is in this moment, I knew Elliot and I belonged together.

Elliot deepened our kiss. Our breathing started to escalate and we both began to pant. I felt my heart thumping loudly as if it was going to jump out of my chest. I was so relieved and excited to hear Elliot wasn't having a baby with Kimber, I could burst. I'd shared my deepest fear with him, and he was not walking away from me.

That knowledge alone was amplifying my level of excitement. The intense passion accentuated the sizzle between us. Together we got lost in the kiss. We'd not made love in over a week and we both were hyper-aware of our longing for each other. The sexual tension between us was building fast. I was caught up in the visceral reaction my body was having towards him yet again.

Elliot placed his hands around my waist, his body melding into mine. Everything after that was instinctive between us. He lifted my leg to his hip, curling his hand up under me to support me. I felt the heat growing in his groin. Elliot backed up two steps, sinking both of us in the oversized winged white leather chair while hoisting me on his lap. I straddled him, moving my hands under his thin t-shirt, fingering the David Yurmen dog tag hanging around his beautiful neck. I loved touching his skin, his rock hard abs. His kisses intoxicated me. Elliot was groaning out loud, his hands moving towards my breasts, pushing up under my bra, his fingers squeezing my nipples. A jolt of electrical shock flowed through me at his touch. I threw my head back with an audible cry.

"Look at me baby," Elliot said, his hands sliding up my thighs where my skirt had crept up around my hips exposing my lower body.

I gently ground against his erection, my body and mind lost in the moment. I forced my heavy eyes to look at him. Elliot pierced my soul with a look of tenderness and reverence.

"This is real, Julianna. You need to know this. My feelings for you are real, baby."

I nodded my head affirmatively at Elliot, grinding myself more forcefully now against his erection.

"Tell me you know this baby."

I shake my head more rapidly now. I'm about to explode any minute now. I could feel my orgasm mounting, and Elliot wasn't even inside of me yet. I opened my mouth to say something, to scream in ecstasy, just as Elliot pulled me to his mouth, slipping his tongue in my mouth, caressing the inside. I moaned in his mouth as he placed one hand on my butt, grinding me hard against him, while placing his other hand on the back of my head deepening our kiss. I caught his tongue, sucking gently, feeling his realness in my body, in my mind, in my heart.

As my orgasm washed over me, I plopped my head on Elliot's chest while he stroked his fingers softly through my hair. Our hearts were beating rapidly. Elliot groaned softly, taking a deep breath, slowing his own pulse down.

"Sweetheart I want to rip all your clothes off right now and take you, but I can't. One, I don't have a condom and two, I'm on call at the hospital. If I start making love to you now, I guarantee you once I start, I won't stop for the next two days, right up unto the hour that you have to be at the opening. But I want you so bad. I plan to make this up to you."

Elliot was smiling down on me with a hungry look, and I knew he was waiting for my response.

"Is that a promise Elliot?" I said, looking up at him, fingering my pink diamond cupcake.

"It is indeed."

I knew Elliot was not in complete control of his schedule as an Obstetrician. Babies come when they want to come which is mostly on their own time frame. But I respected his commitment to his profession, because I know there will be days when he'll have to do the same for me in reverse. Running a business is equally demanding.

"Can I accompany you to the launch opening on Saturday night, Julianna? I've cleared my calendar to be there for you."

I swear this man could read my every thought. My thoughts had gone to schedules and he'd cleared his calendar already. I was tickled pink. And then I giggled to myself realizing I was totally surrounded in pink.

"I'd like nothing more Elliot."

Elliot wrapped his arms around me, scooting me back closer to him when I shifted a little. He threaded his fingers through mine. We sat for a minute relaxing in each other's arms.

"Julianna?"

"Yes?"

"You have a new tattoo."

I realized this was a rhetorical question, so I paused to see if he planned to say more.

"It's in Italian. What does it say?"

I took a deep breath and exhaled before answering. No way I was telling Elliot about Maya, Logan, and my drunken marijuana-infused tattoo session. It was bad enough Nicky still hadn't gotten over it. No way was I going to discuss this with Elliot and be at risk for ruining our beautiful moment. But the more I thought about it perhaps it was kind of poetic. *All Who Wander Are Not Lost.*

"It means I'm found. I'm no longer lost. You've found my heart," I said quietly.

Elliot gave me a puzzled look, but leaned down and brushed his lips against mine.

"And you've found mine."

24

$\mathcal{D}$*exter*

"$\mathcal{M}$r. Esposito, a Mr. Oliver Banks is here to see you," Melissa, my receptionist, spouted through the speakerphone.

"Send him in please."

Oh man, this was perfect. Oliver Banks had come to see *me*, here at the hospital. He must be desperate to talk to Julianna Becker. What a perfect way for me to screw that piss ant Elliot and make some money at the same time. Goddamn, the numbers are all going my way today.

"Oliver, so good to see you."

I shook his hand, which was soft as butter. I would guess the man never worked a hard day in his life.

"Thank you, Mr. Esposito, for taking time out of your busy schedule to see me."

"Call me Dexter. It's not every day the hospital gets a sizable donation for the fundraiser. No reason we can't be on a first name basis, Oliver."

"Dexter it is."

Wow. This guy was straight out of Revenge Of The Nerds. What the hell did Julianna Becker see in this guy? Had to be the money. No, she doesn't need money. Maybe he was good in bed. Either way, I'm going to pimp him good. Take his money, and get all the recognition for bringing in a sizable donation to the hospital. Elliot thinks he's the only one that can get a hospital wing established. I could make that happen too. The Oliver Banks Wing for . . . what . . . I got it . . . anal repairs?

"As you know, I'm planning to make a sizable donation at the hospital fundraiser, specifically during the auction. I understand you're the man to see?"

"I am indeed. The hospital is so grateful to have you as a supporter. Donations of a million dollars don't come around every day."

"Well there's a lot more where that came from, and a little something for you to the tune of ten thousand dollars if you can see your way to helping me to get some private time alone with Julianna Becker."

"I'm at your disposal. You can count on me to help you any way I can. But I'm curious. Why do you need to pay to see Ms. Becker? Didn't the two of you have history? Or was that just media gossip?" I asked.

I knew I was walking on eggshells here with Oliver Banks, but what the hell. He wanted something from me. I was the one Oliver Banks needed right now. I was the man of the hour. I'd Googled him and read all the tabloids. I was well aware that Julianna Becker was one of his women.

"Well we did," he said, getting up out of the side chair and walking towards the picture window to look out, his camel cashmere coat hanging loosely on his shoulders. "Our relationship ended, but our friendship has been momentarily derailed."

"Friendship momentarily derailed? What does that mean exactly? Not that it's any of my business," I said, mindful that I may piss him off.

"Her brother Nicholas keeps her surrounded by security twenty-four seven. Since our break-up, I'm not readily able to get close to her. I see no reason why she and I can't be friends."

Friends? I bet he meant 'friends with benefits'; a fuck buddy piece on the side now that he's a married man. Somehow I'm not quite sure I believed any part of this cockamamie story.

"Oh, I get it. She's royalty and you've fallen from grace?"

Oliver turned away from the window, staring at me with steely eyes. He grit his teeth and I could see he wasn't happy with me exposing his vulnerability.

"Can you make this happen or not Dexter?" Oliver asked, walking over to my desk, planting both knuckles on it, glaring at me eye to eye.

Oliver needed to ease up. It was a fundraiser for Pete's sake. It wasn't like this was life or death.

"Yes I can make this happen, Mr. Banks. Making things happen around here is my specialty."

Oliver absorbed my words and collected himself. He reigned himself in, adjusting his physical appearance. Hell, I could make manna fall from heaven with this kind of money. I reasserted my point with confidence just to make sure he would have no doubt in my abilities.

"Trust me. I will make it happen," I repeated, giving him a smug grin.

Oliver reached into the inside pocket of his suit jacket and lay down a check made out to the hospital for two-hundred and fifty thousand dollars.

"A small deposit," he uttered.

He pulled out another five thousand dollars in cash and slammed it on my desk. "You'll get the rest at the auction," he snapped.

Nerds do have tempers, don't they? I mulled over with myself, debating whether I wanted to slap this rich nerd across his face. But then I looked at the stack of Ben Franklins on my desk. I reminded myself to chill out. I was in the workplace.

Our standoff was interrupted by my phone ringing. It was my receptionist Melissa.

"Mr. Esposito, it's Ms. Lawson. I tried to stop her, but—"

And before Melissa could finish her sentence, Kimber stormed her way into my office uninvited.

What the fuck is wrong with this woman? Did her father, Jefferson Lawson not teach this bitch any etiquette at all? Good Lord.

Kimber blasted through my office doors like a runaway freight train. I was starting to believe this woman had anger issues. Daddy Lawson must have missed a couple of dance recitals. Somewhere in her upbringing, she'd made a road trip to Crazy Town and stayed too long. No wonder Elliot got rid of this woman. She was mad as hell. Frazzled. Deck to the nines, straight off the Ms. New York runway exit ramp. Beautiful. Sexy. Pissed. And yes, out of control.

"Kimber darlin', can't you see I'm in a meeting."

Kimber paused. She took in the scene between Oliver Banks and me. She straightened her back. I could see her momentarily reining in her anger.

I hoped she wasn't here to talk about this pregnancy bullshit. She wasn't having a baby—mine or otherwise. She knew I was still annoyed she told Elliot that she was having my baby. I didn't need rumors like this getting out to ruin my reputation around the hospital. That blabbermouth Babs down in the Becker Wing would have a field day with that kind of information.

"Oliver Banks, may I present Kimber Lawson"

Oliver re-directed his attention from me. I grabbed his check, the cash on the table, and slowly slid it in my top drawer like a stealth fighter. Oliver stood in front of the money so as to use his body to hide our transaction from Kimber's view. I made a mental note to myself that the nerd wasn't as nerdy as I thought, but then again, he didn't get on the list of Forbes' youngest entrepreneurs for nothing. Oliver had some kind of useful skill set.

Kimber glanced at me and then at Oliver. She looked beautiful as always, but Kimber smelled money like the gold-digger that she was.

"You're Oliver Banks," she said, batting those pretty 'I'm helpless' eyelashes at him. She flashed that same helpless look that dragged me under her current. I had no doubt those pageant judges didn't stand a chance. Oliver better get a grip or else he's going to end up like the rest of us with a noose around his neck and a red lacquered manicured hand in his pocket.

"And you are?" Oliver said, mesmerized by all that beauty that captures most men in Kimber's tangled web.

"Kimber Lawson. Former Ms. New York. Remember, yes?"

"Oh yes. Who could forget such a beautiful flower?" Oliver said, making a pass at Kimber, taking her hand and kissing it softly. I suspected he didn't really remember her. He was just a nerd with money faking it until he can take it. I knew his type. Wasn't this joker married? What a loser.

My mistake was thinking she was my woman now. Kimber blinked those pretty beautiful brown eyes at him, positioning her body so as to give Oliver a full frontal view of those beautiful breasts some other foolish man paid for dearly.

"What do you need Kimber? I'm in a meeting."

"It's about my necklace," Kimber said, glancing at her well-manicured fingers, not giving me eye contact.

"What about it?" I shuddered, knowing all hell is getting ready to break loose. This is not a conversation I want to have in front of Oliver Banks.

Kimber reached in her clutch and slammed the Tiffany-like necklace down on my desk.

"I'm not a woman that wears knock-off's Dexter. Do you take me for a fool?" Kimber hissed, her eyes narrowing at me.

"What do you mean baby?" I said, pretending that I was clueless.

"I had Daddy's jeweler appraise it. It's a piece of junk, Dexter. Junk!" she shouted. "What am I supposed to wear now to the Fundraiser?"

Somebody needed to give this woman an acting job, because Kimber was very good at feigning helpless. She and I both knew that she owned tons of jewels, real ones. For her to pretend that she had nothing else to wear was beyond the pale. But I got it. This was a money conversation.

"I need a new necklace now. A real one," she continued, her eyes momentarily veering away from me while she made googly eyes at Oliver Banks.

"I have no idea how that could have happened," I lied. "I had my personal shopper handle that purchase. There must have been some kind of mix-up. But I will look into it, honey."

I couldn't wait to send her back home to her father. I'd grown bored with her financial demands. Kimber's credit line with her father far exceeded mine. But no. She wouldn't be happy until she milked every dime she could out of me, despite the fact that she herself came from money. This was so sick. The bitch had money of her own for Christ sakes. I felt like a stooge. I wanted to give her back to Elliot.

"I need a new necklace to go with my new Ralph Lauren gown. It's a must have."

No way I was going to look like a fool in front of Oliver Banks. I needed to give the appearance that I could support a woman like Kimber Lawson, even though I knew I damn well couldn't afford her. And with all the coke she was doing, she was getting more costly every day.

Kimber looked at me, and so did Oliver Banks. They both were waiting to see how this scene was going to play out. My manhood was on the line. I reached in my pocket and handed Kimber my Gold Card.

"Thank you Dexie," Kimber said to me in her best purring voice, snatching my card out of my hand, pausing only to give Oliver Banks her best come-hither look. Oliver was affected. He adjusted his stance and Kimber caught it. I realized my days with Kimber were numbered. She'd been onto her next prey for a while now. If my intuitions were accurate, she would find herself a place on the Oliver Banks roster, which would suit me perfectly fine. I was ready for her to send me back to the minor leagues. She had fulfilled my purpose for her as far as I was concerned. Fuck over Elliot.

"It's so nice to meet you Mr. Banks," Kimber said, her long lashes blinking.

"Oliver, please. I look forward to seeing you both at the fundraiser."

"My pleasure," Kimber said as she extended her manicured hand to him.

Oliver lifted her hand to his lips, kissing her knuckles. I suppose he thought he was rich enough to totally disrespect me in front of my woman and make a play for her, but I caught on to his slime-ball move.

"Go back to work Dexie. I know you're busy love. Tally ho sweetie," Kimber said in a fake British accent, feigning like a second ago she hadn't just bit the hand that fed her all those Jimmy Choo's.

Why the hell was she faking a Naomi Campbell British accent? This bitch isn't British, and she definitely isn't Naomi Campbell.

I put a fake grin on my face in front of Oliver as I said my farewells to Kimber.

"I realize you're a busy man, Dexter. I should move along. Time is money," Oliver said with a smirk on his face as if he'd discovered a hidden treasure.

I would bet the money in my drawer that he was hoping he'd get out of my office fast enough to try to go catch up with Kimber. One thing for sure, I didn't trust this man. I'd take his money, all of it, but I trusted him as far as I could throw him.

"It was good seeing you Oliver. The hospital is grateful for your generosity, as am I."

I could feel the fake smirk on my own face.

"What would we do without benefactors such as yourself."

I reached my hand out to shake Oliver's hand. He grabbed my hand and clinched it tightly.

"You make sure my money is well spent," he hissed in my ear as he shook my hand and pulled his body close to mine.

I nodded in agreement, trying to release my hand from his treacherous grip.

This is turning into a shitty day. First Oliver. Then Kimber. If it weren't for Elliot, Gabriel, and that prima donna Julianna Becker, I wouldn't have half the headaches I do daily on behalf of this hospital.

I opened my drawer and looked at the five thousand dollars in cash.

But then again, life ain't so bad. Money does make the world go round. I laughed out loud.

I buzzed Melissa to come into my office. I made up an excuse that I needed some legal documents copied. I figure she'd know if Oliver made a play for Kimber after he left, and I needed to know the temperature around here.

Melissa stalked into my office as if she were too busy to be bothered with something so un-important as copy work. She entered my office glaring at me through her red framed eyeglasses, looking annoyed.

"You know Mel, for some reason, I can't seem to remember where I put those compliance documents I wanted copied."

Melissa started shuffling papers on my desk, and I knew she wouldn't find them.

"Where did you have them last Mr. Esposito?"

"I don't know. Ms. Larsen had me on my back heel arriving unexpectedly. I seem to have lost my focus here for a minute. Do you know if she's still in the hospital?"

"No, she stormed off pretty quickly after running into Dr. EZ. He was on his way out of the cafeteria and she was headed into the cafeteria."

"Oh Really? I thought those two weren't speaking anymore after their broken engagement?"

I knew Melissa didn't know that I was in relationship with Kimber. Besides my spilling the beans on myself with Oliver, I hadn't gone around advertising my personal business.

"Well clearly nothing's changed. Story goes those two were exchanging harsh words near the coffee stand over a necklace. Dr. E was telling Ms. Larsen to stay away from him and his new lady friend. The fact Dr. E is off the market again is news all throughout the nursing pool," she said, shuffling papers in different stacks on my desk.

Leave it to the hospital nursing pool to have all the dirty gossip as it relates to Elliot.

"You would think those nurses would have something better to do with themselves than to spend their days chatting it up over Dr. Fischer," I snorted.

"Maybe, but after all, Dr. Fischer is single, available, and hot as ever. Any smart woman would make a play for him," Melissa said, turning the knife into my back ever so slowly.

"Actually who gives a damn," I squinted, my mood getting pissier.

"Well Dr. DeLuca must give a damn. He thinks Dr. Fischer's got better things to do seeing how he was the one that dragged his less than willing buddy away from the dogfight with that woman."

Well this was news. And why aren't I surprised? Elliot was back with Julianna Becker, and Kimber was still rubbing his nose in it, reminding him who's boss. I was hoping Julianna would be done with Elliot over that necklace, making it easier for me to cut a pathway with her to speak to Oliver. Now I was going to have to work my magic around Elliot. I needed to make this moment happen, otherwise Oliver would be back in my face looking for his five grand back, and I needed the other five.

"Ms. Larsen had two cups of coffee in her hand. The nursing pool was taking bets as to whether she was going to throw them on Dr. E. But it appears he was saved by the bell, or rather saved by Dr. DeLuca."

Two cups of coffee? Kimber must have been trying to make a play for Oliver. Why in the world would she have two cups of coffee in her hand headed to the cafeteria?

"Forget the copies Melissa," I snapped.

I didn't want to hear any more of this nonsense. I was done thinking about Oliver, Kimber, and Elliot. The only thing I needed to think on was his donation and my money.

Oh, and Dr. Elliot Fischer and Julianna Becker.

25

Elliot

he weather tonight was cold, but the snowfall previously predicted had yet to arrive. I was glad Julianna wasn't going to have to deal with snow, ice, and slush for her opening, but it was December. Anything could happen with Mother Nature.

Our limousine pulled curbside to *Sugar Mommy's*. The launch party was destined to be a spectacular red carpet affair, having been the buzz around town all week. The paparazzi and media talking heads were outside the cafe scrambling to take pictures at the arrival of the guests who'd arrived by invitation only. Parks and Parks Security had a female security woman named Blue on the door checking off the names of the arriving guests. Julianna said she belonged to her brother's security detail, and if you crossed her the wrong way, you might end up with your face turning blue. Clearly a woman no one with a brain wanted to have to deal with at all. I took Julianna at her word that Blue was effective at her job. A no nonsense woman.

Our driver briefly lowered the window for Craig to speak with

Julianna. We could see the barrage of flashes from the camera lights outside.

Craig ducked his head inside through the window.

"Sorry Ms. Jules. Your sister-in-law's father has arrived ahead of us. We've got Secret Service to deal with tonight. Your Dad's with him."

"No problem Craig. I could use a moment," Julianna said nervously.

Julianna and I would have to delay our entrance for her father Blake Ross Becker, II and his good friend Senator Clayton Lawrence Montgomery to enter first. The Senator's protection detail would have to get in place before Julianna could make her arrival.

"Do Nicky and Harper have to deal with this often?" I asked, pouring us both a flute of Champagne while we waited, rubbing my hand up and down Julianna's smooth legs.

"He and Harper are pretty much used to the hullabaloo that comes with being a U.S. Senator's daughter. Nicky knew that when he married Harper. They've had to deal with it throughout their entire marriage."

"I imagine that can be a lot to cope with regularly."

"Actually Nicky has a harder time coping whenever my father's around. He gets extra cranky whenever Big Daddy's around."

"Then I'll be sure not to take anything Nicky says tonight personally."

"Now that the buzz is that Harper's father is a potential vice presidential contender, security is even more intense."

"I'm sorry you have to wait to get into your own place of business."

"Well I invited them, so this is the price I must pay," she said, swigging her Champagne down quickly.

"It's also the price of good press," I said, topping her glass with more Champagne. "Pay me now or pay me later, right?"

"It comes with the territory. I don't mind waiting. I need a moment to calm myself."

Julianna nodded, completely used to this experience. Still, I could sense she was nervous. She hated life in the golden cage, so I felt the less said about it the better. I quickly changed the subject to something more pleasant.

"You look beautiful baby. Tonight's going to be an awesome night. I'm proud of you. I'm even more prouder to be at your side."

Julianna was dressed to kill in an elegant strapless neon pink cocktail dress with a matching neon pink fox fur coat. Her new zippered diamond necklace with the pink cupcake dangled perfectly against her creamy pale skin. Her beautiful legs were accentuated by a pair of black badass gladiator-looking stilettos.

"You look so hot."

"You can thank Michael Kors," she giggled.

"Well I'm not sure I want to thank Michael just yet. I have a strong urge to handcuff you to my wrist, so as not to let anyone get near you tonight. I know I'm going to have to bat the wolves off my woman all night."

"I wanted to wear something elegant and understated to accent my beautiful necklace. I really do need security tonight," she laughed, fingering the diamond cupcake yet another time, as if she were making sure it was there.

Julianna opened her little black clutch, and slid out a tiny red mirror shaped like a pair of lips, touching up her lips with gloss. I was seconds from pulling her closer to me, desiring to suck those pouty lips hard. She read the hungry look on my face.

"Don't even think about it," she chided me.

"I've got big promises to keep, remember baby?"

"Yes I do remember Elliot, and I pretty much plan to hold you accountable when this night is over," she smiled slyly, "but not before. You look handsome as ever tonight too, Dr. EZ," she giggled, mocking me.

"Oh please, you mean you've heard that nickname already too?"

"You're the talk of the nursing pool at the hospital, Elliot. That's all I heard after I fainted in your arms. And to think you're all mine now," she said, licking her lips, running her fingers down the side of my face.

"I'll always be all yours Julianna."

Craig knocked twice on the window, re-directing our attention, prompting our driver to lower the window.

"Showtime Ms. Jules. You ready?"

"Yes, let's do the damn thing. I've got promises to collect later," she laughed, tapping me on my knee and smiling.

---

*T*he camera lights flashed all around us as Julianna and I made our entrance, taking pictures together on the red carpet. I held her close to me to keep her warm and to protect her from the night air. It was kind of nice that Maya had arranged a mini red carpet extravaganza to celebrate the opening. I momentarily felt like a celebrity, as did all the arriving guests. Julianna wanted each of her guests to feel special.

Once inside, Maya was busy taking everyone's photos as she had the photographer's exclusive for the evening. Julianna and her brother posed together, along with several more shots of Harper, Nicholas, and myself as a group.

"I'll see that these photos make Page Six in the morning," Nicholas whispered in Julianna's ear. "This will be great publicity for the business."

"Thank you Nicky, for everything," she smiled with deep affection.

"We'll build your brand quickly. You think you can keep up, Cookie?"

"I'm ready to make my mark brother."

Nicholas kissed Julianna on her forehead, then released her back into my arms. He grabbed his wife Harper from behind, ignoring the fact that she was talking to other dignitaries, pulling her close to his side. Harper let out a squeal, thumping Nicholas playfully in his chest. Harper was looking uber sexy in a white long sleeve midriff sweater with a matching high-waisted knit skirt that hugged all of her curves. She wore a white belt around her waist that looked like a string of pearls. I didn't know what designer she was wearing, but I knew enough from buying Kimber's shoes to recognize some strappy nude

Louboutin stilettos when I saw them. Nicholas had up his game tonight too, elegantly dressed as always in a black Italian made silk suit, white shirt, and silver tie. They looked like the proper power couple that they were.

"Mine," Nicholas said out loud behind her ear, cupping his hands around her waist, and nibbling slightly on her ear.

I wasn't sure who he was talking to specifically. Perhaps that was some mantra he recited to the universe. Either way, I knew better than to get overly friendly with Harper tonight. She was married to a jealous megalomaniac. But I better understood. Because now I felt the same way about his sister. Mine.

I eyeballed Julianna as she tended to each of her guests personally. Everyone in the room was raving over her delicious desserts and pastries. *Sugar Mommy's* was going to forever be on the map for the who's who of New York after this well planned opening.

It was a stunning cafe filled with stunning delicacies. It reminded me of an upscale Parisian Patisserie. Dimly lit chandeliers hung from the ceiling, making for a nice glow on the cream marbled floors. The seating area wrapped around display cases that were packed with gorgeously decorated pastries. There was something in the display cases for everyone.

The aroma in the air smelled heavenly. It triggered memories from my childhood days, when my mother let me indulge myself in the pastry shops of Paris, especially when she was into that hit book *French Women Don't Get Fat*. The display cases were stuffed with decadent red velvet cupcakes, fluffy éclairs, buttery French croissants, gooey rich chocolate brownies, light as air French macarons; cookies in all flavors ranging from maple cranberry oatmeal, chocolate peanut butter to cinnamon sugar snickerdoodles.

Soft jazz was playing in the background, courtesy of Xavier's infamous Aunt, Zoe Cook Gardner. Zoe and her husband Julian Gardner's jazz trio had arrived from Washington Crossing Pennsylvania earlier in the day.

Xavier was blowing his heart out on the saxophone next to his Aunt Zoe. Logan had joined the merry band of jazz musicians playing beautifully on the electronic keyboards. Apparently when Julianna was acting as my nursemaid, her girlfriends Maya and Logan were working deals with Xavier to get his Aunt's trio to play tonight. It all felt right in this moment. I looked around watching Maya working the room taking tons of photographs for her *Sugar Mommy's* exclusive. The night had come together without a hitch.

My heart was warmed watching Julianna's friends and mine coming together to help her launch party be the pinnacle of success. I had no doubt this event would make Sunday Morning's New York Times Style section. A room full of well-heeled dignitaries and their wives, was sure to make the news.

*J*ulianna walked my direction grabbing my hand, pulling me close to her. I was in seventh heaven happy that Julianna was back in my world after that ugly scene Thanksgiving with Kimber. My necklace around her neck was beautiful. I loved admiring it on her.

"Please Elliot, come meet my father and brother. They're across the room with Nicky and Harper," she said, smiling and waving at another elderly couple across the room.

I was stepping into a huge moment. I was going to meet Julianna's father, Blake Ross Becker II. Julianna's father was the kingpin of chicken. He headed the family's chicken processing empire, the largest in the nation. I straightened my tie as we walked his direction. I was pumped looking at him from across the room.

He struck me as a man of power by his appearance alone. Blake Ross Becker was a large man, late sixties, towering over six feet tall with snowy gray hair and a deep booming voice that commanded the attention of anyone within ten feet of him. He carried himself like a man in charge. A large Cuban cigar hung from his mouth, a whiskey neat in his glass. The fact that Julianna was introducing me meant she wanted me to be a part of her family's inner circle. This was a big step for our relationship as far as I saw it.

"Big Daddy, I have someone I'd like you to meet. This is Dr. Elliot Fischer, Chief of the Becker Obstetrical Wing at New York Presbyterian Hospital. And this is my oldest brother Blake Ross Becker, the third."

"Call me Three," her brother Blake said, extending his hand to shake mine.

Three was mid-forties, the handsome cheery type. A whole lot less serious than her brother Nicholas. I knew he was the Becker family's lawyer, but somehow I pegged him for the family cut-up. Three struck me as a man that didn't take life too seriously with his playful personality. While I knew he had a wife and kids, he struck me as the kind of guy that made family dinners totally interesting.

"And of course you already know Nicky and Harper," Julianna said, beaming from ear to ear.

I extended my hand to Julianna's father, and then to her brother, shaking their hands. I nodded at Nicky, who nodded back at me, as if to silently agree he and I needed to bypass formalities. If his eyes could talk, I was certain they were saying "Yeah yeah yeah, spare me the appearances. I'm not sure I can trust you yet."

"Harper you're looking beautiful as always," I said, kissing her Euro-style on both cheeks.

Harper pulled me in close to her giving me a bear hug, ignoring any formalities. Nicky groaned under his breath, but I ignored him.

"Nice to meet you son," her father said to me warmly. "Glad to meet the man that's running that Becker Wing my son built. You must be the young fella my daughter in law brags about that got my grandkids into this world safely. Good job, my boy. Any man that can put up with my son throwing a fit over another man having access to his wife's vagina deserves a medical wing to run," he laughed heartily with a booming laugh that sucked all the air out of the room.

"Big Daddy, behave yourself," Harper said teasingly.

I laughed out loud, before I realized Nicky was the only one in our little group that was frowning, not finding any humor in the conversation.

"Daddy, try not to poke at Nicky tonight," Julianna teased playfully. "Your love always comes out sideways when you and Nicky get together."

Julianna's father slapped Nicky so hard on his back, I thought he was going to choke on his own vodka martini. Harper rubbed her body against Nicky's chest, flashing those big brown eyes, melting the frown right off his face, getting lost in her soothing gaze.

"C'mon Nicky, let me get you another drink," his brother Three said. "Commandment Number Eleven. Thou shall not let thy wells run dry," Three laughed, mocking Nicky, pulling him out of Harper's clutches.

"I'll send him back, Harper, when he parts the waters again. I've got business to discuss with him," Three teased Harper.

It was well known that Nicky had this quirk of pretending he was God. Everybody in the family apparently liked to tease him about it. I personally didn't think it was so smart for them to tease him. He was a man that had the resources to move mountains if he wanted to, but members of the family didn't take him so seriously. But I knew better. I was the biggest benefactor of the Becker Wing endowment. If he thought he was God, have at it. Who was I to dispute him. His wife Harper was nothing to sneeze at either, equally as powerful and wealthy in her own right.

"Excuse me Elliot, but I'd like to introduce Julianna to some of my friends, do you mind?" Harper said.

"Not at all Harper."

"Baby I'm going to go say hello to Gabriel," I said to Julianna. "I'll be here when you get back. I'm not going anywhere."

Julianna smiled, standing on her tiptoes, giving me a small peck on the cheek. I watched as she followed Harper across the room. I scanned the room for Nicky. He was at the bar with Three watching Harper.

I made eye contact across the room with Gabriel, and slowly began making my way through the sea of people, some sitting, some standing, all having a good time, in order to get to my friends.

When I got through the maze of red checkered table-clothed tables, as servers toting trays of pastries and pink Champagne moved about, I pulled out one of the white wrought-iron cushioned chairs where Gabriel was sitting, glad to have a small break with my friend.

"Hey man, how's it going?"

"I've got no complaints, E. This is the life. Open bar. Delectable pastries. Logan for eye candy. Who could ask for a better life?"

I laughed, shaking my head. "And you have the nerve to call *me* easy."

"You should talk. Does that necklace with the cupcake dangling off Julianna's neck that looked like somebody robbed a Brinks truck have anything to do with you by chance?"

"I call it *Sugar Mommy Couture*," I said with a proud look on my face.

"Sweet Dr. E. You can put that one down in the handbook, in case I have to rip a page one day," Gabe said, his gaze shifting from me, back to Logan on the keyboard.

Maya joined our table almost as soon as I did, her camera slung around her neck. She looked beautiful, charmingly professional, at the top of her game. Maya sat next to me, shot a quick snapshot of Xavier, then tossed back a glass of Champagne from a nearby server, asking for another as she set her empty glass back on the tray.

"Isn't he adorable? Who knew he played the sax?"

"We did," Gabriel and I said nonchalantly at the same time, shaking our heads at Maya's comment.

Gabriel playing the saxophone was old hat to us. He claimed playing the saxophone was the ultimate panty dropper. I was starting to believe him. Gabriel was looking at Xavier as if maybe he should take up the instrument. I knew the feeling.

X was wearing black Raybans, blowing Candy Duffer's song, *Solo Sax*, a song that he'd dedicated especially for Maya. His mahogany colored hair hung loose tonight under a black fedora, framing his olive colored face. He was wearing black pants, and white Italian cotton shirt that accentuated his biceps, a black tie pulling his hipster-cool look together.

Logan was making goo goo eyes, lost in all things Gabriel. I looked across the room, noticing Craig in close proximity to Julianna. He was doing his job, but appearing totally unhappy about Xavier putting moves on Maya. Maya was playing a dangerous game. I didn't expect this triangle merry-go-round of Xavier, Maya, and Craig to last too much longer before things came to a head. It was hard to conceal the appearance of things.

Craig's expression had changed from cool to iceberg cold. He looked as if he wanted to put a bullet in Xavier any moment now. Xavier was having too much fun, stoking the Maya flame adding fuel to Craig's fire. One of these days Gabe and I were going to have to stitch our good friend up after some jealous boyfriend or irate husband decided it was time to take him down a notch. Xavier was the king of cool. He couldn't help himself. He loved all women and all women loved Xavier.

As X's song reached its end, Julianna came to the microphone.

"I want to take this moment to thank all my family and friends tonight for your wonderful support of the opening of *Sugar Mommy's*. I hoped you've enjoy yourselves. Please spread the word amongst your friends and family about *Sugar Mommy's*. Do come back again whenever your sweet tooth calls." Julianna grinned, then giggled playfully, thanking all her guests.

Everyone applauded enthusiastically. Xavier's Aunt Zoe announced the Trio would be taking a short break. I had no doubt *Sugar Mommy's* was going to be a huge hit. Everyone in the room was in awe.

"*A*re you over here with the guys having a bromance?" Julianna said playfully, interrupting my thoughts as she joined our table.

Craig was moving in concert with her, hugging the outer wall of the room. He brought his wrist up to his lips mouthing something to another security person across the room who was hovering over Harper.

"You're the only romance I'm ever gonna need," I smiled.

I brushed my thumb across Julianna's knuckle as Gabriel and I stood while Julianna joined our threesome. Logan and Xavier left their instruments, making their way through the maze of guests, joining our table. This moment felt like a replay from Halloween night with the six of us, except this time Julianna and I belonged to each other. Logan and Maya began fawning over Julianna's necklace. They were momentarily interrupted by several of the guests who were starting to leave and coming over to say their good-byes to Julianna, shaking her hand and wishing her well. Julianna's father and the Senator said their good-byes earlier, thankfully taking most of their security with them. Only a few close friends and die-hards remained. Nicky sent two large magnums of Verve Cliquot over to our table to celebrate. Nicholas, Harper, and Julianna's brother Three were still hugging the bar, immersed in a deep conversation about politics.

Xavier did the honors, popping both bottles open with a quick twist of his wrist, somehow making that simple gesture look totally sensual. Both Maya and Logan were mesmerized by Xavier's moves, but luckily for me Julianna was unfazed. I suppose if my brother was Nicholas Becker it would be hard for any man to impress me too, which meant I'd have to work extra hard to keep her.

As the night wore on, glancing around I became hyper-aware of Craig and another security person across the room quietly closing in on our table amidst the voices echoing throughout the room in an atmosphere of gaiety. Craig's facial expression was telling. He looked as if he were coming unhinged.

I first glanced at Xavier to see if he were behaving unseemly with Maya, enough to provoke Craig into a frenzied state. Nothing unusual was awry. Maya and Xavier were casually thumbing through photos in her digital camera. No real threat there. Logan and Gabriel were feeding each other pastries like a love-struck couple. I wondered if they were a heartbreak waiting to happen.

"Let's toast to a wonderful opening for my favorite *Sugar Mommy*," I suggested.

"To *Sugar Mommy* on top," Logan giggled, brushing crumbs off her mouth, taking her index finger and wiping it across Gabriel's top lip.

"To *Sugar Mommy* on top," we all chimed in unison.

Julianna gazed at me hungrily. I knew that look.

"Yeah baby you can be on top," I whispered in her ear as she fingered the cupcake on her necklace again. "I promise."

The six of us clinked our Champagne glasses when a foreign voice joined our little celebratory soiree. It was Blue, the female guard assigned to Julianna's security detail for the night, tagged with the assignment of monitoring the guest list and invitee entrance into tonight's opening.

"Excuse me Ms. Becker," Blue said solemnly, failing at whispering in her ear. "There's a gentleman at the door, a Mr. Oliver Banks, who wants to speak with you. I told him that this in an invitation only affair, but he insists on speaking with you."

Every part of me began to feel agitated. Oliver Banks was an uninvited guest. I didn't want Julianna's opening to be spoiled by the slime dog that clearly wanted to crawl back into her life.

"Would you like for me to encourage him to leave?" Blue asked, bending over and trying to whisper so that her words were out of earshot.

But it was too late. I heard every word. I had no doubt that Blue would have no problem getting Oliver to leave, but Julianna was looking towards the door with a mixture of disbelief and curiosity. Even I knew she didn't want a scene at her place of business on her opening night.

I couldn't imagine for the life of me why Oliver Banks was here stalking my woman on the most important night of her life. He wasn't invited. He was married now with a new wife. What could he possibly want with her? Oliver was Julianna's history.

My adrenaline was coursing through my veins at high speed leaving me feeling agitated, frayed, and confused. In this moment, there was nobody I disliked more than Oliver Banks. I could feel my face grimace. The mere thought of him rubbed me the wrong way.

"Please excuse me for a second," Julianna mumbled to me. Our friends at the table barely took notice of the interruption, or of her quick exit. Our private moment of winding down, having a good time, downing Nicky's Champagne and eating hot buttered croissants that Julianna's sous chef had set on our table for a late night snack was getting interrupted with late night Oliver Banks bullshit.

"I'm sorry Ms. Becker, but I'm instructed to remain close."

Julianna shrugged her shoulders but said nothing. I stood as Julianna rose.

"I'll come with you," I said through gritted teeth.

"Not to worry Elliot. Blue is with me. I can handle this. I'll be quick," she said, running her soft hand down the side of my cheek.

I grunted, not liking any of this. Julianna excused herself. Gabriel and Xavier stood as well, but not really noticing the change in my demeanor, given their concentration on Maya and Logan.

I watched as Julianna made her way through her crowd of guests, many of whom were thanking her on their way out. She ducked her head out the door, peering at the stragglers of paparazzi who were trying to get more last minute photos before their deadlines closed. Blue followed her out the door. I excused myself and walked closer to the door to see for myself what was happening.

I watched as a large hand pulled Julianna outside on the red carpet. She looked cold as he tugged her close into the side of his body. Blue flexed instinctively, her hand sliding inside her waist, but Julianna nodded to her, mouthing words that must have motivated Blue to step back a bit.

Fuck me. I had so reached the end of my rope with Oliver Banks. I wasn't having this. This was my woman now. No way he was going to come here uninvited and try to steal my woman tonight. And why was she going to see him, giving him the time of day?

My telephone buzzed right at the exact moment I decided I was going to break rank and stomp Oliver Banks right into the red carpet. That slime dog was saved by the bell.

"Dr. E, it's Babs. You need to get to the hospital right away. The Miller triplets decided they aren't going to wait until next month. They're coming now. Time to do your thing Dr. E."

"I can't Babs, I'm busy. It's my night off. Call somebody else."

"C'mon Dr. E. These are the Miller triplets. They aren't going to wait around for somebody's schedule to free up. The resident on call is stuck on the New Jersey Turnpike due to some eighteen wheeler taking a flip. You're next up to bat. Besides, this is going to be hot news TMZ style in the morning baby. Their daddy is the drummer in that famous rock group, 'Deliverance.' This is money in the bank for the Becker Wing and publicity for you."

I groaned, shaking my head in dismay. This was my night to keep my promises. My night to make love to Julianna. Not to be delivering babies in waiting for some rock star daddy, while Julianna got wooed on a red carpet with Mr. Slime Dog Millionaire.

"Babs, can't you call someone else?" I pleaded, looking out the glass door at the flash of camera lights going off.

"Nope. Sorry Dr. E. If you da man, then you da man. You got to ride wit dat, baby, and git those babies here safely."

I paused in silence, not saying a word. I knew I was contemplating way too long for Babs. Patience was not her virtue.

"Okay, Dr. E. I'm gonna put it to you this way. Don't let me have to come over to where you are and slap you into tomorrow. I know you're with that Becker gal, but she'll be there for you when you get done delivering these babies. This is your calling, remember. A woman's got to know that about you, even if she is a Becker."

Babs' words struck a chord deep inside of me. This was my passion. This was what I do. I lived for these moments. Whoever was going to be my wife, these unsolicited moments came with the package of everything that was me, Dr. Elliot Fischer.

"Okay. Okay. I'm on my way."

 *ulianna*

"**M**s. Becker, you're wanted back inside ma'am," Blue said, cutting Oliver off.

Thank God for Blue. This was not a conversation I wanted to have in front of cameras. Between the bright lights and the honking taxicabs in city that never sleeps, I didn't want my private affairs played out on TMZ. Plus, I was cold, standing outside with no coat.

"I'm coming now Blue. Thank you."

I waved at the remaining paparazzi as the flash bulbs continued to pop off.

"Everything's under control here Meyers," Blue spoke into her wrist. I figure she was speaking to Craig, who was likely inside having a fit that I had not returned to get locked back into his peepers. He seemed to think no one could guard me as well as he.

"Listen, Julipop. Am I on some Becker do not call list or what? I've been trying for weeks to speak to you."

Oliver sounded out of control. I knew him better than he knew himself. He was emotionally caught up somewhere between angry and lost.

"Who says I want to speak to you Oliver? Besides, my number has changed. If I wanted you to have it, I would have given it to you."

"You're just mad. Pissed. This can be like old times honey. This is what we do. Make up to break up, Julipop."

"Don't call me that. I'm not your Julipop or your honey," I smiled a fake smile through gritted teeth acutely aware of the cameras. One thing for sure, I was mad. I was done with Oliver, but obviously he hadn't crossed the finish line yet.

"We need to talk."

"There's nothing to say."

"I have plenty I need to say, Julipop"

"No, you want your cake and eat it too."

"The only cake I've ever wanted was yours."

I sensed we were making a scene. I wanted him gone. Whatever he had to say I didn't want to hear it. Especially not tonight. This was my night. I didn't want it tainted with an ex-boyfriend who never really wanted me, who was now sounding like we weren't done.

I pulled myself away from Oliver, heading back inside my cafe, re-orienting myself when I heard the music playing in the background. Oliver followed on my heels behind me, with Blue close on his.

Blue headed across the room toward Nicholas's direction, while Craig mouthed something to Stephen, who then left Nicholas's side headed my direction.

A familiar voice had come to my rescue.

"Well you've said your congratulatory remarks. Now it's time for you to say goodnight," Elliot hissed from over my shoulder, not waiting for me to respond. His fists were clinched at his side, gray eyes narrowing. He pulled me to his side.

I had no idea where Elliot came from, but I didn't mind letting him do the talking because my tongue was frozen in my mouth. I was in shock to even be having this conversation. Seeing Elliot this angry was new for me.

"In case you haven't noticed buddy, I'm having a conversation with Julianna," Oliver sneered, ever formidable.

Oliver Banks wasn't the type of man to be easily rattled. This was going to turn into a pissing match and I could tell Elliot had no intention of losing.

"In case you haven't noticed, *buddy*, this conversation is *over*," Elliot said mockingly, giving his last word an accent, his jaw tightening.

I still hadn't said a word. I was at lost for words stuck between the man that didn't want me and the man that did. I was confused about everything else going on here, but not about that.

Oliver and Elliot resorted to a staring match. You could hear a pin drop between the three of us. Who was going to do or say something next? Elliot and Oliver were taking the notion of pissing contest to a new high. The silence was thick. Awkward.

Please God don't let this moment turn physical in my establishment tonight.

---

*B*efore anyone could say another word, Nicholas joined our space, stepping in between Elliot and Oliver looking nothing less than infuriated.

Craig, Stephen, and Blue were flanked on both sides of Oliver, waiting on the word from Nicky or me to toss him out.

"Banks, if you so much as think about starting a brawl in my sister's place of business on this most important night, I will personally cut your balls off and stuff them down your throat in one of her cupcakes," Nicky glared, his eyes narrowing, his voice dropping down to a low hiss.

But Oliver was ever the gentleman, and never one to lose his cool.

"No harm no foul, Nicky," Oliver said throwing both his hands up in the air before Nicky could speak another word. "You can call off the dogs. I was merely extending my congratulations. I'll see myself out. I will talk to you later, Julipop," he said nodding his chin upward at me, puckering his lips, blowing me a kiss.

SUGAR MOMMY ON TOP

Elliot was flaming. He stepped two paces towards Oliver, fists balled.

"Fischer," Nicky commanded. "Let's all enjoy the evening shall we?" he said, daring Oliver or Elliot to act out in my place of business in front of my guests.

Oliver flashed a look at Elliot. He wasn't done with this yet. Elliot was clearly restraining himself, but on the fringes of losing control any minute now, ignoring the fact that his phone was buzzing wildly. Finally, he answered, snapping "I'm on my way."

"Stephen, please see Oliver out," Nicky ordered politely.

And with that, Oliver was ushered out the front door. Elliot starting texting into his phone, then scurried past me, hurriedly. Gabriel and Xavier were following on his heels like robots. Elliot still hadn't said a word to me.

"Are you okay Cookie?" Nicky said, nodding his head at Harper who was still at the bar with my brother Three.

Thank God, most of the guests had called it a night.

"Yes, a bit caught off guard, Nicky. I wasn't sure what to do in front of the cameras and all. I never expected Oliver would have thought to crash my opening," I said, still in disbelief.

"Oh God Nicky, what about the pictures of he and I?"

"I'll try to work on getting as many of them buried as I can. We'll hire a publicist to help you manage your public exposure in the future. This is as good a time as any for you to learn on the ground floor how to deal with adverse situations. Who knows. We might one-day morph you into a celebrity pastry chef."

"I need to simply get through this night, Nicky, before I start planning out the rest of my future. Right now I'm feeling totally out of control."

"This is just a small hiccup, Cookie. It happens all the time in business. Don't let Oliver Banks spoil your joy. The night has been a total business success."

"Elliot left without saying good-bye. That's not business, that's personal."

"He's emoting. Another man is threatening his relationship with the woman he believes he loves. He's got to sort himself out right now."

"But I don't want Oliver anymore Nicky."

I fingered the cupcake on my necklace nervously.

"I know that. You know that. And, deep down, Elliot knows that. But Oliver is willing to put what you have to the test."

"But why Nicky? He's married. Why won't he move on?"

"Who knows what his motives are Cookie. Once an asshole, always an asshole. Be thankful he's not *your* husband."

Nicky and I watched as Logan and Maya strutted across the room in our direction. Logan slid her hand down the front of her cream colored babydoll cocktail dress, brushing pastry crumbs off the tiny soft organza and Swarovski crystal beaded bodice. She looked like a delicate feminine flower that oozed sensuality as she floated like air across the floor. Maya was rocking a beautiful long sleeved green metallic snake-skin like shimmery cocktail dress that she managed to snag straight off the runway. Maya was getting into the holiday spirit early, wrapped like a beautiful Christmas package.

Nicky used their nearness as an opportunity to quickly change the subject off our delicate topic of discussion.

"Yes, you're definitely going to need a publicist with these two man-eaters at your side" he said, his eyes narrowing. "You're a businesswoman now, Cookie. Time to settle down. Protect your image."

Now it was time for me to be the one to change gears again. I didn't want to open this discussion up again with Nicky going on and on about Logan, Maya and I needing to be married. I especially didn't want to discuss this tonight.

"*J*ules, what in the world was that about?" Logan asked rushing to my side, pushing a strand of her long blonde hair back into the jeweled pin that was holding her elegant up-do.

I was so flabbergasted about the whole scene with Oliver I could hardly get my words out.

"Heeeeeeey Nicky," Logan said, holding up her empty ring finger, flicking it in his face. "You running short of hot body watchers tonight. I can't believe Ollie the loser broke through your gridiron," she said, her eyes sparkly with mischief.

Logan was rubbing it in Nicky's face now, his expression impassive. I shook my head at her not to challenge him if she ever expected us to get out of the golden cage.

"Yeah, Jules, what was Oliver Banks doing here?" Maya asked. "I took a picture of the three of you. It didn't look like the picture of happiness that's for sure."

"Who knows what Oliver really wants? He claimed he was in the neighborhood and wanted to congratulate me."

"Forget about it Maya, the moment is over," Nicky said, trying to force a change in subject.

Logan was still waving her empty ring finger in Nicky's face.

"Logan, I swear you test the patience of Job, woman," Nicky grunted. "But know that I have plenty of it."

"And you Maya, you're up first to bat," Nicky said with a wicked grin.

"Meaning?" Maya asked nonchalantly, totally clueless.

Nicky waved his hand at Craig, who walked like a man in charge getting ready to put us all on lockdown. Craig grabbed Maya's camera from her hand, flicking buttons on her digital camera.

"Oh no you don't, Craig Meyers," Maya said, tugging on the camera straps locked between his big hands.

"I'm doing my job Maaaayaaaaa," he said, drawing her name out, simultaneously deleting the pictures of Oliver and me.

"And I'm doing mine, you big hunk of don't fuck with me," Maya steamed.

"Calm down Maya," Nicky said soothingly. "It's only a couple of pictures."

"Oh hell no, Nicky. Everybody knows you've got a reputation for having photos deleted from photographers' cameras."

"You've still got the exclusive. It's all good."

Maya ignored Nicky, focusing on Craig, rolling her eyes at him. Maya was not the type of woman that was going to be bossed around. Not by Nicky, and certainly not by Craig. She was furious.

"Unless you want a bunch of lawyers up your ass in the morning Meyers, you best make sure you deleted the right pictures. Give me back my camera."

Maya stepped closer to Craig, looking up into that rock hard chest, one hand on her hip, giving him her best threatening gaze.

"I don't take kindly to threats from pretty little naughty packages like you throwing temper tantrums, Maya. Careful, I might spank you before the night's over," Craig said, looking down into those big brown enticing eyes.

"Ohhhh my, a showdown," Logan said, fanning the flames of love. "Boy meets Girl."

I knew better. This was not a coincidence. Nicky was playing God again. Between the three of us, he was going to see to it that Maya the man-eater was going off the market first.

Logan looked at me. I looked at Logan. Maya and Craig were long overdue for a meeting of the minds. They'd been dancing around each other now for weeks.

"My money's on Maya," Logan said cocking her head to the side.

"Hmm. I'll take that bet," I said, grabbing a Champagne off the server's tray, downing it quickly.

"It's time for you to stop—wandering—Maya. You get my drift. I'm getting sick of it," Craig said, emphasizing the word wandering.

Oops. Decoded the Italian. Someone else has been watching the security tape and has seen Maya's tattoo. No doubt, all of our tattoos, for that matter. After all, we were a drunken group effort that night. I took a huge gulp of my Champagne, not knowing where this conversation was headed.

I stuck my hand out in jest to Logan as if to say "Pay up."

Logan snickered, "Tattoo night, Jules."

"I'm going back to find my wife," Nicky said, looking totally exasperated. "I'm having a good night. I'm not sticking around for any more of this."

"You are not the boss of me, Mister," Maya spit out to Craig.

I had to hand it to Maya. She didn't crack, despite being cued into the fact that Craig had seen her ass turned up with our girlfriend tattoos that said, *"All who wander are not lost."*

"Who's going to stop me? You?" Maya said, challenging Craig further.

Logan put her hand out for me to give back all pretend monies taken. Whoa. This really was a showdown.

"I need another drink," I said, but not moving my feet, waiting to see how this was going to end.

"I need a cigarette," Logan said.

"You don't smoke Lo."

"I know, but this is better than watching the People's Couch. Better than sex."

Craig stepped closer to Maya, who didn't back up.

"Let me put it to you this way Maya, I'm getting a little tired of watching you flirt in front of me with personal trainer guy."

"Well boo fucking hoo, Craig."

"Consider me "X-ing" him out of your life. Ya feel me?"

"No I do not feel you, Craig," Maya huffed, still not giving an inch.

"Actually, consider this a warning to every other man for that matter. The only person that's going to be watching your body from now on is going to be me."

Logan put her hand back out for me to give her the pretend money back.

"And why exactly do you think that's going to happen Mister Craig Baxter Meyers?"

Whoa . . . I'm behind. Who knew Craig's middle name was Baxter? This was getting serious. Maya was calling him by his full name.

"Because nobody's going to love you better than me Maya," Craig said, tucking a dark curl behind her ear.

Well damn. I put my hand back for Logan to hand it all over.

"Ka-ching Ka-ching."

Maya and Craig were looking at each other now with hangdog eyes. Maya was grinning like a love struck fan girl about to melt into a puddle right there on my floor. Craig looked like a man in the desert and Maya was a cool drink of water. I knew the way Maya was staring into his whiskey brown eyes, that she wasn't going to be a challenge too much longer. These two definitely wanted to be with each other.

"Time for tequila, Jules," Logan said, knowing we were on the same page about Maya and Craig. "Maya's getting ready to take a dip into all that chocolate."

"Oh hell yeah," I said co-signing Logan's thoughts.

We both agreed it was time to move on from the Craig and Maya throw-down. It was getting too intimate to watch. They wanted each other.

"Yeah, later for those two. My feathers are still ruffled that Elliot left without saying good-bye," I pouted, fingering the cupcake on my necklace again.

"Don't feel bad. I barely got a good-bye myself. Gabriel left with him. Some rock star drummer was having triplets. He claimed 'Duty calls', and kissed me."

"All this male abandonment, I think I'm gonna need to spend some time with Jack and Daniel tonight," Logan quipped.

Logan and I sauntered over to the bar, ordering from the bartender.

"Here's to duty, Jules."

"Here's to un-kept promises, Logan."

We clinked our crystal glasses together.

"Here's to Jack," she said.

"Here's to Daniel," I said.

"Hey Maya," Logan yelled across my now empty cafe, deciding she wanted to ruffle Craig's feathers, "after-party over here!"

Craig shot us both a dirty look. Logan and I clinked our glasses and snickered. Logan yelled across the empty cafe at Maya.

"Surfboard."

*lliot*

"*H*ow's it looking Babs?" I asked as Gabriel and I busted through the doors of the Becker Wing together.

"We've got Mom on a monitor. Her contractions have slowed a bit since I called you last."

"I'll wash up and check on her," I said.

"Yea, and I'll go check in on Big Papa," Gabriel said. "I want an autograph."

"Damn Gabe, Knock it off. Who cares about an autograph?"

"I do. *Deliverance* is going to blow up to the top of the charts any day now. Baby Daddy's John Henry is going to be worth lots of dinero's on Ebay."

I shook my head, looking at Mommy Miller's chart. Her labor was progressing fine, but her blood pressure was beginning to rise from the stress of the labor. It was likely this trio was going to have to be pulled out of their comfort zone. Babies were like that. Little manipulators wanted to come on their own good time, but I had different plans for this squadron.

"I looked at her chart, Gabe. I say we give her a few more hours to dilate. If things don't progress any sooner, we C-section her early morning."

"I agree E."

"Seeing how I missed my night with Julianna, I'm going to find my favorite gurney and catch a couple of Z's. I'm supposed to be off tonight with my woman fulfilling my promises."

"Well maybe you ought to call her and make nice."

"What do you mean?"

"Damn E, are you always so clueless when it comes to women? Did you forget you left without saying good-bye? This was her special night, man."

"Yeah I know. I was just so out of control about Oliver showing up, I guess I took my frustrations out on her. It wasn't her fault that asshole showed up."

"She's not to blame for that scene."

"And then Babs starting blowing my phone about coming in for this delivery. I knew I might need your help too, so now both our nights are ruined."

"You know E, I've never had this conversation with you before, but I'm going to say this to you now, so you won't fuck up this good thing you've got going with Julianna and regret it for the rest of your life."

"Yeah, and . . . ?"

"You have this way of creating these little mini abandonment scenarios with your women, where you duck out without any real warning. How is a woman supposed to take you seriously when you keep doing that thing that you do?"

"What the hell are you talking about Gabriel?" I asked, my mood getting even more pissier than before.

Could he not see that I was trying to calm myself down? He needed to mind his own business tonight.

"Elliot, you left Julianna's launch party in a funk without even saying so much as a good-bye. It was rude. At least I told Logan that

"Duty Calls." But no, you didn't say a mumbling fucking word. Maybe you deserve to be kicked to the curb."

I looked at Gabriel, confused by his unfiltered frankness. Perhaps I had handled myself like a horse's ass. Selfish. Mad that Oliver was making a play for my woman to the point I took it out on her on her special night. Maybe I really am the dick Kimber always said I was.

"So maybe I really am the dick Kimber always said I was," I said, realizing now I was confronting my fears out loud.

"Oh hell no, E. Let's don't get carried away. Kimber Lawson is not a good judge of character or anything else for that matter. Don't get my words twisted here. You're a great guy. I'm just saying, a simple good-bye laced with a kiss wasn't that hard under the circumstances."

"I don't recall you lacing Logan's lips with kisses on your way out."

"I gave her a peck on my way out. But you need to understand Logan and I are on a different playground. We're dancing around each other trying to figure out if we're going to be riding in the same lane."

"Funny it never looks that way to me. What happened to special?"

Gabriel ignored my comment as if he let that go in one ear and out the other.

"But you and Julianna, you guys have long since crossed that bridge. You're over there in the zone of moonlit nights and sunset mornings, brother."

I nodded in agreement. I felt like a heel. Gabriel had called me out on my bullshit. I was so wrapped up in my own feelings I hadn't given consideration to how Julianna might have felt. Not to mention this was her special night. Bad enough she shouldn't have had to deal with Oliver, but then I turned around and acted like a piece of shit too. Rude. Insensitive.

I looked at my watch. It was well past midnight, but I was going to call Julianna anyway. I needed to assure her that I would always be there for her.

"Thanks Gabe, for your honesty. I'm sorry I cut your night short too. I'm gonna catch a few winks and think about how to check myself." I did not mention to him that I was going to call Julianna.

"I hope she'll speak to me tomorrow."

"You've got a very expensive cupcake dangling around that pretty neck. Damn right she's going to speak to you. Put one of those around my neck and I'll talk to you until you're blue in the face," Gabriel howled. He slapped me on the back. "I'll be in the second floor clinical lab. I'm working on some new stuff that's going to turn modern medicine on its head. You know where to find me."

Gabriel was the child prodigy grown up. I knew if he was experimenting with something new in medicine, I best leave him to it. He was a brilliant physician. Far be it for me to interrupt his creative juices, except to get these triplets here safely.

"I'll call you when Mommy Miller's boys decide they're tired of being in the huddle and are ready to make a break for the goal line."

Gabriel and I gave each other a high five. I made my way to my favorite hideaway room in the Obstetrics wing, plopping myself down on a gurney.

I slid my phone out of my breast pocket and dialed Julianna's number. My anxiety started to build as it rang four rings before she picked up.

"Hello," Julianna's answered, her sweet voice now sounding tired and weary.

"Baby?"

"Elliot," Julianna answered softly.

"Did I wake you?

"Yes."

"I'm sorry I didn't say good-bye tonight. That was plain wrong of me."

"Okay," Julianna said coolly.

I could tell by the sound of her voice she was miffed with me. She had every right to be disappointed in me.

"Baby?" I whispered slowly.

"Yes?"

"I'm at the hospital waiting on a set of triplets to make their appearance."

"Yes," she whispered softly.

"I wish with all my heart, they were our babies."

I heard Julianna intake a deep breath through the phone. She paused.

"Julianna?"

"Yes?"

"I'm sorry. Forgive me. I was having a jackass moment."

I heard her take another deep breath.

"Julianna, you own my heart. I'll never ever need anyone but you." Silence filled the space between us. "It was just that when I saw you with Oliver, I got so jealous," I continued. "He wants you back. I didn't like seeing him with you."

Julianna still hadn't commented. These long pauses were testing my nerves to the breaking point.

"I love you Julianna."

More silence.

"I love you too, Elliot."

"Baby?"

"Yes Elliot?"

"I'll be by in the morning to deliver on my promises as soon as this trio arrives, I promise. Is that still okay?"

"I don't know, Elliot," Julianna chuckled teasingly. "The newborns see you more than I do."

Where was this conversation headed? Was she going to break up with me?

"Perhaps we'll have to make one of our own if I ever expect to see you."

Oh my God. Julianna was talking about making a baby with me. Something big had changed between us. Newborns scared Julianna. Newborns send her into panic mode. Was this her way of telling me that she loved me? She trusted me? Because if she was, I was totally on board with where this relationship was headed. My spirits were starting to rocket through the roof upon hearing her words.

"Baby we don't have to make one right away, but I promise to start practicing at it really hard in the morning."

Julianna chuckled some more. I could feel the smile on her face. I was sure she could feel the smile on mine.

"Good night Elliot."

"Good night *Sugar Mommy*."

"**W**ake up E, we've been granted a reprieve by the Baby Gods," Gabriel said, nudging me out of my sleep.

"What time is it?"

"It's 7:30 am. We've caught a break. Rock star's Obstetrician has arrived, and is going to perform the C-section on the Miller triplets. We can go home."

"Oh thank God," I yawned. "I promised Julianna I'd come by this morning when I was done here."

"So you took my advice?"

"I did. She and I are cool."

"Well I'd say this was turning out to be a stellar Sunday morning. No surgeries for us. I still got my autograph, and you got yourself out of the dog house with Julianna."

"Yeah. So let's get the hell out of here," I said, sitting up on the side of the gurney.

Gabriel grabbed my hand, pulling me to my feet.

"I'm outta here. But I need to make a stop on the way out at the gift shop to pick up the morning papers. I'll grab a couple of coffees. I'll meet you at the Emergency Room entrance."

"X is going to meet us out front. He and I are going to the gym. We'll drop you off at Becker Towers on the way."

I nodded at Gabriel as he and I headed different directions with plans to meet each other in ten minutes at the Emergency Room entrance. I headed out of the Becker Wing saying my good-byes to Babs and Patty.

I ducked into the gift shop, grabbing the morning paper, but not before stopping to pick up one of those pink beanie babies. It was a bunny rabbit that was praying. I wanted to give it to Julianna to put on her nightstand.

"Your job is watch over my woman when I'm on call," I said to bunny.

I asked the cashier for a small gift bag, knowing if Gabriel saw what was in the bag, I would never hear the end of it. Cupid had me all in the way in her clutches, my heart totally on lockdown down. There was no denying that I was a man in love.

I headed towards through the emergency entrance doors with the newspaper, stopping at the coffee stand to grab two coffees, both black. I sat the coffees down on the brick wall and began flipping through the pages for the style and entertainment section. It was work reading and holding on to the paper at the same time, as a gust of cold wind hit me in the face. The skies looked gray, but still no snow. Damn weathermen. I was better at predicting when babies were born than they were about forecasting the weather.

Sure enough, Maya had gotten her exclusive, because there were pictures of Julianna, her family on the red carpet, the senator with Julianna's father, Nicky and Harper, and a shot of Julianna and I together. Maya had done well. This day was getting even better, because as far as I could tell, there were no other pictures that showed anything but a highly successful launch opening. The editorial text gave testimonials praising the quality of the pastries from some of the celebrity foodies that were on the guest list.

Gabriel headed out the emergency room door just as I was folding the newspaper up under my arm. He pulled the top of his leather bomber up over his ears.

"Damn man it's cold out here," he said rubbing his hands, grabbing his coffee out of my hand.

"You think? Where the hell is Xavier? I don't want to stand out here too long freezing my nuts off."

"Yeah, well if you don't make nice with Julianna this morning, you may not have any nuts let to freeze.

Xavier pulled up in his SUV, screeching his tires loudly as if he had an emergency. A tall, lanky, red-headed woman passing Gabriel and I turned back around to see who was making all the commotion. Xavier flashed his million-dollar smile at the woman. Like most women that found Xavier irresistible, the redhead grinned sheepishly back at him. Xavier winked. She blushed. And I shook my head at him in disgust.

"Good morning fellas. How'd did it go last night since I saw you last? You save any lives? Bring any babies into the world?" Xavier spouted.

"God you're such a flirt. You really can't help yourself can you?" I said to him, ignoring his question, and climbing inside, placing my coffee in his cup holder.

"I can't help it. I woke up like dis," Xavier crooned in his best imitation Beyoncé voice. "Besides I've got a thing for redheads."

"Ha. More like redheads, brunettes, and blondies," I said, certain I left something out.

Gabriel ignored Xavier, choosing to answer his question instead.

"I worked in the lab most of the night. I only came to help E out, but he was granted a reprieve from the baby Gods. By the time the mother got ready to deliver, her own doctor arrived," Gabriel said.

"Yup it's a good morning all right X," I said. "Drop me off at Becker Towers. I've got a workout of my own planned."

"Well I hate to be the bearer of bad news, but maybe you should look at this first," Xavier said, sliding me his phone that was set to an Internet site called GossipBoss.

I snatched Xavier's phone, only to see a picture of Julianna tucked under Oliver's side, with the caption that read, *"Guess What Very Married Social Media Mogul Is Out For His Late Night Sweets?"*

"Fuck," I said out loud as Gabriel grabbed Xavier's phone.

I opened my own phone to look at the blog post.

"It was too good to be true. This blogger is trying to make it seem like something scandalous is going on between Julianna and Oliver."

I read further down.

"Nobody will believe this shit," Gabriel said.

"Maybe we should go run that dickhead Oliver down and put the fear of God in him," Xavier said, pulling the SUV out into the flow of traffic, one cabbie honking loudly at him, while another threw him the bird.

I was hardly through the blog post when my text messenger dinged. It was Mario.

Mario: "Hey Dr. EZ."

Elliot: "Hey Mario, what's up?"

Mario: "Yo peeps have been on da run. @illegalpapi greased @olliegator's palm with 5K in Benjamin's. @olliegator tryin' to snag @kimmykazi into being one of his side baes, and Shorty is still on his dance card.

God I felt like I needed an interpreter to decipher what the hell Mario was saying. I wasn't that old, but felt like I was getting old just reading this shit. It took me a minute using my Urban Dictionary app to figure out what he was saying. Apparently Oliver had paid five thousand dollars to Dexter, and was hitting on Kimber. I wasn't sure how to take that news. The world was getting too small. I suppose Kimber had the abortion and was back riding in the trophy saddle. Julianna was still on Oliver's bidder's list for the hospital fundraiser scheduled in two weeks.

"Yeah X. I've reached my limit with Oliver Banks trying to get back with the same broken heart I've worked to heal."

I texted Mario back.

Elliot: I appreciate the heads up Mario. Anything else I should know?

Mario: One more thing Dr. EZ.

Elliot: What's that?

Mario: Dance card gonna be rigged in @Olliegator's favor. Save yo dinero's, Bro.

Elliot: Fuck me

Mario: Not interested. I like the punani.

Elliot: That's not how I meant that Mario.

Mario: ROFL. Geez Dr. EZ. I'm not stupid. Just fuckin wit you bro.

Elliot: Bye Mario. Thanks.

Mario: Bye Felicia.

Who the hell is Felicia? Mario must be high again. Sounds like he's losing track of who he's talking to for Christ's sake.

"Maybe it would be wise to ignore Oliver and hope he goes away. It's not like Julianna wants to deal with him. Maybe this problem will fix itself," Gabriel said.

"Good Lord, may I never have to talk to anybody under eighteen for the next year," I said out loud. My thoughts were spinning in between Mario's text and Xavier weaving in and out of traffic like a mad man.

"You're not listening to me. Who are you texting?" Gabriel asked.

"It's Mario. Oliver's co-opted Dexter into doing some of his dirty work for him at the hospital fundraiser so he can get close to Julianna."

"When's the fundraiser E?"

"In two weeks."

"See Gabriel, I'm telling you man, we need to confront that geeky guy and tell him to back off E's woman," Xavier said, screeching his tires curbside.

As we came to an abrupt halt in front of Becker Towers, I left the newspaper in X's jeep, but grabbed my hospital gift bag for Julianna.

"What's in the gift bag man?"

"Nothing."

I should have known that Xavier would notice. He rarely misses anything.

"You got a little sumthin' sumthin in that bag for your sugar pie?" Xavier teased, making his voice sound all girly.

Gabriel starting laughing out loud. I didn't care that they were teasing me. Buying praying bunny felt like a good idea. I was rolling with my heart and not my little head for once. I was learning quick to stop ignoring my intuitions like I did with Kimber. Could have spared myself a lot of grief.

"None of your business," I say to X.

"Glad to see you're still taking my advice E. Don't pay any attention to X. He doesn't have a woman."

"Because I have a harem in waiting, and when they leave me, there's always Bubbles and BabyDoll," Xavier laughed heartily.

"Xavier, you're a certified man whore."

"What can I say E, I--"

"Yeah I know already. You woke up like this," I said.

"No man, I woke up like dis. It's I woke up like dis, man. Do you even listen to music anymore man?"

"Seriously X?"

Xavier laughed heartily.

"I'm only fucking with you man. You need to relax, let the steam out a bit. You're taking this Banks business too seriously."

"Yeah, E. Put this blog and Mario's news on the back burner. Go in there and play nice," Gabriel said, stretching his arms and yawning loudly.

"Yeah E, go in there knock it out the park, baby," Xavier teased.

"You want us to wait outside in case she throws you out E?" Gabriel shouted.

"Bye Gabe. Later X. Thanks for the lift."

I didn't care that they were making fun of me. Too many hours had gone by since I was last in Julianna's arms. It was time for me to start practicing making my own babies for a change. I had promises to keep.

ulianna

opened my door, awaiting the elevator doors to open into my foyer. Rick had already called ahead requesting permission for Elliot to come up. I glanced up at the cameras, giving the finger to whoever was watching on Stephen's team, just because. Hopefully it wasn't Craig. He was growing on me. Plus, Maya liked him. But the rest of Parks and Parks body watchers would have to put up with me.

I whipped my body away from the camera, glaring at his huge smile; cool gray eyes flickering over me.

Elliot pulled me into his body, kissing me passionately, letting whoever was watching us on the camera know that he was staking his claim to me.

I felt the familiar wave of warmth engulf my body. A body that was practically half naked, bare-legged, wearing nothing else but Nicky's faded out NAVY t-shirt that I'd hi-jacked off his yacht last summer.

My choice of clothing reminded me of the day Elliot and I made love for the first time. Maybe this shirt was slowly becoming my good luck charm.

My thick brown locks were pulled up in a scrunchie pinned to top of my head. Normally I would be more concerned about my appearance in front of my man, but it was early morning and I was not a morning person. This was me, Julianna alá naturale. This is who I was under all the glitz without the glam squad.

Elliot was looking over the real me again, much like he did the week I first took over his home, nursing him back to good health. And I very much liked the look that was mirroring back at me.

Gray eyes peered at me as if I made his world go round. I no longer felt the hole in my heart left by Oliver. Instead I felt warm and gushy all over, my heart fluttering with unrestrained excitement. And wouldn't you know ComputerLuv was playing Al Green and Joss Stone's *How Do You Mend A Broken Heart* in the background, ringing throughout my home.

"Hey Baby," Elliot whispered, stepping inside my door.

He looked handsome as ever, wearing a grey knit hoodie sweater with a sleeveless navy puffer on top, his blue scrubs underneath both, messenger bag strapped across his torso.

"Nice music," he said obviously affected too by my choice of early morning music, or maybe it was just me.

"Hey Elliot."

"Good morning."

"Best morning."

"Can I get you anything? Coffee? Mimosa? Fresh strawberries?"

"Nope. I'm here to fulfill promises this morning."

"Promises, huh? Aren't you a day late?" I asked, my smile widening.

"Yes, but I come bearing gifts."

"Well I never look a gift horse in the mouth," I said in a hushed tone, mesmerized by his devastating smile.

Elliot's smile widened as he handed me a tiny gift bag. I turned away leading us both into my living area, making a fuss over the tissue, excited to see what was inside. Elliot slapped me playfully on my butt, and I yelped like a playful puppy, totally giddy with anticipation. I opened the bag, pulling out the cutest pink beanie baby bunny with praying hands.

"Someone to watch over you when I'm not around."

"I loveeee him Elliot," I said kissing the top of Bunny's head.

"And Bunny loves you."

I glared back at Elliot, blushing, feeling the heat of the lust and desire that was rolling off of him in waves. I wanted to pinch myself to make sure this wasn't a dream. He was mine. I was his. And we both wanted each other.

I jumped into his arms, saying nothing. Elliot took the bunny out of my hands, setting him on my cocktail table next to one of the vases of pink roses that remained from his last visit. He was all over me, kissing me in the space between my neck and my shoulder. With one hand around my waist, the other was running through my hair pulling it down. He was kissing my lips hard as I wrapped myself around his body like an anaconda, squeezing him tightly, not willing to release him.

Elliot walked us further into the living area, the heat from the fire crackling in fireplace warming what was left of the cold outdoor chill left on his skin.

"You're so beautiful, woman."

I ran my fingers over his head, lost in his love.

"Kiss me Elliot. Make love to me."

He kissed me harder, tasting like honey.

"I'm here to fulfill all of your promises babe. Tell me what you want—what you need."

I kissed my lips passionately against his, both of us caught up in our own heated reverie. He grabbed my nipple, reaching his hand up under my t-shirt, twisting it hard. His wet lips were on mine before I could mouth a word.

"Elliot—" I gasped. "I want—I want—" I said, breathing heavily, unable to form a coherent sentence.

"Julianna," he said, both of us panting and breathing heavily.

"I want to make love to you."

"Do what you want with me baby. I'm all yours."

"Condom," I whimpered. "This is practice remember?"

"Uh, huh," he said, patting at a condom lodged inside his top breast pocket of his scrubs.

I let out a breathy moan as his tongue trailed down my neck towards my breasts, moving slowly down my naval. I was losing it. Elliot grabbed hold of my waist pulling me closer to him, his lips pinching my ear, his erection poking past the flimsy fabric of his blue scrubs and into my stomach. I leaned into him, rubbing him, grinding into his body, wanting more of him.

Elliot licked my neck, using his right arm to grab my ass. I was on fire from his touch. I yanked the condom out of his top pocket, ripping it with my teeth, sheathing him quickly.

"Julianna, I have to have you. I'm going to make a son."

"I think we should make our daughter."

"Twins it is, baby."

We both laughed at our inside joke, except part of me wasn't sure that Elliot wasn't serious. His fingers were playing in my wetness, plunging deep inside me, like he was the composer to a rhythm playing in his head, my body moving to his beat. Moaning, I grasped Elliot's neck as he brought me to an orgasm. Twice. No three times. My head was spinning in such ecstasy I couldn't remember anymore.

My legs were weak, but Elliot held onto me plunging inside of me with deep thrusts and little effort. My head whipped back in pleasure as my eyes rolled back into my head. Elliot fucked me harder and harder as he came, grunting loudly.

"Fucking Christ Elliot," I screamed in pleasure, locking my legs tighter around him.

"Say my name baby."

"Elliot."

"Elliot what?" he commanded as I screamed more loudly.

"Elliot, I love you."

"I love you too Julianna," he said loudly capturing my lips at the moment we reached our climax together. He bit my lip, nibbling on me, slowing down his pace, both of us riding the wave of pleasure together.

I fell on top of Elliot's chest as he wrapped me into his arms. Elliot kissed the top of my forehead, running his fingers through my hair.

He exhaled loudly in contentment.

"Mmm, your promises feel good," I beamed.

"Good. I'll be sure to make some more."

---

*E*lliot and I found ourselves making love again in my shower, and then my bedroom, nourishing ourselves in between our love-making with bacon and eggs, strawberries, and Mimosas. Pink bunny came with us, landing on my nightstand watching over the both of us now as we drifted in and out of sleep, tangled in each other's arms enjoying our lazy Sunday morning. I nuzzled my nose in his neck, watching him sleep so peacefully. I placed my hand on his chest feeling the rhythm of a heart in love. Butterflies fluttered in my belly as I thought about what our pretend practice babies would look like.

Babies. I couldn't believe I was thinking about babies. The fact that I was thinking about babies was reinforcement that I was a woman in love. Practicing baby making was making me crazy.

I turned away from the heat of Elliot's body, only to have him turn and snuggle against me in the spoon position. But we wouldn't spoon for much longer, as my phone buzzed on my nightstand next to Bunny.

My ringtone was playing Gino Vanelli's *'People I Belong To.'*

Elliot tightened his grip on me.

"Hey Nicky," I said sleepily, wiggling a bit out of Elliot's heated body.

"Good Morning Cookie."

"What 'sup?" I said, feeling Elliot moving closer to me, his cock twitching against my thigh.

"I see you are bright eyed and bushy-tail this morning."

"You should know. Who's on duty? Stephen or Craig?"

"Stephen."

I was glad he didn't say Craig. Stephen wouldn't take my throwing the bird at him to heart. He would laugh, getting a kick out it. He'd been watching over my brother for years, so he saw me more as a little sister than he did as his charge.

"So what do I owe the pleasure of this early morning call brother? You know I have company."

"I do."

"And?"

"And I'm giving you a heads up that your sister-in-law is headed your way. She's decided she's going to kill two birds with one stone. She's coming down to discuss the fundraiser."

"Fuck. Who wants to deal with that subject this morning?"

"She does. You know she's a Type A work-a-holic. No rest for the weary with that one. She's been on China time for several hours already this morning. It's mid-afternoon for her."

"You should talk. You're as bad as her. How exactly do you two even make a marriage work?" I asked with as much early morning sarcasm as I could muster.

"We broke the rule on opposites attract," he laughed. "We're exactly alike."

I laughed with him because I knew that was exactly the truth.

"So sister, you've been duly warned. Get your ass up and moving. Pour some coffee down Elliot. Harper's on a conference call with the Chinese Minister of Finance, but she'll be wrapping up soon. She doesn't know I'm giving you a heads up."

"Thanks Lancelot."

"Don't mention it Cookie."

I could feel Elliot's finger running circles over the top of my tattoo above my butt, his way of letting me know he was awake.

"Bye."

"Bye Cookie."

I turned over to see darkening gray eyes and a full erection both looking at me, desire and passion flowing out of those beautiful eyes.

"Wanna make another baby Sugar Mommy?"

"I hate to break it to you darlin', but Harper's on her way down from the Penthouse. That was Nicky. He says she wants to talk to us about the fundraiser."

"Ummm, next time I need to sneak in here, and you need to stop aggravating security. We drew too much attention," he chuckled.

"You should be the one to talk," I said, as he kissed me passionately like a crazed man who was lost but found. I giggled.

"I was lost, and I am found," Elliot said, slapping me hard on my buttocks.

"We could make a run for it you know, not be here when she comes," I said, starting to strategize our escape.

"I could never do that to Harper and keep a straight face the next time I see her."

"Jesus Elliot, what kind of straight laced childhood did you have sweetie?"

"I never learned the art of running away," he laughed. "It's not like I've lived a life with an army of Seals chasing after me on the daily."

"Perhaps you should come hang out with me and the gals for a change," I grinned wickedly. "We got game baby. We're very skilled in the art of the great escape."

"I know, and it scares me. I never want you to ever feel you have to run from me baby," he said, suddenly getting all serious while getting out of the bed.

God I loved looking at his fantastic ass. I couldn't decide what I liked better. The front or the back. It was all finely chiseled.

"I would never run from you Elliot," I said, following him out of the bed, reaching up on my tiptoes to kiss his lips.

"Good, because if you do, I will follow you to the ends of the earth. I'll hunt you down like prey," he laughed picking me up over his shoulders, my legs kicking behind me, tossing us both in the shower.

Ohhh, wet baby making was my favorite position.

"Good morning Jules," Harper said, looking too business-like for a Sunday morning, wearing a white low cut blouse, a wide gold belt clinching her tiny waist, with a navy blue pencil skirt.

Did she ever relax?

"I hope you don't mind, my showing up unannounced, but I needed to talk to you about the fundraiser."

Elliot walked down the hall from my bedroom, barefoot, wearing jeans and a t-shirt. He had changed out of his scrubs, a change of clothes apparently stuffed in his weekender messenger bag. He entered my living area where Harper and I were drinking coffee.

"Oh Elliot, I didn't realize you were here," Harper said, standing up, embracing him in a big hug.

Boy my sister-in-law was shrewd. She played the moment off like it was all an accident. But my brother had ratted her out. I would give her a pass because I accepted the fact that her work-a-holic ass couldn't help herself.

"It's good to see you Harper. Did you have a good time last night?"

"I did. It was a perfect launch opening. Everyone invited had a wonderful time. Maya's photos made this morning papers. Everything went exceptionally well despite the glitch with the negative blog post with you and Oliver."

"Blog post? Oliver?"

"Yes. Surely you two know this by now. It's afternoon for Christ-sake's. Where have your heads been?"

I could feel the shock rush across my face.

"Never mind, don't answer that question," Harper said, showing little to no emotion on her face, waving her hand in the air dismissively.

But what I especially didn't like was the look on Elliot's face. He didn't look surprised at all, his cheeks flushed with what, guilt? No. He looked pissed. Noooo, I wasn't sure what the hell he looked like other than I knew that he knew. And I didn't like it.

"You knew about this? You didn't tell me?" I quizzed.

"You know baby, it didn't feel . . . Oliver wasn't worth . . . I didn't think . . . "

I stormed into my kitchen area, opening my MacBook on my kitchen countertop. I Googled last night's event opening. Fuck me. There it was. *GossipBoss's* daily blog with a gigantic picture of Oliver and me looking like a motherfucking couple.

"Why the hell didn't my brother say something to me this morning?" I shouted. "This is my reputation on the line!"

Elliot shook his head at me realizing I was letting on that Nicky had warned us she was coming. It was too little too late. I didn't give two shits. I was too hysterical. This was just another one of those times where everybody in this bitch ass family treated me like I was some fragile porcelain China doll that had to be shielded from the truth. I was sick of it.

"Nicky? You spoke to Nicky this morning?" Harper asked quizzically, her face unable to conceal her expression that was changing to a slow burn.

Too late. That train had left the station. Harper was going to kill Nicky when she got back to their Penthouse. And you know what? Too fucking bad for him. If he was going to keep secrets from me, I was going to tell all of his. Shit rolls downhill, or in this case, uphill to the penthouse.

"Yes, he warned me you were coming."

"He did what?" she asked, as if she really believed Nicky wouldn't dime her out. She and my brother loved being able to get one up on each other. It was a turn on for the both of them. Everybody knew it but them. She was probably going to go upstairs, tear him a new ass, and then they were going to fuck each other's brains out.

"He said you knew Elliot was here. That you were on a mission to talk about the fundraiser. Frankly, I started not to be home, Harper, so as not to deal with this shit today, but I can see now that was a stupid decision on my part," I fumed. "I needed to be right here to hear this bullshit. Everything happens for a reason."

Elliot moved closer to me, grabbing my hand.

"Don't touch me," I said, watching him flinch like he had put his hand in a burning flame.

"Well actually Jules, this is a good thing," Harper said calmly.

She was hardly moved by the tantrum I felt I was getting ready to wage.

"Better to hear bad news from family, than to hear it out on the street in public where you're unprepared. Nicky's hired a publicist to do damage control. It's a tiny bump in the road."

"A tiny bump in the road?" I shouted. Are you kidding me? All of New York thinks I'm sleeping with a married asshole."

"Yes, and rule number one, don't sweat the small stuff. And this is small."

"How would you know? It's not your reputation or business on the line," I pouted, my voice cracking.

I was fighting off the tears. Harper dismissed my remark. Of course she of all people would know what was small and what was not. She was Fortune's Forty Under Forty only a few years back. If anybody knew, she did.

"Oliver needed some publicity. He used your event to get it. And in the tech industry, for some—negative attention is as effective as positive attention."

"I'm sorry, baby, that I didn't tell you first," Elliot interrupted. "I was so excited to see you, it completely slipped my mind in the heat of the moment," Elliot pleaded.

"Well that was a pretty fucking long heated moment don't you think?" I said, still not letting up on releasing my anger towards him.

"It was a lot of heat," he said, not backing down from his position, his balls showing up, peaking their head out amidst my fiery storm.

I glowered at him. Do I cut his dick and balls off? Hmm. Maybe that's a bad idea? I was kind of getting used to having them around. Maybe not. But then again, everybody in this family was going to have to start learning not to treat me like a freaking baby. Might as well start with him, if he planned to be the man at my side. Baptism by fire this morning. It was Sunday.

"Well you two can work that out when I leave," Harper interrupted. "But you would be fools if you let this business with Oliver and some rag tag blogger get in between what you're building with each other. Take it from me."

I plopped back down on the couch in total disbelief of this entire news. Elliot moved to sit next to me, grabbing my hand again, rubbing his thumb across my knuckles in an attempt to comfort me. He knew I was terribly upset. I wanted to pull away from him and everyone else. I could feel myself withdrawing, but he wasn't going to let me. I shouldn't have been surprised. Five minutes before, he told me he would follow me to the ends of the earth. I had no doubt I had the look of a gazelle getting ready to make a run. Running was the one thing I knew how to do well.

"I tell you what," Harper said. "In the spirit of this is not such a good time, I'll email you both my thoughts and details for the fundraiser. Time is closing in on us and we only have two weeks until the event," she said. "How does that sound? Work for the both of you?"

"Sounds good to me," Elliot said, his foot tapping nervously next to mine.

Elliot was stepping up to the plate in agreement with Harper. They both knew it was a waste of time to talk about the fundraiser right now. I was far from being in a listening mood. I wanted to know who to shoot first. Maybe I'd line Oliver, Elliot, and Nicky all up against a wall, make like the firing squad and take all those jokes out in one fell swoop. Then Logan, Maya, and I would take Nicky's jet and go chill in the Mediterranean. But after I thought about it, that was a bad idea. Harper would hunt us down like dogs and she had the brains, pedigree, and resources to do it. Nobody messes with what's hers, and my brother was definitely hers.

"Fine," I muttered, cursing under my breath, pouting.

"Good. I'll email you both. I need to get back home to set up a play date for the twins, so I don't have to worry about killing their father in front of them," Harper said casually.

I shrugged her words off. Elliot looked at me as if he were actually mortified. Too bad, he didn't know Nicky and Harper intimately. Those two were like Mr. & Ms. Smith. Neither played fair in love and

SUGAR MOMMY ON TOP

war. One day I would have to tell him about their love affair and the war they waged with each other over a Japanese conglomerate that almost ended them both.

Harper stood up, kissing Elliot and I said my good-byes.

"Enjoy your Sunday kids."

And with that, my loving sister-in-law, the whirlwind known as Harper Montgomery Becker, was out the door.

29

*E*lliot

I hardly understood how a beautiful Sunday morning could start to turn into a certified crap sandwich so fast over Oliver Banks, but it had. I truly had forgotten to say anything to Julianna about the blog post. The minute I laid eyes on her this morning, all my worries and woes went out the window. I was on a mission to make her happy. After last night's fiasco with Oliver, I didn't want to end up back in the doghouse with Julianna. As far as I was concerned, Oliver was basically an all-around piece of shit that wanted my woman. I didn't want to spend my time with her discussing him. And now on the strength of Harper's news about the gossip blog, Julianna was mad at him, me and everybody else in the world. Hell I hadn't done anything but try to make her happy.

But one thing for sure, I wasn't going to let our happy moment get too far out of hand. She had a crazed look in her eye. She wanted to cut my jewels off. I was starting to walk around her place getting myself coffee, filling my mug, and consciously covering my balls. I'd never seen my baby this mad. But I was getting a good dose of what a petite stick of dynamite looked like this beautiful Sunday morning. But I needed to take my head out my ass fast. I had to grow my balls back real quick because this news of Harper's was spinning our happy morning totally out of control. *Sugar Mommy* was ready to take everybody out. Kill now. Ask questions later. And if word got out to her posse, it wouldn't take long for them to go nuclear on everybody around them.

I fully understood how she and Nicky were related. This was some deep down DNA shit. I was gaining insight. Kill ran in this family's gene pool, because my *Sugar Mommy* was mad to the tenth degree.

This morning started off wonderful. I intended to keep it that way. I was going to fix this problem, and fix it fast. I didn't need some hot to trot high paid publicist to make that happen either.

I scurried into the kitchen out of earshot of Julianna who was chatting it up on Facetime with Logan, filling her in about Gossip-Blog. I grabbed my phone, dialing Mario's digits.

"Hey Mario."

"Hey Dr. EZ. You're a surprise this morning. I don't have any new information for you right now."

"I've got another matter for you Mario, if you're interested."

"You know I'm always interested in helping you out anyway I can Dr. EZ. My dad thinks you're the greatest thing since sliced bread. He'd be happy to know that you're helping me with my take home biology exam."

"Take home biology exam?"

"Yeah, you know that exam you're going to do for me, while I do a little sumthin' sumthin' for you."

"Oh yeah, *that* exam," I said, playing along.

Little motherfucker was bribing me. Nothing comes free with this generation. What happened to favors? I was surrounded by mad women and crazy teens.

"Right . . . Dr. Ez."

"Mario, there's a blog called GossipBoss."

"Yeah I know of it," Mario said, popping bubblegum in my ear. He let out a screeching whistle to somebody in the background.

"I think the site is going to be down today and everything on it unrecoverable."

"Yeah, Dr. EZ, I got that same email too. Something about website under construction for maintenance."

"Right. That's the one," I said, smiling though the phone. "Okay Mario, it was nice talking to you."

"It was nice talking to you too, Dr. EZ. Check your Dropbox."

"Bye Mario."

I knew it wouldn't take long for Mario and his crew to bring that site down. He was that good. He was better than good. But motherfuck. I sure didn't contemplate doing a high school biology take home test. Jesus. Maybe I would email it to Gabriel for him to do. He was the child prodigy. He could do it with his eyes closed. I wanted to spend my time with Julianna, not screwing around with some high school biology exam this afternoon. I opened my phone to text Gabriel.

Elliot: Dude, need help.

Gabriel: Anything for you E, what's up?

Elliot: File attached. Complete and return.

There was a brief pause in our texting. I waited, praying that Elliot would help me out. I was going to owe him big time.

Gabriel: R U freaking joking ace? Lol

Elliot: No. Don't ask. Will explain later.

Gabriel: SMH :)

Oh well. What could I say? Mission with Gabe accomplished. I'll owe him a couple cold beers in the man cave when this was over. Maybe I'd even throw in a lap dance or two at Maximillion's.

I headed toward Julianna's kitchen, opening the refrigerator, pouring us both a glass of cold Champagne, slicing some fresh strawberries. She was ending her Facetime conference call with Logan and Maya, still looking pissed. While she hadn't run out of this house away from me, she was running away internally. She was still fragile with this whole relationship and love business. Oliver had threatened her ability to trust, and now my ass was on the chopping block because I failed to tell her that I knew about that dip shit blogger. But one thing I was confident in—I knew how to dig myself out of this deep hole.

My phone text messenger dinged, to my surprise. Who the fuck wanted me now? I'm not delivering any more babies today, unless you brought me in the hospital hog-tied and laid out on a stretcher.

Gabriel: See attached. U owe me!

Elliot: Got it. Thanks buddy.

Gabriel: Maximillion's will do.

Elliot: Are you a mind reader too?

Gabriel: I'm a lot things rolled up in one. Enjoy your day.

Elliot: You're my boy! Saving grace.

Gabriel had my head spinning. I knew he was a genius, but even I expected that high school exam to take a little bit longer to complete. But how the hell did I know what child prodigies were capable of? Seriously? I didn't care. All I wanted was to be free to focus on my woman, who I might add, was throwing daggers at me with her eyes. She was traveling up the pissdom scale to nuclear, in a slow burn.

***

J walked to Julianna's side, confidently handing her a Champagne flute, rubbing the back of her shoulders. I could feel her tensing up at my touch. I bent down low. I whispered in her ear.

"Let's toast baby."

"What are we toasting to, Elliot," she said snippy.

I was standing behind her. She was sitting in front of her laptop. A chair stood between us, but still I put my hand over the jewels. I wasn't going to take any chances. after all, this was Nicholas Becker's baby sister. Navy Seals were subject to jump out at me at any moment. And if they did, they would have to take me down, because I love this woman. My woman.

"To the end of gossipy bloggers," I whispered in her ear.

Julianna turned towards me confused. Perplexed actually, her brow knitted quizzically.

All of this was a lot to absorb. I understood. She'd have to wade through her fog of pissdom to get to where I was in this moment. Which was why I rubbed her skin softly on her shoulder, my hand making my way down the front of her cleavage. Her nipple responding to my touch. A telltale flush of desire passing across her face.

I tapped Julianna's MacBook out of the sleep mode, waking it, my fingers typing in the URL for the *GossipBoss* website. And what do you know. The whole Goddamn motherfucking site was down for some kind of maintenance bullshit.

Julianna's eyes got big as her mouth dropped opened. Champagne spurted from her mouth spraying her top. She turned to face me.

"What did you do Elliot?" she asked, her face looking happy as hell.

Now, that was the look I was aiming for. Home Run. I wanted *that* face back.

"Taking you to the land of kept promises, baby."

"Oh, Elliot, I love the promise land," she swooned, wrapping her arms around my neck.

I grabbed her, grinding her body into my hard on, plunging my tongue deeper into her mouth, drinking in her air, her hair falling free around her face. We had babies to make. Ones that had smiley faces just like hers.

---

*J*ulianna and I made love, lounging around the rest of Sunday afternoon. At one point we both pulled our MacBooks out to review Harper's emails about the fundraiser. We only had two weeks until the event, which took us to one week before Christmas. Christmas was hectic enough as it was. I couldn't believe that we had to do this event one week before Christmas. But I refused to complain. Harper reminded Julianna that the

SUGAR MOMMY ON TOP

whole event would also be good for *Sugar Mommy's* so who was I to complain.

Julianna's staff was taking on most of the heavy lifting for her part of the process. She was in charge of the dessert portion of the menu. My job was to generate a donor's list from the contacts and address book of the physicians on staff. I could handle that part pretty easily. Mostly I was worried more about the auction side of the fundraiser, and how to penetrate whatever evil play Dexter had cooked up with Oliver. I already knew the process was rigged from my conversations with Mario, but I couldn't tell Harper that Dexter and Oliver were trying to taint the auction and that her sister-in-law was targeted for Oliver's personal interests. I wasn't supposed to know these things. I happened to have a hacker in my back pocket, a fact I didn't want disclosed.

So I read Harper's emails with Julianna with feigned interest, going along with the game plan. I proceeded as if everything was under control. I needed time long enough to collect my thoughts to figure out what the hell I could do to stop the ugly train called Oliver Banks that was coming for my woman.

The whole fundraiser event was an unwelcome distraction. I wanted to focus on what to get Julianna for Christmas, not on this damn fundraiser. Julianna was back on happy Sunday morning mode, and I didn't want us to get too engrossed in work today. The only saving grace was the fact that the Fundraiser would be over in two weeks, and I could get all of these people out of my hair and get back to the business of focusing on my woman, and doing what I loved, delivering babies.

"Elliot?"

"Uh huh," I mumbled flipping through my contacts to create a physician list on Excel.

"I'm sorry I got mad at you for not telling me about the blog."

"We kissed and made up. I forgot about it. Besides I could have been more thoughtful about you not hearing it out in public. I wasn't thinking."

"It wasn't your fault that blog was posted."

"It wasn't yours either," I said.

"I know, but I never said I was sorry for snapping. I should have."

"I heard you say you were sorry," I said, still pecking on the keys.

"No you didn't."

"There lots of ways to say you're sorry. And you know what baby, you were really really sorry," I said reaching out, grabbing her hand and kissing the back of it.

Julianna busted out laughing loudly.

"Well good. But in case you didn't hear it, I think I needed to say it again."

I stopped pecking on the keyboard, laying my laptop in the bed next to me. Julianna laid her MacBook down on her nightstand, setting Bunny on top.

"I'm all ears, baby."

And so was my cock, which was twitching through my boxers. Julianna climbed on top of me, as I wrapped my arms around, kissing her lovingly.

Nothing felt better than a Sunday afternoon sorry. My woman was so good at sorry, I was going to be sorry back myself. I wanted her to get lost inside my sorry.

exter

" *I* look forward to seeing you on Saturday night," the CEO
of the hospital said. "I'm expecting good things from you
Dexter."

"I have the biggest donor in the room in my back pocket. Yes sir,
you can count on me."

"I know I can," he said, winking at me on the way out of my office.
"We wouldn't want a repeat of last year."

Oh fuck this shithead. Did he not see I handed him a check for
two-hundred and fifty thousand dollars? So what that last year my
donor list gave the smallest amount of money? So what that Elliot's
donor friends threw millions at the hospital? Elliot and his sidekick
Gabe weren't the only people around here that had rich friends. I
needed to get through this fundraiser in one piece. I only had to deal
with this crap for five more days.

The CEO of the hospital was looking at me, Dexter Esposito, to
haul in the cash. He wasn't looking to pretty boy Elliot in bed with

that Becker family, nor that child prodigy whose only claim to fame was a big brain and some famous parents. The CEO was looking to me, Dexter king of the road Esposito. *I* was going to be the man that walked on water around this motherfucker. People were going to fear me. They were going to be singing my praises by Saturday night.

The way I saw it, if things went as planned, I'd do this deed for Oliver Banks, then I'd be the head man in charge bringing in the largest donor this year. Who knows, it everything went as planned, I might even get a promotion to the corporate office out of this deal. I could be running the legal department for all the hospitals owned by the parent corporation. I'd be the shining star. I would raise the largest donation, and everyone would know I was the most powerful player around this bitch. I would finally get what I wanted for a change. Power, recognition, and the two ass clowns out of my sight and out of my league. I only had a few loose ends to tie up first, and Kimber was one of them.

*K*imber had led Elliot to believe she was pregnant by me. But she and I knew she wasn't. The last thing I needed was for anybody to think that trophy bitch was pregnant by me. I needed to put a bullet in this rumor before it got out of control. She was going to be my date for the fundraiser. I needed to remember to put a little bug in Elliot's ear at the event. As an Obstetrician, a conversation about the state of Kimber's so-called pregnancy would invoke interest on his part, distracting him from the things I needed to make happen at the auction for Oliver. If I played my cards right, it was going to be the perfect distraction that I would need in order to swap Elliot's bid with Oliver's for Julianna.

I'd made a smart move volunteering with Harper Becker to be in charge of the auction. She was happy to have me volunteer for the role. As long as I was careful to stay out of the way of that crazy husband of hers, I could pull this off. Nicholas Becker was a powerful man. If he knew what I had planned for his baby sister, it would be like the walls of Jericho tumbling down. All hell would break lose. But I was smarter than the average bear. Everybody thinks I'm a moron. But by the time I get finished moving these pawns around on my little chessboard, at the end of the day this moron will be the one getting paid.

I needed to do one more thing. I fired off a text message to Oliver.

Dexter: You only have four days left. Need credit card number you plan to use for the silent bid.

Oliver: Why?

Dexter: Need to be able to recognize the numbers.

Oliver: Check your email. Don't fuck it up.

Dexter: Relax. This is under control.

Oliver: No Julianna. No donation.

Dexter: Chill. You just write the check.

I will be so glad when this crap is over. Oliver reminds me of those privileged college frat boys that you hate to be around too long because they think they rule the world and everybody in it because they have money.

By the end of Saturday night, he'll have his little fuckfest date with Julianna, I'll be in the good graces of the CEO, Elliot will be deemed a has-been, I'll be rid of Kimber, and ten thousand dollars richer to boot.

I heard my email notification ding on my computer. Finally, Oliver's credit card number. I replied with my bank checking account number I set up specifically for this transaction with a note saying *"Don't forget to show me the money."*

Now. Four more days to go.

31

J ulianna

"Y ou guys are coming to the fundraiser Saturday night, right?"

"Hell yeah," Logan said. "I'm Gabriel's date."

"Yeah, well I'm kind of your body-watcher's date who'll be on the other side of the room, Jules. The best thing about dating Craig is where you go, I go. He watches you and I watch him. All of a sudden, I'm your friend with benefits," Maya laughed.

Logan, Maya, and I fell out laughing. We were hanging out in the back kitchen of Sugar Mommy's after hours, sipping cognac and stuffing our faces with croissants.

"Yeah, three more days and I'll have my freedom back. I know my sister-in law said this whole fundraiser crap would be good for business, but truthfully I'm over it. I have to deal with stuffy hospital heads all day long. This is not my idea of fun I tell you. I'd rather be here."

368

"Who said making money was fun Jules?" Logan said.

"Exactly why I work the trust fund Daddy set up for me," Maya chuckled. "I take pictures, I play, I travel, dip into the fund, I take pictures, I play, I travel, dip into the fund," Maya said.

"Shut up Maya. Everybody knows you're actually good at what you do. You could open your own gallery with all that so-called dipping you do in your trust fund. Who are you fooling?" Logan asked.

"So what. Jules is good at what she does. She has her own patisserie to prove it. Look around you. What's your point Logan?" Maya snapped.

"My point is getting serious about your passion in life is hard work. It's not always fun."

"It's fun if you enjoy what you're doing," Maya said, tossing back her cognac. "Your passion is supposed to be fun."

"What's your passion Logan, besides giving Gabriel DeLuca a hard on, huh?" Maya said.

I looked at Logan and then at Maya. I hoped this conversation was going to have a good outcome. The three of us were as smart as they come, as far as our IQ's were concerned, but we very rarely dealt in the business of challenging each other intellectually to underscore the point. We knew what we knew and we left it at that.

"Well if you insist Maya on backing me into a corner, I'd have to say that my passion is—my passion is—playing. That's it. I play, I dip, I play I dip. I'm like you Maya," Logan said, swinging her cognac like she said something profound.

I was confused. What the hell did that mean?

"You play and dip what Logan? Come clean."

Logan straightened her back upright as if she was about to say something profound.

"I play the keys and I dip into the trust fund, Jules. Who dropped you on your head?" she said looking at me as if I had an IQ of 40. Her serious face was waiting on a response.

Maya and I cracked up laughing, falling all over the barstools in the *Sugar Mommy* kitchen, while Logan poured each of us another round of Remy Martin, stuffing another croissant in her mouth. We were seriously getting drunk.

"Oh God, we are so bad," I laughed.

"Yeah bitches, by the time we get forty, we're going to be having this same conversation. I'm not planning on growing up anytime soon."

"Yeah well you tell that to Craig," Logan said. "I think he's got plans for you Missy."

"Uh uh. Jules is the one in love with Dr. EZ on the eyes," Maya said. "She's closest to the altar."

"No, don't sell me cheap Maya," I said. "I've seen how Gabriel looks at Logan. And you Maya, stick a fork in you, you're done, sister."

It was in that moment that I finally got what all the fuss with my brother Nicky was about. He wanted all of us to grow up and get a life, much like the one he had. Maybe he knew there would be some new element of richness to be added to our life if we learned to share ourselves with someone other than ourselves. I think I finally understood his sense of urgency now. I really could see myself building a life with Elliot. I was starting to put pretend faces with the pretend babies we were making. I was feeling like I wanted more from my life than just hanging out with my girlfriends hiding and running from a bunch of hired body watchers.

No doubt, Maya was definitely falling in love with Craig, even though it would take an act of Congress to get her to admit it. Logan could hardly deny that she wasn't smitten with Gabriel. And me? I was in madly in love with Elliot.

"So what do you think Maya? Logan? Do you think it's time we settle down?"

"Hell to the no," Logan protested. "I would kill myself first. I am not a one-woman man."

"You look like it to me," Maya said, sipping her drink slowly. "Every time you get around Gabriel it's like everybody else in the room disappears. You don't have to hide your feelings with me Logan. It's me Maya," she said with a straight face, but looking like she was holding back a huge laugh.

"Who are you trying to fool Maya? Between Craig and Xavier vying for your attention, you don't have time to know what's going on around you. You're stuck in the middle of what popsicle flavor you want to try out first. Deep chocolate or caramel baby," Logan laughed, throwing back her drink.

All this talk about hot guys was making me think about Elliot and how much I wanted to be lying next to him right now, throwing caution to the wind, letting myself fall head over hills deep into his love.

"What about family? Don't you both want a family one day?" I queried them innocently.

Maya looked at Logan. Logan looked at Maya, and then they both looked at me.

"Jules, we *are* each other's family, bitch. This is the way it's always been," Maya barked.

"Don't get all emotional Maya. I realize that's the way it's always been. I talking about the fact that we all might want to, you know— expand our circle of family," I said, looking at both of them, waiting on their response.

A weird silence floated over my industrial kitchen where we sat tossing back drinks and eating hot pastries coming out of the oven. Maya and Logan looked at me as if they were clueless. Who would have believed in this moment they were highly educated women?

"Look, we're all in our early thirties. The baby meter is running. If we want to find a husband, this is our age appropriate best window of opportunity, you know, before the field gets picked over," I murmured.

"You mean seriously take it to the next level Jules?" Maya asked.

"Yes, that's exactly what she means," Logan said, her expression still impassive.

"I thought I was going to open this gate with Oliver, you know, but it wasn't meant to be. Loving someone who doesn't love you back is like waiting for a ship at the airport. But that doesn't mean I should give up on the dream because he chose to be a lying cheating manwhore," I said, reaching under the counter and pulling out the serious stuff.

Jack and Daniels were invited to our party.

"I could see myself making babies with Craig," Maya chipped up, pouring herself three fingers of Jack Daniels in one of my crystal glasses under the cabinet.

Maya was my girl. I could always depend on her to come down on my side in these tense moments when we both knew we had to win Logan over. It was always the three of us on the same page. One for all and all for one.

I placed a glass down, filling it for Logan.

"What do you think Logan?" I said quietly.

"I think Gabriel is holding back. So it doesn't matter what I think. You may have found the love of your life with Elliot, and Maya may have Craig on lockdown, but Gabriel's a different kind of beast."

"Shut up Logan, all men swoon over you. You've got the magic coochie, bitch," Maya said.

A look of uncertainty flashed across Logan's face.

"Well if he likes it then he better not try to put a ring on it," she said.

Maya and I stared at each other, perplexed. We both thought Logan had gotten Bey's lyric wrong, but then she busted out laughing hysterically. Maya and I followed suit in the craziness. It was time for us to stop drinking.

"You really are a commit-a-phobic, woman," Maya giggled.

I agreed, rolling my eyes up in my head. Too much truth for one night. It was definitely time for Silas to pick us up and pour us into our beds. This discussion had gotten way too heavy for Jack and Daniel to join us. We had no experience in doing heavy. It was foreign to us. We were the fun machine that typically ran when the opposite direction when things got too heavy. But tonight we were knee deep in alligators talking about men, building relationships and family. Something was changing. We were on the road to settling down.

*S*aturday had come too soon, but not soon enough. I was anxious about everything related to *Sugar Mommy's* participation in the hospital's fundraiser. I needed everything to go perfectly. The fundraiser was being held in the Hammerstein Theatre in midtown Manhattan at the Manhattan Center. So I went early in the morning to supervise my setups and pastry deliveries. Things had gone seamlessly well. I was pleased everything was perfect by my standards and expectations.

There is nothing more to do, I told myself as I shuffled through my closet looking for the white zippered garment bag enclosing the gown Harper's stylist had hand delivered yesterday. Harper said it was the right look for a group of medical professionals and their deep-pocketed friends. It was her thank you gift to me for all my hard work and participation on the fundraising committee. I'd been so busy the last few days I hadn't had a chance to peek at it, but I trusted Harper's judgment. She always looked like a million.

I wanted to look sexy for Elliot, but mentally reminding myself I was being auctioned off tonight to some lucky winner for a dinner date. Elliot was totally unhappy about the auction, despite all my attempts to remind him that this was for charity, and therefore a good cause. I told him I only had to venture out of our love bubble for one night, but for some reason he was totally unsettled about the whole idea of my being auctioned off. By the end of the week he was irritable and grumpy.

I found the garment bag, stretching it across my bed, and held my breath. I was mentally slapping myself for waiting until the last minute to deal with tonight's choice of apparel. I unzipped the bag and gasped. The gown was beautiful. A pink satin Dina Bar-El gown flown in from Beverly Hills. It was a floor length mermaid silhouette with a sweetheart neckline and spaghetti straps. The straps were crisscrossed in the back revealing a cut that dipped low in the back. It was a luxurious gown with very sensual and glamorous lines. A pair of pink studded five carat diamond earrings were tucked inside a petite meshed drawstring bag, tied around the satin hanger with a card from Nicky that read *The Becker Wing Thanks You.*"

I was tickled that I was going to be dressed in pink tonight. Christmas was less than five days away. I figured most of the women would be wearing a lot of red tonight. I didn't want to walk around looking like a carbon copy of everyone else.

The earrings were a perfect match to the pink zippered diamond necklace Elliot had given me. I had the perfect pair of rhinestone studded silver Prada stilettos. They were going to be gorgeous with this gown. The look was totally elegant and sexy. It was a good thing I was going to be meeting Elliot at the fundraiser. I'd take bets he wouldn't want me anywhere near an auction block in this outfit. I reached for my phone to thank Harper and Nicky.

"*H*ey Cookie," my brother Nicky answered.

"Is Harper there? I want to thank her for the dress, I love it. I love the earrings too, Nicky."

"I'm glad you do Cookie. Harper and I wanted you to feel special tonight."

"You always make me feel special Nicky."

"Harper's putting the twins to bed, but I can have her call you back. We're both getting ready. Big night huh?"

"Yeah Nicky, I'm totally nervous. I've been working on the dessert menu forever, but I believe I've nailed it."

"Well if you did as well as you did for your opening, I'm sure it's all going to be good."

"So do you think I'll bid out a high price tonight, brother?" I could hear Nicky growling under his breath. "I take it you're not fond of this idea of an auction this year." I could just imagine how this was sticking in his craw. He paused before speaking.

"It was a good idea, until I heard you were on the auction block. I would have preferred my wife not have agreed to that."

"That would be both you and Elliot. He's been sulking all week over it. It's one dinner date. Probably I'll end up with some crotchety old geyser for a night. You guys worry too much."

"I'm sure Elliot will have every reason to worry. No doubt you'll be the best dressed woman in the room."

"You mean next to your wife that is," I laughed.

"You both are beautiful."

"And we both love you too Nicky."

"I hate to cut you off Cookie, but she's gonna kill me if I don't get dressed and make us late."

"I gotta run too Nicky. I'm meeting Elliot there. Tell Harper to be on the lookout for me."

"Will do Cookie. Try to keep your girlfriends to behave themselves tonight will you? I recognize that's asking a lot from your crew."

"I'm working tonight. It's all about the brand. This is business for me too brother. It's not all fun and games."

"I'm happy to hear it. You're focused and that pleases me. I'll see you later Cookie.'

"Bye Nicky."

An hour and half later, Craig was knocking at my door.

"You ready Ms. Jules?" he asked. "We've got to stop and pick up Maya and Logan on the way."

I grabbed my cream colored satin clutch and full length ranch mink.

"Ready as I'm going to get, Craig."

"You look beautiful Ms. Jules. He's going to have a hard time taking his eyes off you for sure tonight."

"Good. Maybe that means I'll go for a high price tonight," I giggled.

Craig frowned at my little joke. I waved my hand, shrugging my shoulders.

"Gotta keep that Becker Wing in tip top shape," I continued before he could speak. "Dr. Fischer and his staff love new equipment."

"Well you're owning it tonight Ms. Jules. The way you look, it will be state of the art for those docs next year."

I let out a breath I didn't realize I was holding.

"Thanks Craig. You're very kind. Wait until you see what Maya's wearing tonight."

Craig swiped the security card and we both stepped on the elevator together. He spoke into a gadget on his wrist, a small white cord running from under his shirt to his ear.

"Stephen. We're probably are gonna have to kill some people tonight. Twinkle Toes, Pretty Is, and Pretty Does are going to generate a lot of heat tonight," he said, pressing the down button on the elevator keypad.

I glanced in Craig's direction as he stood next to me. He looked stoic in his expression so I wasn't sure if he were joking or not.

And then he cracked a half smile. I blushed, grinning widely. I had a feeling this was going to be a good night.

 *ulianna*

" $\mathcal{L}$ ooks like Harper's managed to get all the deep pocketed movers and shakers out tonight," Logan said as we checked our coats, Craig and Stephen close on our heels.

Harper's contacts reached far and wide. She must have put out a siren call given the number of big dogs that had turned out for this black tie soiree.

"Yeah, I think I see your Mom and Dad across the room Logan," Maya whispered amusingly.

"Where?" Logan said, her smile quickly vanishing and replaced with a look of frustration.

"Three o'clock, table 45. They're talking to the Maestro of the Metropolitan Opera and the Ambassador from the UN General Assembly."

"It's gonna be that kind of night," I said, my head bobbing left and right as I tried to spot Elliot out of the thick crowd.

"Well I hate to alarm you Maya, but your folks are seated next to ours, according to these place-cards," Logan said picking up the tiny white card at the place-card table identifying our table number.

"Thankfully, Harper thought to put the three of us all together," I said.

The last thing I wanted was to sit at the same table as my father, sandwiched in between Nicky and Blake. They would spend the entire night talking business.

It appeared the evening was well underway with many of the guests milling about at the silent auction tables, while red coated servers shuffled among the distinguished guests with cocktails and hors d'oeuvres. The next hour would soon be followed by an intimate dinner and dance. The melodic sound of instrumental music was playing softly from the small band located on the opposite side of the room.

Kudos to the decoration committee. The venue was beautifully decorated. Each table was lit with soft candles inside tall vases with white flowers intermingled with festive gold ribbon, each bellowing out in a lovely floral arrangement that sparkled underneath the dimly lit crystal chandeliers. A large ten foot white Christmas tree with silver balls, tinsel, feathered white angels, and small twinkling lights looked almost magical in the far corner of the room. A huge flat screen TV hung from the ceiling, flashing pictures of the Becker Wing and its newborn babies in some kind of day in the life piece. Cute.

I spotted my brother Nicky across the room, talking with the Chairman of the Global Health and Social Medicine for Harvard Medical School. I recognized his face from last year's fundraiser. He was a huge contributor to this event that loved cozying up to Harper, taking advantage of all opportunities to hob nob with her father the U.S. Senator and his wife, Elizabeth. I had no doubt that a ton of money would be raised for the Becker Wing tonight.

As I expected, Harper looked stunning in a midnight blue sequined gown with an off the shoulder silhouette. Nicky was handsome as ever in his made-to-order Armani tuxedo, white shirt, and midnight blue silk bow tie. They both looked great, but not as great as the handsome man exiting their conversation circle and headed my direction. I grinned widely, pleased that man was mine. My breath hitched as he sauntered closer to me.

"Hey baby," Elliot said, pulling his body close into mine, kissing me gently on the lips.

Elliot grasped my hand, twirling me around in a tiny circle, his heated gaze running up and down my body, gray eyes wide.

"You look good enough to eat, sweetheart. Pretty in pink and utterly gorgeous"

"I could say that about you tonight handsome. Prada?"

"Dolce and Gabbana," he hinted as I admired his black peak lapel one button tuxedo, black grosgrain tie, and black leather lace-ups.

"Where's Maya and Logan?"

"Bar. Both of their parents are here tonight. They needed some liquid courage."

"Something stronger than Champagne, huh," he said, grabbing two glasses from a passing server and handing me one.

"Pretty much. Matthews, Matthews & Matthews have their own table. The Kennedy family has their own as well."

"Does that mean your gals will be laid back in light of the strong family presence tonight?"

"Gotta protect those trust funds," I chuckled.

Elliot laughed with me. He tucked me closer under his arm, at the same moment Dexter Esposito approached us. Dexter was wearing a blue velvet tuxedo with a matching blue velvet bow tie.

"Good evening Dr. Fischer. Ms. Becker," he said with all sincerity, raising my hand to his lips.

"Oh good evening Mr. Esposito" I said, speaking first.

"Dexter," Elliot said, acknowledging him coolly.

Elliot's body stiffened. He really did need to try loosen up if he was going to have a good time tonight. But I could understand this wasn't the best moment for that, his nemesis standing in front of him.

"You're looking stunning tonight. No doubt every man in the room will want to bid on you," he said with a wicked laugh. "So kind of you to donate yourself to the cause."

"You be sure you keep your money in your pocket Dexter. She's all mine," Elliot hissed.

"So who are you with tonight?" I asked innocently, hoping to take the emphasis off me and change the subject. This conversation was going to sour Elliot's mood.

"Oh, I'm here with Elliot's ex, Kimber Lawson. There she is over there across the room," he said, pointing to Kimber talking to some man whose face I could barely see through the crowd.

Kimber was wearing a sleek red gown that was ruched at the midline with a sparkly broach underneath the breast line on her side. Very Ralph Lauren. She looked every bit the beauty pageant model. She was beautiful, yet hardly looking pregnant. I expected her to be further along by now. But, she was flat as a board. She actually appeared thinner than when I saw her last.

"Funny, she doesn't seem to quite have that pregnancy glow," Elliot said snappily, his brow frowning at Dexter.

Elliot must have read my mind. I thought the same thing about Kimber. The animosity radiating between both of them was so thick you could cut it with a knife. Suddenly I no longer wanted to be a part of this conversation. It felt too personal. It was obvious it was a subject Dexter did not want to discuss. Especially in front of me.

"Sorry Elliot. That's a baby you won't get to deliver. Kimber was never pregnant," he laughed, tipping his glass up to his lips and gulping hard.

"What do you mean Kimber was never pregnant?"

I tried to tug my hand loose from Elliot, but he held on more tightly, not letting me go, his eyes darkening with anger.

"You really are a puppet, Dr. EZ. Kimber was doing what she does best. Pulling strings."

"You mean she wasn't pregnant by you?" Elliot asked, both of us now registering surprise.

"Not only was she not pregnant by me, she wasn't pregnant at all. You didn't really believe she was going to mess up that banging body with a baby did you, man?"

God I didn't want to be here for this conversation, but Elliot was clutching me so tight. He must have sensed I was ready to run. I was lacing my track shoes up in my head.

"But I'm cutting the lady in red loose after tonight," Dexter chuckled. "Look at her," he said. "She thinks she's got bigger fish to fry."

Elliot and I glanced back in Kimber's direction as Dexter took a huge gulp of his drink. I gasped so loudly I could hear myself. I could see the man very clearly now. Kimber was fawning over Oliver. What was he doing here? Why were both our exes here, and flirting with each other? This town was beginning to get too small.

"And to think Oliver's my guest tonight," Dexter said, his brow furrowed. He took another huge sip of his drink, moving his head as if he were shaking off his thoughts.

"I don't recall seeing Oliver's name on the hospital invite list I collected from you," Elliot said, his face grimacing.

"It was one of those last minute additions. Guess I forget to tell you Doc. What can I say? I'm a busy man, focusing on this auction and all. Speaking of which, I need to check on the set-up's for tonight's bids."

"Go fuck yourself Dexter. You didn't forget to tell me. We both know that was deliberate on your part."

"Elliot, Elliot, Elliot," Dexter said, his voice barely audible now. "Control yourself in front of this beautiful cupcake," Dexter hissed, rubbing his hand slowly down the side of my arm.

"If you put your hands on her again, I'll break your fingers right here and now," Elliot said through gritted teeth.

"Oh this again, Dr. Fischer. We're gonna do a replay of our elevator scene tonight? You wanna take it outside, asshole?"

My heart started to race even faster. Elliot was teetering on the brink of going thermonuclear. Elliot drew his fist back, right at the moment Nicky stepped up behind him, grabbing his hand, putting it in his, and shaking it.

"Good to see you tonight Elliot," Nicky said as Dexter departed quickly, not sticking around to address Nicky.

"You look beautiful tonight Cookie," Nicky said, deliberately seizing the moment to lighten the atmosphere. "I especially love the earrings," he winked, totally not embarrassing Elliot by mentioning his near physical exchange with Dexter.

I was so glad Nicky was able to calm Elliot down man to man. My nervous anticipation had skyrocketed through the roof listening to Elliot and Dexter's exchange. What was worse, my mind was still processing the notion that Oliver was in the room, and Elliot's ex fiancée Kimber was all over him like a vine.

Before the three of us could say any more to each other, Harper approached the microphone, encouraging everyone to find their seats. Nicky shook hands with Elliot, whispered something in his ear, while Elliot nodded. Nicky then excused himself.

"I'm sorry baby that you had to witness that scene with Dexter and me. He's had it out for me for a long time now, and I've reached my limit."

I nodded, letting out a deep breath. Elliot and I made our way through the crowd to our table. Gabriel and Logan were already seated, locked in their mutual obsession with each other, hardly noticing our arrival. Maya was seated on the other side of Logan. Xavier was sitting next to Maya. Elliot pulled out the chair for me. Gabriel and Xavier rose to their feet while I was seated next to an elderly husband and wife power couple from academia at Columbia University. I scanned the room for Craig. He was up against the wall staring at Maya who was grinning back at him with a sparkle in her big brown eyes.

Harper was still talking at the microphone as the servers placed plates of lobster with filet mignon, scalloped potatoes, and asparagus around for each guest.

"I so love surf and turf," Maya said in a low voice.

"Me too," I said softly, acknowledging Maya.

Harper continued speaking, detailing the Becker Wing's accomplishments over the last year, showing a brief video tour of the wing with Elliot and his staff on the big screen.

Elliot's expression was impassive for the most part, except when his phone buzzed and he slipped it under the table to read his text message. I squeezed his hand in support under the table. Surely he wasn't planning on delivering any babies tonight. Who could be texting him?

"Is everything okay?" I whispered in his ear.

"Nothing I can't handle," he answered, his voice clipped and stern. He pocketed his phone back in his breast pocket, resuming his attention back on his surf and turf. I pushed my food around my plate with my fork nervously. Elliot must have sensed my discomfort. He placed one arm around the back of my chair, placing his hand on my thigh and squeezing it.

"Don't mind me baby. I want to get this night over, that's all."

"I know," I sighed, pulling my glass of Cabernet to my lips, sipping slowly.

By the time Harper got close to the end of her speech, it was dessert time. I'd planned the dessert menu so that each guest got to choose between decadent chocolate cheesecakes laced with fresh strawberries, or tiramisu. I'd been mindful of keeping the dessert choices elegant and simple.

I heard Harper tell the guests that desserts were the compliments of *Sugar Mommy's*. One thing about Harper, she always had business on the brain. I kindly lifted my glass in a small salute to her in thanks, appreciating the fact she was looking out for my business.

I put a spoonful of cheesecake to my mouth when Harper mentioned the silent auction. Elliot's body stiffened as my picture and all the other date volunteers' pictures flashed across the wide screen. Logan and Maya giggled under their breath. I rolled my eyes so as not to encourage them. The academic's wife patted my arm in restrained glee.

"That's so sweet of you to volunteer," she said. "Isn't it honey?" she asked her husband.

"I'm sure you'll raise a lot of money my dear," he said, smiling in his awkward attempt to compliment me.

I could feel the flush pass across my face. Elliot shifted in his chair uncomfortably, inhaling deeply. This was not a subject I wanted to discuss. The whole idea of the auction had been a sore subject between us all week.

Harper wrapped up her speech. The music was playing again as many of the guests were making their way to the silent auction table, the bids for which were starting to post on the electronic bid boards scattered around the room. Other guests were getting out on the dance floor. The die-hards were making their way to the cash bar.

Logan and Elliot were still in deep conversation. Maya was making small talk with the power couple, and Xavier's eyes were tracking someone across the room. I followed his eyes across the room, looking in the same direction as he. Xavier's eyes were fixated on Kimber, who had sashayed across the floor looking annoyed at Dexter. Dexter was in deep conversation with Oliver at the bidding booth. From across the room, their conversation looked contentious. I recognized that look on Oliver's face. Elliot was back to typing in his text messenger, watching the bid board as the price started to tick upwards by my name.

"Will you excuse me for a moment baby? I'd like to put my bid in for the evening before somebody tries to make off with my woman."

"Well I'd hope that you would," I smiled, running my hand down his cheek as a knot started to form in my stomach from excited anticipation.

***

*E*lliot grabbed my hand, pulling it to my lips and kissing it, before he rose to head toward the bidding table. But before he could leave, my father stepped towards our table, resting his hand on my shoulder.

"Hey young man," he said to Elliot, shaking his hand.

"Good evening Mr. Becker. Good to see you again sir," Elliot said to my father.

"Hey Daddy," I said, rising from my chair to embrace my father.

"I dropped a ton of money on you baby. You spend so much time with this young man and your brother I figured I'd have to drop some serious cash in order to see my own daughter," he laughed, his Cuban cigar hanging out of his mouth.

"You'll have to outbid me first sir," Elliot smiled respectfully. "I'm going to give you a run for your money sir."

"Thank God it's for a good cause. A win-win for you son, either way."

"Yes, it is sir. The Becker Wing is the finest obstetrical wing in all of Manhattan."

"That it is my boy, but you have Nicholas and Harper to thank for that," Big Daddy said.

Elliot glanced up at the bidder's board, his face wincing, and my father laughing a hearty laugh.

I gasped.

"Oh Big Daddy you didn't," I said, noticing my bid price had gone up triple since Elliot and I last checked. I was up to a hundred thousand dollars already. Who would pay such an obscene amount of money for a date with me?

"Afraid that's not me baby. I threw fifty thousand in the pot, but it's cheaper for me to send my driver to the Tower and fetch ya myself."

"I don't believe it," I said, not realizing I was talking out loud.

"The numbers speak for themselves, daughter," Big Daddy roared with laughter.

My father was getting a kick of out the look on Elliot's face. Elliot didn't know it but my father was testing his mettle, much like all the Becker men did when it came to me. He was going to push the envelope to see what kind of balls Elliot was packing.

"Umm, you've got your work cut out for you son. Somebody wants a date with my baby girl pretty bad," Big Daddy laughed in-between smoke filled coughs.

I could feel my heart thumping inside my rib cage. Elliot had a look of focused determination in his eyes.

"Not as bad as me sir, I'm headed to the bidders table now."

"Good luck my boy," he said, patting Elliot on the back. "Julianna, call me next week. Wanna talk to you about donuts."

Donuts? What in the world could my father want with donuts?

"Yeah Daddy. Donuts," I said sarcastically.

I kissed my father on the cheek as Elliot helped me back in my seat, tucking the hem of my gown away from the foot of the chair before he proceeded towards Dexter's bidder's table. I wasn't sure it was a good idea for him to go alone. He was so mad with Dexter earlier. I looked over my shoulder at Gabriel in a silent plea. He must have read my thoughts.

"Hold up E," he said. "I've got a couple of bids of my own to make on some of the wine cases."

Thank God for Gabriel.

33

*lliot*

"*E*, I'm coming with you," Gabriel said, loosening up the knot in his bow tie. "I'm over this penguin suit and this fundraiser, man."

"I'm over this entire function," I squawked. "The bid is being rigged for Oliver Banks to win the date with Julianna. It doesn't matter how much money one bids. Oliver's coming out the winner."

"How do you know this E?"

"Mario's been texting me all night. He's hacked into Dexter's computer."

"Does Julianna know this?"

"Hell no. I couldn't tell her I know about this. She wouldn't understand."

"Who else knows E?"

"Me, Mario, and now you."

"Fuck man, who's behind this bullshit scheme?"

"I'll give you one guess."

"Dexter?"

"Yeah man."

"Damn E. Don't beat the shit out of him. I'm off duty. I'm not trying to stitch him up again tonight. I've got plans with Logan."

"Yeah, right," I said, with as much interest that I could muster in light of the circumstances.

"What does Oliver want with your woman? Married life not satisfying him? He's got to have every woman all to himself?"

"I don't know why he won't move on. Maybe I should ask him. Get this bullshit over once and for all. Now that Dexter's working for him, things have gotten complicated."

"Kimber's been all over Oliver tonight," Gabriel said.

"Deep pockets."

"Told you that bitch was a gold-digger. I have no idea why you thought you could ever marry her," Gabriel sighed with renewed frustration.

"Would you believe according to Dexter she was never pregnant?"

"Get the hell out of here E? What was that whole pregnancy stick business about?"

"If you ask me it was a ruse to break Julianna and I up."

"Man those two are ruthless."

"Kimber's not the real threat here. She and Dexter are playing games with each other if you ask me. Dexter's is Oliver's pawn tonight and Oliver's pulling the strings."

"So what's the plan, E? You need a plan. Please don't let that asshole Oliver get a date night with your woman. I like Julianna too much to think she'd have to end up with him for an evening, charity or otherwise."

"When Julianna volunteered, she likely never contemplated Oliver Banks in the picture. Otherwise, I suspect she would have never agreed. It was all about charity to her," I said.

I glanced at the bidder's board again. Good grief. Julianna's bid was up to one hundred and fifty thousand dollars. Dexter was grinning ear to ear. I sent Mario another text.

Gabriel and I approached the auction table Dexter was manning.

"Dexter, we'd like to enter a bid," Gabriel said with the straightest face he could muster.

It was everything I had to hold my peace.

"Give me your credit card, asshole," Dexter said to Gabriel. "You too, pretty boy," he said, referring to me. "Whatcha bidding on Gabriel?" Dexter snorted.

"I want that case of Dom Perignon '63."

"That bid opened at thirty-three hundred. It's at thirty-five right now. What's your bid? I'll play up to five-thousand. And what about you E? What's your poison tonight?" Dexter smirked, ignoring the fact that Gabriel was muttering under his breath.

Gabriel slapped his credit card on the table so Dexter could input his numbers. Dexter took the card and entered his numbers in the computer, his fingers pecking away in between gulps of an amber liquid in his cocktail glass.

"I'm bidding on Ms. Becker."

"I don't know E. Maybe you should quit while you're ahead. Somebody other than her Daddy wants some quality time with that one. She's already up to one-hundred and twenty-five thousand. Not sure you got the money or the balls for that kind of action," he snickered.

"Maybe you should quit while you're ahead, Dexter," I snarled.

Dexter had no idea I came from a wealthy family. I didn't ride on my father's name, so neither he nor Oliver would have any idea I could play this game as well as anybody here.

"So when should I put the brakes on your little show? I doubt you'll be able to keep up. I think you're out of your league ole buddy."

I knew from Mario that Oliver had a stop order on his bid at two-hundred and fifty thousand dollars for a date with Julianna. Dexter never once considered I could play hardball with Oliver. Oliver was going to be pissed. Dexter wasn't going to get paid. And Julianna would be spending her time with me. As soon as Dexter would try to swap the credit card numbers, Mario would be changing it back to mine and their little game would be over.

"Three-hundred and fifty thousand dollars," I said.

"Three-hundred and fifty thousand dollars?" Dexter questioned, his face turning pale.

"You heard the man asswipe," Gabriel said, totally enjoying the look of horror on Dexter's face.

"What the fuck, you rob a bank or something?" Dexter snapped.

"No. I *am* the bank," I said, handing him my Black Card.

My phone was buzzing in my pocket. I knew it was Mario. I eyeballed the bidder's board. Bids for Julianna were up another fifty thousand to one hundred and seventy-five thousand dollars. I needed to get back to Julianna's side as soon as possible. I wanted to be next to her to see the smile on her face when I win this bid.

"C'mon Gabriel, let's get back to our table."

I slapped Dexter on the back who still appeared to be in shock.

---

*G*abriel and I headed back to our seats. The fundraiser was in full swing. The band was playing an upbeat song, couples had joined other couples on the dance floor including Xavier and Maya. Logan and Julianna had played musical chairs now sitting next to each as the once seated elderly couple had moved to the main bar. Craig was up against the wall talking into his wrist, his facial expression stoic. He was probably plotting on how to kill Xavier. Xavier was playing with fire. It had to be hard for Craig to have a love interest in Maya, all while having to perform his job of guarding Julianna. Part of me felt sorry for him. The other part of me didn't because I knew Xavier was a walking man whore that would make Craig work for Maya's affection for kicks. He'd see himself as helping Maya out playing a pitiful role of wingman.

"We're back baby. Did you miss me?" Gabriel said to Logan.

Julianna slid over one seat to let Gabriel sit next to Logan.

"We're talking about the insane amount of money that is being tossed around for the date with Julianna tonight."

"Who does this?" Logan said out loud, her face looking smug, not matching her words.

"Oliver Banks does, but I'm sure I'll win the bid," I said.

"Oliver Banks?" Julianna and Logan question, both speaking at the same time.

Julianna looked shocked, right as the bid board jumped to two-hundred and fifty thousand dollars.

She gasped, but I remained calm. Logan's eyes were wide. Gabriel and I smiled at each other. The music still playing loudly, the moment of truth upon us. I glanced at the bid table where we'd left Dexter. From a distance, I could see Oliver arguing vehemently with Dexter. I grinned, grabbing Julianna's hand and squeezing it. My phone buzzed again. Mario. Julianna's bid jumped to three hundred thousand dollars. I was winning. I needed to read Mario's text message in private.

"I'm going to the bar, baby. Can I get you something?"

"I'll have whatever you're having," Julianna said, her voice low and weak. She was scared Oliver was going to win a date with her.

I winked at her, excused myself and headed to the bar. When I reached the bar, I ordered two cognacs, and pulled out my phone. It was a text from Mario.

Mario: *"You're good to go Dr. EZ. Those guys are toast. He won't be the one dating your Bco."*

Me: *"Thanks Mario. You're the best."*

Mario: *"Damn right homey!"*

I glanced at the bidder's board. Julianna's bid was at three-hundred and fifty thousand. I knew that was my bid, but I was confused. If Oliver was out at two-fifty, who was still bidding?

I glanced back at Julianna, only to catch Oliver storming towards her.

What the fuck? I waived my hand at the bartender wildly in an effort to get his attention amidst the crowd. I needed him to hurry with my drinks. The bidder's bid for Julianna ticked up again, this time to four-hundred thousand dollars. Fuck. I'd been outbid. This was horrible. Not the outcome I'd planned. And what was worse, Oliver was dragging my woman by the hand through the crowd, walking towards the Christmas tree in the corner of the room. Craig was shadowing her. I looked at the bid screen. Julianna sold at four-hundred thousand dollars. But to whom? Finally, my drinks arrive. I glance through the thick crowd. But, where was Julianna?

34

Julianna

J was stupefied in disbelief, along with both Logan and Maya, when they told me how much I'd sold for. Four hundred thousand dollars to the Becker Wing for one date with me was astonishing. The names of the winning bidders were seconds from being announced on the big board. I glanced towards the bar to locate Elliot with the drinks, when I caught a glimpse of Oliver storming towards me.

"I need to talk to you Julianna," he said, grabbing my hand forcefully, pulling me up from my seat looking me eye to eye.

"There's nothing to say," I said, rebuking him.

"Get your dirty paws off her," Logan said, interrupting him.

"I need to talk to you in private," he hissed, ignoring Logan.

Oliver grabbed my hand, pulling me across the room close to the corner where the large Christmas tree stood. We both knew he only had a matter of seconds before Craig would arrive, so I wasn't totally worried. I was more worried about Elliot finding me gone when he returned with the drinks.

"What is your problem Oliver? We're done. You left me."

"I should have never left you," he pleaded. "She and I, we don't fit," he stammered, the smell of alcohol on his breath.

"Oh really? Last I recall of your conversation, your exact words were "She gets me." What happened to that Oliver?" I fumed. "Go back to who gets you."

Maybe Oliver wasn't done, but I had my closure. I didn't want or need him anymore. I wasted far too many years waiting on him to love me the way I loved him. I had no idea, the days and months I'd spent loving him, that I was a placeholder for whatever he was looking for in a woman. All I ever heard from him was that he didn't want to be married. The reality was he didn't want to be married to me.

"I know it feels unfair that I didn't tell you that you weren't the one, but now I know better."

"Telling me? Know better? You didn't tell me anything. You called me and said "Guess what? I got married." Who does that Oliver? Did I mean so little to you that you couldn't talk to me first?"

"I didn't want to hurt your feelings I suppose," he said, shamefaced.

"That wasn't about you not wanting to hurt my feelings Oliver. You wanted to have your cake and eat it too. You're selfish. You only care about yourself. And I was foolish enough to let you string me along for your ride. Well I'm permanently off the merry-go-round called Oliver Banks!"

"It's not like that at all Jules. I made a mistake."

"Leave me alone Oliver. You and I are done. I've moved on."

I turned my back on Oliver, totally in a state of disbelief that we would even be having this conversation, not to mention this was neither the time nor place. Oliver grabbed my arm hard, pulling me forcefully back to him. The spaghetti strap on my dress ripped, exposing part of my breast. I pulled my dress up in horror to cover myself, slapping him across the face hard.

In a split of a second, Elliot caught me by surprise, brandy glasses flying, leaping on top of Oliver, his fist plowing him in the face. They both of them toppled into the huge decorative Christmas tree that was threatening to fall over, its lights blinking. Craig rushed to my side, pulling me away from the brawling mayhem.

"I gotcha Ms. Jules," Craig said, yelling into his wrist, "Tinkerbell secured."

Stephen stepped in-between Elliot and Oliver, both of whom were still throwing fisted blows at each other. Stephen was dragging Elliot off the top of Oliver, tossing him back like a rag doll. Three men in black approached Oliver in a rush, another man struggling with a tugging Dexter in handcuffs. Nicky rushed to Elliot's side, refraining him from bum rushing Oliver again, ordering Xavier and Gabriel to stand clear, both ready and willing to jump into the fight. The two men in black flashed their badges at Oliver, handcuffing his arms behind his back.

"Oliver Banks. You're under arrest for fraud, theft, interstate wire transfer fraud, and money laundering. You have the right to remain silent. Anything you say may be used against you in a court of law."

Some young teen-age boy with a red and green streak running through his hair ran out from under another man dressed in a dark suit, rushing to Elliot's side.

"You did it Dr. E, you did it," the young boy exclaimed gleefully.

"No, we did it Mario," Elliot said, rubbing the boy's tousled multi-colored hair.

The man in the dark suit shook Elliot's hand, saying "C'mon son. You and Dr. Fischer can catch up later. We promised to help some Feds with their incident reports."

The young boy nodded. The man gave Elliot a big hug as the boy beamed ear to ear, winking at Elliot.

Elliot's lip was busted, his clothes disheveled. One of the men in black was speaking to Elliot while taking notes. Gabriel was holding a handkerchief over a small cut above the top of Elliot's left eye, trying to stop the blood that was seeping down his face.

Maya and Logan rushed to my side, my hands shaking from the rush of adrenaline, as I tried to cover my exposed breast. Logan, having found a stapler, successfully stapled the strap of my dress, giving me some semblance of decency. The guests in the room were all abuzz as to why a fight had broken out in the fundraiser and with whom. Many were chattering about the undercover police presence that was surrounding Oliver and Dexter. Kimber was crying, running clumsily after Oliver and Dexter, both of whom were being shuttled out the room in handcuffs. The whole affair had suddenly turned into a room full of chaos.

The bar was suddenly overcrowded with patrons rushing to drink something stronger than Champagne. Harper rushed over to the band, instructing them to start playing music again. I doubt she was going to let this night turn into a total disaster. That was Harper. Never losing sight of the business.

"*B*aby are you okay?" Elliot said, his expression worried, kissing me lightly on my lips.

"Oh Elliot, I'm so sorry you're caught in the middle of my baggage with Oliver. But I don't understand. Why were the police involved? What's going on?"

Before Elliot could explain, Nicky joined the two of us.

"Cookie, you okay?" he asked, his green eyes narrowed, looking me over head to toe.

"I'm fine. I'm fine. Craig managed to pull me out of the fray."

"Thank you, Elliot, for protecting my little sister. Oliver's never had her best interests at heart, but I see you do. If you hadn't caught wind of his dirty scam, the Becker Wing Fundraiser would have been tainted with all kinds of scandal giving our fundraising attempts a black eye."

"Well I had good motivation. He was after my woman," Elliot said, pulling me by the waist, tucking me under his arm.

"What's this all about Nicky? I thought this was only about Oliver wanting me back."

"Oh he wanted you back all right. So badly, that he attempted to rig the outcome of the auction bid for you, but Elliot, with a little help from his friend, uncovered his scam."

"Well that's a lot of effort to go through just to get me back."

"Yes, it was, but he had help from Dexter Esposito," Elliot added.

"What's Dexter got to do with this?" I asked, still trying to put all the pieces together in my head.

"Dexter is an ambitious man who harbored animosity towards me," Elliot replied. "So Oliver was paying him under the table to rig the auction to get you to date him. Oliver's company is in financial trouble. His wife is leaving him."

"Oliver was covering his bases, thinking if he could get you back before his financial woes were publicly exposed, talk you into marriage, then he'd have immediate access to enough wealth to bail out his company," Nicky grunted.

"Wow. I didn't know," I gasped, covering my mouth with my hand.

"You couldn't have known. Nobody could have known."

"Elliot let me in on Oliver's scam. I contacted John Matthews, who has friends downtown at the bureau."

"The FBI?" I asked.

"Yes, they had Oliver's company under surveillance. They asked Elliot and Mario for their help to fill in the blanks for them. The wheels were set in motion to bring Oliver to heel," Nicky said. "Dexter was collateral damage."

"I headed them both off at the pass bidding three-hundred and fifty thousand dollars for a date with my woman to his two-hundred and fifty thousand dollars."

"Sadly, Elliot was out-bidded," Nicky grimaced, shaking off some unspoken thought that was going through his head.

"I can't believe it man. Who the hell out-bidded me for Julianna? I thought I was the only serious competition in this auction."

"It appears otherwise," Nicky said, tossing back the last few swallows in his drink and ordering another.

"*W*ho would bid that kind of money on me?"

"It's posting on the board now," Nicky said. It appears you're going on a date sister with . . . with . . . a Matteo Kenn."

"Who the hell is Matteo Kenn? What does he do? Is he a doctor? Lawyer? Banker? I've never heard of this guy," Elliot groaned.

"Well we'll know any moment now. Harper's coming to the microphone shortly to reveal and thank the winning bidders," Nicky said, looking at his wife with affectionate eyes.

Elliot looked frazzled, disgusted and defeated.

"It's only one date sweetie, and not with Oliver. And it's for a good cause too. Think of all that new equipment you baby catchers will get to buy."

I grabbed another Champagne from a passing server, squeezing Elliot's hand.

"I'd rather go another year without new equipment than sacrifice my woman to some man that's got the hots for her."

"I can't say that I blame you, Elliot which is exactly why you'll never see my Harper being auctioned off, lest I throw a million dollars into the deal to ward off all serious contenders," Nicky chuckled, then slapped Elliot on the back. "Let that be a lesson."

Harper was rattling though the list of winners, calling them to the stage, thanking them and introducing them to their dates. There were a lot of happy faces pairing up on the stage. I felt bad that Elliot's face wouldn't be one of them.

"Julianna Becker will you join us on stage please?" Harper said through the microphone.

I pried my hand out of Elliot's hand, who was totally not receptive to the idea of my going on a date with another man. I headed to the stage, a tad self-conscious knowing my dress was being held together by staples. But at the end of the day I didn't have to be perfect for a one-time date with another man. Elliot was my man and that was all that mattered, and he thought I was beautiful just as I was.

"And the winner for the date with Julianna Becker, owner of Sugar

Mommy's, the dessert caterer for tonight's fundraiser is . . . Matteo Kenn."

Matteo Kenn. Who was he? What did he look like?

Everyone's head in the room turning around to see which man would stand and come forward, joining me on the stage. I looked around at the men in the room, holding my breath to see who would be coming forward.

Surprisingly Logan and Maya bum rushed the stage, both jumping up and down gleefully, their hands waving frantically. What were they doing on stage? Why were they up here with me? Did they have too much to drink in all the hysteria?

"We're Matteo Kenn," they said waving their auction receipt card, stilettos clanking.

I started jumping up and down with them, laughing wildly. Matteo Kenn. I get it. Matteo as in Matthews and Kenn as in Kennedy. Matthews and Kennedy. Holy smokes. This was awesome news. The three of us were jumping around in a circle on the stage like little kids in the ice cream store. Harper had a huge smile on her face, and folks in the audience were clapping loudly, laughing along with us.

I glanced at Nicky and Elliot. Nicky was shaking his head in bemusement. He threw both his hands up, acknowledging his surrender. Elliot's mouth flew open wide. Gabriel and Xavier had rushed to his aid at the bar, slapping him on the back, as if the joke was on him. Even Craig had cracked a small smile on his face. This was turning out to be a good night. Saved by my gals.

"I love you guys," I said gleefully.

"We love you too Jules," Maya said with a wide grin.

"Now we've got a date to tear up the town," Logan said with a wicked glint in her eye. "Wherever shall we go?"

"Party over here!" I whooped.

Harper shooed the three of us off the stage in an effort to move on. We were moving too slowly for her. She was ready to bring the fundraiser to a close.

Yes. A good time was going to be had by all. I had a hot date with Matteo Kenn. A gal couldn't ask for more.

35

*E*lliot

*I*t was snowing outside. Very fitting for Christmas Eve. Nicholas and Harper didn't know it yet, but I was soon going to be family. The eight carat pink diamond was burning a hole in my pocket. After almost losing my woman to Oliver Banks and the mysterious Matteo Kenn, I was done with fun and games. I no longer wanted to compete with another man for my woman. Ever. I was taking Julianna off the market.

Things were feeling like they were starting to get back to normal. Dexter had been fired from the hospital. Oliver was being indicted. Kimber had headed back to Long Island to her family's home, distancing herself from both Dexter and Oliver, waiting for her next fish to fry. Craig and Maya were officially a couple. Logan and Gabriel were still circling each other, and Xavier was . . . well . . . Xavier.

I'd been working double shifts 'round the clock since the fundraiser. Seemed like every baby in New York decided to be born the week of Christmas. I hadn't seen Julianna in three days. I had reached my limit of days I could go without seeing my *Sugar Mommy*. Yes, things were getting back to normal. A new normal. And I intended for my new normal to include Julianna. I wanted her for a lifetime.

I walked through the doors of Nicholas and Harper's penthouse at Becker Towers. The soft scent of pine filled the room, as lights twinkled from the humongous Christmas tree that had a little sandy brown curly-haired boy and girl underneath it giggling at a toy train that wrapped around the base of the tree. They had to be Nicky and Harper's twins, Miles and Milania.

Harper rushed up to hug me, shoving a dirty martini in my hand, kissing me on the cheek and welcoming me to their home. Harper looked as beautiful as always, wearing a long turquoise oriental dress with two slits on the side that showed off her beautiful caramel colored legs, her hair pinned up in a ball with two chopsticks, her bangs wispily falling to the side of her face.

"C'mon on in Elliot. Julianna's on her way up. She had some sugar cookies in the oven for the twins that she's bringing up. I'll tell her you're here," Harper grinned, looking and sounding a bit buzzed. It was strange seeing her so loose.

Nicky walked down a spiral staircase wearing a white shirt, jeans, and barefoot. I was glad he was on casual mode as I too had put on my favorite blue jeans, a warm Ralph Lauren shawl collared sweater, and black Ugg moccasins.

"Hey Elliot, Merry Christmas," he said shaking my hand, then picking up his daughter, who was dressed like a pink fairy princess with a tiara in her head. He sat her down, then grabbed her brother, tossing him up in the air, planting a wet kiss on his face.

Both twins giggled, taking turns saying "Daddy Daddy we're playing train ride."

Nicholas walked towards Harper who handed him his own dirty martini, tugging her hard into his body, nuzzling his nose against her neck, sniffing her, then nibbling on her ear. Nicholas tucked a loose lock into place.

"Behave yourself honey, we have company," Harper giggled like a schoolgirl.

I was glad my new family was in a good mood, because my news was going to come as a surprise to everyone. My heart was beating rapidly in anticipation.

Before I could gather my thoughts away from this picture perfect family, Julianna burst through the doors like gangbusters.

"*Sugar Mommy* has arrived!" she shouted. The twins tore themselves away from the train set like gangbusters, jumping up and down begging for sugar cookies. Nicholas plopped down in the oversized chair, pulling Harper down in his lap with him.

"Nicholas, the twins," Harper said, setting her cocktail down on the side table so as not to spill it.

Julianna set the cookies down on the table as the kids dug in deep, each of them taking cookies in both hands.

"Hey baby," she said, eyeballing me. "Your *Sugar Mommy* is here." She was looking at me with those big brown sexy eyes. I was drooling inside with thoughts too dirty to even think in the presence of kiddies.

Julianna took three long strides across the room jumping in my arms, saying "Merry Christmas my Dr. EZ."

"The only thing easy is my love for you," I said, kissing her back passionately.

"Ewwww," Milania said with a mouth full of cookies. "Mommy, Auntie Jules is kissing a man."

"Yeah baby, like Mommy and Daddy do when we love each other, Auntie Jules loves Doctor E.," Harper said.

Harper moved to brush the crumbs off Milania's face, but Nicholas pulled her back into his lap refusing to release her.

A woman dressed in a gray pantsuit called out to both twins, telling them it was bath time. I suspected she was their nanny. Nicholas must have read my thoughts.

"Nanny," he said out loud before I could speak, his fingers playing with one of Harper's curls. Both kids followed behind the woman, their mouths and hands filled with cookies. Nicholas was a lucky man. Tonight I wanted to be just as lucky.

"I hope one day we have a couple of kids like that," I whispered in Julianna's ear.

She blushed, moving towards the large wrap around sofa, pulling me down with her, patting her hand on the soft leather for me to sit next to her. I dropped to my knees instead.

Nicky and Harper froze. Julianna's eyes grew wide and teary.

"Julianna Becker, you make me question myself on why I ever thought falling in love was not a good idea. From the first day you fainted in my arms, Cupid shot an arrow straight through my heart. My heart stopped every time I looked at you. I love you. I want to be your family. I want to make a family with you."

Tears filled my baby's eyes.

"I want to come home to you every night for all my nights. I can't promise that I won't have days where I'm tired, cranky, or hard to get along with, but I promise that I will love you for all that you are, with all that I am. Marry me?"

Julianna gasped, placing her hand on the side of my face, smiling through tears of joy. You could hear a pin drop in the room.

I pulled the pink diamond ring out of my pocket, opening the blue case, pulling back the velvet lid, still on bended knee.

Her eyes grew wider. She caught her breath.

"More diamonds," she whispered, her eyes focused on the ring, salty tears steaming from her eyes.

"A girl's best friend," I said quietly, painfully waiting for her answer, my stomach rumbling. "And yes, I'm a very wealthy man. Please baby. Change your name to mine. Let's be a family and make sugar babies."

Julianna let out a laugh and released more tears. She bent low, kissing my lips tenderly.

"I love you too, Elliot Fischer. Yes, I'll marry you."

I rose to my feet as she came up with me, putting her arms around my neck, kissing me deeply, our hearts thundering. I slipped the ring on her finger.

Harper and Nicholas rushed to their feet, embracing our embrace until we all found ourselves in a group hug.

"Welcome to the family, Elliot," Nicky bellowed out.

"Congratulations you two," Harper said with excitement.

"One down, two more to go," Nicholas said beaming.

I had no idea what he was talking about. But it didn't matter. My heart was overflowing with joy. *Sugar Mommy* was all mine.

 *he End*

A WORD ABOUT THE AUTHOR

I am Jude E. McNamara. Virtual adventurer. Keyboard ninja. Guardian of sassy romantic encounters. I am the alter ego of that other woman, Jude. You know, the one that loves snowy nights, is in a relationship with love, and looking for her own hero. While by day she's off being the disciplined scrappy businesswoman with the mind of a shark, I gallivant her keyboard by night, running wild and free on the down-low. I figure she'll have to catch up to me. Because once that blue power button turns on, I'm far too busy breathing life into those colorful characters that run around in her head, incessantly telling me their stories even if it's at the break of dawn.

You can find me and my merry band of jet-setting girlfriends running from the paparazzi at the high-end cocktail bars in Manhattan, drinking Patron Silver. I'm the flashy one wearing the sparkly tiara on my head. Like clockwork, when she faithfully dons her track shoes to catch up with me, I usually have to listen to her lecture me about my behavior over a glass of champagne. She loves champagne. Actually I love champagne too—except I like mine with a side of tall, handsome hunk begging me to stop at the intersection of heartbreak hotel and romantic encounter road, demanding a happily ever after.

It's an arduous race to "The End" before her blue button goes dark and I cease to exist. But once the blue light appears, the race is on, right up to the point when we two Judes meet on the same page, often in a book like this one.

For more about the author, visit: www.judeemcnamara.com
Two Judes Publishing
668 Stony Hill Road Suite 339
Yardley, Pa 19067

STAY CONNECTED WITH JUDE

Thank you again for your readership and support. If you enjoyed this book, please leave a review at your favorite retailer. If you would like to learn more about my other books, below are excerpts for two of my recently released novels. Also, you may wish to sign up for my **newsletter** to be notified when my new novels are released.

Visit me online at http://www.judeemcnamara.com where you can learn more about me, find book trailers, my blog posts and other new upcoming work.

Best Regards
    Jude E. McNamara

http://www.judeemcnamara.com
    Email Jude: jude@judeemcnamara.com
    Follow me on Twitter @judeemcnamara
    Follow me on Instagram: iamtwojudes
    Follow me on Facebook: Jude E. McNamara

AN EXCERPT FROM MILK MONEY

For more about Nicholas and Harper and how their love story began, read MILK MONEY from Jude E. McNamara.

CHAPTER 1

$\mathcal{N}$icholas

"$\mathcal{T}$he second best thing about this New Year's Eve night, next to my getting married, is the fact that you're my best man, Nicky. Thank you for standing up for me," Mico said, giving me a bear hug.

I tapped the rooftop of the limousine, waving my hand to let my driver Silas and my security chief Stephen Parks know that we were ready to head to Saint Patrick's Cathedral. Stephen was following behind us in the black armored Chevy Suburban. His security team were positioned ahead of us in another Suburban. Tonight's wedding celebration was a huge affair. My good friend Noah "Mico" Dunham was marrying Riley Nelson Cook. This time last year, my friend and his new bride's son had both almost lost their lives in a serious motorcycle accident.

"Silas, get us to the church on time!" I yelled. "If we're late, Mico will put me in one of those famous headlocks he was known for at the Naval Academy."

"Yeah man, how's our time? Riley will have my ass if I'm late."

"It's 10:15pm. Don't worry. Silas will have us there on time. Your bride is scheduled to arrive at 11:30pm."

"I take my vows at midnight, Nicky."

"Don't worry about it Mico. I've got the ring. We're on schedule."

Tonight was a big deal for my good friend. It was a bigger deal for me because I was standing up for him. Best Man. I wanted this night to go without a hitch.

"Here, take a shot to calm your nerves," I said, grabbing the crystal decanter off the limousine bar, pouring Mico and myself a shot of vodka.

"Thanks for the wedding present, Nicky. Loaning us the Milk Money jet so we can spend our honeymoon in the South of France is beyond wonderful," Mico said.

I could tell by his huge grin my gift had made him happy.

"Not a problem Mico. Riley's company was a great investment decision. I'll get it back from you one way or the other," I laughed heartily.

"Thanks Nicky. I earned major cool points with her when Milk Money took her company on as a client. That was a really good decision."

"Nah man. I should be thanking you for bringing Riley's business to my attention. Of the ten companies Milk Money has provided angel investment funds to this past year, hers has been one of the more profitable businesses on my leader board."

"Riley's worked really hard to make her business a success."

"Well it shows. That investment is showing lots of promise right off the bat. Even Lucia is happy," I said proudly.

"Well if Lucia is happy, then life is pretty good. Lucia is one badass woman. She is not to be messed with, Nicky."

"You're telling me? Dude, you're preaching to the choir."

"Does she ever chill, or does she always work herself into oblivion?"

"Rarely chills," I said, shaking my head back and forth.

What Mico didn't realize, was that "badass" didn't even begin to appropriately describe my business partner Lucia Falco's talents.

Lucia had been with me from the early days eight years ago, when I formed Milk Money. Together, she and I nurtured the firm, having started it on a shoestring budget. Today Milk Money was one of the most premiere angel investment firms on Wall Street. And Lucia Falco was central to the company's success. She was a beautiful, smart, no nonsense workaholic. When it came to business, we were a lot alike.

"Mico, I have nothing but good things to say about Lucia. She's a wonderful business partner. She keeps me on the straight and narrow. Lucia is the Yin to my Yang. I could not survive without her."

"Yeah, Beauty and the Beast," Mico grunted.

"Just like the POTUS needs a body man, Lucia is my body woman."

"Well somebody needs to keep you in line, Nicky. I suppose it might as well be Lucia," he said casually. "Everywhere I turn, you're in the gossip columns with this heiress or that model."

"Oh, don't believe everything you hear Mico."

"I don't. But I know you. No doubt, most of the gossip is true. You even give the foreign press a workout. Nicky, don't you think it's time to slow your roll?"

"Why should I?" I said, glancing at Mico quizzically.

"Look, I know you've got this whole "I'm not going to commit to any woman" thing going on, but dude, you're forty-one."

"Give it a break, Mico."

"No Nicky, I think it's time you retire that 'playa' card of yours. Get on with it. Settle down. Tie the knot. Make some babies."

"Babies?" I said, choking on my drink. "Good Lord."

"You're Big Willie now. You are on Forbes' list of the top one hundred richest men. You are the most eligible bachelor in Manhattan. Quit the shenanigans, man, and settle down," Mico pleaded.

"Jesus man, you're starting to sound like Big Daddy."

The mere thought of my kingpin father brought memories of his recent communication today.

"How so?" Mico said, glancing at his own watch, clearly getting more nervous the closer we got to the cathedral.

"I received a very lengthy voicemail earlier today from Big Daddy. He was dribbling on and on about why I needed a wife and kids. He claimed I need to focus on the family legacy."

"See Nicky, even Big Daddy and I are on the same page."

"Mico, please. You know there has only been one woman that has ever meant anything to me. And, she has managed to walk away with my heart. Matter of fact, she stomped on it, crushed it into a thousand pieces, and beat the heel of her pricey stiletto into it." I sighed and took a big swig of my drink, wondering how the hell things got so messed up between me and her. "And as far as Big Daddy is concerned, he wants me to do what he wants me to do, when he wants it," I babbled. "You know how he is."

"So?" Mico said sharply, shifting nervously in his seat.

"Sooooo, some people respect him, some people fear him. Big Daddy doesn't care which you choose, as long as you stay out of his way and give him what he wants. He forgets that I'm not other people. I don't have to give into his demands."

"Not the wisest move for you to be getting on the bad side of Big Daddy Blake Ross Becker II," Mico chuckled, putting full emphasis on my father's full name.

"Yeah yeah yeah," I said, waving my hand wildly in the air.

I was ready for this conversation to end. I could hardly deny that my father was starting to put his foot on my neck over my state of singleness.

"Man, you best to get with the program with Big Daddy. I'm not really sure you should be poking that bear, if you know what I mean. How hard can it be Nicky, for you to find a woman and settle down?"

"After Harper, I don't give my heart away anymore. She feels like unfinished business," I said solemnly.

"You've got to start somewhere Nicky."

AN EXCERPT FROM BLACK
SEQUINNED BOWS AND CHAMPAGNE
NIGHTS

Find Jude E. McNamara's debut novel: BLACK SEQUINNED BOWS
AND CHAMPAGNE NIGHTS.

CHAPTER 1

*R*iley

"*I* told you I don't mix business with pleasure."

"C'mon, Riley. It's time to get out from under your rock and find a date to escort you to the Memorial Gala."

Damn. Madison's persistence was getting on my last freaking nerve. The mere mention of my taking a date to the Memorial Gala was causing me to get dizzy. I could feel the sweat building on my palms as I right clicked my mouse, surfing the net for images for my new food and wine book.

"I'm not under a rock, Madison. Don't forget, my company is doing the event planning for this gala. I have no intentions of turning my most significant business event of the year into 'date night'."

"All you think about is business. I'm starting to worry about you."

"Madison, if this gala goes well, I'll be able to springboard my business to new heights. I can leverage this event by pitching my five-year growth plans to some angel investors. This will catapult my business to the next level."

417

"That's what you always say, Riley."

"I say that because it's going to be a very important night. One in which I need to be focused. Business is the only hat I plan to wear."

"Well there's no reason you can't focus on business and a man too."

Madison's mind was in overdrive. The fact that she was browsing intently through my choices of graphic covers didn't mean she was giving up on this subject. I had no doubts she was not backing down on this business of my dating.

"Riley, you of all people know how to multi-task."

Yep I called that one right. Madison was pulling out her big guns. A look of determination flashed on her face. It was hard to argue against a crazy person settled on her ideas. Madison wasn't going to let this discussion go without a win. She was on a roll. She was going for the gold medal this time.

"Attending the Memorial Gala without a plus one doesn't bother me one bit. It will be hard enough sitting through the reading of the names of the 'Fallen.' Lucas is posthumously receiving the Navy Cross Medal commendation for heroism and meritorious service. The night will be difficult enough as it is," I sighed.

"You can do this, Riley. I have complete confidence in you. Having a date will make it all that much easier."

"Have you gone loony tunes? Easier how?"

"Umm. Emotional support for one. Eye candy to stare at for two," she said, trying to appear thoughtful, but failing. She was holding back a laugh, big time.

"Madison, I've spent the first half of my life as Lucas's wife, never having to deal with this business of having to date. Dating feels like taking on some new challenge that I don't have a lot of experience in, frankly. It means work."

"It's not meant to be work, Riley."

"So you say," I grunted.

"Dating is intended to be fun. You haven't had fun in so long you've forgotten what it's like to have a man fawn over you. A little male attention can be a good ego booster, girlfriend."

SUGAR MOMMY ON TOP

"Easy for you to say, Ms. I always have a man."

"Riley, you've gotten way too serious these last few years."

"Since Lucas's death, I've managed to have a pretty funky track record in picking the right guys."

"Only because you haven't picked the one, Riley," Madison said, motioning her fingers in imaginary quotation marks. "You're too young to be alone sweetie."

"In case you've forgotten, we're middle age."

"I know how old we are, Riley. But that doesn't mean we both aren't beautiful, young at heart, young in spirit, and can still knock 'em dead. Woman, we could be trophy wives ten years from now," Madison laughed with a wink.

"Well I might be young, beautiful, and alone, but I'm not lonely," I blabbered.

"Says who?"

"Says me."

"Woman, you haven't been out with a man since the dark ages. Would you even recognize loneliness if it stared you in the face? Look at you. You're held up in your own private world like some suburban princess on lock down, dedicating your entire existence to these kids and work."

Madison waved her hands out in front of her, pointing wildly at my laptop, multiple computer screens, graphic images, and a desk full of paperwork. She pointed her index finger at my paper trail of work spread out across the floor leading to my chair. The room did look like a workaholic lived here. She was playing hardball now, determined to take complete advantage of my surroundings, using my work area as props to make her point.

"I've been busy building an empire, Madison."

"Doesn't mean you're not a full-fledged, bona-fide, certifiable, Type A workaholic. It's high time you played the get out of jail free card now honey. Have some fun for Christ sakes. It's been eleven years since Lucas's death, three years since you broke off your engagement with Warren."

"Oh please Madison, don't remind me."

"Life is too short, woman. You need to inject some testosterone into the mix. Stir things up," Madison said, tossing a couple of the graphic covers aside. "Besides, most of the time you lace up your track shoes and go running for the hills any time a man shows you the slightest bit of interest."

"That's because I attract the crazy guys," I said nonchalantly, stacking the graphic covers up neatly that Madison was tossing aside.

"It's because you're so lovable Riley, and everybody knows that crazy people need love too," she giggled. "They do seem to find you sweetie. But honey, you need to weed through that haystack in order to find that needle. It's like playing the lottery. You can't win if you don't play the game," Madison demanded.

Madison was right. She knew me better than anyone. We'd been best friends since seventh grade, roommates in college, and now lived on the same cul-de-sac two houses apart. When we were teenagers, we pricked our fingers, meshed the redness together, and promised to remain loyal to each other forever. There wasn't anything that we each didn't know about the other. Madison was my whenever, wherever, whatever friend.

"Madison, I've resigned myself to the fact that I may not ever find another life partner as wonderful as Lucas. Those days are long gone. Frankly, if my broken engagement with Warren is any clue, I'm not so good at picking them now either. Besides, where is it written that I have to have a man?"

"Warren doesn't count. He came along when you were grieving the loss of Lucas. You were on the rebound. Who knew he was going to turn out to be dog shit," Madison snorted.

"Obviously I didn't."

"He was a rebound relationship. Everybody knows rebound relationships don't count."

"Yeah right," I said sarcastically, rolling my eyes up in my head.

"Every woman has had at least one rebound relationship in her lifetime where we fail to hit the 'eject the loser' button. We all get that one relationship that doesn't count," Madison said, smiling to make me feel better.

"Well it sure as hell counts to me. Sadly, it took me far too long to realize I was on a sinking ship."

WINGMAN

Find also for your reading enjoyment, Jude E. McNamara's WINGMAN (A Black Sequinned Bows and Champagne Nights Prequel Novella). This and all her other novels are available now at your favorite book retailer.